MW00770733

"What do you mean, what happened?" asked the woman—who Jack remembered had been called Maisy. She was hovering next to the bed, looking at him in concern. He liked that. A lot. Had he ever had anyone seem that concerned about him before?

But at the simple question, his mind blanked. He wasn't *sure* what he meant. He looked into Maisy's eyes. "I don't know."

"*What* don't you know?" she asked gently.

"Anything," Jack blurted. "I mean...I know my name is Jack, but that's about it. Why does my head hurt? Where am I? Who are you? What happened to me?"

An almost delighted snort sounded from Jason on the other side of the bed, and Jack quickly turned his attention to him.

"Sorry, I just...I didn't expect this," the man said.

Jack's eyes narrowed as he took him in. If he wasn't mistaken, the man was trying to hold back a smile. But that couldn't be right. Why would he be happy that Jack couldn't remember anything?

"As I said, my name's Jason Feldman. You're at my house in Seattle, Washington. You were in an accident and hit your head." He nodded to the woman. "That's my sister, Maisy. And you're Jack Smith—my brother-in-law."

Jack's head spun. The only thing sticking him was the brother-in-law thing. That meant...

He turned to look back at Maisy.

She was staring at her brother with what Jack could only call a stricken expression on her face. But that emotion wiped clean when she looked down at him.

"Hi," she said weirdly.

"We're married? You're my *wife*?" Jack blurted, frantically searching his mind for the tiniest memory of this woman...and coming up blank.

But instead of Maisy answering, it was her brother who said, "Of course she is. You two have been married for a couple years. You were out hiking together and you fell. Were out for hours. The doctor said you'd be fine, but we've been extremely worried...you don't remember *anything?*"

Jack slowly shook his head. Everything was a complete blank. His breathing sped up as alarm spread through his body. But then he felt a light touch on his arm. Maisy.

"It's okay...you're okay," she said urgently.

"Well, shit. Guess that means the vow renewal ceremony you've been planning is off," Jason said.

Maisy bit her lip as her head shot up and she stared at her brother.

"What?" Jack asked.

"You two lovebirds were planning to renew your vows. The ceremony was supposed to be this weekend. Then you got hurt. And my darling sister, who's spent a ton of time working on the details, was so excited. I guess we'll have to postpone...although we could simply downsize things. Instead of the hundred guests Maisy invited, we could do a smaller ceremony, stick to just family."

"Jase," Maisy protested weakly.

"*Jason*," he corrected immediately. He looked down at Jack. "She can never remember that I hate that stupid nickname from childhood."

"Maybe we should give him time to get his memory back," Maisy suggested.

"Are you going to stand there and tell me that you don't want to do this?" Jason asked his sister.

Jack could feel tension in the air between the siblings, but he couldn't begin to understand why.

Jason didn't give Maisy time to respond before continuing. "You two love each other more than any couple I've ever met. You were both so excited about this. We'll scale it down. I've got a friend who's ordained, we can bring him in. It's your new start. You know Mom and Dad would want this."

The color leeched from Maisy's face at the mention of her parents.

Frustration swam through Jack. He hated not knowing what was going on.

"Our folks died in a carjacking years ago. Maisy was their baby. Spoiled rotten. She was lost without them. Had to drop out of high school because she couldn't handle losing them. I moved back here to the family home to help her out, and we've been here ever since."

"How long have we been married?" Jack asked Maisy in a gentle tone. He felt terrible for her. He didn't know if his own parents were still alive or not, but he imagined losing your parents had to be awful, and if it happened while you were a minor, it must be even worse.

But again, her brother answered for her. "Only about two years, and things were rough between you for a while, but they've been a lot better recently. So you guys decided to recommit yourselves to each other. Hence the renewal of vows ceremony."

Nothing Jason said rang a bell within Jack. In fact, it felt...wrong. If he was married to this woman, if he loved her as much as Jason insisted he did, surely he'd feel something deep down inside? Instead, it felt as if he was meeting two strangers. It was disorientating.

"Are you hungry?" Maisy asked softly.

"Starving," Jack admitted.

"I'll get Paige to make something and bring it up," Jason said. "She's our cook." Then he looked at his sister as he said, "I'll leave you two to bond...and I'll call my friend about this weekend."

"Jason, please," Maisy said.

"It's for the best," Jason told her. "You know it is. I'll take care of everything. You know how overwhelmed you get. The last thing we want is you having a relapse and for the doctor to have to come and sedate you. Relax, sis. I've got this."

Once again, Jack felt as if he was in the dark. He didn't understand what the hell Jason was talking about, and he hated it.

As soon as the man left the room, Jack turned to Maisy. "Relapse? *Sedate* you?"

Maisy licked her lips nervously. "I don't deal well with stress."

That didn't really answer his question, but because she looked so uncomfortable, Jack let it drop. For now. His eyes swept the room, desperately willing himself to recognize something, but nothing about the somewhat austere space felt familiar.

"Can I have some water?" he asked, spying a jug on a small table on the other side of the room.

"Oh! Of course. I'm sorry, I should've gotten you some the second you woke up," Maisy fretted as she turned to head toward the table.

"It's okay. So...my last name is Smith?" Jack asked.

Maisy shot him an uneasy look before turning her back on him to pour a glass of water. "Yeah," she said.

"Jack and Maisy Smith, huh?"

This time, she simply nodded.

Something wasn't right about this situation, but Jack couldn't figure it out. Not when his head was pounding so hard. He brought a hand up and felt the back of his head where the pain seemed to be coming from, wincing as he encountered a large lump.

"Does it hurt?"

The question came from his wife as she hovered next to his bed once more, this time with a glass of water in her hand.

"Like a bitch," Jack said as he reached for the water.

Their fingers brushed as he took the glass from her, and she gasped slightly.

Jack inhaled sharply as well when a jolt of what felt like electricity shot down his arm. Without thought, he reached out with his free hand as Maisy pulled away. His fingers grasped her wrist, and she froze.

Jack ran his thumb over the racing pulse in her wrist. Her skin was soft and felt a little chilly to him. But he couldn't deny touching her felt right. The *only* thing that had felt right since waking up in this room. Would he feel like this with a stranger? No way. At least he didn't think so. He hadn't been sure he'd believed the story Jason was feeding him, but as he watched pink blossom in Maisy's cheeks at his touch, satisfaction filled him.

This woman was his wife. He might not remember anything about his life, but he knew without a doubt this woman was *his*.

Suddenly, he was as anxious as she apparently was about their vow renewal ceremony.

"I don't remember getting married," he said gently

after taking a sip of water and putting the glass on the table next to the bed.

"It was a spur-of-the-moment thing. We didn't have a big ceremony."

"I'm not surprised."

She frowned. "Not surprised about what?"

"That I was too anxious to make you mine to wait for you to plan a big shindig."

Her blush deepened.

"I'll do it," Jack told her.

"Do what?"

"Marry you again this weekend. I don't remember our first ceremony, and this will be a new start for us, like your brother said."

She stared at him for a long moment. "We don't have to," she whispered.

"I don't remember you, or the life we had, but deep down I know you're mine. My soul recognizes you. Not knowing who I am or anything about my life sucks. But for some reason, simply having you here makes the blackness in my brain not seem so scary. I know you, Maisy Smith, and it would be my honor to marry you...again."

Tears filled her eyes and dripped down her cheeks. "Jack," she whispered.

"Too much?" he asked as he gently tugged on her hand and brought it toward him. He kissed her knuckles.

"I just...this is all so overwhelming," she said.

"Will you sit with me? I want you to tell me everything about yourself. What your likes and dislikes are, your dreams...hell, I don't even know how old you are."

"I'm twenty-eight."

Jack opened his mouth, then sighed as he closed it.

"What? Too young?" she asked.

He chuckled, but it wasn't a humorous sound. "Not at all, I was just going to make a joke about *my* age, but then I realized I don't know my own birthday. How old am I, love?"

She stilled, her eyes wide as she stared at him.

The door opened, and a woman walked in carrying a large tray. She was around the same height as Maisy, in what he figured to be her sixties, and had black hair she'd pulled back into a messy bun at the back of her head. She was slender and regal looking, and he thought he saw a bit of Native American in her features. She looked at Maisy with a small frown as she juggled the tray in her hands. Jack couldn't interpret the look, and the confusion and uneasiness he felt when he first woke up once more swept over him.

Maisy tugged her hand out of his and hurried over to help with the food.

Jack didn't understand the tension between the two women. Paige looked concerned and he wasn't sure why. He was no threat to his wife. And why did Maisy clearly not want to tell him how old he was? Was he much younger than her? Older? He didn't feel as if he was in his twenties, but he didn't feel as if he was in his forties either.

"I made you some hearty vegetable soup. You'll feel better once your belly is full," Paige told him after she put the tray down on the table next to the bed.

"Thank you. It smells wonderful," Jack told her.

"Oh, I almost forgot. Here," Maisy said.

Jack saw she was holding out a pair of glasses. He automatically reached for them and put them on. He didn't even remember that he wore glasses, but as soon as they were on his face, he relaxed a little. Yeah, his sight wasn't awful, but everything was much clearer now.

He stared at his wife and willed himself to remember, but he still had no memories before waking up, other than his first name.

"I hear we're having a wedding this weekend?" Paige asked tentatively.

Maisy bit her bottom lip and turned to Jack.

"We are," he said firmly.

He didn't understand the look Paige gave Maisy, but she said, "Great. I'll start planning a menu."

"Nothing big," Maisy warned the older woman. "It's just going to be family."

"I understand," Paige said.

Again, there were undercurrents to the conversation that were way above Jack's head, and he was so confused. Before he could ask questions, Paige turned and left the room without saying anything else.

"I should go," Maisy said uncertainly.

"Stay," Jack insisted. The thought of her leaving made his heart rate speed up. If he didn't know better, he'd think he was having a panic attack. But that didn't make sense. He wasn't the kind of man who panicked at the slightest provocation...was he? Then again, he couldn't really know that for certain.

"Are you sure?" Maisy asked. "I just thought maybe you'd want some privacy."

"You're my wife, I don't need privacy from you. You know me better than anyone. Have seen me at my worst and best, I assume. Stay."

It took several seconds before she nodded.

"While I'm eating, you can tell me more about our

lives together. What we do for a living, about your brother, your mom and dad, and anything else you can think of." When she remained silent, he gently clasped her hand. "Maisy?"

"Yes?"

"I might not remember you or our marriage...but I'm looking forward to getting the chance to fall in love with you all over again."

Her eyes filled with tears. "I don't deserve you, Jack."

"Of course you do," he told her. "We deserve each other."

CHAPTER TWO

Maisy stared at Jack as he slept. The last hour or so was absolutely horrible. Every word out of her mouth was a lie. She wasn't his wife. She'd never even met the man before Jason dragged him into her room and dumped him on the bed.

Her brother was awful. Terrifying. Nothing like the boy she'd looked up to when they were growing up. Somewhere along the way, he'd changed from the protective older brother to the monster he was today. And she was trapped.

It was true that their parents had been killed when she was only fifteen years old, and that her brother had moved in to care for her because she was a minor. Also, because she'd been out of her mind with grief.

Somehow, one year had turned into two, into five, into ten. And now, thirteen years later, she was still living in the house she'd grown up in with a brother who hated her.

For the most part, it was just the two of them all those years, with Paige and a few other daily staff members on the payroll. Though Jason *did* get married five years ago... but his wife had mysteriously disappeared just four months after she and Jason were married. Her brother claimed Martha had left him without a word, but Maisy wasn't convinced. She'd spent the night before Martha's disappearance with her sister-in-law, and she'd seemed...okay. Not super happy, as she'd admitted she and Jason were having some issues, but Martha was determined to work through them. She'd genuinely loved Maisy's brother, which made her disappearance all the more confusing.

As for Jason, instead of seeming heartbroken, he'd appeared...satisfied.

That was when Maisy's suspicions *really* started. She hadn't wanted to think Jason had anything to do with his wife's disappearance...but how could she not?

For years, she'd kept silent about what she'd seen the night Martha had supposedly left...but if she truly believed Jason's story, that he'd gone to bed next to his wife and when he'd woken up, she was just gone...

Then how did she explain his behavior that night?

Why had she kept the pictures she'd taken all those years ago, still carefully hidden?

Just in the last several months, as the drugs she'd been on for over a decade started to clear from her system, allowing her to think clearly for the first time in years... she'd begun to wonder about her parents' deaths, as well.

Jason had received a hefty life insurance payout after their parents died. Money he seemed to go through rather quickly. Then, three months after getting married, he'd finally been able to access additional money their parents had left to him in a trust.

Now that money was apparently long gone, as well. It

was a pretty hefty sum, yet he'd managed to spend it all. If she had to guess, she'd say he ran through the last of his inheritance close to a year ago...around the time he started to ween Maisy off her meds. Started encouraging her to find a boyfriend.

But apparently his patience was wearing thin. Just two months ago, Jason began outright insisting she needed to get married. Of course, because she was old, fat, and ugly, *he* was going to find her a husband.

She hadn't expected him to literally drag in a stranger off the streets.

Maisy didn't know what her brother had done, or where he'd found Jack, but it seemed to be a stroke of unbelievably good luck for Jason that Jack had amnesia. The man didn't even know his last name wasn't Smith.

Her brother was smart; the story about them planning to renew their vows was ingenious. Maisy had no idea how Jason had planned to get Jack to marry her if he *hadn't* lost his memory, but because he had...it made things much easier.

Jason wanted her inheritance. The money her parents had left for her, sitting safely in a trust since their passing. She received a stipend every month—which her brother took—but he wanted the rest, and unfortunately for him, it had the same stipulation as Jason's own inheritance.

She couldn't access the money unless she was married.

It was why Jason had married Martha, she now realized. Maisy had learned there was a three-month waiting period after the marriage was official before the money could be released, and it hadn't been too long after that when poor Martha had supposedly "left."

Maisy had already come to the realization that her

brother would have skipped her sham marriage to a stranger, and she'd probably be dead right now, if it wasn't for the fact that upon her death, her inheritance wouldn't go to her brother—it would go to charity. Her parents had been eccentric, but also very clear in their wishes as far as distribution of their assets. They knew that money could make people do terrible things.

But Maisy didn't think they'd ever believe it could make their own *son* do such awful things to get his hands on their millions.

Now Jason was forcing her to get married so he could gain access to her money.

Maisy wanted to stand up to him. Wanted to go to the police with her suspicions. But her brother terrified her. He had a lot of nefarious friends. People who wouldn't hesitate to break the law. People he'd probably hired to kill Martha...and maybe even their parents. People who'd probably kidnapped poor Jack.

Jason was a greedy asshole, and Maisy had no idea how to get out from under his thumb.

She had no college education, no friends, no driver's license or money of her own—no way of escaping his clutches. No matter where she went, he'd find her. And the second she signed her name on a marriage certificate, the clock was ticking for her poor husband...and probably for her too.

Three months. That's how long she had before every cent her parents had left her would be under Jason's control.

And she'd be expendable.

As would Jack.

Turning her attention back to the man resting on the

bed, Maisy studied him. He was exceptionally good-looking. She guessed he was in his thirties. Built. His stubble enhanced his square jawline rather than hiding it. And the glasses? She was a sucker for a man who wore them as well as Jack did. Back in high school, the last time she'd had any interest in boys, she'd always been drawn to the smart, nerdy-looking guys. Not that Jack looked like a nerd. Far from it. But the glasses took him from handsome to crazy hot. She'd also caught a glimpse of a tattoo on his right shoulder.

In short, he was way out of her league, and there was no way a man like him would tie himself to a woman like her if he didn't already think they were married.

Which brought up another issue...her lack of sexual experience. Thank God she wasn't a virgin. *That* would be impossible to explain away when they'd supposedly been married for two years.

She'd had sex exactly once, not long before her parents had died. She'd been young, *too* young, and sneaking around had felt liberating. She'd felt so grown up at the time. But the experience had been awful. Was over in minutes and had hurt horribly.

Then her parents had been killed and her brother moved back into their family home and before she'd realized what was happening, Jason had taken over her life. Had arranged for her to be homeschooled and earn her GED, sequestered her away from the few friends she'd had, and had brought in a doctor who kept her sedated with drugs, at first to manage her grief, then allegedly to help her deal with stress. And she hadn't complained. It was easier to just go with the flow, and the drugs helped her avoid thinking about everything she'd lost.

She sighed. Jack would discover they hadn't been intimate when she balked at sleeping with him. How the hell Jason thought she could make this man believe they'd been married for two years was beyond her.

"Maisy? Come here."

As if thinking about her brother had conjured him out of thin air, Maisy turned toward the door.

"Did you hear me? *Now.*"

Sighing, Maisy nodded and turned back toward Jack. He was still sleeping. Without thought, she reached out and gently took his glasses off his face and placed them on the small table next to the bed, so they wouldn't get crushed if he turned over, before walking toward her brother.

As soon as she was within reach, he grabbed her upper arm in a cruel grasp and hauled her out of the room. He closed the door softly, then dragged her downstairs and toward his office.

Maisy hated the room. It used to be her dad's, and once upon a time she'd had wonderful memories of sitting on the sofa, playing while her father worked. Or sharing the oversized armchair with her mom while she read to her.

But now, the room was filled with bad memories and pain. Her brother liked to bring her there to yell at her. To tell her how stupid she was, how lucky she was that he was around to manage her life. Remind her that she'd be homeless if it wasn't for him. He also had a tendency, more so in the last few years, to use physical force to get his point across. Slaps, shoves, and he particularly loved pinching her, bruising her skin.

The brother she used to know was nothing but a memory, and in his place was this cruel, greedy man who thought he was entitled to whatever he wanted, whenever he wanted it.

"We need to get our stories straight," he said as soon as the office door shut. "Tell me what you talked about. What you've already told him."

"This isn't going to work," she said with a small shake of her head.

Pain burst in her cheek when Jason smacked her with his palm.

"It'll work if you want it to," he growled, then got in her face as he squeezed her upper arm hard enough that Maisy knew there would be bruises on her skin later. "You owe me," Jason told her. "I wasted my entire fucking life coming back here to make sure you were okay after Mom and Dad died. I gave up my dreams to babysit you. And we need the money you'll get for marrying this guy."

Maisy didn't dare show the doubt she was feeling on her face. She'd learned over the years to not show emotion, to hide what she was thinking from her brother. She really had no idea how Jason had managed to spend not only the life insurance payouts, but his trust money as well. The amount had been in the millions.

"Besides," Jason said, letting go of her arm and giving her a shove away from him. "It's not like *you* need the money. It's just sitting there gathering dust, and I'll be damned if it goes to charity. Mom and Dad worked hard for that cash, it would be a slap in their faces for it to go to strangers."

Maisy resisted the urge to rub her arm. That was one more thing her brother loved; proof that he'd hurt her. "He asked questions that I didn't know how to answer," she admitted.

"Like what?" Jason asked.

"How old he was."

Her brother waved his hand in the air as if brushing off her concern. "Doesn't matter. Just tell him he's thirty-six or something."

"He's gonna be suspicious when there aren't any clothes or IDs or even a toothbrush of his own in the bathroom," Maisy warned.

"Way ahead of you. I've arranged to get some shit brought in. Remember, I told him that you guys had been having a rough patch. If nothing else, just tell him you decided not to move back in together until after the ceremony."

"But isn't he still going to want his own stuff? Or to see where he was living?" Maisy asked. This plan was horrible. How in the world did Jason think they could pull this off?

"Shit, Maisy, don't be so goddamn annoying. Figure it out! Right, sorry, you're too fucking stupid to do that. Fine —say that he lived in Spokane or something, somewhere that isn't too close, and the place burned down. So all he owns is what's here. He just moved back in right before his hiking accident."

Maisy stared at her brother. He was sitting at their father's desk now, and she was standing in front of it as if she were a kid being reprimanded by the principal or something. He had an ability to make her feel small, and she hated it. Hated *him*.

The thought startled her. She'd spent her life giving Jason the benefit of the doubt. Brushing off her concerns about him even as he got rougher, scarier. After all, he was her *brother*. The only blood relative she had left. And he had taken care of her, had been there for her when she'd been at her lowest.

But she knew that wasn't enough to excuse his behavior toward her. Not in the least.

And here she was, a grown-ass adult, living under Jason's thumb.

In her defense, Jason wasn't the kind of man you defied. She'd learned that well over the years. But kidnapping a stranger to force him to marry her, just to get access to her inheritance...it was unbelievably crazy. The monthly stipend she received was generous. It went straight into Jason's account and was more than enough for most people to live on comfortably. But now that he'd blown through his own inheritance, his greed had obviously gotten the better of him.

She hadn't been around Jack more than an hour or two, but she already had a feeling he wouldn't be fooled by any of her brother's stories, not for long. It was only a matter of time before he figured out that something was very wrong. It was possible he'd get his memory back too. And when he did, he'd be gone so fast it would make her head spin.

Which was the main reason Jason wanted them married so quickly. It didn't matter if he left...as long as they were married for at least three months, her inheritance would be released.

But in the back of her mind, Maisy knew that Jason had no intention of ever letting Jack go. If he was dead, he couldn't go to the cops with any accusations that he'd been kidnapped and forced to marry a stranger.

"Right, so what else do I need to figure out for you?" Jason sneered.

Maisy didn't want to be here. Didn't want to be having this conversation, but she did need help. She wasn't good at lying. Never had been. "What do I tell him he does for a living? He's bound to ask. Wonder if he has any work friends he should invite to the ceremony this weekend."

"Hmmm," Jason mused. Then he snapped his fingers. "Bounty hunter."

"What?"

"Bounty hunter," he repeated. "They're loners. He never got too close to anyone because in his profession, that wouldn't be smart. And you were a stay-at-home-wife. It's not like you can do much of anything, anyway."

His barb hit its mark. Jason always complained that she did nothing but sit around the house, but it wasn't as if she'd been given the opportunity to do anything else. Having a job meant possibly making friends, and that wouldn't do. It would mean people asking questions about why an almost-thirty-year-old woman was still living with her older brother.

And that was a good question. Over the years, her brother had done a great job of convincing her—and others—that she was fragile. And when necessary, he used drugs to keep her from caring too much about what was going on around her. But when he'd stopped insisting she take her pills every morning, her newfound clarity came not only with suspicions about her brother, but also a glaring truth...

She was ashamed of herself.

She should've left long before now. Should've gone to the police the second she had suspicions about her sister-in-law and her parents. But she didn't have access to her money, had no friends to help her, and while she was close to the staff in the house, especially Paige, she refused to put them in danger by enlisting their help to escape.

And now there was Jack. Maisy knew without a doubt if she didn't go along with the scheme her brother had come up with, *Jack* would pay the price. And if she did anything right in the world, it would be to protect the innocent stranger upstairs in her bed.

Jason continued giving her answers to questions that Jack would inevitably ask. And while on the outside it looked as if Maisy was listening, her mind frantically wandered. She couldn't pull this off for three months. There was no way.

But the ugly truth was, she only had to string Jack along until his signature was on a marriage license.

During a lull in the ridiculous stories Jason was spewing, Maisy blurted, "How would this have worked if he didn't have amnesia?" She couldn't stop thinking about that. It wasn't as if people actually had shotgun weddings anymore, and if someone had kidnapped *her* and told her that she had to marry someone, she would've laughed in their face.

"I was going to give him one chance to do as I asked," Jason told her with a straight face. "If he refused, I would've had to use more drastic measures to convince him."

"Like what?" Maisy reluctantly asked when he paused.

Jason grinned. "It's not like you need *all* your fingers."

Maisy stared at him in shock.

Her brother laughed. *Laughed.*

Yes, she was an idiot for giving him the benefit of the doubt for so long.

"If that didn't work..." He shrugged. "Having the barrel

of a gun pressed against your temple goes a long way toward making someone see the benefits of signing their name on a piece of paper."

Maisy felt sick. She couldn't believe she was related to this man. Someone who was so ruthless and coldhearted.

"All we need is his signature on that marriage certificate. After that..." He stared at Maisy for a long moment. "You need to keep him compliant. If he suspects what's happening, it won't end well for him."

Maisy swallowed hard and nodded.

"Good. Now get out. You're making my head hurt."

Maisy turned toward the door without another word. She felt sick inside. She didn't know what to do. If she admitted to Jack what was going on, he'd leave in a heartbeat...if Jason even let him out of the house, which she doubted. But if she went along with her brother's scheme, she was as bad as he was.

"Maisy?"

At the door, she turned to look back at her brother.

"Don't fuck this up. You won't like the consequences if you do. And once we have this money, you can get your own place. I know you'll like that."

Oh, he was good. The old Maisy would be thrilled at the bait he'd just dangled in front of her. But now that her eyes were finally opened, now that the fog of the drugs had faded, screw an apartment of her own. All she could think of was getting the hell away from the evil that was her brother. Getting out of the state.

She nodded obediently because it was what was expected of her.

"Good. Glad we're on the same page. And, Maise?"

She wished he'd just shut up and let her leave. She

needed some time to think. To try to figure out a way to save not only herself, but Jack as well. He might be a stranger, but when he'd touched her, she'd felt...a connection.

He didn't deserve what was happening to him. She might be complicit in a lot of things her brother had done, but she'd do whatever she could to help her "husband," no matter what the consequences turned out to be.

"When he asks questions you're too dumb to answer with something convincing, suck his dick and spread your legs. Sex works wonders as a distraction."

Bile rose in Maisy's throat, and she quickly walked through the door and shut it quietly behind her.

She leaned against it and shut her eyes, her mind spinning. For the first time in years, she wished her parents hadn't been wealthy. Maybe if they hadn't had millions of dollars in the bank, they wouldn't be dead. She'd be married for real, with a family, and her brother wouldn't have turned into a monster. Money had its perks, but she wouldn't wish her life on anyone.

"Hey there, sexy."

The three words had Maisy's eyes popping open and pushing away from the door.

Don Coffey stood way too close to her, leering. He was one of the many men Jason "worked with"...and someone who had always given Maisy the creeps.

"Jason's in there," she said, gesturing toward the office with her hand.

"Thanks. You want to meet up later?"

Maisy shuddered. Don was always hitting on her, and it made her feel the need for a shower. "Sorry, busy," she told him.

His eyes narrowed. "One of these days, you're gonna regret turning me down."

That definitely sounded like a threat. Don was a big man. Tall at six-three, and muscular. Jason told her once that he took steroids to stay so bulky, and she didn't doubt that for a second. If he wanted to, he could seriously hurt her. She'd always tried to stay out of his way.

Maisy wasn't sure why her brother didn't just have one of his friends marry her. It would be a lot less risky than kidnapping a stranger. She could only guess it was because his friends were just like him. The possibility that they'd double-cross or blackmail him after the deed was done was high. They weren't exactly model citizens and would probably do anything necessary to get more money.

Maisy didn't respond to Don's comment, simply sidled around him, trying not to touch him in the hallway, and headed for the stairs.

"That's an ass I wanna tap."

It was obvious Don wanted her to hear his crude comment, but she didn't react, simply kept walking up the stairs. She needed to get out of here. Even though she didn't have any money, she'd leave today if she could. But now there was Jack. She wouldn't leave him in this viper's nest. She'd do her best to convince him that they were a loving couple, do this farce of a vow renewal ceremony, then play things by ear.

Three months. That's all she needed. After that, she'd be free. Jason could have her money. She just wanted out.

She slipped back into her bedroom and her eyes immediately went to the man lying on the bed. He had one arm flung to the side and his head rolled back and forth in agitation. It looked as if he was having a nightmare.

Wincing, because it was likely he was probably dreaming about something her asshole of a brother had done, Maisy hurried to the side of the bed. She sat on the mattress and put her hand on the arm that was by his side.

He startled at her touch, and Maisy questioned what she was doing. He could hurt her through no fault of his own, if his dream was violent. But when a whimper left his lips, she leaned toward him as if drawn by the vulnerable sound.

"It's okay. You're okay," she murmured.

To her surprise, his eyes popped open, but his gaze was unfocused. "Don't. Please don't! No more...*Hurts*."

"I won't hurt you," she soothed. "I'm going to do everything I can to help you. To get you out of this."

His eyes closed, and it seemed to Maisy that he calmed. His head stopped thrashing and he stilled on the mattress. But when she went to stand, his hand shot out and grasped her forearm.

She gasped in surprise, but his hold didn't hurt. She'd gotten so used to Jason grabbing her and squeezing hard that she automatically recoiled anytime someone touched her. But Jack's fingers around her arm, while firm, weren't causing any pain.

"Stay," he whispered. "Please."

Maisy settled back down on the mattress. "I'm here," she told him softly.

His fingers relaxed around her arm, but he didn't let go. Maisy watched him sleep and wondered what his story was. Where Jason had found him. If he had friends who were worried about him. If he had a family, a real wife.

At that thought, she frowned. What if he was already married? When Jason submitted the marriage certificate, would that come up somehow, despite the fake last name? If his marriage to her couldn't be registered with the state, he was as good as dead. Because there was no way Jason would simply let him go.

Surprisingly, the thought that this man belonged to another woman made a pang of jealousy spear through Maisy. It was irrational. She didn't know him and he didn't know her. He might be the kind of man who would beat his woman. Or maybe he was an asshole.

But from the little she *did* know of him, Maisy didn't think so.

"Please don't be married," she whispered. She hated to think of a woman out there frantic because her husband was missing.

Even if Jack wasn't married, he had to have people who would notice he was gone. Someone as charismatic as Jack seemed to be wouldn't live in a bubble like she did. They'd eventually discover where he was and come for him. And when that happened, Maisy vowed to do what she could to aid them. It was the least she could do. Jack had somehow crossed paths with her brother, and she might not have done anything for poor Martha, but she could do something now.

However, as much as she hated to admit it, the best thing for Jack right now was to go along with her brother's plan. It was the best way to keep him safe. She just prayed he didn't regain his memory in the next few days. Or at least until she could come up with some way to get them both out of this mess.

The second she signed that marriage certificate, the countdown clock would start. As soon as Jason had her money, both she and Jack would be expendable. Shivering at the thought, Maisy took a deep breath.

The longer Maisy sat next to Jack as he slept, staring at his fingers around her arm, the more she understood this man's fate was entirely in her hands.

CHAPTER THREE

Jack woke up when something brushed against his face. Opening his eyes, he was confused for a moment, but then he inhaled and his memory returned. Not that he had many memories in his head at the moment, but the woman sleeping in his arms wasn't something he could forget anytime soon.

He was on his side and Maisy's back was to his front. He had his arm around her waist and his nose buried in her hair. She smelled like...apples. The sweet red ones. And she felt absolutely perfect against him. Jack hated that he didn't have any memories of their life together. How they'd met, how he'd convinced her to give him a chance—because he was absolutely sure she could do so much better than him.

What she sounded like when he made her come.

The thought of sex with Maisy had his cock lengthening, but he didn't make a move to act on his arousal. He was content to hold her while she slept. She was still fully dressed, while he wore only a T-shirt and boxers. He inhaled again, the scent of apples burying itself into his psyche.

Time ticked by, and Jack had no idea how long he lay with Maisy sleeping in his arms, but eventually she began to stir. He could just see the sun rising outside the window, indicating that he'd slept away the evening and through the night. When Maisy had joined him, he had no idea, but he loved the thought of her coming to him while he slept.

It was obvious when she realized where she was, because she tensed in his arms. Not liking that, Jack scooted back and rolled her toward him until she was on her back. Then he came up on an elbow and hovered over her. His gaze ran over her face, trying to memorize her features. Her cute, pointed nose, the scattered freckles. The dark circles under her eyes, which bothered him.

"Morning," he said after a long moment.

"Hi."

"Sleep well?"

She stared up at him for a beat, before nodding. "You?"

"Like a log. Must've been because I was holding my wife all night," he joked.

But she didn't crack a smile. Instead, she looked even more worried.

"I'm okay," he told her, thinking she was concerned about his accident.

"Have you remembered anything?" Maisy asked.

"Nothing," Jack said with a shrug. "But my head hurts a little less this morning, and I woke up with the smell of apples in my nose...I can think of a lot worse ways to wake up," he said, trying to make her smile.

"It's my shampoo," she whispered.

"I like it."

She stared up at him, her body tense, her fingers digging into his upper arm as if she was scared. Wait, was she afraid of him? The thought made Jack frown. "Are *you* all right?"

"I'm not the one who hurt my head and has amnesia," she replied.

Jack frowned a little deeper at that. It didn't escape him that she hadn't actually answered his question. He tried again. "Does this make you uncomfortable?" he asked. "Sleeping with me?"

"We're married, it's what married people do," she said.

There. Again, she'd deflected his question. Jack scowled.

Something caught his attention on her upper arm, where her shirt had ridden up. He pushed her sleeve up a little more with his finger and exposed a pretty nasty bruise. "What's this? What happened?"

"Nothing, I'm fine," she said breezily. "I bruise easily. I need to get up."

But instead of scooting back and letting her swing her legs over the edge of the mattress, Jack moved closer, straddling her thighs and caging her under him. "What happened? I didn't do that, did I?"

"No! Of course not." She tensed even further, if that was possible.

"I won't hurt you, *Stellina*."

"I know."

Jack relaxed when he heard the sincerity in her response.

"Are you scared of me?" he couldn't help but ask. She

hadn't relaxed under him, was stiff as a board. And he hated it.

"No."

"Are you sure?" he asked with a tilt of his head.

"What does *Stellina* mean?"

"Little star. It's Italian."

"Why'd you call me that?" Maisy asked.

"I don't know. I'm guessing I haven't used that term before?" When she shook her head, he said, "It just seems to fit. In my head, everything's dark. Shadowy. My memories are there, but they're shrouded in blackness for some reason. But you, you're like a shooting star, a light in that darkness. I might not remember what kind of man I am, or my past, but I must've done something right to have you as my wife."

To Jack's alarm, tears filled Maisy's eyes.

"What? What's wrong?" he asked, feeling panic rise up within him for the second time in as many days.

"Nothing. It's just...that was really sweet."

Jack studied her. He didn't like that such a simple compliment could have her reacting so emotionally. It was apparent he hadn't given her nearly enough of them during their marriage if she reacted like this. He made a mental vow to do better.

"What's on our agenda for the day?" he asked.

She blinked up at him. "Um...I don't know."

"What do we usually do?"

Maisy bit her lip and her gaze slid away from his.

Jack's eyes narrowed. Yet more evasiveness.

She looked back at him. "I guess we should get up, change, go down for breakfast. We can see how you're feeling after that."

"I feel fine."

"Jack, you hit your head. Hard. You lost your memory. I'm thinking we shouldn't push things."

"I'm okay. Have been through a lot worse than a knock on the head."

They both froze.

"You have?" Maisy whispered.

No matter how hard he racked his brain, Jack couldn't remember any other injuries he'd suffered. "I guess? I don't remember."

"It's okay," Maisy soothed, rubbing her hand up and down his biceps. "Don't force yourself to remember. It can't be good for your head."

Jack rubbed his forehead and sighed. "Yeah. Anyway, a shower sounds amazing. As much as I love lying here in bed with you, we probably should get up. Do we shower together?"

She blinked up at him. "Um...no."

"Shame," he teased. Then something occurred to him. "I'm assuming my clothes are here?" He looked around the room. "This room looks decidedly...feminine."

"Uh...yeah. You weren't actually living here...um...you had an apartment in Spokane."

"Spokane? That's hours away!" Jack exclaimed.

"Yes. Jason told you yesterday that we were having issues. We'd been working through them, but you, um, had a lease that you couldn't break. So until we renewed our vows, we thought it best to continue living apart. We were, um, dating."

"Why were we having issues?" Jack demanded.

"Um...we just were," she said, avoiding another question.

"Did I cheat on you? Was I abusive?"

"What? No!" Maisy said without hesitation.

Jack relaxed, relieved beyond measure that he hadn't done either of those things to his wife. He didn't feel like the kind of man who would break his marriage vows, but since he didn't have any memories to back up those feelings, he didn't know for sure. "Then why? Why would I live so far away from you?"

"Maybe I cheated on *you*, and you got pissed," Maisy said.

"You didn't."

"Jack, you don't know that."

"Are we really arguing about this?" he asked with a small smile.

Maisy sighed. "Fine. I didn't cheat. It wasn't any one thing. But...you were gone a lot. With your job."

"My job?"

"You were a, ah...a bounty hunter. You were always hunting down bad guys. Gone all the time. I didn't handle it well."

Jack blinked in surprise. "A bounty hunter?"

"Yeah. You liked working for yourself. Don't have a lot of friends. Spent a lot of time watching people... um...surveillance."

Nothing she was telling him struck a chord in Jack. Why in the world would he spend so much time away from home, especially with a woman like Maisy waiting for him in their bed?

"So, I, um, moved back into our family home with Jason, and you went to Spokane. But...I hate to tell you this after everything else...but your apartment complex had a fire. It burned down. So all your stuff...it's gone."

Jack stared down at her. "*Seriously*? All I have is this T-shirt and one pair of underwear?"

She giggled nervously. "No, of course not. And Jason is getting you more stuff today."

Jack carefully mulled over everything he'd just learned. Everything sounded so bizarre. But he couldn't put his finger on why; plenty of married couples separated these days. Regardless, he felt off-kilter and confused.

Maybe because it almost sounded like Maisy was making things up as she went along. He was fairly certain she was lying through her teeth, but since he didn't remember anything about her, he couldn't say for sure. Nor did he have any idea why she might lie to him. "So, I have no clothes, no belongings, nothing."

"You have me," Maisy said quietly but firmly. "And I'm going to do everything I can to make sure we're okay from here on out."

Her words sounded sincere and almost desperate.

"I have a feeling I don't deserve you," Jack said.

To his surprise, she looked sad at his words. "You don't," she replied. And she didn't give him a chance to reply. "Now, are we gonna get up or what? Paige is gonna be upset if we don't get downstairs in time for breakfast."

"In time?" Jack asked.

Maisy shrugged. "My brother likes to eat at certain times."

Jack wanted to know more about Jason. Hell, he wanted to know everything about his wife and her family. He hadn't moved from his position over her, nor did he feel any great need to shift away. Despite his misgivings, he liked being this close to her. Liked the way her fingers unconsciously rubbed his arm. "Tell me more about yourself, *Stellina*."

"Um, what do you want to know?"

"Everything."

She giggled nervously once more. "I'm not that interesting."

"I highly doubt that. Tell me about your family."

Her smile faded. "My parents died when I was a teenager. Carjacking. They were both shot and killed. Jason moved back home to look after me. You might remember him saying yesterday that I don't do well with stress. I was kind of out of it for a while, couldn't function well without medicine to keep me from freaking out all the time. I dropped out of school, got my GED...and here I am."

"I'm so sorry about your parents, Maisy. How did we meet?"

It was a simple question, but she looked like a deer in headlights. "Um...online."

"Online? Don't tell me I was on a dating site," Jack said with a laugh.

But she didn't crack a smile. "No, um, a friend of my brother's set us up. We talked for a while online, then we met, and that was that."

As far as explanations went, it was extremely lacking, but because she looked so tense and stressed, Jack let it drop. He supposed it wasn't important. They'd met, fallen in love, then got married. "What's the plan for this weekend?" he asked.

She relaxed under him, proving that it was a good idea to stop asking about their courtship.

"I don't know the details. Jason said he'd take care of it."

"Right. Well, I can't say I'm thrilled that I got hurt, or that my apartment complex burned down, but I *can* say that I'm thankful for a second chance with you. I promise I'll do whatever I can to make our marriage work. But I need you to talk to me. If I do something you don't like, tell me so we can work it out. I don't want to get to the point of another separation. Okay?"

Instead of answering, she pinched his upper arm.

"Ow," Jack complained, even though it hadn't hurt. "What was that for?"

"Just making sure you're real and not a dream," she told him. "Men don't say things like that. They don't like to talk."

"I do. I mean, I think I do," Jack told her. "If it means you don't want to move out of my house, my bed, my life, I definitely do."

Maisy brought a hand up and cradled his cheek. "I'm going to make this right."

It sounded like a vow. A vow he didn't fully understand. He leaned down and kissed her. It wasn't a passionate kiss, but he lingered for a long moment. The electricity he'd felt when he'd first touched her yesterday was back in full force. Shooting down his spine and going straight to his cock. It was surprising, really. The kiss was chaste, merely a meeting of their lips. And yet it felt life-changing.

When he lifted his head, she licked her lips as if mesmerized. Then she took a deep breath and said, "Come on, we really do need to get up."

Jack let her slip out from under him and he followed.

He swayed a little when he stood, but Maisy was there, putting an arm around his waist. "You good?"

"A little light-headed, but I'm all right."

"Come on, I'll walk you to the bathroom. I think there's an extra toothbrush in there. If not, you can use mine."

"You'll let me use your toothbrush?" he asked.

"Well, no. I'll let you have it. Sharing toothbrushes is gross," she said with a small smile, looking up at him as they walked.

Jack laughed out loud. "So sharing toothbrushes is gross but you want me to use yours?" he asked, still grinning.

She blushed a little. "Right. Sorry, didn't think that through."

She wasn't really giving him a ton of support. At a good five inches shorter than his five-eleven, she didn't have the proper angle or strength to keep him from falling. But Jack liked the feel of her against him all the same.

"I mean, is sharing a toothbrush any different from sharing...other bodily fluids?" he asked, still smiling.

To his surprise, she blushed a fiery red.

"Yes. Now, don't go falling and hitting your head again," she warned as they entered the small bathroom.

"Maybe you should stay and shower with me," Jack teased.

The blush on her cheeks didn't abate. "Whatever. I'll shower in the bathroom down the hall. I'll see if I can borrow a pair of sweats from Jason for you to wear until he gets you other clothes today. Is that okay?"

"That's perfect, *Stellina*."

She stared at him for a long moment before taking a deep breath and heading back into the bedroom.

"Maisy?" Jack called, reluctant to see her go for some reason.

She stopped and turned back toward him. "Yeah?"

"Thank you."

"For what?"

"For being so good to me. For marrying me. For being willing to marry me again after I neglected you. For being you."

Tears filled her eyes once more. Then she turned and left the room without a word.

Instinctively feeling as if something was very off, Jack frowned and closed the bathroom door. He stared at himself in the mirror above the sink. It was an odd feeling to see a stranger looking back. He didn't recognize himself. His glasses were still out on the table next to the bed, but he could see his reflection well enough. He had a small scar under his chin, and his beard was a little too long to be comfortable. His skin was tan, as if he spent a lot of time outdoors in the sun, which made sense if he was a bounty hunter who liked to hike.

If he was a bounty hunter? Did he doubt his wife's story about what he did for a living? He had no reason not to trust her, but deep down, he couldn't see himself spending his life chasing down bad guys. He wasn't sure why, but that didn't feel like something he would enjoy. Not to mention, he didn't think he was the kind of man who would neglect his wife.

His head throbbed as if a memory was desperately trying to surface, but no matter how much he tried, he couldn't bring it to the surface.

Frustrated, confused, and in pain, Jack abruptly turned away from the mirror and reached for the knob in the shower. He felt grubby, still had blood in his hair, and he needed to get clean. Maybe the day would bring more clarity to his situation. If nothing else, he'd get a chance to get to know his wife better.

Jack didn't understand the tension between Maisy and her brother, but he remembered the way Jason had spoken to her before he'd known Jack was awake, and he didn't like it one bit. His wife needed a champion, and he may not have been there for her before, but he was now. If he discovered that Jason didn't respect Maisy, as soon as their renewal ceremony was over, Jack would look for a new place for them to live. He might not know who he was, or anything about his past, but he wouldn't stand back and let someone he cared about be abused in any way, shape, or form.

And Maisy Smith was definitely someone he cared about. For better or worse, in sickness and health, he'd vowed to stand by her side, and he'd do just that. He'd protect her from himself, her brother, and anyone else who dared try to hurt her in any way.

Where his fierce protectiveness was coming from, Jack didn't know. But he assumed it was a product of being her husband. Memories of loving her in his unconsciousness. *I'll do right by you,* Stellina*, this I vow.*

Satisfied by his internal promise, Jack stripped off his clothes and stepped into the shower. Today was literally the first day of the rest of his life, and he was ready to get on with it...with his wife by his side.

CHAPTER FOUR

The rest of the week had been extremely stressful for Maisy. She felt as if she was walking on eggshells. Every time Jack asked her a question, she was sure the jig was up. That she'd say the wrong thing and his memory would suddenly return.

Now it was Saturday morning—her wedding day.

It was ironic. She'd dreamed about this day for so long. One of her favorite games when she was little was dressing up and using a towel or blanket as a "veil" and walking down the stairs as if she was descending toward her soon-to-be husband. Her mom used to play the part of the officiant, and Maisy would repeat the vows word-for-word to her imaginary beau.

And now here she was, going through with this sham of a marriage. She pretty much hated herself. Hated Jason for making her too afraid to say no to him.

She didn't care about the money...would give it up in a heartbeat if it meant Jack wasn't in this situation. But he was. And that sucked because in the last week, Maisy had discovered that she *liked* the man.

He was considerate, smart, polite, and protective.

It was the last trait that gave her pause. He truly thought she was his wife, and anytime Jason crossed the line—which he was very careful not to do around Jack very often—he'd intervene, getting her away from her brother.

There was no way he'd forgive her for what she was doing. Lying to him, pretending to be someone she wasn't.

But it was mornings like this one, lying in his arms, feeling loved for the first time since her parents had died, when Maisy could almost forget this was all a charade. Hearing his heart beat under her cheek as she lay against his chest, smelling his manly scent, feeling his arms around her...she felt safe.

She already knew she didn't want to give up Jack, but she also knew the inevitable moment would come. He'd remember that they weren't actually man and wife, that he'd been kidnapped, that he'd been tricked into marrying her. And he'd leave.

On one hand, Maisy prayed for his memory to return. She wanted him to get out. To get away from Jason. If he was still here after the requisite three months had passed, he was a goner. As was Maisy. She knew that down to her very bones. And yet, here she was. Complicit in anything Jason was doing.

She was a horrible person. Being afraid of what her brother might do to her if she messed up his plan was no excuse. Not when she suspected what he'd done to her sister-in-law, or even their parents. But what were her options when she was literally penniless? She supposed she could go live on the streets, though Jason would never stop trying to find her. He needed her to gain access to her money.

Jack jerked under her, and Maisy turned her thoughts from her own depressing situation to the man who'd gotten under her skin in just a few short days.

There hadn't been one night so far when he hadn't endured a nightmare. She had no idea what they were about, but if his reactions were anything to go by, they were horrific. And she hated the idea that this man—this strong, compassionate, caring man—was traumatized by something so horrible that he suffered over it every night.

She prayed that whatever Jason's nasty acquaintances had done to get Jack here wasn't the reason for his nightmares.

"You're okay," she murmured soothingly, moving a hand up to his face and palming his cheek. "You're safe."

"Owl! Are you okay? Talk to me, man!"

Maisy didn't know who Owl was, but this wasn't the first time he'd said the name while in the middle of a nightmare. And it was obvious he was someone Jack cared about deeply. "He's all right," she said, praying she wasn't lying. But then again, it would be just one more lie piled on the heap she'd already told him.

"They're hurting him!" Jack moaned as his head thrashed on the pillow.

The arm that was around her tightened, almost painfully so.

"What's wrong with him?"

Maisy jerked at the sound of Jason's voice. She'd been so focused on Jack, she hadn't even heard her brother enter the room. She wasn't surprised he'd come in uninvited. He invaded her privacy all the time, but he hadn't done it since Jack had woken up after being brought into the house. She didn't know why he was there now, but she didn't like it. Not at all.

"Nightmare," she said brusquely, keeping her eyes on Jack.

"Wake up!" Jason exclaimed loudly.

Maisy glared at her brother. She didn't think that was an appropriate way to wake someone who was having a bad dream.

Jason stepped to the edge of the bed, not caring that she was lying there with her soon-to-be husband, and put a hand on Jack's arm, shaking him almost violently. "Hey! Snap out of it! You need to get up and get ready for your wedding!"

Jack moved so fast, Maisy wasn't at all prepared. He pushed her to the side and swung at Jason, his fist making contact with her brother's cheekbone with a loud thud.

Jason grunted as his head whipped back.

Then Jack did something Maisy had a hard time understanding. Instead of pushing her brother away, he grabbed hold of his shirt and pulled him *toward* the bed. And he hit him again.

Maisy could only watch with wide eyes as Jack did his best to beat the crap out of Jason.

Even though he was strong, and apparently had a very mean right hook, Jason was able to yank his shirt out of his grip and stumble backward.

"What the fuck?" he exclaimed.

"No more!" Jack said. "Stop!"

Unbelievably, Jack still seemed to be asleep, caught in the grip of whatever horrors he saw in his mind.

Not thinking about her own safety, only wanting to

soothe him, Maisy scooted back up next to Jack and put her hand on his chest. "It's okay, he's stopping!"

Amazingly, Jack stilled at her touch and voice.

"Seriously, what the fuck?" Jason seethed as he stumbled backward a little farther. "I think he broke my nose!"

"He's dreaming, he didn't know it was you," Maisy said defensively.

"He's lucky I need him to marry your ass!"

Feeling relieved now that Jack had flopped down next to her again, she asked, "What are you doing in here so early?"

"The sooner I get you married, the better. The officiant is downstairs."

"Now?" Maisy asked, looking over at the clock. "It's not even seven o'clock."

"One hour," Jason warned. "I want your ass downstairs by eight. Hear me?"

Maisy ground her teeth as she pressed her lips together.

"Trust me, Maise. You'll be downstairs at eight, or you'll be fucking sorry," Jason threatened. Then he turned and walked out of the room, bitching about his nose under his breath.

The thing was, Maisy was already sorry. Sorry she'd let herself get into this situation. Sorry that she hadn't already confessed to Jack. Sorry that she hadn't helped him get the hell out of this house and away from her.

But even if she had, Jason would've kidnapped someone else. He didn't care who she married, as long as it was done. It was likely he'd find someone horrible too, just to show her that she had no control over anything.

Someone who would beat and rape her. Someone like his awful so-called *friend*, Don.

Determination filled her then. For the first time in years, she had someone else to worry and care about other than herself. If it was just her, she'd probably continue on as she'd been doing for the last decade. Doing whatever Jason wanted, turning a blind-eye to the horrible things he'd done, hiding behind a drug-induced haze, just so she'd have a place to live. But now, she was responsible for the safety of someone else.

She'd marry Jack and do what she could to protect him from Jason. It would buy them some time. If she didn't marry Jack, her brother would kill him and kidnap someone else.

She had three months to figure out what to do and how to tell Jack what was going on. She had every intention of telling him...if nothing else, so he could protect himself from her brother. She'd help Jack find where he came from; she had no doubt he had lots of people who were probably worried sick about what had happened to him. He'd hate her, of that Maisy had no doubt, but if he was outraged enough to leave her, to get away from her brother...

It was the best thing she could do for Jack.

She hoped it would keep him safe.

She didn't need Jack with her at the bank, in person, to gain access to her inheritance. The marriage certificate should suffice. Jason would still get her money, and she'd either be free or dead. At this point, it didn't really matter which.

Jack shifted under her, and Maisy realized her hand had slipped under his shirt and she'd been caressing his chest, both to soothe him and because his warm skin felt amazing against her palm.

"Morning," he said in a deep, rumbly voice that seemed to pierce straight into her soul. He shifted against her so his arm was around her back and his other hand pressed against hers, keeping her from removing it from under his shirt.

"Morning," she said cautiously. It wasn't that long ago that he'd been decking her brother. Would he remember?

"What time is it?"

"Seven. And I have to tell you, Jason's anxious for our ceremony and wants us downstairs by eight."

One of Jack's brows lifted in surprise. "That doesn't give you much time to get ready. What's the rush?"

She shrugged. "I guess he's excited?" Understatement of the century. The sooner he got her married, the sooner the countdown to him getting millions of dollars started.

"Are things...all right between you two?" Jack asked gently.

Maisy stilled. She had no idea how to answer that. She couldn't be honest and tell her soon-to-be husband that she hated her brother. That he was an awful human being.

"It's just that I've noticed he doesn't exactly treat you with care. I must've really hurt you if you chose to come back here to live with him."

Maisy felt tears spring to her eyes. She hated that Jack thought he'd done something to alienate her.

"Don't cry," Jack begged. "I can handle anything but that. I'm sorry, this is our re-wedding day. I'll back off. But you should know...I want out of here. I want to get a place just for us. I don't like how he talks to you sometimes, and while he's family, it's not cool. I need to see about getting a replacement ID and accessing our bank account and talking to my landlord about lease deposits and getting a replacement cell phone."

His words made her tears stop as she stared at him. Of *course* he'd want to do those things. Anyone who was renting an apartment that had burned down would do the same. But the issue was that he *had* no bank account, there *was* no landlord, and she had no idea where his previous cell phone had gone. Not to mention identification. Jack Smith didn't exist, and he would find that out pretty quickly once he started trying to re-claim his nonexistent life.

"Breathe, *Stellina*. I'm sorry, I didn't mean to stress you out today of all days." Then he smiled. "I have to say, I like waking up to you touching me."

Maisy swallowed hard.

"I won't push, but tonight...I'd really like to make love with my wife. Though it sucks, because I don't remember what you like."

"What I like?" she whispered.

Jack grinned. "Yeah. Do you like it hard and fast? Slow and easy? How sensitive is your clit? Can you come with nipple play or do you need more stimulation? I don't know what your favorite position is, or whether you like to be in control, or if you like it when I'm more dominant."

Maisy squirmed against him, and he chuckled.

"I kind of feel like one of those men of old...desperately wanting his woman but having to wait until his wedding night to uncover all her secrets. But this time, I feel like *I'm* the virgin. It'll be like our first time all over again—and I can't wait."

Maisy hadn't allowed herself to think too much about

this part of the ruse her brother had foisted on them. Yes, she'd been sleeping at Jack's side since her brother had dragged him home, but she'd blocked out the sex part of being married, assuming she could come up with some reason to put it off. Now she realized how foolish she'd been. Again. Of *course* she couldn't put off sex with her husband for months.

He wanted to make love tonight. And it would be their first time together, but she couldn't exactly tell him that.

"*Stellina*? I'm sorry, did I shock you?"

She forced herself to breathe. The only thing shocking about what he'd said was how much she wanted it. She could feel how wet she was between her legs. "No," she lied.

"Liar," he accused gently.

It took everything in Maisy not to flinch at that word.

He leaned up, keeping her hand trapped under his shirt as he moved closer and closer. Maisy's eyes closed at the last second and she lowered her head, meeting him halfway. She needed his kiss more than she realized.

The second his lips touched hers, she felt as if she'd come home.

He'd kissed her before, several times now, but they'd all been chaste touches. This kiss was completely different. His tongue traced the seam of her lips, and she opened to him immediately.

He surged inside, taking control, and all Maisy could do was hold on and moan as he took her mouth like a man possessed. He nipped, sucked, and explored every inch of her mouth. Her nipples were hard under her shirt and her fingernails dug into his chest as he devoured her.

When he pulled back, they were both breathing hard, and all Maisy could do was stare at him.

"I'm not letting you go again," Jack said, the words sounding like a vow. "Whatever happened between us is in the past. From this day forward, it's us against the world. I won't let you down, and I'll always be your champion. Thank you for giving me a chance to make things right. This time, I promise to be the husband you deserve."

His words sounded like something straight out of a movie. Like...marriage vows. The pesky tears sprang to her eyes again. He wouldn't be saying those things if he knew everything was a lie. That they'd known each other for less than a week. That her brother had kidnapped him to force him into marriage. That he'd planned on torturing them both if either of them resisted.

"I promise that I'll do right by you," Maisy told him in a low, husky voice. "That I'll do what I can to support you and keep you safe."

"That's my job," Jack said with a small smile as he ran a hand over her hair. "To keep you safe, that is."

Maisy closed her eyes and lowered her head to his shoulder. This man. He was killing her.

They lay there for a couple of minutes, lost in thought. Then he finally said, "If we're going to be downstairs by eight, you need to get up and start getting ready."

He wasn't wrong. But the thought of the enormous wrong she was doing to this man was overwhelming.

"Come on, *Stellina*, up. The sooner this is done, the sooner we can come back up here and start our honeymoon."

Her head came up at that, and she saw the sparkle in his eye.

"That is, if I can get this erection to subside long enough to not look like a pervert in public."

Her eyes moved without conscious thought. And when Maisy saw the bulge in his sweatpants, she swallowed hard. To be honest, his size scared her. The one time she'd had sex, it had hurt. A lot. And that boy was nowhere near Jack's impressive proportions.

Jack's finger under her chin lifted her face back up so he could look into her eyes. "I won't hurt you. Surely you know that."

He *would* hurt her, devastate her when he turned his hate toward her after he understood the deception that had taken place. But she nodded anyway.

"I don't remember our sex life, but you've obviously taken me many times—I can't imagine I was able to resist you—so it's gonna be good. Better than good. I give you my word."

She nodded. And suddenly, she wanted this. Him. Wanted to feel every inch of him deep inside her body. Wanted to know what it felt like to be cherished in bed. She'd read a lot of books, knew what sex was *supposed* to feel like, and for once, she wanted to experience what the fuss was all about. And she knew without a doubt that sex with Jack would be unforgettable.

"Right," she said firmly. "I'm getting up. We're getting married, then we're having sex."

He grinned. "Re-married, and yes, we are."

Shoot. She had to remember that this was supposed to be a renewal of vows ceremony, and not an actual marriage. Jack was smart, really smart, and if she screwed up too many times, he'd get suspicious.

"Get up, Mrs. Smith. Get ready. We'll walk down together."

Sliding her hand out from under his shirt, Maisy nodded. He picked up her hand, kissed the palm, then grinned at her as she scooted over to the edge of the bed.

When she was halfway across the room, Jack said, "Maisy?"

She turned around to look at him.

"I feel like the luckiest man in the world that you're willing to give me a second chance. Thank you."

Shit, Maisy felt like the worst fraud. Her throat was so tight, she couldn't speak, so she simply smiled at him, then turned back toward the bathroom. As soon as the door was shut behind her, the tears fell.

CHAPTER FIVE

"Do you, Maisy Smith, take this man to be your lawfully wedded husband, to have and to hold, for better or worse, for richer or poorer, through sickness and health, till death do you part?"

"I do." Maisy's voice was soft, and it quivered the smallest bit.

Jack squeezed her hand in support. She smiled at him as their gazes stayed locked together.

"Do you, Jack Smith, take this woman to be your lawfully wedded wife, to have and to hold, for better or worse, for richer or poorer, through sickness and health, till death do you part?"

"I do," he said, surprising himself with the depth of feeling he experienced at those two simple words.

This morning hadn't gone as he'd expected. He'd thought Maisy would spend all morning getting ready and then they'd have a leisurely brunch before their vow renewal ceremony. But instead, he'd woken up with not only his head hurting—which was still fairly normal—but his knuckles as well, for some reason. Then Maisy had her hand on his bare chest, which made his cock hurt in the best way. And the kiss they'd shared had been life-altering.

There were things about his wife's situation that bothered him greatly. The most important was the clear disdain Jason showed for his sister. It felt incredibly wrong and had Jack on high alert. He didn't like the disrespect he'd shown by insisting this ceremony take place so early in the morning, but since he didn't understand the undercurrents, he didn't feel as if he could really interject his opinion.

But he'd been dead serious this morning when he'd told Maisy that he wanted out of this house as soon as possible. There was something about Jason he didn't trust. Not only that, but he didn't want to have to worry about his brother-in-law busting into their room anytime he felt like it. He wanted his wife to himself.

For the ceremony, she was wearing a simple lavender dress that came down to her knees. It clung to her upper body and flared out at her hips. She looked beautiful, and he hadn't hesitated to tell her so the second he'd seen her. The blush on her face and shy look she'd given him had made Jack want to throw her on their bed and show her *exactly* how pretty he thought she was, but he also didn't want to deal with an annoyed Jason, so he'd simply offered his wife his arm and they'd headed out of the room.

They'd walked down the stairs together, and the second they'd entered the dining area, Jason had said, "Good, I was just about to send someone up to find you two. Let's get this done." And the officiant had started speaking.

Jack had taken one look at the "officiant" and the hair

on the back of his neck had stood up. He didn't know the man, but he definitely didn't look like someone who performed marriages for a living. He was bald, had a scraggly goatee, and his gaze lingered on Maisy's chest a little too long. Other than his inappropriate interest in Jack's wife, the man seemed almost bored.

As far as vow renewals went, this one wasn't exactly ideal. But Jack did his best to ignore the awkward aspects and concentrate on what was important.

Maisy.

Now, the ceremony was over almost as soon as it had begun.

"You may kiss your bride."

He'd been holding Maisy's hands while her brother's friend performed the ceremony, but now he palmed her face. She braced herself on his chest as she looked up at him.

The entire "ceremony" had taken about five minutes, if that. Jack hadn't had a chance to tell Maisy how proud he was to be her husband. How thankful he was that she was giving him a second chance. He hated that they'd grown apart, but he mentally vowed to do everything in his power not to let it happen again.

"You really do look beautiful," he said softly.

He felt her lean into him a bit more. "Thanks. You look good too." Jason had brought him a bunch of clothes earlier in the week, and Jack had put on a pair of slacks this morning instead of the jeans he felt more comfortable in...since this was a special day and all.

"For God's sake, kiss her already!" Jason exclaimed.

Jack didn't take his gaze from his wife as he slowly lowered his head.

Her chin tipped up as he got close.

Keeping his eyes open, Jack did his best to memorize this moment. He didn't have a lot of memories with his wife, so now he cherished each and every one. Like the way she lay boneless against his chest in bed and curled into him like a contented cat. How she worried about him, was extremely concerned about his memory and whether any memories had returned yet, and how she had no problem sitting at his side for hours and simply talking. He enjoyed being taken care of by his wife and wanted to do the same right back. He was protective of her, she seemed...fragile. Jack wasn't sure why, but the feeling persisted.

Their wedding kiss was short but extremely heartfelt. Jack poured all his feelings into the embrace. This felt right. He was still getting to know Maisy again, and because of his lost memories, it felt as if he'd just met her. But a part of him deep down had recognized her as his. If it hadn't, he might doubt every single thing he'd been told after waking up.

"All right, you two, that's enough. You can have sex after we do the paperwork," Jason said crudely. It was an intrusion on a beautiful moment, and once again, Jack resented his presence.

He reluctantly lifted his lips from Maisy's and stared down at her. She met his gaze and licked her lips sensually. Her fingers had curled into little claws, and she was leaning into him as if he was the only thing keeping her upright.

"Hi," he said inanely.

"Hi," she whispered back.

"Here," Jason said, once more ruining the moment by waving something at them.

Frowning, Jack turned and saw his brother-in-law was holding out a pen.

"It's time to sign the paperwork," Jason told them.

"Paperwork? We're already married," Jack said, frowning.

"Right, you are. But I thought you'd like a memory of today, something to put in a scrapbook. It's all good. It's just a memento. It's not as if you guys can be married twice."

Jack narrowed his eyes at Jason. It seemed to him that the man was speaking a little fast, as if he was nervous...or excited. He couldn't tell which.

"Here, you first, Maise," Jason told his sister, practically shoving the pen at her.

She dropped a hand from Jack's chest and turned to accept the pen her brother was holding out. Jack didn't let her go. He turned her in his embrace but kept an arm around her waist, holding her against him.

She peered up at him shyly, and Jack knew he'd never get enough of seeing that small blush on her face. He walked her a few steps over to the dining room table, where he saw an official-looking document laid out.

Jason leaned in next to Maisy and pointed at a signature line at the bottom. "There. You sign there," he ordered.

Jack felt Maisy stiffen, but she didn't hesitate to lean over and sign where her brother indicated. Then she turned and looked up at Jack, offering him the pen.

For some reason, Jack hesitated. He looked down at the paper, then at Jason. The man seemed a little too eager for them to sign whatever these papers were. Excited. Almost smug. Like a kid who was about to get a giant ice cream cone or something. It sent warning bells clanging through Jack. It was frustrating as hell not to know why he felt this way about his brother-in-law.

"Jack?" Maisy whispered.

Looking at her hand holding the pen, he saw it was shaking. Was she nervous? If so, about what?

"Usually the groom has the jitters *before* he gets married," Jason joked. "What, you regretting tying yourself to my sister again?" Then he laughed as if he'd said the funniest thing in the world.

If Jack hadn't already been looking at Maisy, he would've missed the affect Jason's barb had on her. She flinched, but it was a fleeting move. Her brother's words obviously hurt more than she'd ever let on.

Jack moved before he thought about what he was doing. He took the pen from Maisy's hand and leaned over the table, scribbling his name on the line above Maisy's then slamming the pen down on the table. "I don't regret anything about marrying Maisy. Now or the first time."

"Right, of course you don't. I'll just go and get this framed for you," Jason said, not seeming to care that Jack was pissed at him. He snatched up the piece of paper from the table, gesturing to his friend who'd performed the ceremony as he went.

The man's eyes came up from where he was obviously checking out Maisy's ass, and he smirked at Jack before following Jason to the door. The silence that filled the room after their departure seemed huge.

"Well," Maisy said nervously, but she didn't expound on what she was thinking.

"Hello, Mrs. Smith," Jack said, pulling her close until she was plastered against his front. He looped his arms around her and held her gently against him.

Maisy looked up at him, but instead of happiness he saw apprehension in her eyes. Which was unacceptable. Damn her brother for making today anything less than joyous. "You hungry?" he asked.

At that, her lips twitched. "Starving."

That was another thing, Jack didn't think his wife ate enough. He hadn't had many meals with her and her brother here in the dining room, but during the few that they'd shared, he hadn't missed the disapproving looks Jason had given his sister while she'd been eating.

"I think Paige was going to make us a special breakfast," she told Jack.

"You want to go somewhere?"

Maisy frowned. "Like, to a restaurant?" she asked in confusion.

"Yeah, *Stellina*. Like out to a restaurant. We haven't been out since...you know, my accident. I thought maybe we could take a drive, talk, have a nice meal somewhere. You could tell me more about you. There's so much I still want to know. It'll be a good chance for me to court you all over again."

"Like a date."

"Exactly." Jack didn't like how shocked she seemed that he wanted to take her out.

"Okay. But we need to talk to Paige. She's probably already started making brunch for us."

That was one more thing Jack liked about his wife. She was very cognizant of others' feelings. Didn't like to put them out. Was very considerate. Every day, he learned something new about her. She loved animals, wasn't much of an outdoor girl, didn't like seafood but for some reason could eat tuna from a can. She didn't snore, but kind of snuffled in her sleep, and she didn't sleep well unless she was plastered against his side. That last one, Jack loved more than he wanted to admit.

It felt...strange. Good, but odd. As if it was something new for him, someone sleeping at his side. Which was confusing since he was a married man, but then again, he'd apparently been living in Spokane while she'd been here in Seattle, so maybe it wasn't so unusual after all. Every night when they went to sleep, she seemed hesitant to climb into bed with him, but after she fell asleep, she inevitably migrated over to his side and clung to him like she was drowning and he was her own personal flotation device. And Jack loved it. Loved the feel of her in his arms. Loved having her close.

"All right, let's go find Paige, then we can get going. It sucks that my car was stolen while we were hiking. Piss-poor timing for sure. I need to get that replaced soon. I appreciate your brother renting one for us to use. You'll have to drive though, as I haven't replaced my driver's license yet."

"Um...shoot. I didn't think about that. I, ah, don't have a license."

"You don't have a driver's license?"

She shook her head. "No. I wasn't old enough when my parents died, and after, I didn't have an interest. It was all I could do to get through every day. And considering they were carjacked, I had even less desire to get behind the wheel of a vehicle."

Jack could understand that. Frustration pulled at him.

He needed out of this house. He didn't know why, but he felt like a prisoner here. Which sucked, because this was Maisy's current home.

"Fuck it," he muttered. "If I get pulled over, so be it. I'll take the ticket for not having my license, but you'll have to tell the cops who I am so I don't get arrested."

Jack was joking, but the stricken expression on Maisy's face made him regret making light of the moment.

"We can stay here," he quickly said.

"No! It's fine. I'm sure you're sick of the house. I trust you, Jack."

"That means the world to me. You're safe when you're with me."

"And you're safe with me too," she responded.

He smiled at her and pulled her against him once more. He loved the feel of her against his body. She was soft to his hard, the yin to his yang. It was hard to believe he'd forgotten this woman. She seemed to take up every inch of his headspace now. His brain was full of all things Maisy Smith. His wife. It was unbelievable, but so right at the same time.

He lowered his head without a word and felt satisfaction rise up within him when she went up on her tiptoes to eagerly reach his mouth. One of her hands came up and caressed the back of his neck as he kissed her.

What had started as a way to show her how pleased he was that she was his wife, that he honored and cherished her, blossomed into so much more in a heartbeat. It was all Jack could do not to lay her back on the table behind them and take her right then and there.

He wanted this woman. His wife. He yearned to see her body. To find out what she liked in bed. To feel her clasping his cock as he pushed deep inside her warm, wet sheath.

She was his wife, he'd had her hundreds of times before now, but he didn't remember a damn one of them, and that made everything a little more exciting. How many men had a second chance to have a first time with his wife?

They were both breathing hard when Jack forced himself to lift his head. One of his hands had pulled up the hem of the pretty lavender dress she wore and was kneading her scrumptious ass cheek. The other he'd wrapped around her hair, holding her head still as he ravished her mouth.

Her pupils were dilated, and her lips plump and red from their kisses. She looked up at him in a daze even as her fingers caressed the sensitive skin on the back of his neck. Her nipples pressed hard against the bodice of the dress and it took all of Jack's control not to lean down and take one of them into his mouth.

"Nice."

The low voice had Jack moving before he understood what he was doing. He spun, putting himself between Maisy and whoever had dared interrupt them, letting go of her ass so her dress fell back down, covering her thighs once more. Turning, he glared at the man who stood just inside the door. He was tall and muscular. Had blond hair and ice-blue eyes that seemed lifeless. He wore a smirk on his face that rubbed Jack the wrong way and made him want to remove Maisy from his sight immediately.

Jack didn't recognize the man, hadn't seen him in the house before.

"Don't stop on my account," the man snickered. "Things were just getting good."

"Who are you?" Jack barked. The man gave him the creeps, and he didn't want him even in the same room as his wife.

"No one," the man said with that same mocking smile on his face. "I was just looking for Jason."

"He's not here," Jack said gruffly.

"Right. I'll just be off to find him then. I hear congratulations are in order?"

Why he said that as a question, Jack didn't know. He gave a single curt nod.

"Right. Then congratulations. And sorry about the memory problem...but it looks like things turned out better than planned for you. Lucky."

Jack didn't understand what the man meant, but he definitely didn't like him. He didn't say anything, just continued to glare at the stranger.

The man tipped an imaginary hat to them, then left as quietly as he'd arrived. But it was the laughter that echoed through the hall and into the dining room that had Jack gritting his teeth.

"Who was that?" he asked, turning and pulling Maisy into his embrace once more.

"I don't know. I've never seen him before. But Jason has lots of...associates...that I've never met."

Jack's head was pounding harder than before. It was as if his unconscious was screaming out a warning, but he couldn't decipher it. It was frustrating and irritating.

"Jack?" Maisy asked. "If you don't want to go anywhere, that's all right. I'm sure whatever Paige has planned will be wonderful."

Taking a deep breath and willing his pounding headache to fade, he shook his head. "No, we're definitely going." Then he looked down at his wife. His gaze ran over her face, her still plump lips, her mussed hair, knowing it had been his hand that caused it. He blurted, "Tonight, I'd like to make love to my wife again...if that's acceptable to you." Yes, they'd talked about this before, but after vowing to love and honor her, he felt as if he needed to get her permission.

She looked nervous, even a little scared, which bothered Jack. But then she licked her lips and nodded.

"We don't have to, if you aren't sure," Jack felt compelled to say.

"I'm sure. I...I want you. But...it's been a while for me."

Jack frowned. "A while?"

She nodded and bit her lip. Her eyes flicked to the left for a split second, before she met his gaze again. "We haven't...you know...in several months. Since you moved out to Spokane. And I'll probably be...rusty. Can we...will you...go slow?"

Jack's heart turned in his chest. "I won't hurt you, *Stellina*. I give you my word."

She nodded. "Then yes, I'd like to...consummate our marriage tonight."

Jack chuckled at her words. "It'll be our second honeymoon. I'd love to hear all about our first one over breakfast. Shall we go find Paige then get out of here?"

Maisy swallowed hard and nodded.

He leaned down and kissed her forehead reverently, inhaling the scent of apples into his lungs once more. He'd forever associate that smell with this woman. It sucked that not even her scent could break through the fog covering his past. Wasn't smell supposed to be one of the strongest triggers for memory?

It didn't matter. He'd make more memories, starting now.

Jack wrapped his fingers around hers and pulled her away from where Jason's "associate" had gone. He didn't want to see that man again.

Maisy's brother wasn't what he seemed, of that Jack was sure. The longer he was in this house, the more uncomfortable he became. And he definitely didn't like the fact that his wife had lived here without him.

Something was off about this place. Jack couldn't put his finger on it. All he knew was that he wanted out. Wanted Maisy out. And he'd do whatever he could to speed up the process of getting his life back. He needed to get an ID, a car, and figure out how to do a job he didn't even remember, so he could provide for his wife.

There were a lot of things he didn't yet know about who he was, and about his wife, but he'd do whatever it took to be the best husband he could be. And if he could make the worry and fear he sometimes saw lurking behind Maisy's eyes disappear, he'd be a satisfied man.

CHAPTER SIX

Surprisingly, Maisy had an amazing day. Paige hadn't been disappointed in the least that they were forgoing the meal she'd planned. In fact, she'd seemed downright gleeful Maisy was getting out of the house.

Jack was a very safe and competent driver. She'd never been comfortable in a car because of what happened to her parents, but with Jack behind the wheel, she'd been able to relax a little. His head was constantly on a swivel, he was aware of where all the cars and people were around them.

They ended up stopping at a hole-in-the-wall diner that Jason never would've stepped foot inside. He was a snob when it came to food and only ate in uptight, expensive restaurants.

The diner smelled like grease, and even now, hours later, Maisy could still smell the fried food in her hair. But the meal was absolutely delicious. She'd ordered waffles with whipped cream and strawberries, a glass of chocolate milk, and a plate of fried Oreo cookies for dessert. Jack didn't comment once about how many calories she was consuming or even raise an eyebrow at the unhealthy food choices. For himself, he'd ordered a hamburger with home fries and had a slice of apple pie afterward.

But the best part about the meal was how at ease Maisy felt. Jack peppered her with question after question, and talking about herself normally made her uncomfortable, but at no time did his questions venture into uneasy territory.

When she'd first met Jack, she was reluctant to answer *any* questions about herself, not wanting to get too close to the man. But the more time she spent with him, the more relaxed she became. What would it matter if she talked about her likes and dislikes? If she opened up just a little?

She talked about her favorite foods, what books she liked to read, how she spent her free time, and shared a little about that awful time immediately after her mom and dad had been killed. How she'd been a basket case before Jason stepped in so she didn't have to move out of the only home she'd ever known.

Maisy even felt comfortable enough discussing the years she'd spent in a depressive haze. How the prescription medicine had been the only thing getting her through most days. Jack had been understanding and empathetic, not judging her for using medication so she wouldn't have to deal with the emotional pain of her grief.

It was as if he truly understood, which was a relief—but it also made Maisy feel even guiltier. There had to be a reason he was as empathetic as he was, and she hated that she didn't *know* the reason. Didn't know the man behind the lost memories.

Before she could feel even worse about marrying him

under false pretenses, wondering about the friends or family who were probably worried sick about him, he suggested they see what else they could find to do before heading back to the house.

Maisy paid their bill—it bothered Jack that he didn't have his own money to pay for them—and he held her hand as he walked them back to the car. They went to a big box store, where she impulsively bought him a prepaid smartphone. She might live to regret that decision—especially if Jason found out—but she wanted Jack to have access to help...just in case. Then they stopped at a large park and walked for a couple of hours. People-watching, laughing, holding hands.

It had been one of the best days of Maisy's life.

And she felt guiltier still. Because while she hated her brother for kidnapping Jack and forcing him to marry her, she'd never felt as content as she did right now. With Jack by her side, kissing her, holding her hand, and making her feel as if she was normal for the first time in years. And she had no right to feel that way. Not about a man who wasn't truly hers to begin with.

It sucked. Because sooner or later, Jack would remember everything. It was inevitable. And when he did, she'd be right back in the same situation as before. Well, not entirely the same. As soon as Jason got his money, she'd most likely experience some sort of horrible accident, and her brother would be free to spend her money as he pleased.

But now, after getting a glimpse into a future she might've had if she'd fought harder, instead of despair filling her...anger rose.

How *dare* Jason treat her the way he had! She didn't

give a crap about the money, she simply wanted enough so she could leave Seattle and start her life over. Maybe meet a man who would love her for who she was. Who would kiss her as if his life depended on it. Hold her hand, laugh at her stupid jokes.

Shoot, who was she kidding? Jack *was* that man, but their relationship was a lie. He had no idea he'd only met her a week ago. That he was a pawn in her brother's appalling scheme. It was horrific, and Maisy had no idea how to fix things, or if they even *could* be fixed. She was too deep into the scam now. She was just as bad as Jason. She should've tried to talk to Jack that first day he woke up. Explained why he was in pain, that her brother had kidnapped him. Done what she could to free him from the danger that shrouded her childhood home.

But she hadn't. And now she was just as guilty as Jason. She'd married Jack under false pretenses, for God's sake. There was no way he'd ever forgive her for that.

"What was that sigh for?" Jack asked.

They were sitting outside the house. Neither had wanted to go back inside just yet and by unspoken agreement had remained in the car, talking for the last thirty minutes.

"It's just...it's been a good day," she told him honestly.

"It has," Jack agreed and reached for her hand. He brought it up to his lips and kissed her knuckles. "And it's not over yet."

The way he looked at her, as if she was the most desirable woman in the world, had Maisy squirming in her seat. She wanted him. It was crazy, probably stupid, but his memory could come back tomorrow, for all she knew. And if she had only one night with Jack, with a man who seemed to want her with a desperation she'd never experienced before, she was going to be greedy and take it. She'd be able to pull up the memories of their wedding night when she was alone once more, trapped in the nightmare that was her life.

"We should probably go inside," she said softly.

"Yeah. You think your brother has planned a dinner? A reception of sorts?"

Maisy shook her head immediately.

Which made Jack frown. "Why not? Doesn't he want his little sister to have an amazing memory for her renewal of vows?"

Realizing she should've made up some excuse rather than simply saying no, Maisy racked her brain to come up with something that might make sense. But her mind was blank. As she'd told Jason once upon a time, she wasn't good at lying. Didn't like doing it and never was able to think fast on her feet. In the end, she just shook her head.

"Whatever. Doesn't matter. I'm not sure I want to spend my night with your brother, no offense."

She gave him a small smile. "It's okay. I don't want to spend my wedding night with him either."

"So...maybe we can raid Paige's kitchen and bring some snacks up to our room? Lock the door and celebrate our own way?"

Her heart felt as if it would beat out of her chest. Maisy gave him a small smile and nodded.

"Great. Let's go," Jack said, sounding eager. He jumped out of the car, and Maisy giggled as she did the same. He grabbed her hand as soon as she walked around the vehicle and pulled her toward the door.

Half expecting Jason to be waiting for them with a

frown on his face and a scolding on his tongue for being gone so long, Maisy was pleasantly surprised when the hallway was empty. They headed for the kitchen and found Paige and two of the housekeepers chatting.

They made small talk, and Jack sweet-talked Paige into making them a charcuterie board with various kinds of cheese, crackers, pickles, olives, carrots, chocolate, a few cookies, and some nuts. He carried it up the stairs to their room, and after putting it on the bed, walked determinedly to the door and locked it.

Maisy was well aware that locking the door wouldn't keep her brother out if he really wanted in. She'd learned that the hard way last year when he was yelling at her and she'd fled to her room to get away from him. He'd laughed and used a key she didn't know he had to enter her room without any difficulty whatsoever. He'd told her how stupid she was, that there was nowhere she could go that he wouldn't find her, and swore that if she ever walked away when he was talking to her again, she'd regret it.

But now wasn't a time to think about her brother and all the bad things he'd done. She was married, and she wanted this time alone with her husband more than she'd ever thought possible. It was stupid, she should put him off, tell him she had her period or something. Sleeping with him would only make him hate her more when his memories returned, but Maisy needed Jack more than she needed air. If she only had this one night, she was taking it, selfish as that might seem.

Jack walked toward her and put his hands on her shoulders. Then he gently pushed her backward until her knees hit the mattress. "Climb up," he said with a small smile. "We'll have a picnic."

Doing as he requested, Maisy sat so she was on one side of the large cutting board Paige had used for the finger food. Jack joined her on the mattress and sat next to her instead of across.

Then he proceeded to feed her one little snack at a time. They laughed and talked about her favorite TV shows as they ate. But each time his fingers brushed against her lips, Maisy's need ramped up. Before long, he stopped being coy about touching her while they ate. His free hand rested on her knee, and each time he fed her a piece of food, he ran his thumb over her bottom lip or caressed her cheek.

And of course, Maisy gave as good as she got. She fed him as well, loving the way his pupils dilated as she teased him back.

The next time he gave her a piece of chocolate, Maisy reached up and grabbed his wrist, keeping him from pulling his hand back. She licked his finger, ridding it of the small bit of melted chocolate that had been left behind.

Jack moaned, and the sound went straight to her pussy. She stared into his eyes as she took his index finger into her mouth. Feeling extremely wanton, she licked around the digit and sucked, hard.

Maisy squeaked in surprise as Jack moved. He had her on her back before she knew what he was doing. He loomed over her, and she stared up at him in anticipation. Then, without a word, he leaned down and kissed her. Hard, deep, and with complete dominance. And she loved every second. She melted under his touch, giving in to whatever he wanted.

And what he apparently wanted was what *she* wanted

too. Maisy had never felt so...alive. Every nerve ending tingled. She could feel how wet she was between her legs, her underwear positively drenched. She needed Jack. Now.

Not realizing she was clawing at him, trying to get closer, she mewed in disappointment when he pulled back.

"Easy, *Stellina*. We have all night."

She shook her head. "No. I want you, Jack. Now. If you don't get inside me right this second, I think I'll die."

To her frustration, he grinned. "Yeah?"

Her eyes narrowed. "Are you laughing at me?"

He sobered. "Never. Don't you know? I want you just as badly. But this is our first time, I want to savor it. Savor *you*."

For a split second, Maisy panicked. Did he know? Did he remember that they weren't married? That she was basically a stranger to him? But then he continued speaking.

"You might remember the feel of me, but for me, this is all new. I don't want to miss a thing. The way you squirm when I touch you, if you arch into my touch when I suck on your tits, how you look and feel the first time I make you orgasm."

"The first time?" Maisy blurted.

"Please don't tell me I'm a selfish lover," Jack said with a frown.

"Um...no, you aren't. I just..."

He let her off the hook. "Shhhh. It's okay. And yes—the first time. I plan on seeing you come several times tonight. Is that all right?"

Was it all right? This man couldn't be real. "Duh," she blurted.

He smiled again. "Good. Now lie there and don't move. I need to get the food off the bed."

Maisy kept still as Jack went up on his knees then stepped off the mattress. He quickly moved the charcuterie board to the dresser, then nearly stopped her heart when he took his glasses off and placed them on the table next to the bed, peeled off his shirt...then reached for his pants.

Before she was ready, he was naked. His cock was swollen and the head almost purple as it stood out hard and firm from between his thick thighs. She didn't get nearly a long enough look at him before he was back on the bed, caging her in.

His lips were curled upward in a grin as he looked down at her. "It's almost like that's the first time you've seen me naked. Surely it hasn't been so long since we've been together that you've forgotten."

Maisy's heart pounded in her chest. Jack was beautiful. And intimidating. And because he thought they'd had sex many times before, he obviously had no problem baring himself to her without a second thought. "I just...you're beautiful, Jack."

He looked surprised for a moment, then he gave her a soft smile. "May I?" he asked, even as he began to slowly pull her dress up her legs.

Maisy held her breath as he undressed her. It was extremely difficult to lie there and not try to cover herself. She hadn't been naked in front of someone else even once in her life since becoming an adult...that she knew of. Now, the overhead light was on and there was no hiding.

Besides, Jack wouldn't expect her to be shy...they'd been supposedly married for two years. She did her best not to squirm in discomfort as Jack helped her get the dress over her head, then tossed her underwear and bra off the side of the bed. She lay on her back and tried to read his expression. Was he disappointed?

"*You're* the beautiful one," he said after a long moment. "I don't know what I did to get lucky enough to be your husband, but I'll do whatever it takes to make sure you never regret re-marrying me."

Maisy wanted to cry. This man...he was everything she'd ever dreamed about. And it was all a lie.

The guilt was eating her alive. She couldn't continue to lie to him. Couldn't let him keep on thinking they were something they weren't. She actually opened her mouth to tell him that they'd met less than a week ago and her brother had kidnapped him in order to force this marriage —but the words got stuck in her throat when Jack crawled between her legs and ran his hands up her thighs, pushing her legs apart as he went.

She was as exposed as she'd ever been, and Maisy wanted to die of embarrassment. Jack was staring at her pussy as if he'd never seen one before. He moved one of his hands and ran his thumb up her seam. She jolted when he ran his digit over her clit.

"Easy, *Stellina*," he murmured.

Maisy moaned as she arched into his touch. She'd masturbated, but nothing she did to herself felt as good as Jack's fingers on her. Closing her eyes, she lost herself in sensation.

"I can't believe I ever forgot this pussy. So fucking perfect," he said reverently.

Maisy jerked when he pushed her thighs even farther apart. Her eyes popped open and she looked down. The carnal view that greeted her made another moan slip from between her lips. Jack had dropped down to his belly and his gaze came up to meet hers just as his tongue came out and he licked her.

"Jack," she whispered, as her hands went to his head. She'd planned to push him away, this particular act feeling far too intimate...but when he licked her again, she instead gripped his hair tightly and pulled him closer.

He chuckled, and Maisy felt his breath against her extremely sensitive folds. Then he devoured her. There was no other word for it.

When women talked about men eating them out, she hadn't thought much about that particular crude phrase. But now she understood. Jack used his nose, his lips, his tongue, even his fingers to stimulate her. He slurped, licked, and sucked, bringing her to the brink in minutes.

All she could do was hold on for dear life as he literally blew her mind. She felt no embarrassment. Only pleasure at this man's hands. When he latched his lips over her clit and used his tongue as a vibrator, she let out a little screech and tried to pull away from him. But he wouldn't let her, his hands clamped around her hips and held her still.

And when his finger slipped inside her body, Maisy whimpered.

She exploded a second later. It was the most intense and pleasurable orgasm she'd ever had in her life. And it seemed to go on and on. Her fists in Jack's hair had to be painful for him, but he didn't let up the assault on her bundle of nerves.

She went limp under him as her orgasm waned. Maisy felt Jack moving but didn't have the strength to open her eyes. It wasn't until she felt him wrap her legs around his waist that she managed to pry up her lids.

And the vision that greeted her would be burned in her mind forever. Jack's hair was mussed and his upper chest was red from exertion. He licked his lips as if he couldn't stand to waste even one drop of her release that was smeared all over his lips and chin.

"I need you. Can I?"

It was then Maisy realized he had his hand around his cock and was slowly stroking himself as his chest heaved with desire. And suddenly, she needed him inside her just as badly as he obviously wanted to be there.

She nodded and put her arms above her head and arched her back. Showing him nonverbally that he could take what he needed.

In response, Jack kneed her thighs even farther apart as he scooted forward. Maisy couldn't take her eyes from his cock. It was leaking precome and actually looked painful. He leaned over her, bracing himself with one hand, while the other guided himself to her core.

* * *

Jack had never felt this way before. True, he didn't have memories of making love with his wife to compare to, but he knew without a doubt he'd never been this eager to get inside a woman. It was an honor to get to experience a second first time with Maisy. And she was absolutely glorious. She'd gone off like she hadn't orgasmed in years... which made him feel like shit because he'd obviously neglected her for far too long.

And she came so beautifully. She tasted like heaven

and was so damn responsive. He felt like the luckiest man in the world. He'd wanted to make this last, wanted to explore every inch of her, reacquaint himself with his wife. But he couldn't wait. He was two seconds away from exploding and he wanted to be inside her when he did.

Scooting forward, Jack looked down and grimaced. He was leaking precome nonstop and it was only a matter of time before he lost control. He ran the head of his cock through her folds, loving how wet she was. Pride swelled in his chest. *He'd* done that. He'd made her come so hard she'd soaked not only his face, but the sheet under them as well.

He could smell her muskiness all over him, and he grinned. He pressed the head of his eager and willing cock to her opening and pushed.

Even before Maisy squeaked in alarm, he'd already paused. She was so damn tight! If he didn't know better, he would've said she was a virgin. But that was impossible.

"Jack," she whispered in a wobbly voice.

Tenderness and concern swamped him, making the urge to come recede just a bit. Enough for him to regain control. "Easy, *Stellina*. You're okay."

"I just...you're so big."

"I am, but you can take me. You've done it before. Relax."

His words didn't seem to have any effect. She was tense under him, and Jack hated that fact with every fiber of his being.

He could feel the blood pumping through his cock, but he resisted the urge to plunge inside the heaven he knew without a doubt was waiting for him. Instead, he moved the hand that had guided himself into her and began to lightly caress her sensitive clit.

She jerked against him, and his cock slipped inside her hot body another inch.

"Look at me, Maisy," he ordered. Her gaze came up to his immediately, which sent satisfaction coursing through Jack. "Don't take your eyes from me, understand?"

She nodded.

"Good. You know what I thought when I was going down on you?"

Her cheeks were bright pink as she shook her head.

"How damn good you taste. How I could spend all night between your legs and die a happy man."

"Jack," she protested with a small wrinkle of her nose.

He grinned, and was immensely pleased when her inner muscles relaxed around him a smidge. "I've never experienced anything as amazing as when you came for me. I could feel you tighten around my finger and all I could think of was how incredible it would feel when you did the same around my cock." He continued to caress her clit as he began to gently ease the head of his cock in and out of her pussy.

"You were made for me, *Stellina*. I promise not to let so much time go by again so you forget the shape of me deep inside you. Move your legs up for me. Put your feet flat on the mattress. That's it, perfect. Now spread your thighs more. Give me room. Oh yeah...just like that."

The next time Jack gently pushed inside, he got almost all the way in. "Almost there, you're doing beautifully. Just a little more and you'll be taking all of me."

Her gaze hadn't wavered from his, and it made this experience all the more intense. Her brown eyes seemed to sparkle and her pupils were slightly dilated as she tried to do as he asked.

He began rubbing her clit hard and fast, and Maisy's eyes widened, her breaths coming faster as she stared up at him. "Again, Maisy. Come for me again."

As if his words were the permission she'd been waiting for, Maisy's muscles tensed and she flew over the edge with a shout.

As she was coming, Jack pushed through her spasming muscles until he was seated to the hilt. Then he held still and gritted his teeth as he reveled in the feel of her hot, wet sheath rippling around his cock.

"Are you in?" she asked in a shaky voice a few seconds later.

"I'm in, baby, and it's so damn good. You feel amazing."

"So do you," she admitted in what seemed like a surprised tone.

It irritated Jack. He'd obviously been a horrible lover in the past. For her to be so tight, it meant he hadn't made love to her in way too long. And her surprise at him wanting to give her multiple orgasms, even her shock that being inside her could feel so good...He vowed then and there to do better. To show her how incredible sex between them could be.

"Are you...are we done?" she asked.

Again, that feeling that he hadn't done right by his wife struck him, but Jack pushed the feeling back. He'd analyze it later; right now, he needed to pleasure his woman. "Not even close," he told her, lifting his hips before sinking back inside her. Their pubic hair meshed together, and he could feel the wetness from her pussy coating his balls.

"Oh!" she exclaimed, reaching up to grab hold of his

upper arms. He'd lowered so he was bracing himself on his elbows, cupping her shoulders so he still had good leverage.

"I'm not sure how long I can last," he admitted. "You're so hot and wet that it's all I can do not to lose my load right here and now."

At his words, her inner muscles fluttered around him.

He rocked his hips back and easily glided out of her until just the head of his cock was inside. "You okay with this? I'm not hurting you?"

"Yes. And no. Jack!"

"Jack what?" he teased.

"Move!" she exclaimed.

Letting out a long breath, he relaxed for the first time since he'd realized she was having trouble taking him. "Gladly," he said reverently. "Watch," he told her.

"I thought you told me to look into your eyes."

Jack smiled, and it hit him how much he loved this. Loved that she could tease him. Loved that he could talk dirty to her and she seemed to like it. Loved that he could be fully in control in their bed. He wasn't sure why he *needed* that control, and he didn't realize until right this moment that he did, but he was relieved that his wife could give that to him. But then again, she was probably very used to his ways in bed.

"And now I want you to see me take you," he told her. "Look at how wet my dick is. It's covered in your come. You're so slippery and hot. You're perfect."

Jack adjusted again to hold his upper body up and just moved his hips, pushing in and out of his wife's pussy. The sight of his come-covered cock was so erotic, and he had a feeling he'd never seen anything so beautiful in his life.

"Jack," she whispered as she dug her nails into his arms once again.

"You take me perfectly. You were made for me," Jack told her, feeling the rightness of those words down to his soul. "I'm not letting you go," he informed her. "No matter how things go between us, I'm never leaving you again. I'm not living across the state from you. We're going to work things out before I let that happen again. Maybe I'll just keep you in our bed, your legs spread, and my cock stuffed deep inside you until we figure out our differences."

"Harder, Jack."

"You want more of me?" he asked, loving how desperate she seemed for his cock.

"Yes! *Please*."

He might like to be in control, but he instantly disliked the sound of her plea. He wanted her desperate for him, yes—but for some reason, he didn't like hearing her beg.

"Eyes back to mine, *Stellina*," he ordered.

She obeyed without hesitation.

"You want something, you've got it. You don't beg me for anything. Ever. Understand?"

She nodded.

"Good, now hold on. This is gonna be hard and fast. That okay?"

"Yes, Jack. Take me. Make me yours."

"You *are* mine," he said. "Just as I'm yours."

And just like that, his control was gone. He began to fuck her hard and fast, just as he warned. And his wife took all of him. She dug her fingernails into his arms as the pleasure came over him without warning. Shoving himself as far inside her as he could get, his balls contracted, and he exploded so hard he felt dizzy. Jack shot load after load of come deep inside of Maisy, marking her from the inside out. He came so hard, he could feel it leaking out from where they were joined. And somehow it still wasn't enough.

Shifting over her, he reached a hand between them and roughly began to manipulate her clit once more.

"Jack, no..."

"Maisy, *yes*," he countered. "I need to feel it again. Milk me, *Stellina*. Take all I have to give."

Her eyes closed, but he didn't reprimand her. His gaze lovingly ran over her features as she strained to reach the pinnacle once more. When she finally came, it wasn't as intense as the last, but it was no less pleasurable, for her or him.

She was dewy with sweat by the time he rolled them over, so she was lying against him like a weighted blanket. And nothing had ever felt so right. Reaching down, Jack managed to pull the covers over them.

She sighed, and he felt her warm breath gust over his neck. "I should move."

"Why?"

"Because I'm too heavy."

"Says who?"

She lifted her head at that, and Jack couldn't keep the masculine sense of satisfaction from coming over him. She looked thoroughly ravished. He'd done that. He'd turned her inside out. And it felt amazing.

"Me. Um...Jack?"

"Yeah?"

"You're still inside me."

"I am," he agreed.

"Is that...don't you have to get up and clean yourself or something?"

"Why? Is that what I usually did? Leave our bed after filling you up and giving you three orgasms?"

"Um..."

Once more, Jack was overcome with the feeling he was missing something. Something huge. When she didn't respond further, he finally shook his head. "Well, that might be what I did before, but not anymore. I don't want to move. I'm comfortable. Your pussy feels amazing around my cock, even when I'm not hard. I want to stay right where I am for as long as I can. Unless...am I hurting you?"

"No."

He breathed out a sigh of relief. "Good. I'll slip out soon enough. For now, it would please me if you'd let me stay."

"How can I say no to that?" she asked.

Even though it was a rhetorical question, Jack said, "You can't."

They lay snuggled together for a minute or two, then Maisy stiffened.

"What? What's wrong?" he asked, totally in tune with her, especially when he could feel every inch of her because of how she was lying on top of him.

She lifted her eyes. "We...we...didn't use protection."

Jack blinked. "Shit. I assumed...I just thought since we've been married for so long that you had that covered. I'm sorry."

Maisy didn't respond, just continued to look at him with furrowed brows.

"You aren't on birth control?" he asked.

She shook her head.

"Did we use condoms before?"

She paused before resting her head back down on his shoulder. "It's okay," she said softly.

"Look at me, Maisy," Jack ordered. He waited until she'd reluctantly lifted her head to look at him once more. There was worry in her eyes, and he hated that, especially after what they'd just shared. "I'll go and get tested tomorrow. I don't think I would *ever* cheat on you, but since I can't remember anything about my life until after the accident, I want to make sure. I'd never do anything to put you at risk."

She hesitated a fraction, then nodded.

And the fact that she didn't balk at him going to get tested for any sexually transmitted diseases told him louder than words that she *had* actually been worried about that. "And I'll get condoms while I'm at it too."

"I...it's not the right time for me," she blurted. "And honestly, I like feeling you. All of you. It's messy, but...does it make me weird to say that I like it?"

Jack smiled at her. "No. I like it too. You want a baby, *Stellina*?" he asked gently.

"I shouldn't," she whispered.

"But you do," he said, satisfaction coursing through his veins. He could imagine her pregnant. She'd be absolutely beautiful.

"Maybe."

At the soft admission, Jack felt his cock twitch deep inside her channel. It was as if his dick wanted to make a baby right that second.

She grinned at him.

He returned it. "Thank you," he said softly. "Thank you

another chance. For not giving up on me, on
not to let you down again."

n't let me down," she protested.

k didn't let her continue. "I did. I obviously didn't live up to the marriage vows I gave you the first time. I was living on the other side of the state, doing who the hell knows what, while you were here, in your brother's house. It's unacceptable. I promise not to leave you again, *Stellina*. We'll work out any issues that come up. Together."

Her eyes filled with tears.

Jack moved a hand up to the back of her neck and held her still as he lifted his head to kiss her. When he started to get hard again, he pushed the blanket off them and said, "I don't have the willpower to pull out of you. So we need to stop until I can get tested."

Maisy bit her lip, then slowly sat up astride him, pushing his cock deeper. She braced her hands on his chest and stared down at him even as she wiggled until her knees were on either side of his hips. "I trust you, Jack."

"Maisy," he warned, his hands going to her hips. He wanted to pull her off, but he didn't have the willpower. And when she lifted up an inch before sinking back down, they both groaned.

Jack stared at her tits, which were perfect. They weren't overly large, weren't too small, and when she moved, they jiggled enticingly. He captured one in his hand and squeezed.

She lifted off his dick once more, sinking down harder this time.

"That's it, *Stellina*. Ride me. Fuck your husband good and hard."

His words made her inner muscles tighten around him once more as she began to move faster. He memorized this moment. His wife taking him, her head thrown back, her tits bouncing with every move. Even though he couldn't remember, he had a feeling he'd never seen anything so goddamn sexy in all his life.

She took him hard and fast, her movements quickly becoming uncoordinated, even clumsy, making the moment more memorable. It was as if this was her first time being on top, which had to be impossible. With a woman like this as his wife, Jack was positive he'd had her in every position imaginable. But since his memory had failed him, he had no problem learning all over what they liked best.

And he definitely liked this.

"Touch yourself," he ordered. Her hand moved immediately, going between her legs and manipulating her clit as she bobbed up and down on his cock.

The second he felt her muscles tense, he rolled them, fucking her hard through her orgasm until his own came upon him. Once more, he filled her with his release. Except this time he couldn't help but think about the possibility of getting her pregnant. It should've scared the crap out of him, but instead it felt...right.

After catching his breath, Jack slipped out of bed and went to the bathroom. He wet a washcloth and cleaned himself up before returning to the bedroom and cleaning their combined release from between her legs. Jack didn't miss the blush that swept over his wife's face. One more thing he obviously hadn't done before. He'd been an idiot, that had to be the only answer to why she sometimes acted so surprised at the things he did.

After returning the washcloth to the bathroom, he slipped back into bed and pulled Maisy into his arms. They were both naked, and it felt wonderful to have her lying skin-to-skin against him. She fell asleep almost immediately, snuggled close, but Jack lay awake for quite a while, thinking.

He still couldn't remember anything past waking up in this room, but for some reason, holding Maisy felt...odd. It was amazing, and he loved it, but it felt *new*. Not like something he'd done for years.

The feeling worried him.

Berating himself yet again, Jack made a mental vow to be a much better husband. If he hadn't slept with her in his arms every single night, he was a fucking idiot. Because there was nothing better than the feel of this sleepy, snuggly woman against his heart.

Did he love her?

Jack thought about that question for a long moment. He was married to her, so he had to love her at one point. But the fact that he had no memories of their life together was a little disconcerting. He wanted to say of *course* he loved his wife, but honestly, with his memory gone, it felt as if he'd only known her for a week. He cared about her, yes. He worried about her, and the obviously strained relationship with her brother. Something was off about that, but he hadn't been able to put his finger on what the problem was, exactly...yet.

He felt protective of her...but love? He was ashamed to admit that he wasn't sure he was there yet. He'd never admit it to Maisy, as that would probably gut her. She was a woman who loved hard and deep. He could tell that about her even after only a week.

Love would come. He'd fallen for her once, he would again. Of that he had no doubt. For now, the connection he felt with her, both emotionally and physically, was enough. The sex was amazing, and that *had* to be because they'd been in love before. His body obviously remembered her, even if his brain didn't.

Maisy stirred against him, and Jack turned his head and kissed her temple. She immediately settled and that warm feeling in his chest grew. Yeah, he could definitely fall back in love with his wife. It was only a matter of time.

Jack had a lot of other shit he needed to figure out, but this? His marriage? It was solid. He'd make sure it stayed that way, no matter what.

CHAPTER SEVEN

Maisy blushed when she looked over and caught Jack's eye. They were eating dinner with Jason and were sitting next to each other. Jack had his left hand on her thigh, as if he couldn't bear not to touch her for more than a moment. And Maisy loved it.

A week had passed since they'd gotten married, and he'd been insatiable. They'd spent more time *in* bed than out of it, not that Maisy was complaining.

But her brother's snide comments when Jack wasn't around—like when he'd gone out to get a test to prove that he didn't have any STIs; he didn't—about her whoring herself out and warning her not to fuck anything up, were getting to her. With every day that passed, Jason seemed to get meaner. It was as if having Jack in the house was turning her brother into even more of a monster.

He was impatient and resentful that he had to wait three months to get his hands on what he thought of as *his* money.

Jason had used some of his criminal connections to get

his new brother-in-law a "replacement" ID. He'd also added Jack to her bank account, so he could get a credit card. Jason was further disgruntled because that meant he'd actually had to put money *into* her account, so Jack wouldn't get suspicious when he saw how little there was in their supposed joint account.

Now she had more money than she'd ever had in her life, almost ten thousand dollars, but Jason made sure she understood that it was an advance on the tiny stipend he gave her every month. Which was ridiculous, because the stipend she *should* be receiving was double that ten grand. Jason took it for himself every month, leaving her pennies...and more importantly, making sure she was reliant on him.

But now that she was married to Jack, things were different. And Jason knew it. He was losing control over her, and he hated it.

"We're going to go look at apartments tomorrow," Jack announced out of the blue. He squeezed her thigh when she turned to look at him in shock.

"Why?" Jason asked in a hard voice.

"Because. It's time. We've been in your way long enough."

"You aren't in my way."

Maisy would've snorted at the comment if she felt safe enough to do so. But she didn't, so she kept quiet.

"Maisy and I need to be on our own. I appreciate you letting her stay here while we worked through our stuff, and for letting me recuperate from my accident, but we need to be in our own space," Jack said firmly.

"Maise, this isn't a good idea," Jason said. "What if you have a relapse? When Jack goes back to bounty hunting, you'll be alone again. And you know what happens when you're alone. You get depressed and need to take meds so you don't do something stupid. And when you're on meds, you're a space cadet. Remember that time you lit all those candles and almost burned our house down?"

Maisy pressed her lips together. Her brother wasn't exactly wrong. She *didn't* like being by herself. And the meds the doctor had prescribed *did* help. But they left her feeling disconnected from just about everything. She was on meds for years and years after her parents died, and had lost so much of her life because of them.

"I'll take care of her," Jack said. "I'm going to find something else to do. Obviously, my previous job wasn't good for our relationship. And if Maisy needs to see a doctor, I'll get her to one. I don't know what meds she was taking before, but there's no reason for her to be a 'space cadet,' as you call it. She probably didn't have the right dosages or combination of medicine. She's *my* wife, *my* responsibility. Not yours."

The tension in the room was sky high, and it made Maisy extremely nervous. She knew why Jason didn't want her to move out. Because with her around, he could keep an eye on her and make sure she wasn't doing anything that would betray him. She had no doubt that he hadn't expected a man like Jack when he'd kidnapped him. He'd wanted someone he could control, and Jack *wasn't* that man. Not even close.

Without a word, Jason scooted his chair back from the table and stood. He shot Maisy a look so full of threat, she flinched. She'd need to do what she could to avoid being alone with him for a while. Because when he was like this, he always took it out on *her*. And now that she was married, and sleeping with her husband every night, there was nowhere her brother could mark her that Jack wouldn't notice. His days of being able to bruise her arm by holding her too tight, or pushing her so hard she fell on the floor or against a piece of furniture, were gone. Another way he was losing control. Which just made him even angrier.

Jason would have to find another way to hurt her—and Maisy had a feeling that would involve threatening Jack.

It would work. Maisy had already gotten to the point where she would do *anything* to protect her husband. He hadn't asked to be here. He'd been taken from his real life and thrust into this farce. Jason wouldn't hesitate to do anything necessary in order to get his hands on her money, and if there was even a one percent chance that Jack was regaining his memory, or that he'd do something to threaten Jason's plans, her brother would act.

He'd lock Jack in the basement—or worse, straight-up kill him and not report his death or disappearance to the authorities until three months had passed. She only needed to be married for three months. After that, it didn't matter if Jack divorced her or if either of them ended up dead.

"You okay?" Jack asked quietly when they were alone.

Maisy did her best to wipe the dread she was feeling from her expression before looking at him. "Yeah."

His hand tightened on her thigh. "You don't look okay."

That was another thing, this man could read her like a book. She couldn't seem to hide any of her emotions from him. She sighed.

"I'm sorry."

Maisy tilted her head in question. "For what?"

"For not talking to you about moving out before I informed your brother."

She couldn't remember the last time *Jason* had apologized to her. If anything, when he was in the wrong, he seemed to get more defensive rather than apologetic. "It's okay."

"Is it?" Jack asked. "Do you want to get an apartment with me?"

"Yes." Maisy couldn't think of anything she wanted more than to get out of this house. At one time it had been a refuge. Filled with memories of her family. But over the years, it had become a prison. Her brother wasn't the same person she'd looked up to when she was young, and she'd been terrified of him for a long time.

"Your brother...he's not nice."

She wanted to snort. That was a complete understatement if she'd ever heard one. But what did Jack know? What had he heard? Anxiety threatened to overwhelm her.

"This is a big house, but it's not *that* big. I've heard how he talks to you when he thinks no one is around. It's not cool, Maisy. It's abusive, and I can't stay quiet about it anymore. I know he's your brother and you love him, but he's a bully. If you were just some random woman, and he was some guy you were in a relationship with, I'd advise you to get the hell out before he did something other than just use words to hurt you."

Maisy stared at Jack and felt the tight band she always seemed to have around her chest loosen a fraction of an inch. She was both glad and frustrated that Jack didn't know the actual extent of Jason's volatile personality.

Glad because if he knew that her brother *did* get physical with her, he'd probably lose his mind. He'd seen a few small bruises on her arm the first week he was in the house, but she'd blamed them on her clumsiness. Fortunately, he seemed to accept her excuse.

And frustrated because she knew the second Jack regained his memory, his concern about her would disappear in a puff of smoke. Because abused or not, she was complicit in what Jason had done. She hadn't been involved in the plot to kidnap a stranger, hadn't wanted to get married, but she also hadn't spoken up. Hadn't gone to the police once she'd realized what had occurred...or with her other suspicions about her brother.

She'd agreed to get married knowing full well Jack didn't have any idea he'd been kidnapped, and she'd lied to his face over and over about their so-called life together, all because she was afraid to stand up to her brother.

She was ashamed of herself. And tired. So damn tired.

For the first time in months, the desire to lose herself in the medications she used to take rose hard and fast within her. She wanted the easy out they gave her. Wanted to numb herself to what she could feel coming on the horizon...namely, having to face the consequences of Jason's actions—and her own.

Losing Jack would destroy her. She loved him already. It was ridiculous, and the odds of her brother choosing a man for her who would end up being the love of her life were astronomical. And yet, here she was.

Jack treated her as if she was the most important person in his world. He was constantly checking with her to make sure she was all right. Wanting to feed her. Making sure she was getting enough sleep and was staying hydrated. He listened to her. Laughed with her. Supported her.

In short, he was perfect. And he'd hate her forever once he understood the depths of her deception.

"You can tell me anything, *Stellina*," Jack said gently as he brought her hand up to his mouth to kiss her knuckles. He did that all the time, and it never failed to make her want to melt. "No matter how scared you are, how uneasy you are about a situation, you can tell me about it and I'll do what I can to make it better. You aren't alone, I'm here. Understand?"

Maisy stared at him. Yeah, he was here...now. But without a doubt, as soon as his memories returned, he'd leave and never look back. She gave him a small nod anyway.

"Good. I don't know about you, but I've kind of lost my appetite. What do you think about going upstairs and snuggling under our covers?"

She smiled. She would never turn down a suggestion like that. "Yes. That sounds amazing."

"I have a present for you," Jack blurted.

He looked nervous, which wasn't like him. And his nervousness made Maisy feel anxious in return. "I don't need anything. Except you."

Jack's lips twitched. "Which is one of the things I love about you. You don't demand trinkets. You don't collect useless crap. You're content to sit in the window and read, or just soak up the sun, watching the world go by. It's awesome. But I got you something anyway. Come on, we'll stop by and apologize to Paige for not finishing this amazing dinner before going upstairs."

"And see if we can steal a snack for later?" Maisy asked,

knowing Jack fairly well by now. They'd spent the last two weeks barely away from each other's side. She knew that he had a sweet tooth and liked having a snack a couple of hours after dinner.

He grinned. "Maybe." Then he stood and pulled her up with him. But instead of heading for the door, he pulled her against him and hugged her tightly.

She felt him nuzzle her hair before he said quietly, "I hate that you have anxiety. That you have to take meds because of it, because I wasn't there for you. But I give you my vow that I'm here now. I'm going to be a better husband this time around."

Maisy wanted to blurt out the truth then and there. This wasn't right. Wasn't fair. Jack was beating himself up for something he hadn't even done.

Determination rose within her. She might not have done the right thing before, but she couldn't continue on this way. Couldn't let this man think he'd let her down. He'd done *nothing*. Had merely been in the wrong place at the wrong time.

She needed to tell him everything. About how they'd just met, how their renewal ceremony had actually been a fake marriage—but legal as far as the government knew, especially since "Jack Smith" now had ID to back it up, she assumed. How her brother had kidnapped him and possibly killed his own wife. About her inheritance, how Jason wanted it for himself, which was why Jack was here in the first place.

Figuring out who Jack was and where he came from would be a harder task, but she could give him the ten thousand dollars Jason had reluctantly put into her account and he could use it to hire a private investigator.

Surely *someone* out there was looking for him, worried about him. He could find his people and forget all about her.

Feeling better than she had in a very long time, now that she had a plan, Maisy squeezed Jack hard. Giving him up would hurt, but it was the right thing to do. She should've done it already, but maybe the fact that she was finally pulling her head out of her ass would mean something.

She opened her mouth to tell him everything, but he spoke before she could.

"Come on, let's find Paige. The sooner we do that, the sooner we can get under the covers...and snuggle."

"Snuggle?" Maisy asked with a heartbreaking chuckle as she tilted her head up to look at him. Her husband was so damn handsome it made her heart hurt. His eyes sparkled behind the glasses he wore, and she did her best to memorize the moment.

"I don't know if I was the kind of husband who liked to snuggle with his wife before, but now I find it's the best part of my day."

"Mine too," she admitted without hesitation, deciding it was best if she told him everything in their room, anyway. Away from anyone potentially eavesdropping.

"And when we're done snuggling, you can ride me."

Maisy snorted in surprise as he turned them toward the door to the dining room. "I think you're obsessed with me being on top," she told him.

"I don't hear you complaining," Jack said easily. "And you have no idea how gorgeous you are when you ride me. I can see all of you, have easy access to your clit, and you take me so deep that way. Besides, you hate sleeping in the wet spot and when you're on top, you don't have to deal with that."

Maisy stopped and stared up at Jack. She'd gotten wet just hearing him describe their lovemaking, but it was his consideration of her that made her pause.

"What? Too much?" he asked with a small, sexy grin.

"No, I...I'm falling in love with you," she admitted. It was another lie in a long list of lies, but she wasn't brave enough to tell him that she wasn't falling—she was already there.

"It's a good thing, since we're married. Come on, *Stellina*, I have a need to cuddle with my wife sooner rather than later."

* * *

An hour later, Jack couldn't stop smiling as he stared up at his wife, who was riding his cock with unbridled lust. She was lost in sensation, her head thrown back, desperately grinding herself on his dick as she approached her orgasm.

He hadn't lied earlier, this *was* his favorite position with her, although they were all amazing. His Maisy was beautiful. And the kicker was, she had no idea of her appeal. She was self-conscious about her body, and even though her brother tried to convince her she was fat, Jack thought she was perfect. He loved everything about her.

Loved.

Yes. He loved his wife. It hadn't taken him long to come to that conclusion. It was hard to believe a week ago he was questioning his feelings for her. Jack felt as if he'd loved her forever. And it wasn't a superficial kind of thing, not brought about because of how good sex was between them. He was so damn grateful he'd gotten a second chance to prove that he could be the kind of husband she deserved. He had no idea what his problem had been, why he'd felt it was a good idea to live hours away from her, why he'd put his job ahead of his relationship, but that was done now.

"Jack," she whispered almost desperately.

Knowing what she needed, he moved. Flipping her over so she was on her back, he slammed his cock in and out of her until they were both panting. It was hard to believe a week ago she could barely take him without pain. Now, she took everything he had to give and demanded more.

She loved when he took her hard, and the way her pussy squeezed his cock as if it didn't ever want to let him go was the most incredible sensation.

"You want to come?" he asked as he fucked her.

"Yessssss," she hissed.

"Then touch yourself. Get yourself off while I take what's mine," Jack demanded.

Her hand immediately moved between them. She didn't have a lot of room to maneuver but didn't seem to care. Her fingers brushed against his belly every time he bottomed out inside her, and it was sexy as hell. He felt her frantically fingering her clit, and it only heightened his pleasure.

Gritting his teeth, Jack barely held onto his control. He wanted her to come before he let himself go. Needed that. She came first, always. It wasn't a feeling that felt familiar, but it did feel right. Maisy was his everything. He'd do whatever it took to see to her needs. No matter what they were.

The moment he felt her pussy fluttering around his dick, he pulled her hand out from between them and lifted her legs over his shoulders. Then he leaned down until they were face-to-face. She was almost bent in half, completely open to him.

Her ass shook as she continued to orgasm and Jack's hips pistoned up and down as he took her. It didn't take long for his own pleasure to overwhelm him, and when he finally let loose, he shoved himself as far as he could inside her and groaned.

His orgasm almost hurt. Every time with her felt like the first time. He still hated that he had no idea what their sex life was like before his accident, but he was convinced it couldn't have been anywhere near as good as it was now. If it was, there was no way he would've forgotten. The feeling of being torn inside out every time he was deep inside her body wasn't anything he'd experienced before. He'd bet his life on it.

This time, instead of rolling over so Maisy was on top of him, Jack lowered her legs and braced himself over her on one elbow while leaning over to the nightstand. He was careful not to let his dick slip out of its warm, wet home. Every time he came, he expected to lose his erection, but he always stayed half hard, as if his cock had a mind of its own and was determined to stay in Maisy's hot pussy.

"Jack?" she questioned when he moved back over her.

"Yeah?"

"Not that I'm complaining, because I love being under you, surrounded by you like this. But...what's up?"

"That surprise I mentioned downstairs?" He held a small box up between them.

Maisy's small gasp made Jack smile.

"What is it?" she asked, making no move to reach for it.

"Why don't you open it and see?" he suggested.

Reluctantly, she reached for the box. She looked up at him, then slowly opened the lid.

"I noticed you don't wear a ring, and I don't have one either. I guess it must have been destroyed in the fire. But I find that I want everyone we meet to know that you're mine. And I want to show the world that I'm taken as well," Jack said when Maisy didn't reach for the rings nestled in the box between them.

"They aren't fancy, but you don't seem like the kind of woman who would like a huge, gaudy ring." Jack began to get nervous as Maisy simply stared at the set of wedding rings in the box. "If you don't like them, I can take them back and get something else."

"No!" she exclaimed suddenly. "I love them. I just...Jack."

There was sorrow in her words that Jack didn't understand. He thought she'd be thrilled with his gift. He'd noticed that neither of them wore rings and it hadn't sat well with him. But now he second-guessed his surprise. Maybe they'd agreed before not to wear them for some reason.

He watched as she pulled out the three rings. She lifted her left hand and went to put the band on her finger, but Jack stopped her. It was a little awkward balancing on his elbow above her as he reached for her hand, but he wouldn't miss this moment for the world. "Let me?" he asked.

Maisy nodded and gave him a small smile.

She held her hand out for him, and Jack slid the thin

gold band down her ring finger. Then he slowly added the band of diamonds he'd thought fit her personality perfectly. Seeing his rings on her finger made his heart beat faster, and his cock harden deep inside her.

She gasped and licked her lips sensually. Then she held up the ring he'd bought for himself.

Moving his weight to his right side, Jack held his hand out for her. The feel of her sliding the ring down his finger was like coming home. "You're mine," he breathed.

"And you're mine," she replied.

"Damn straight."

A knock on the door startled them both, and Jack turned his head and frowned at the door.

"Maise? We have that appointment with the banker in the morning. Don't oversleep!"

"Go away!" Jack barked, scowling as he heard his brother-in-law's steps retreat down the hall. "After your meeting, we're going apartment hunting," Jack informed Maisy.

"Okay."

"Okay," Jack agreed. Then he moved, reluctantly pulling out of her body and climbing to his knees. "Up," he ordered. "On your knees, facing the headboard."

Maisy's cheeks were pink, but she didn't hesitate to do as he asked. She turned away from him and settled on her knees and elbows in front of him, exposing her perfect pussy and ass.

Jack's dick jumped at seeing his come slowly leaking out of her. Reaching out, he used a thumb to catch it before it could fall to the sheets and push it back inside her channel. The image of her heavy with his child made his heart lurch in his chest. She'd admitted that she wasn't on birth control, and while she'd claimed it wasn't the right time in her cycle to get pregnant a week ago...it could be now.

The urge to tie her to him in such a fundamental way was strong. So strong, Jack inched forward on his knees, grabbed her hips with a grip that was probably too tight, and sank into her sheath with one quick thrust.

They both gasped.

"Shit, sorry...too much?" Jack asked. It took every ounce of control not to move. To give her time to adjust to his size.

"No, you're perfect. More, Jack. Please."

There was that word again. Most men would revel in their women begging them for more. But not him. He hated when she pleaded.

"You don't have to beg me for more," he told her as he began to move. "I'll gladly give you anything you need."

"All I need is you," she said.

Neither spoke anymore and the only sound in the room was the slap of skin meeting skin as he took her hard and fast from behind. Jack's eyes were glued to his cock as it slid in and out of her slick folds, covered in their juices. It was hot as hell, and it made Jack even harder.

But because of how good she felt, it was only a matter of time before his balls drew up in preparation for letting loose. Gritting his teeth, Jack draped himself over Maisy's back. She came up to her hands and began to move, rocking herself on and off his dick, fucking him as she desperately reached for her pleasure.

Looking down, Jack saw their left hands next to each other on the mattress. Their wedding rings shining in the overhead light he hadn't bothered to turn off. Seeing the tangible reminder of their commitment to each other made his heart beat faster.

He leaned down and nuzzled her ear and wasn't able to keep the words from spilling past his lips. "I love you, *Stellina*. I don't know what I would've done without you these last couple of weeks. You're my everything, and I vow that I'll always be by your side. No matter what, I'll be your rock."

She froze under him. "You can't promise that," she said softly.

"The hell I can't," he growled. "You love me?" he asked.

His heart stopped beating for a moment while he waited for her answer.

"Yes."

"That's all that matters. We'll figure out things as we go. Together."

"Okay."

Jack relaxed at her acquiescence. "Okay," he agreed. Then he snaked a hand under her body and she jerked in his grip as he tweaked her clit. "Come on my cock, *Stellina*. Mark me as yours."

"You *are* mine," she hissed, just before she exploded.

Her possessive words and the feel of her milking his dick was all it took for Jack to come too. He held himself deep as ropes of come burst from him. When he was finished, he felt as weak as a kitten. He fell to the side, holding Maisy against his chest as he did. He held her close until his cock slipped out of her body, then he turned her. She eagerly assumed the sleeping position they'd found was the most comfortable. Plastered against his side, head on his shoulder, one leg slung over his, his arm around her.

"How's your head?" she asked groggily after a moment.

Jack smiled. She was always worrying over him. When she'd found out the headache he'd had since waking up two weeks ago hadn't abated, she'd been instantly concerned.

"It's fine."

"Still there?" she asked.

"Yeah."

"Maybe we should take you to see a doctor."

"I'm okay," he told her.

Maisy sighed in frustration against him, her warm breath gliding over his chest. "It shouldn't still hurt," she told him.

"If the headache is still there in a week, I'll go. Okay?"

She immediately nodded against him. "Okay. Promise?"

"I don't make promises I don't keep," he reassured her. He played with the ring on her finger as it lay on his chest.

A minute or two went by before she spoke again. "You really love me?" she asked quietly.

Jack didn't know why she sounded so surprised. "Yes."

"But you just met me."

He frowned at that. "Not really. I mean, we were married before I lost my memory, and it's obvious my soul recognized yours. I might not remember what we did day in and day out, but a love like ours obviously can't be held back by something as trivial as memory loss."

"I'm going to do right by you," Maisy said solemnly. "I've made mistakes. Huge ones, but I'm going to make this right if it's the last thing I do."

"Shhhh," Jack soothed, not liking the distress he heard in her voice. "Sleep, *Stellina*. Tomorrow you'll have your meeting at the bank, then we'll find a realtor who can help us apartment search. We have the rest of our lives to figure things out."

"I love you, Jack. I do."

The words settled into his soul. Jack kissed her forehead before closing his eyes.

He had no idea how long he'd been asleep or what had woken him up, but one moment he was sleeping peacefully, and the next, his eyes popped open and he stared not at the ceiling of his and Maisy's room, but at a dark, dank metal box. He heard the sounds of yelling and moans, and his heart began to race.

"Stone? You okay? Hang in there, buddy! We're not dying here, you hear me? We aren't! The Army's coming for us. They wouldn't leave two of the best Night Stalkers here to die. Don't you give up on me, Stone!"

After blinking several times, the dark cell gave way to the comfortable room he'd shared with Maisy for the last two weeks. The overhead light was still on, and Maisy snored lightly in his arms. Jack was covered in sweat and his head was pounding so hard it hurt to even breathe.

What the hell had he just dreamed? *Was* it a dream? The crazy thing was that he knew the person speaking was someone named Owl. But he had no idea who Stone was. Nothing in the dream made sense.

Closing his eyes, Jack did his best to slow down his breathing and heart rate.

It was a nightmare, nothing else.

Deep down, he suspected it was much more. But he couldn't think about it right now, instinctively knowing if he did, his head would literally burst. So instead, he counted Maisy's breaths. Concentrated on the feel of the puffs of air from her exhalations against his bare skin.

Inhaled the smell of sex and apples that permeated the air and bed. Listened to the faint sound of vehicles outside the house. Licked his lips and tasted Maisy's musk from when he'd eaten her pussy earlier, before they'd had sex.

Swallowing hard, Jack allowed himself to fade back into an uneasy sleep. This time when he dreamed, it was of a beautiful mountainside filled with trees, cabins interspersed throughout the forest, laughter, the smell of food cooking, and a cow mooing impatiently from inside a big red barn. It felt peaceful, and it calmed him into a restful sleep.

* * *

"I can't believe we haven't found anything!" Owl said as he ran a hand through his hair in agitation.

Brick wasn't happy either, but he had to be the voice of reason here, otherwise Owl would go off the deep end. It had been two weeks since Stone's kidnapping. And since then, there hadn't been any sign of where he'd been taken —or by whom.

Lara had gone over and over what had happened in that hangar in Seattle, and nothing she could remember had given them any clues as to where Stone could be. She had given them a pretty good description of the man who'd taken him, as well as the car, but she hadn't been able to catch a license plate number. And without that, they were as much in the dark as they'd been when they'd started. They knew a serial killer had hired a man to kidnap Lara, and that man had sold Stone. And that was about it. Both the serial killer and his hired hand were dead, taking any secrets to their graves with them.

The surveillance cameras at the regional airport hadn't been working, and the one camera that had caught the car leaving the hangar was too far away to be able to read the plate.

Stone had disappeared into thin air, and there hadn't been any clues as to where he could be. And Owl, his former Army Night Stalker partner and fellow prisoner of war, was on the verge of completely losing it.

"I can't believe that with the best people on this—Tex, that Elizabeth woman he works with, even Ry the supposed computer genius—we can't find hide nor hair of him! He has to be out there somewhere, Brick! And he's probably wondering why the hell we haven't come for him. We need to find him. *Now!*"

"I know, Owl. And we're trying."

Owl crumpled into a chair at the table in the smaller conference room at the main lodge at The Refuge. "We *have* to find him," he said in despair. "I can't bear to think of what he's going through. It makes no sense. Who would've taken him? And why? If they haven't asked for a ransom, why kidnap him?"

Brick didn't have any answers. "I don't know. But I promise you, Owl, we aren't going to stop looking. No matter how long it takes or how much it costs, we aren't giving up. Ever."

"I'm gonna go talk to Ry again. She said she had an idea last night. I want to see if she's found out anything new," Owl mumbled.

Brick wished he could do more. Wished he could help his friend. Owl and Stone were as close as two men could be. They'd been to hell and back together, and Brick knew Owl was blaming himself for Stone's kidnapping. Even though he'd been unconscious at the time of the abduction, he still blamed himself.

Ryan, otherwise known as Ryleigh or Ry, had been working at The Refuge for a while now, and apparently she was some sort of computer hacking prodigy. There was definitely a backstory with her, but with Owl and Lara both recovering from being kidnapped by a serial killer—an evil bastard who'd been hell-bent on making Lara his sex toy for a second time—and with Stone missing, no one had much time to get to the bottom of why Ryan was working at the lodge and what she was hiding from.

Brick put his hand on Owl's shoulder and squeezed. "How's Lara doing?"

"She's good. No sign of any morning sickness yet," Owl said. Talking about his new pregnant wife seemed to take some of the anguish from his eyes.

"Good. Let me know if Ry's found anything."

"I will. Brick?"

"Yeah?"

"Thanks."

"For what?"

"For not giving up."

"I will *never* give up. Stone's out there somewhere, Owl. He's strong. I have no doubt he's hanging in there, just waiting for us to find him. And we will."

Owl took a deep breath. "Yeah, we will." Then he nodded at Brick and headed for the door.

Brick stood in the middle of the room for a beat after Owl left. He closed his eyes and took his own deep breath. He had no idea who would want Stone, or for what. Every day that passed with no word of where he'd disappeared to wasn't a good sign. But he hadn't lied to Owl, Brick would never stop trying to find answers. Stone was one of his best friends, and he didn't deserve what had happened to him.

The thought of him being held hostage, *again*, was like a ball of acid in his belly. The man had been through enough, and whoever was responsible for kidnapping him would pay. Brick would personally make sure of that.

Letting out the breath he'd taken, Brick opened his eyes and headed for the door. He wanted to call Tex once more, check on his other friends to make sure they were all hanging in there, and he needed to make sure the guests at The Refuge this week were having a good time. He had a lot of balls in the air and didn't want to drop any of them.

But first, he needed to see Alaska. She was his rock, his light. Just being around her made things seem not so bad. She and the other women were just as worried about Stone as the rest of them, but because of her own experiences, she had nothing but confidence in his ability to get to the bottom of what happened and bring their friend home.

He needed that boost, because right now, it really did seem as if Stone had disappeared into thin air. There were no clues, no signs about where he could be. With every day that passed, the likelihood of bringing their friend home alive got slimmer and slimmer.

CHAPTER EIGHT

Maisy was uneasy. Not only because she had to go to the bank with her brother this morning, but because Jack was acting...different. And she didn't think it was because of the words of love they'd exchanged last night.

Something had happened, but she had no idea what. He seemed wary this morning, on edge. When they'd gone downstairs to have breakfast, he'd flinched at every little sound. Maisy worried it was because his head hurt worse than before, but he'd denied it.

The last thing she wanted to do was go anywhere with Jason by herself, she'd gotten very used to having Jack around to run interference and act as a buffer between her and her brother, but it was obvious he was completely miserable. She'd convinced him to stay home and take some over-the-counter painkillers so they could go out and look for apartments when she returned.

The second she shut the door to Jason's Land Rover—that he'd bought with *her* money, all the while telling her that buying her a car would be a waste since she never went anywhere—he unleashed his nastiness.

"Not even a thank you for your brother?" he asked with a sneer.

"What?"

"I bought you a cock and you haven't once said thank you."

Maisy's stomach churned, and she gripped the armrest on the door so hard her knuckles turned white.

"Seriously, sis, the sounds coming from your room at night almost make me jealous. Jack-o certainly seems to know his stuff."

"Shut up," Maisy mumbled, embarrassed that her brother would be so crude.

The palm to her face came out of nowhere. Jason then shoved her shoulder hard enough that her head smacked the window next to her.

"Don't you talk to me like that! Show some respect, Maisy," Jason growled before putting the car in reverse and backing out of the driveway.

Her cheek stung, and Maisy put her hand over what she knew was probably a red mark. She was shocked he was willing to leave a mark for Jack to find. Proof that Jason was becoming more and more volatile. It was a reminder that she needed to tread very carefully. She probably should've insisted that Jack come with them today, but he really did look like he was in pain and she hadn't wanted to make it worse. Selfishly though, she wished he was there because this trip was a mistake. She knew it down to her bones.

Jason drove toward the bank in silence, but when he didn't turn on the road she knew he should've, anxiety made her belly churn. Eventually, he pulled into the parking lot of a shopping mall. It was busy, cars coming and going everywhere. No one would take notice of them sitting in the nearly full lot. Maisy shivered.

Jason turned toward her—and the look on his face made goose bumps rise on the back of her neck.

"We need to talk," he told her seriously.

Maisy nodded. It wasn't as if she could say no, he'd brought her here for a reason, and she'd have to sit here and listen to whatever it was he wanted to say.

"Don't fall for him."

"What?"

"Don't fall in love with that asshole you married. He's not going to be around long."

"What do you mean? Why not?"

"You know why not."

Maisy swallowed hard. "Jase, no. Please."

His hand swung out and he slapped her again. "I told you not to call me that!" he thundered.

A small whimper escaped, and she was ashamed of herself. She should open the door and run. Should stand up for herself. But she was more scared of what he'd do if she dared defy him than what he'd already done.

"Look, the entire goddamn plan has gone sideways. I didn't expect him to lose his memory, although that's been a nice bonus for sure."

"What *was* your plan?" Maisy asked quietly.

"Don has a friend of a friend who was able to work a deal with this guy. The guy knew you needed to be married, and he arranged to have someone delivered. I have no idea who the fuck Jack is or where he came from, and I don't care—but as I told you before, he was going to marry you one way or another. It didn't matter if he was chained to the fucking wall in the basement, you two were getting hitched. It was a nice surprise when he woke up and had no idea who he was. And don't tell me you aren't enjoying the benefits, because you'd be a damn liar. I've heard you at night. I wonder if *prostitutes* enjoy cock as much as you seem to."

Bile rose in her throat, but Maisy swallowed it down.

"I mean, I paid good money for him to be your husband, so when you think about it, you're paying him for sex. Might as well enjoy it." Jason laughed. "Anyway, the deed is done. You're married and the countdown has started to get your money. Mom and Dad never should've tied it up in that stupid trust with its ridiculous stipulations. In three months, when the money's released, we won't need lover boy anymore."

"Jason, please don't hurt him. I'll break up with him, divorce him, anything you want!"

"You're so naïve," Jason said with a patronizing frown. "You think we can just let him go? His memory is gonna return eventually, and what then? He's not gonna be happy that he was kidnapped, thrown in a trunk, and lied to for weeks. And if you think for a second he might learn to love you, that's not gonna happen when he realizes you're a part of all this. How you lied to his face every day. How you knew what happened, but pretended you were already married to trick him into going through with that so-called renewal ceremony. You're in this up to your eyeballs, Maise. There's only one choice here."

Her brother was right. There *was* only one choice.

Maisy needed to do the right thing for once in her life.

She needed to set Jack free and make sure her brother paid for all the wrongs he'd done in his life.

"Understand?" Jason asked in a cold, hard voice.

She nodded.

"Good. Three months. Even *you* can keep your mouth shut that long. Just keep doing what you're doing, keep spreading your legs, and a few weeks after that money is released, we'll tell everyone he ran off. That he abandoned you."

Maisy bit back the words she wanted to say. That there was no way the police would be stupid enough to believe the same story twice. That Jack had just left the same way Jason's wife had, a few months after they were married and conveniently after the trust money was released.

"After a while, we'll ask the authorities to declare him dead, you know, when he hasn't used any credit cards and there hasn't been any sign of him. Oh! I know, maybe he can leave a suicide note, saying how much he loves you and after learning that you don't want to be with him anymore, he can't go on living. I can plant a seed that he went to the coast and threw himself in the ocean or something. That way his body can't be found. Anyway, once he's officially been declared dead, we can collect on his life insurance policy."

Her brother was insane. That was the only explanation for the calm way he was plotting the death of another human being. Then, his words finally registered. "Life insurance?"

"Yeah," Jason said, leaning into the backseat and grabbing a folder. He took out several pieces of paper then shoved one at her. "Here, sign that."

"What is it?" Maisy asked, trying to read the paper. It

was obviously the last part of some sort of official document. There were two signature lines, one for her and one for Jack. Jack's had already been filled out. At the top of the page in the margin, it said this was page fourteen of fourteen.

"Jack's life insurance policy, of course," Jason said with a smile.

"He signed this?" Maisy asked, her brow furrowing in confusion.

"Of course he did, don't you see his signature?"

Maisy studied the paper in front of her, and when she looked up at her brother, she realized of *course* Jack hadn't signed this. It was forged, probably like most of the papers that had to do with money and their inheritance. "This isn't his signature," she said bravely.

But Jason simply laughed. "So quick on the draw," he mocked. "No, it isn't. But no one will know. I just need you to sign and I'll get it submitted...and backdated, can't have the cops thinking we took this out right after you were married. That wouldn't look good when Jack disappears."

Maisy shook her head and tried to shove the paper back at her brother. "No."

"No?" he asked in a low tone, making no effort to take the sheet of paper she was trying to give back to him.

"No," she said, trying to sound firm. "It's not right, Jason. You're already getting the money from my inheritance. This isn't necessary."

He moved faster than she thought possible, coming across the console and grabbing her throat. He shoved her against the side of the car, smacking her head against the window again. He got in her face and snarled. "What the fuck do *you* know, Maisy? You've been sleeping for the last decade and a half. I've been the one worrying about the mortgage, the bills, making sure our reputations are pristine. You think that's been easy? It hasn't. There's no money left. *None*. Without the money from your trust, we're screwed! We'll be kicked out of the house we grew up in and destitute.

"You *owe me*, sis. I took care of you. Moved back into the house. Hired all those doctors to make sure you didn't kill yourself in your grief. You've been a good girl up to this point, so don't fuck things up now. And don't even *think* about turning on me. If you do, you'll end up just like poor Martha. Now—sign the fucking paper."

Maisy had no idea where the courage came from, but she managed to ask, "What if I don't?"

To her surprise, Jason let go of her throat and sat back in the driver's seat as he laughed. It wasn't a humorous sound. It actually scared her to death. "If you don't, I'll go home, tell lover boy that you tricked him into marrying you, that you only did it for the money, then I'll lock him in the safe room in the basement like I was going to do if he *hadn't* lost his memory. I'll give him a piece of bread a day and a cup of water. Maybe. By the time three months have passed, he'll be nothing but skin and bones, sitting in his own filth. Then I'll put a bullet in his brain and get rid of his body where no one will ever find him."

Maisy stared at her brother in horror. She used to play hide-and-seek with this man when they were little. He used to hold her hand when they walked to school. Had accidentally told her there was no Santa Claus, then hugged her when she'd cried. He'd stood beside her at the funeral home after their parents died, his arm around her, and promised to take care of her for as long as she needed him.

Now he was a monster—and she hated him.

"And you?" Jason went on. "I'll fill Jack's head with stories of your treachery. I'll make sure he hates your guts and knows it was *your* plan to kidnap him. I'll tell him that you laughed at how pathetic he was for falling for every word, how shitty he was in bed. And in the end, I'll lock you up with him for his last few days. Gagged, of course, so you keep your big fucking mouth shut. He won't care what's happening to you by that point, I promise you that. I'll make you watch as I put that bullet in his skull. Then, because I can't have you blabbing to anyone about what you know, you'll join him. You can rest in not-so-peace till death do you part, after all."

Maisy felt numb. This couldn't be happening.

"Sign the fucking paper, sister dear," Jason growled, leaning over the console and pinning her in place with his evil gaze as he held a pen out for her.

As if in a trance, Maisy took the pen and, with trembling fingers, signed the paper.

"I knew you'd see things my way," Jason said with satisfaction as he tucked the signed document back into the folder and threw it back onto the seat behind him. He turned to her once more. "Three months, Maise. That's all. Then this will all be over and we can go back to how things used to be.

"Oh, and another thing—when we get home, you're gonna talk to Jack. Convince him that you don't want to move out. You're staying right where you are until the three months are done. I don't trust you not to fuck up. And because I know how stressful all this has been, I've picked up refills for you. You'll start taking your anti-anxiety pills again today. Trust me, it'll be better for you."

It didn't take a rocket scientist to know why Jason wanted her and Jack to stay until the three-month waiting period was up. He wanted easy access to Jack to make him go away. Permanently. And there was no way in hell was she going to go back to being the zombie she used to be on those pills. She was clearheaded now, and Maisy knew without a doubt that her brother would somehow use her supposed relapse as a way to get her out of the picture altogether. It would be easy enough for her to "overdose."

Urgency shot through her. She needed to get away. Away from Seattle, away from her brother. Needed to get *Jack* away from him. She needed a plan, and at the moment, she had no idea where to start.

"Maisy? Do you understand me? When we get home, I'll tell Jack that you had a panic attack and you need to start taking your meds again. Tonight, you can get on your knees, suck lover boy's cock, and convince him you don't want to leave. Got it?"

Maisy nodded. Anything to get Jason to shut up.

"Good. Now, we're going to the bank and filling out the paperwork to get the ball rolling on releasing your trust. You sign what's put in front of you without question, or you won't like the consequences."

She nodded again. She couldn't fight him, not now. He'd do exactly what he said he would. He'd hurt her husband.

Jason was right, she was just as guilty as he was in tricking Jack. She shouldn't have gone along with everything. But now that she had, she needed to do what she could to make things right. She'd figure out a way to save

Jack. Even if it meant she'd end up as dead as her former sister-in-law.

"It's nice to see you compliant. Things are going to work out just fine," Jason said in what anyone else would consider a soothing tone. But to Maisy, he sounded sinister.

"Leave the thinking to me, Maisy. You've always been too stupid to figure shit out. I've got this, and in a little over three months, all our problems will be behind us."

Three months. It wasn't enough time. Maisy began to panic as Jason started the car and got back on the road toward the bank. Mentally, she took a deep breath. She had money, thanks to her brother needing to trick Jack. She could use that to...to what? Fly somewhere? Her brother could find her if she used her own name. And what about Jack? What would she tell him?

Maybe she could post on social media about Jack and how he'd lost his memory, asking if anyone knew who he was. A lot of those things went viral. Maybe it would find its way to his people.

But Jason or his friends could also see it before Jack's friends did, and that wouldn't go well for either of them.

She and Jack could literally get into the car and drive away, but where would they go that Jason couldn't find them? How would they live once their small amount of funds ran out? Yeah, they could both find jobs, but how long could they stay under the radar under their own names? She wasn't a criminal like her brother. Or at least... she hadn't been. She didn't know about things like false IDs and new identities.

Her shoulders sagged. Getting away from Jason seemed more impossible with every passing second.

Maybe Jack would have some ideas...if she told him everything. She truly had intended to do just that last night. She lost her nerve right around the time Jack started kissing her, caressing her...stripping her out of her clothes.

God, she was weak.

And even more terrified than before, if that was possible. She hadn't been sure that Jason had anything to do with her parents' carjacking, but now she was almost certain. And Martha was a given, after his crack about Maisy ending up just like her.

Her brother was a psychopath. Didn't care about anyone other than himself. He had enough connections that he easily could've hired someone to fake a carjacking and shoot their parents in the process. As easily as he'd found someone to kidnap Jack.

She sat up and stared sightlessly out the window. She had to tell the police. It was her only option...though it seemed unlikely Jason would let her out of his sight too often now.

He might succeed in stealing her money, and maybe even killing her...but if she wrote out everything she knew and *left* it for the police, they'd have to investigate, right? It would at least be justice if Jason ended up behind bars, unable to spend the money he'd worked so hard to get his hands on.

It wasn't the best solution, Maisy would prefer to live, but she was pretty sure that wasn't in the cards for her.

Her first goal would be to save Jack. He didn't ask to be involved in any of this. Second, she wanted Jason to pay for killing poor Martha, and likely their parents.

The more she thought about it, the more she warmed to the idea. She'd write down everything she could remember, every sin she believed her brother had committed, giving details and specifics that could hopefully be used against him. Names of his friends, doctors who'd written prescriptions without question, people who she thought might've helped him take out the life insurance policy on Jack...and now that she thought about it, he probably had one on her too.

"Remember, keep your mouth shut as much as possible, let me do the talking," Jason told her as he parked in front of the bank.

Maisy nodded. For a split second, she envisioned standing up in the bank office, in front of the manager and the executor of her parents' estate, and blurting that it was all a lie. That Jack had been forced to marry her and her brother was a total psycho.

But then she pictured Jack sitting in the basement, chained to the wall, starving and staring at her with hatred...

It made her flinch just thinking about it.

She couldn't do it. For now, she'd do whatever Jason forced her to do, simply to buy some time. There was a one hundred percent certainty Jack would hate her in the end anyway. As long as he was back with those who knew and loved him, and he wasn't living a lie...it would be worth it.

Maisy had made lots of mistakes in her life, but it was past time she owned up to them. It was too little, too late, but it was all she had.

With no other choice, she got out of the SUV and followed Jason into the bank.

CHAPTER NINE

Jack was worried about his wife.

In the last week, ever since she'd gone to the bank with her brother and he'd stayed home to try to get rid of his headache, she'd been different. Far more subdued.

And that was saying something, because his Maisy wasn't exactly Ms. Outgoing in the first place. But she was even more introverted now. And frankly, it was scaring the shit out of him.

She'd come to their room when she'd returned, where he'd been lying on the bed with his eyes closed, trying to relax, and she'd snuggled up against him without a word. Then she'd told him that she wasn't ready to move out yet.

She'd sounded so sad, so defeated, that Jack had agreed without hesitation.

Over the last week, she'd been completely different from the woman he'd been getting to know. She had an almost permanent line in her brow from worry, and she barely left their room. When she did, it was to sit outside in the sun, quietly staring into space and not engaging with anyone. Either that, or writing in the diary she'd started the day after her bank visit.

He'd pleaded with her to talk to him. Tell him what happened. All she'd said was that she'd had a panic attack at the bank, and an ER doctor had recommended she go back on her meds. She refused to discuss it further, and Jason claimed to have her hospital paperwork locked away in his office. Telling him in a condescending tone not to worry about it, that he'd always taken care of his sister, and Jack didn't need to trouble himself.

Jack was furious. Even more so about the red mark on her cheek, which hadn't escaped his notice. He immediately wanted to confront Jason the second he saw it that afternoon. But when he'd attempted to get out of bed to do just that, Maisy lost it. Cried and begged him not to say anything to her brother.

It was more than obvious that she was scared of him. Terrified, actually. Which was all the more reason to get the hell out of this house, but Maisy seemed more fragile than he'd ever seen her before. And the last thing Jack wanted to do was stress her out more than she was already.

The undercurrents in the house were more concerning every day. He didn't understand them, but they definitely gave him bad vibes. Anytime Maisy interacted with her brother, she kept her head down and barely said two words. She left most conversations up to him and Jason, which were now awkward at best.

But when it was just the two of them in the dark, in their bed, Maisy was even *more* different. She was demanding, almost desperate in their lovemaking. She clung to him as if she was afraid he would leave—which wasn't happening.

Jack had no idea what was going on, but he didn't like it. Oh, he certainly liked how affectionate and passionate his wife was, but not at the expense of whatever was going on. Jason claimed her mental health was fragile, and around her brother, that certainly seemed to be the case. But at night, when she begged him to take her harder, to fuck her in every conceivable position, she didn't seem fragile in the least.

If he didn't know better, he'd think she was putting on an act...but he wasn't sure which was the real Maisy. The delicate girl who barely said two words during the day? Or the insatiable woman who took everything he had to give then demanded more each night?

Not only was he worried about his wife, but he was getting more and more concerned about his own health. His headaches hadn't lessened, and he was getting flashes of things he didn't understand. He assumed they were memories, which he was thrilled about; there was nothing he wanted more than to remember his life before he'd woken up in this house. But what he saw didn't make sense. The flashes included people he didn't know and places he didn't remember. And most confusing of all was the sensation of flying. But instead of making him sick, the visions of being in the clouds, flying above cities and oceans, made him feel *free*.

It was puzzling and disorienting, and each new image made his head pound. Jack wanted nothing more than for the pain to stop.

Maisy jerked in his arms. They'd made almost frenzied love earlier. His wife had knelt between his spread legs and given him a blow job that turned his world inside out. She hadn't let him pull away, swallowing every ounce of his release without hesitation. He'd returned the favor until she was sweaty and writhing on the sheets after two orgasms. She'd then ridden him almost frantically, until he'd once more come deep inside her body. Then she'd dropped against him and fell asleep almost instantly.

When he'd tried to shift her off him to make her more comfortable, she'd clung to him and whimpered in the back of her throat. So he'd let her stay right where she was. And now she was shaking in his arms. Her eyes fluttering behind her lids, obviously in the throes of a nightmare.

For a brief moment, he felt empathy that was so strong, it could only come from understanding exactly what she was feeling. But when she moaned his name, the feeling vanished.

"No! Jack! Please, let me explain!"

"Shhhh," he soothed, hating how anguished she sounded. But she couldn't hear him.

"Jason, stop! I'll do anything! Please don't hurt him!"

Jack frowned. He didn't like what he was hearing. "Wake up, *Stellina*!" he ordered.

She didn't wake, but she *did* stop speaking. Instead, a constant whimper left her lips. It was heartbreaking, and she sounded so damn miserable, Jack was beside himself.

He rolled over, pinning her under him, cradling her face in his hands as he braced himself on his elbows. "Maisy!" he said, louder than before. "Wake up! You're dreaming. You're safe with me. I've got you. I won't let anyone hurt you."

He wasn't sure what he expected, but it wasn't for her eyes to pop open as if she'd been faking sleep. But she hadn't been faking. He knew that down to his bones.

"Jack?" she whispered as she continued to stare up at him.

"Yeah, *Stellina*. It's me. You're all right. You were dreaming. Want to talk about it?"

Once again, the question seemed familiar, as if it was something he'd heard all too often. And he wanted to snort, because the last thing he ever wanted to do was talk about his nightmares. Where that thought came from, he didn't know.

To his surprise, Maisy nodded.

"You have to know...I didn't want this."

"Want what, hon?"

"I mean, I *did* want this. A husband. A family. But not like this!"

Jack was confused, but he nodded, wanting her to keep talking.

"I love you," she admitted. "And that's no lie. I'd do anything for you."

"I love you too," Jack told her.

She smiled sadly. "I'm sorry. I'm so damn sorry."

"You aren't making sense, *Stellina*. It's your nightmare that has you so turned inside out."

She stared at him for a moment, before closing her eyes and nodding.

Jack didn't like the loss of eye contact. It felt like she was shutting him out, like she did during the day when they moved about the house. "Look at me," he ordered.

Her eyes opened immediately.

"I love you, Maisy. You've been the one constant in my life since my accident. You're the one person I know won't lie to me, who will tell me things as they are. And I'd do anything for you. Getting to fall in love with you a second time was a gift. Hear me?"

Her eyes filled with tears and they overflowed, coursing down the sides of her face into her hair. "The best day of my life was when I met you," she whispered.

Jack leaned down and kissed the salty tears from her face. "Then why are you crying?" he asked.

"When your memory returns, you're going to leave," she admitted in a barely there whisper.

Jack shook his head. "No, I'm not."

"You are. But it's okay. I'll understand."

"What aren't you telling me? What happened with us? Why'd I move to Spokane?" he asked. Then he shook his head. "No, you know what? It doesn't matter. That's behind us. We started over two weeks ago. Our renewal of vows was just that. A new beginning. I'm not leaving you, *Stellina*. And I'm not letting you leave me either."

She gave him a watery smile. "I'm going to make this right. I give you my word on that."

"We're already right," he said firmly. Anxiety rolled through his gut. Something was wrong. Very, very wrong. Even though he'd just said it didn't matter why he'd up and left his wife, deep down, he knew it *did* matter. And he couldn't fix whatever happened between them if he didn't know the details.

She took a deep breath, then brought a hand up to her face and brushed the tears off her temples almost impatiently. Smiling slightly, she said, "So...it's the middle of the night and we're both awake...whatever should we do?"

Jack didn't want to change the subject. As much as he enjoyed making love to his wife, he had so many questions. Why she all of a sudden was taking so many pills again.

He'd seen the bottles Jason had brought to her. He *hated* that she felt the need for medication, wanted to do something, anything, to lessen her anxiety. He couldn't fathom needing so many different drugs for a bout of anxiety, but...surely her doctor knew her medical history better than he did. Wouldn't prescribe her something that would be harmful to her, would he?

The hand that had wiped her face snaked down their bodies and managed to squeeze between them to close around his cock. Like usual, all it took was one touch and he was hard.

"Make love to me, Jack," she said, licking her lips.

He couldn't resist her. Anything his Maisy wanted, she'd get. "How do you want me?"

"Like this. You looking into my eyes. Long, slow, and deep."

Fuck, her words got him so hot. Jack moved his hips back and unerringly found himself at her opening. Then he was all the way inside. He didn't even remember moving. But his cock obviously knew what it wanted, and that was to be buried inside her warm sheath.

She was still wet from his earlier release in her channel, and the thought of his come filling her to the brim was so carnal, and satisfying as hell. "Like this?" he asked as he slowly caressed her from the inside.

"Yesssss," she moaned.

Jack made love to his wife just as she requested. Long, slow, and deep. He stared into her eyes as he did so, and she didn't break eye contact, not once. He felt closer to her than ever before...but at the same time, it almost felt like some kind of goodbye.

That wasn't happening. She was *his*. He wasn't letting

her go. That was unacceptable. This woman was the other half of his soul. He had no doubt whatsoever about that.

He might not remember his life before Maisy, but he didn't need to. She was his past, his present, and his future. And he wouldn't let anyone or anything stand in the way of keeping her by his side. He'd forgotten her before, but that wouldn't happen again. He'd tie her to him so tightly there was no way either of them could extricate themselves. If that meant keeping her delirious with pleasure, so be it. It wouldn't be a hardship to give her multiple orgasms every night for the rest of their lives.

Speaking of which...Jack reached between them and tweaked one of her nipples and felt a corresponding tightening around his cock. He loved how responsive she was. But he needed her to come. He was on the brink himself, and he didn't want to go over the edge without her.

He moved his hand farther down and began to caress her clit. She moaned and shook her head, but Jack didn't let up. Within a minute, she shattered. But throughout it all, she didn't take her gaze from his own. When he released inside her body, it felt even more intimate because of their eye contact.

It wasn't until he felt himself softening inside her that he leaned down and buried his face in her neck. He inhaled, smelling her apple scent and the subtle—or not so subtle, considering how often they'd made love recently—scent of sex. It was burned into his memory. No matter how hard the next knock on his head was, Jack vowed never to forget it. Or her.

Instead of getting up to get a washcloth to clean them, Jack pulled out, arranged her against his side in their usual sleeping positions, and held her against him.

"Jack, I need to clean up."

"No. You don't."

"But...I'm leaking," she said with a smile against his shoulder.

"Don't care. Not moving," he told her.

She nuzzled his skin and tightened the arm around his belly. "I love you, Jack. If you believe nothing else, please believe that."

"I do, *Stellina*. I do."

She fell asleep quickly, and Jack felt his heart swell with love. The trust she'd shown in him made him determined not to let her down, as he'd obviously done in the past. Things were different now. He was a different man than the one who'd moved across the state for whatever idiotic reason he'd had at the time. It didn't matter if he regained his memory and remembered what had happened between them. He'd always love her. He couldn't imagine anything that might change that.

* * *

Jack woke up with a start. Maisy still slept like a log next to him. She didn't stir when he jerked against her. Turning his head to see the clock, he saw it had been two hours since he and Maisy had made love. The sun was just peeking over the horizon outside their window.

He closed his eyes and took a deep breath. The dream had been so vivid. He'd been on a hospital bed. Everything hurt. he had no idea why he was there or what happened, but the beeping from the machines next to his bed were irritating, and he was sick of doctors and nurses looking at him with pity.

The next scene that flashed in his head...he was in a small, cozy bedroom of some sort. Owl was sitting on the floor with a hand over his nose. Jack's hand hurt, and he knew instinctively that he'd just hit him.

"Are you awake now, Stone?" Owl asked.

"I told you not to touch me when I'm having a nightmare or sleeping," Jack growled at his friend.

"Fuck you. I'm not gonna let you lie there and scream in pain. I'm fine. Want to talk about it?"

"No."

"Right. I had to ask. You sure you're awake now?"

"Yeah, I'm awake."

"Good. I'm gonna go make some pancakes. Take a shower. I'll see you in fifteen minutes."

Jack winced. The dream felt as if it was overwhelming his brain. It felt so incredibly real. He opened his eyes again and saw that he was still with Maisy in her room. He wasn't in the hospital and he wasn't wherever that cozy-looking room was.

Sweat beaded on his brow. Because the dream didn't feel like a dream at all. Except he had no idea who the man called Owl could be, or why he kept dreaming about him. And who was Stone? Was it really *him*? It sure *seemed* as if Owl was calling him Stone. But the name meant nothing. He had no idea if it was a nickname or his last name or what.

He was Jack Smith. Wasn't he?

His stomach rolled. What the hell was happening? If this was his memory coming back, Jack wasn't sure he wanted it to anymore.

It was ironic that in his dream, he'd been asked the same thing he'd asked Maisy after she'd woken up from her nightmare. No, he didn't want to talk about the demons in his head that seemed to only come out at night.

Then something else occurred to him. He'd obviously punched the man called Owl for trying to touch him while he slept. It *couldn't* be a memory, because he had no problem with Maisy at his side every night. He obviously didn't mind *her* touching him, in fact, he slept like a freaking baby with her plastered against his side. Whatever he was dreaming had to be something he'd seen in a movie or on TV.

Maisy stirred against him, and Jack turned his attention to her, glad to concentrate on something other than whatever the hell was going on in his brain.

"What time is it?" she mumbled.

He loved her like this. Sleepy, open. Not hiding from him.

"Early. Too early to get up. Close your eyes, hon. You can snooze for a while longer."

"M'kay, but we need to go down for breakfast. Jason expects us."

Jack gritted his teeth together. Fuck Jason and his demands that they present themselves for breakfast. They were grown-ass adults, and if they wanted to sleep in, they should be able to do so. But he already knew from experience that if he said that to Maisy, she'd get upset, and it wouldn't be a good way to start the morning.

Instead, he simply said, "I know. I won't let you oversleep."

She sighed against him, and the feel of her warm breath against his chest made his cock twitch, but Jack ignored it. His wife needed sleep more than she needed sex.

He didn't fall back asleep, just stared up at the ceiling until it was time for them to get up if they were going to make breakfast by Jason's schedule. And just as he'd thought, as soon as Maisy was up, she morphed back into the introverted, submissive woman she'd become in the last week.

He hated it. He wanted the happy, smiling wife he'd gotten to know before she'd had that outing with her brother. He'd let Maisy talk him into staying at the house, but Jack was second-guessing that decision now. He needed to get Maisy away from her brother. Their relationship wasn't healthy, that was more obvious than ever. Maybe that was what they'd fought about before, the thing that had made him move to Spokane.

Well, he wasn't doing that again. He'd do whatever it took to protect his wife, even if it was from her own flesh and blood.

Determined to do what was right this time, Jack waited for Maisy to finish getting ready so he could walk her downstairs to start their day.

CHAPTER TEN

Breakfast was a disaster. Maisy was more aware than ever of Jack's growing suspicions. He didn't like Jason, with good reason. Her brother was acting more smug and superior by the day, and when Jack said something about how he was looking forward to their picnic in the park, Jason had snorted under his breath.

If looks could kill, Jason would've been a dead man. Lately, neither man was hiding his disdain for the other, and it made for a very tense living situation.

When Jason finally got up from the table and left—after sending Maisy a not-very-hidden warning glare—Jack turned to her and said, "We're done."

"What? But you love Paige's biscuits and gravy."

"I'm not staying here another week. I know he's your brother, and you love him, but I can't do it."

"I'm sorry he's been...gruff lately," Maisy said desperately, already thinking about how her brother had told her in no uncertain terms that if she left before the three months was up, she'd regret it.

"Gruff? Maisy, he's an abusive asshole. I don't care what he says to me, I've heard worse, but I can't stand him treating *you* the way he does. I can't understand why you've stayed here for as long as you have."

Honestly, Maisy wasn't sure either. No, that wasn't true. At first, it was because she was a minor. Then, she was drugged to the gills, unable to take care of herself. She also had no money, thanks to Jason. No way to take care of herself elsewhere. She had no education beyond a GED, had never lived on her own, had no idea if she could make it in the "real world."

All that...and she was terrified of her brother.

"Look at me, *Stellina*."

Turning, Maisy stared at the man who'd become the center of her world in such a short period of time.

"I'm not going to let him hurt you. I know this is hard for you. When your parents died, he was your rock. If he hadn't stepped in, you would've gone into foster care, been ripped from this house and everything you knew. You're grateful for him, and he's done a lot of good things for you. But you aren't fifteen anymore. And you have *me* to look after you. Trust me, hon. I'm not going to let you down. I might not remember the man I used to be, but I know down to my toes that I can provide for you. Protect you."

Maisy knew that too. She had no idea who this man was, but she had no doubt that whoever his people were, they were the luckiest people on the planet. "How...where will we go?"

"I'm not sure. But I'm actually meeting with a guy this morning about that job I mentioned a few days ago, the one on a ranch? It's not ideal, but it'll bring in some much-needed cash so we don't have to rely on your brother anymore. And...he mentioned something about a small cabin on the property that's available."

"What do you know about leading tours? About horses?"

"Honestly? Nothing. But I'll figure it out. And the thought of being out on that beautiful property, living a simple life...it appeals more than I thought possible. I won't go back to my bounty hunting job, and not because I have no recollection of what it takes to even *be* a bounty hunter. I don't want to do anything that will take me away from you for long stretches of time. This guy has assured me that the tours are mostly during the day, with only a few overnights. I messed up before, sent you back to this house alone. It's not happening again."

Maisy's eyes watered.

"Don't cry, hon. What is it that *you* want to do?"

"Me?" she asked with a sniff.

"Yeah. I don't want you to be bored while I'm off fixing shit and schmoozing with the ranch guests."

Maisy shrugged. "I don't know."

"Sure you do. What do you like?"

"Reading. Animals. Flowers. Kids."

An emotion Maisy couldn't read flashed over Jack's face. "Right, so maybe we can foster animals for a shelter, get them used to living in a house before finding them homes. Or you can learn how to arrange flowers and work for a florist. Or we can talk to the ranch owner about you helping with the kids who show up with their parents. And if none of those things spark your interest, you can sit on our porch and read books, surrounded by the hundreds of flowers you planted, with our loyal mutt Randy by your side and our baby strapped to your chest."

"Jack," Maisy whispered, completely overwhelmed.

"The truth is, I don't give a shit what you do, *Stellina*. I just want to come home to your beautiful smile and know that you're happy."

She wanted that too. More than he'd ever know. But it was a dream. Like trying to catch hold of the fog. It was right there in front of her face, but impossible to grab.

"Now I've freaked you out. Come on, you said you wanted to talk to Paige before we headed out. I'll walk you to the kitchen, then head upstairs to change. You sure you want to have a picnic in the park for lunch? We can go out somewhere."

"I'm sure."

For the last week, Maisy had tried really hard to act the way she always had while on drugs. Spacey, as if she didn't notice anything going on around her. But she hadn't taken a single pill. She needed her head to be as clear as possible if she was going to figure out a way out of the shithole her life had become. And to get Jack away from her brother. It was hard to keep the neutral mask in place when Jason started in on her. When he reminded her what would happen to Jack if she defied him.

Jack stood and held out his hand. Neither of them had eaten much for breakfast, but Maisy wasn't hungry. She wasn't sure what was going to happen in the next few days, but with Jack's determination to leave and Jason's equal desire for them to stay so he could keep control over her, something had to break. She just hoped it wasn't her.

Jack opened the door to the kitchen, and Paige and the other two women who helped with the meals turned to look at them. Satisfied that Jason wasn't around, Jack took Maisy in his arms. He stared at her for a long moment, before leaning down and kissing her forehead. "I'll be upstairs waiting."

The moment he was gone, Maisy walked toward Paige. She didn't have much time, and she needed to tell the older woman something important.

"Maisy, what's wrong? Was something off with your breakfast?" she asked with a furrowed brow.

"No, it was great, as usual. But I need to talk to you," she blurted. "Alone."

Bless Paige, she didn't miss a beat. She turned to her assistants. "Can you give us a moment, please?"

Without hesitation, the two women nodded and headed for the door. When it was just Paige and Maisy in the kitchen, the cook turned to her. "Now, what's going on? What did you want to tell me?"

Maisy looked around, not sure what she was looking for. Cameras? Audio recorders? She wouldn't know what they looked like if they were there. But she couldn't risk being overheard. She gestured with her head toward the large walk-in pantry and headed that way.

Paige followed with a confused look on her face, but she didn't protest. Maisy closed the door behind them, then turned to the woman she'd known practically her entire life and took a deep breath. "I need you to do something for me. Something huge. And maybe dangerous. But I wouldn't ask if I didn't think it was important."

The woman studied her for a long moment. Then surprised the hell out of her.

"When I first started working for your parents, I was twenty-five. It was supposed to be a bridge-job. Something I did until I found a 'real' career. I'm now sixty-one, and I'm still here. I loved your mom and dad, and when you were born, they truly felt their family was complete. Some of my best memories are with you, Maisy. Baking cookies, watching you and your friends squeal in joy over the birthday cakes I made for you. And some of my worst memories are here too. Crying with you after hearing about the carjacking, worrying about you when you were so depressed you couldn't get out of bed...and watching that brother of yours abuse you so horribly."

Maisy's mouth dropped open in shock.

"I see it all," Paige said fiercely. "I would've left years ago, but I couldn't leave you alone in this house. So whatever you have to tell me stays between the two of us. You're the daughter I never had. I love you, child, so whatever you need to say, just say it."

The desire to tell Paige about Jack was difficult to tamp down. It was bad enough she was going to do what she was going to do. She was putting Paige in as much danger as her and Jack, but she had to do *something*. It wasn't enough, but it was the only thing she felt she could do at this point.

"I have a diary. It's not actually a diary, but a confession. I've written it all in the last week. I included as much as I could remember, all the details that will hopefully help. It's in my room. There's a loose board directly under the window. I don't think Jason knows about it. If anything..." She swallowed hard then forced herself to continue. "If anything happens to me or Jack...I need you to get it. And the other things I've hidden there with it. Give it all to the police."

"Maisy," Paige whispered in a tortured tone.

"Not that I think anything will happen," Maisy lied quickly. "But if it does..."

Paige reached out and grabbed her hand. "I understand. And don't worry, I'll take care of it. But I need you to hear me. Are you listening?"

Maisy looked into the face of the woman who'd always been there for her. It was full of lines and wrinkles, and she looked like she'd lived an extremely difficult life, but she'd shown up day after day without fail. Making soups, delicious bread, desserts, and filling Maisy's belly when she didn't feel like eating. She was putting her in great danger by not fully explaining, but as she stared into Paige's hazel eyes, Maisy had a feeling the woman already knew the dark and dangerous secrets that filled this house.

"Maisy? Look at me. Fight through the fog of those damn drugs he's been giving you and concentrate."

She felt bad that Paige thought she was distracted because of the medication she was supposedly taking. Jason had probably warned her she was depressed and back on the meds. Setting the stage, so to speak. "I'm listening," she told her old friend.

"I know," Paige said softly but firmly. "I'll take care of that diary for you. I give you my word. But if the chance presents itself, get out. Away from this house and the ghosts that live here. You deserve to fly, and you've always been tethered to the ground here. Take that husband of yours and get out. You hear me? *Get out*."

"I will."

"Good," Paige said with such satisfaction and relief, it made Maisy blink away tears.

"And take care of that man of yours. He's a good one," Paige added with a nod. "He'll look after you."

Maisy wanted to say so much, but she didn't have the time, and she wasn't sure what she'd say anyway. Paige knew that Jack wasn't her husband before he'd appeared a few weeks ago. She wasn't stupid. But she hadn't said a word. Had kept quiet, just like everyone did around her brother.

A small part of her felt a teensy bit better at that knowledge, as awful as that was. That she wasn't the only one who was afraid of Jason. It didn't absolve her of her wrongdoings toward Jack, but at least she didn't feel so alone anymore.

Paige reached for her and hugged Maisy hard. Since they were about the same height, she could easily whisper in her ear as she did so. "Go. Get as far away from here as you can."

Maisy pulled back and asked, "What about you?"

"The second you're free, I will be too. I've only stayed because of you."

Her words almost brought Maisy to her knees. Knowing that this woman had been looking out for her for almost thirty years had a profound effect on her. She could stay, but that would mean Paige would too, and that wasn't fair. "Love you," she told Paige.

It was the other woman's turn to get teary eyed. "Love you too, child. Your secrets are safe with me. Now, go upstairs and get ready for your outing with your man. I'll have a basket ready for your picnic when you come back down."

"Thank you."

But Paige shook her head. "I knew this day would come. Prayed for it. And you have no idea how thrilled I am that it's almost here."

Maisy wasn't sure what to say about that. She had no plans. No idea how her escape from this house would work. Anywhere she went, Jason would follow, of that she had no doubt. He wouldn't let anything come between him and the money that was almost his. He needed her to sign the papers after three months of marriage had passed in order to get the funds released. After that...she was as good as gone.

She turned and opened the pantry door, relieved when the kitchen was still empty. She blew a kiss to Paige then headed up the back stairway toward her room. Thankfully, she didn't encounter her brother on the way. He'd probably take one look at her face and know something was up.

She slipped into her bedroom and smiled when she heard Jack humming in the bathroom as he brushed his teeth. Closing her eyes, she memorized the moment. It was so...normal. In a life where *nothing* had been normal, it felt amazing.

The water came on and she heard him spit into the sink. Then a moment later, he was standing in the doorway of the bathroom.

"I didn't hear you come in," Jack said with a smile as he walked toward her.

Pushing off the door, Maisy had a sudden need to touch him. To reassure herself that he was real. That he was here. She collided with his chest and hugged him hard, resting her cheek on his shoulder.

"You okay?" he asked as he returned the embrace.

Maisy looked up at him. "I am now," she blurted honestly.

He studied her for a long moment, just as she did the same with him. One of her hands moved into his hair and she stroked his nape. "Your head still hurt?"

Jack shrugged.

Maisy frowned. "Did you take something?"

"Yeah."

"This isn't normal. We need to get you to the doctor."

"I'll be fine," Jack said.

Maisy didn't like that he was still having headaches so long after his head injury. Her brother's contact had hurt Jack, badly. Had hit him hard enough for him to have a concussion and cause him to lose his memory. The fact that his head still hurt now, weeks later, had to be a bad sign. "Maybe a doctor will be able to have some explanation as to why you haven't regained your memory. Or will be able to tell you if it's permanent or not."

"I don't want anyone messing around with my head," Jack said firmly. "My memory will come back or it won't. It's not going to change anything."

Maisy couldn't hold back the wince. His memory returning would change *everything*.

"I'm good," Jack told her, misinterpreting her wince. "Promise. I'll tell you if I think something's wrong and I'll go to a doctor. Okay?"

She'd have to be all right with that. She nodded.

"Good. Go do what you need to do to get ready. Paige still okay with packing us a picnic?"

"Yeah."

"Cool. We'll grab that on our way out. Maisy?"

She looked up at him.

"Today's gonna be a good day. I can feel it. It's the first day of the rest of our lives."

She gave him a wobbly smile. It wouldn't be as easy as that, she knew that as well as she knew her name. Jason wasn't going to let them waltz out of the house and off into the sunset to start their new lives. No, he'd do something to prevent that. The clock was ticking, and he couldn't afford to let them out of his sight.

"Stop worrying, I've got this," Jack said, then he kissed her hard and fast on the lips, before turning her and giving her a playful shove toward the closet. "Don't dawdle, I don't want to be late for my interview."

She gave him a wobbly smile and entered her closet. She was already wearing jeans, but picked out a dressier long-sleeve blouse she hadn't worn in years. It was bright red, and she needed the flash of color to maybe boost her mood.

Jason wouldn't know what they were up to today, they often went out grocery shopping or to get Jack new clothes, and he already knew about the picnic. He shouldn't be suspicious about their outing. But if Jack got this job, he'd learn they were planning on leaving soon enough.

Maisy shivered but did her best to put thoughts about her brother aside. She wanted to enjoy today...because she knew the clock on her relationship with Jack was ticking as well.

CHAPTER ELEVEN

Jack was in a good mood. He'd loved the ranch. The owner seemed pretty laid-back and cool, and the other employees he'd met were down-to-earth and seemed eager to have someone else to help out around the place.

His job duties would entail pretty much doing any kind of work around the ranch that needed doing. Mending fences, mucking out stalls, plumbing in the guest cottages, general maintenance, and, once he learned the trails, leading guests on hikes around the property. The ranch was on about a thousand acres that had both forest and flat land, where the houses and cabins were located, along with an arena where the horses could be trained by staff and ridden by guests. It was a big operation, and Jack was impressed.

But...there was something missing. It wasn't until he and Maisy had arrived at the small park not too far from her house that he realized what it was.

Mountains. There were hills and valleys, but the true mountains were west of the city. A pang hit Jack, and he felt homesick. But for what? Or where? It was frustrating not understanding what his brain was trying to tell him.

A jolt of pain flashed through his head, and he winced, glad that Maisy's back was turned as she spread the tablecloth that Paige had included in their basket. It felt as if he was on the brink of remembering everything, but for some reason the door to his memories was staying stubbornly shut.

Nights were now the worst. He dreamed such disjoined and terrifying things, but had no context for them. Names and people's faces flashed through his nightmares, names and people he felt as if he should know, but their connections to him remained a mystery. The only thing that kept him sane was Maisy. Holding her in his arms somehow kept the worst of the nightmares at bay. Having her near, smelling her apple scent, feeling her naked skin against his own, kept him from lashing out.

He smiled as she looked up at him from her position on the ground. She sat on her heels and pushed a lock of hair behind her ear. "Paige made peanut butter cookies," she said happily.

Jack lowered himself to the ground next to her and reached over to grab a container of grilled chicken. "How about we start with something a little more nutritious?"

"Peanut butter is protein. And there's eggs, and dairy, and carbs in the cookies," Maisy teased.

Jack chuckled and pulled the baggie of cookies out of her hand and placed it on his other side, holding the container of sliced chicken out to her.

She pouted. "You're mean."

"Nope. I care about your health and well-being. How

about this...you eat the healthy stuff first, and then you'll get a reward."

Her eyes sparkled and she teased, "I'm thinking what I want as a reward isn't flavored like peanut butter and isn't in that little baggie."

And just like that, Jack's cock twitched in his jeans. On the night of their vow renewal, his wife had been...reticent. Not unwilling, but unsure about sex with him. His size, his desire for her, all of it. He'd been away from her for too long, and that was abundantly obvious. But now? Her sex drive matched his own, and it was all he could do not to push her onto her back and take her then and there. But they were in a public park and there were people all around them. He'd never do anything that would embarrass her or put her in danger. And having sex in a public park would do both.

"I'll take a rain check on that, *Stellina*. For now, cookies will have to do."

"Darn," she said with a small smile.

As they ate, Jack kept things light. Talking about the people around them, the gorgeous weather, how beautiful she looked in her red blouse...anything that wouldn't stress her out. But eventually he needed to talk about their next steps.

"I'm going to take the job if it's offered to me," he told her solemnly after they'd finished their lunch and had thoroughly enjoyed the cookies Paige had included in the basket.

She sighed and nodded. But she didn't look at him, instead focused on a family kicking a soccer ball around on the grass not too far away from them.

"Do you really not want to leave?" he asked. He had to

know. She had to see how horrible her brother was to her. If it was anyone else, he had no doubt she'd be begging them to leave the situation. He didn't understand why she wanted to stay.

"No, I want to leave. But it's not that simple."

"It is," Jack insisted. "You're twenty-eight, Maisy. An adult. He can't control you forever."

"When I was eight...I was sick. *Really* sick. Jason slept on my floor every night, even though my parents forbade him to do so. They were worried that he'd get sick too, but he didn't care. He snuck in every night after they went to sleep."

"Maisy," Jack said, but she didn't stop.

"When I was twelve, there was this kid at school who picked on me. Spread nasty rumors that I was adopted and my real parents were serial killers. It was ridiculous, but when you're twelve, everything seems like the end of the world. Jason went to that kid's house and had a talk with him. I never found out what he said, but the rumors stopped. Immediately."

She sighed and lay back on the blanket and stared up at the sky. Jack lowered himself next to her and took hold of her hand. They lay like that, on their backs, staring up at the clouds lazily blowing overhead as she continued to speak.

"When Mom and Dad were killed, I was so lost. Scared out of my mind that I'd go into the system. Jason had just graduated from college, but he moved home, did the necessary paperwork to become my legal guardian. When I wanted to die, he got me to a doctor and got me the meds I needed to keep going day after day."

"The meds that made you a zombie," Jack couldn't help but say with a frown.

She shrugged. "Yeah. But the fact is, for years he was my rock. The only person I saw. He kept me going, even when I didn't want to. His life hasn't been easy, Jack. He gave up everything to come home and take care of me."

"I understand that, Maisy, I do. But you aren't eight anymore. Or twelve, or fifteen. And you've got me now. I don't understand this hold he has on you, and it scares the crap out of me. Is this why we were separated?"

Maisy sighed but didn't respond for a long moment. Then she turned her head and locked eyes with him. "I want to leave, but I'm scared."

"Of what?" Jack asked.

She frowned. "He's different. He's not the big brother I remember anymore. He doesn't like you, and I'm afraid he's going to do something to...ensure we can't stay together."

"There's nothing he can say or do that will make that happen," Jack vowed.

Instead of reassuring her, his words seemed to make Maisy even sadder. She turned her gaze back to the sky. "You're the best thing that ever happened to me, Jack. I mean that," she said quietly. "No matter what happens, that's the God's honest truth. Take the job, you'll be awesome at it. I wouldn't be surprised if you weren't part-owner of that ranch in a couple of years."

"I won't do it if you really don't want me to. We can find another way to make ends meet," Jack said, her belief in him warming him from the inside out.

She shook her head and turned back to him. "No. I don't want to stay. I want to leave. With you. Start a new life. It won't be easy, but I'll do whatever I can to help. I'll get a job, I have no idea what, but I want to contribute."

"All I need is for you to support me," Jack told her honestly.

"I do."

"Good. The owner is supposed to call in a few days after a couple more interviews. If he offers me the job, I'll accept and we'll figure out our next move. I'll tell Jason that we're moving out, and I don't want you anywhere around when I do. If he protests, I'll set him straight. I won't give him another chance to abuse you. *No one* hurts you, Maisy. You're mine to protect. To provide for. As your husband, I take my vows seriously."

She swallowed hard. "And you're mine to do the same."

Jack brought their clasped hands up to his mouth and kissed her knuckles, but made no move to get up. "It's such a nice day," he sighed.

She chuckled. "Yeah, it is."

Jack felt more content at that moment than he had in what seemed like forever. He had his wife by his side, a future with her to look forward to, and a knowledge in his bones that he was right where he was supposed to be.

A noise in the distance caught his attention. Turning his head, Jack couldn't see anything in the sky, but the sound seemed incredibly familiar to him.

Sitting up, he stared in the direction the noise was coming from.

Ten seconds later, a helicopter came into view. It was flying fast and seemed to have a specific destination in mind. Jack recalled Maisy telling him about a hospital that wasn't too far from the park.

The sound of the rotor blades settled in his soul—and

he had to close his eyes because of the intensity of the pain shooting through his head.

Pictures flashed through his mind...of a strong and sturdy cabin nestled among the trees...sitting around a large table laughing with a group of men...sitting at a console of switches and lights as he stared out the windshield at the ground far below...men in uniform and weapons, climbing in and out of a chopper he was flying... his friend and copilot, Owl, sitting next to him, frantically trying to keep the helicopter from crashing...pain, blood, a hospital...Owl laughing with a blonde-haired woman... warning that same woman not to touch Stone if he had a nightmare...joy at being at the controls of the chopper they were buying for The Refuge...waking up in a trunk, panic...

A gasp left his lips as his memory returned hard and fast. It didn't gradually come back, letting him acclimate to the sights and sounds his unconscious mind had been keeping from him. No, it played back like a horror movie on full volume.

"Jack?"

He heard Maisy calling his name as if from a distance. His given name, not the one he'd used for years—Stone.

He was Stone. Not Jack Smith. No, his last name was Wickett. He had no siblings, his parents were retired and living in New York. He was owner of The Refuge, a kick-ass retreat for people suffering from PTSD. Co-owner, actually, along with Brick, Tonka, Spike, Pipe, Tiny, and his best friend, Owl.

Shit, Owl! Was he all right? What about Lara?

So many questions ran through his brain...but then the most important one surfaced.

Who the fuck was the woman at his side, holding his hand? Because she sure as hell wasn't his wife. At least, she hadn't been a few weeks ago—before he was kidnapped.

Feeling sick, Stone thought about the renewal of vows ceremony he'd happily participated in. He had a feeling it wasn't a renewal at all.

He'd actually married the liar beside him.

"Jack? What's wrong? Are you all right? Do we need to go to the emergency room? Talk to me, you're scaring me."

Swallowing hard, praying the pain would recede, Stone turned to look at Maisy.

She was frowning, looking worried as she stared at him, her hand gripping his tightly. If he hadn't remembered everything, he would've believed that she was actually concerned about his well-being.

The level of betrayal he felt would've brought him to his knees if he wasn't already sitting.

He had no idea what to say to her. Not knowing the purpose behind her deception kept him from lashing out. He needed information. Who was she? Why had she and her brother kidnapped him? Were they working with Carter Grant, the serial killer who'd vowed to get revenge against Lara? Where was she and Owl? Shit, he needed to call Brick. Find out what the fuck was going on.

"Please, say something!" Maisy pleaded.

"I'm okay," he managed to get out, but even to him, his voice sounded flat and hard.

"Are you sure?"

"Yeah...we should get back."

"Oh, um...okay," Maisy said uneasily.

He felt a twinge of guilt that he was obviously scaring her, but he pushed it down. He'd been fucking *kidnapped.*

Duped into thinking he was this woman's husband! That his last name was Smith. He couldn't trust anything she said or did. She was obviously an extremely skilled liar.

He dropped her hand and stood. She did the same, and he began to pack up the picnic. She bent to help, and he said in a clipped tone, "I've got it."

Maisy nodded and stood back, watching him.

Stone's mind spun. He needed to figure out his next steps. He had free run of the house, so it wouldn't be hard to leave. But he needed answers before he disappeared. Needed to know *why*.

His head hurt. His heart hurt. Hell, it felt as if every nerve ending in his body hurt. The memories of his past wouldn't stop running through his brain like a bad B-movie. His time as a prisoner of war, the torture, the harrowing rescue, the calmness he felt in the mountains in New Mexico, his respect for his friends who'd settled there with him.

But along with those memories were new ones of Maisy. The way she looked above him as she rode his cock. How she felt against his side as she slept. How scared she looked around her brother. The mysterious bruises she claimed were from her clumsiness. The way Jason spoke to her when he thought no one was listening.

Stone was confused as hell. The feelings he had for Maisy hadn't disappeared the moment his memory returned. Instead, he felt even *more* protective of her. Which was crazy. She was obviously a part of whatever plot was afoot with his kidnapping. She'd deceived him from the moment he'd woken up in her bed. But he couldn't understand why. What the end game could be to this elaborate ruse.

They walked in silence toward the car and Stone got behind the wheel, barely waiting for her to shut her door before pulling out of the parking spot. Things were tense all the way back to the house, but Stone couldn't think of one thing to say that wouldn't give away what he was feeling and thinking. He needed some space. To try to figure everything out. To decide his next move.

One thing was for sure, he wasn't spending another day in that prison of a house. He might not be in chains and may not have been physically tortured, but lying to him, telling him that he was someone he wasn't, was a form of torture all the same. Mentally.

"I'll bring the basket back to Paige," Maisy said quietly after he'd parked.

"Okay," Stone told her.

"Jack? Are you sure you're okay?"

"Yeah, I'm just tired. I'm going to go lie down; see if I can get this headache to go away. Give me some time, all right?"

"Oh, yeah, I can do that. Do you think you'll want to come down for dinner?"

"No, I'm not hungry. I'll see you tonight. We'll talk," Stone told her. He looked at her then, for the first time since the park. Her cheeks were devoid of color and she looked extremely worried. As well she should be. Her life was about to be turned upside down...and she had no idea of how ruthless he could be.

Maisy nodded.

Stone turned from her then and headed for the stairs. He needed to make some calls. His friends had to be worried sick about him. And he needed answers. If Owl and Lara were still in the Seattle area, he'd find them and break them out of whatever fucking hole Carter Grant had stashed them.

"Jack?"

He wasn't going to turn around. Wanted to ignore the small and soft way she said his name. But he couldn't do it. He stopped and turned to look at Maisy.

"I love you more than I'm indebted to my brother. Whenever you want to leave, I'm ready."

Her words confused the hell out of Stone. But instead of storming over to her and shaking her and demanding answers to the hundreds of questions rattling around in his head, he merely nodded and continued down the hallway, walking away from her.

Every step he took felt like torture, and he didn't know why. She'd lied to him. Had married him against his will... no, that wasn't fair. He was willing, he just thought he was a different man than he actually was. But he couldn't block out the way she clung to him as if she was truly in love. The way she opened up to him. The things she'd shared, sounding so damn earnest about every confidence.

Gritting his teeth, he took the stairs two at a time, relieved he didn't run into Jason. He wasn't sure what he'd do or say to the man if he saw him right this moment. Before he did something rash that might get him thrown into the safe room Maisy said they had in the basement—he hadn't even been down there, he had no idea what he might find, but he had a suspicion he wouldn't like it—Stone needed to think. Needed to touch base with Brick, find out what the hell was going on.

After that, he'd make the decision whether to disappear like a thief in the night, or metaphorically burn the place down before he made his exit.

Either way, Stone was out of there. He'd vowed he'd never be a prisoner again. He wouldn't stay, not even for a woman he was afraid had already gotten way too far under his skin.

* * *

"Stone?! Holy shit, is that really you? Where are you? What happened?"

Stone couldn't help but smile at hearing Brick's stunned words. "I didn't think anything could flap the unflappable Brick," he couldn't help but say.

"Shut the fuck up and start talking," Brick ordered.

Stone sobered. "I'll tell you everything, but first, is Owl okay? And Lara?"

"They're fine. They're here at The Refuge. Holy shit, I can't believe you don't know. Grant hired a guy, Ricky Norman, to kill both you and Owl, and to fly Lara to his island lair. Norman sold you instead. And the man who bought you was supposed to take Owl too, but turns out, he just took you. So this Norman guy flew Owl and Lara to Grant, who was pissed way the hell off. They got into a shootout, Owl stole the chopper while those two assholes killed each other, but not before taking a round. He promptly passed out as soon as they were in the air. Lara flew them to an airport and now they're married and Lara's pregnant. Your turn. What the hell happened? Where have you been?"

"You aren't going to believe me when I tell you," Stone said, his mind reeling over everything he'd just learned. He was thrilled for Owl and Lara, but pissed they'd had to go through such a harrowing experience.

He spent the next five minutes explaining everything that had happened to *him*.

"Jesus! But you're okay? Not hurt?" Brick asked.

"No, I'm fine."

"Thank *fuck*. And you have all your memory back now?"

"I'm thinking so, yeah. I remember having a panic attack when I was in that trunk. I think my mind must've turned off to protect itself. I was being kidnapped again, and maybe I thought I was going to be tortured or something. So I just...forgot who I was."

"And these people, Jason and Maisy, they tricked you? Said you were her husband?"

"Yes."

"Shit, Stone, that's insane! Why?"

"I don't know."

"Do they know who you are? Like, where you're from or your name or anything?"

"I'm not sure. I obviously haven't seen my wallet or anything."

"Hmmm."

Stone waited. But his friend didn't say anything else. "That's it?" he asked impatiently. "Just, hmmm?"

"It doesn't make sense. There has to be a reason. Lara said the guy who dragged you away said his boss only wanted one guy, not two. That's why he didn't take Owl."

"I'm leaving tonight. I'll buy a ticket at the airport and be home tomorrow."

"I'm thinking we need to consider all the angles first," Brick countered.

Stone was stunned. "You don't think I should come back to The Refuge?"

"No, you're *absolutely* coming back home. But we need to figure out why you were taken. Were you targeted, or would any guy work? If you leave, will they come after you? We need more answers, and I don't like the thought that they'd be able to track you here if you buy a ticket. Give me an hour or so, let me tell the others that you're safe. I know Ry can get you home without leaving a trace."

"Who?"

"Oh, shit, I forgot you don't know. You know Ryan, the newest housekeeper?"

"Yeah?"

"Her real name is Ryleigh. She's a computer genius. Tex admitted she's even out of *his* league—which pisses him off. She's been close-lipped about why she's here or what she's hiding from, and she's definitely hiding from something or someone, but she refuses to say. Has been working day and night to try to figure out what happened to you. She's going to be relieved as hell that you're okay, but pissed that she wasn't the one to find you," Brick said. "Tiny's been keeping an eye on her. Making sure she doesn't run."

Stone was stunned. "Holy crap, seriously?"

"Yup. Okay, lay low, don't let on that you've remembered who you are. Let me talk to the others and Ry, and I'll get back to you. This number okay to call back?"

"Yes."

"You'll probably have to dump the phone when you leave. If your kidnappers are smart, they could probably get the phone traced and figure out that you called here, but that will take a while, I'm thinking. Not everyone has a Tex or Ry in their back pocket to do their illegal computer hacking shit for them." Brick snorted. "And, Stone?"

"Yeah?"

"Fucking thrilled you're okay. We were all going out of our minds here. I don't like the situation, not at all, but it's a huge relief that you're all right. Lara's going to lose it. She blamed herself for not being able to stop that guy from taking you. And Owl's gonna want to hear for himself that you're good. I'm thinking you'll have us all on the line when I call back."

Stone closed his eyes. It felt amazing to have such good friends at his back. He hadn't realized how alone he'd felt until that moment. "Thanks."

"Don't thank me," Brick grumbled. "Stay close to your phone, I'll call back as soon as I have more info for you."

"Ten-four." Stone ended the call and sat down on the bed.

As soon as he did, he could smell apples.

Sighing, he leaned over and rested his elbows on his knees and stared at the floor.

He wanted to believe that Maisy had nothing to do with this fucked-up situation. But what else *could* he think? She'd lied to his face time and time again. She might not have planned his kidnapping, but she'd perpetuated the farce when he'd woken up and discovered he had no memories.

Straining to remember the moment he woke up, Stone frowned. He recalled Jason speaking to Maisy harshly, issuing a veiled threat when she begged him not to do "this." Was she referring to whatever Jason had planned for Jack? He could only assume so.

He also remembered the way she'd stumbled over what

he'd thought were the easiest of questions. She'd been coached by her brother, he had no doubt of that. But why? To what end?

Rubbing his temples, Stone sighed again. There was no doubt that Jason Feldman was an asshole and a bully. He was abusing his sister, mentally and probably physically. Did she deserve it? Stone honestly didn't think so. He'd spent almost every minute of the last few weeks with her. And now that he had a moment to think it through, he knew how scared she was of her brother. She'd even come out and told him that today, but with everything else that had happened, namely his memory returning, he'd blocked it out.

He didn't know *why* he'd been kidnapped, and if he left without a trace, where would that leave Maisy? He shouldn't care. She'd participated in the scam to keep him in the dark about their sham of a marriage. But he couldn't help the feeling that if he left her alone with her brother, serious harm would come to her.

Then another thought shot through him—and he sat up straight on the bed.

He'd had unprotected sex with Maisy every night since their farce of a vow renewal. Sometimes several times a night.

She could very well be carrying his child right now.

And there was *no way* he was leaving his son or daughter to be raised in this house, by his kidnappers.

His decision made, Stone felt as if a huge weight had been lifted from his shoulders. He hadn't realized how anxious he'd been about leaving Maisy behind. It made no sense. She'd lied to him and pretended to be his wife...but he couldn't stop hearing her say she was afraid.

Well, she might be scared of her brother, but she'd be terrified once she met Brick and his other friends. They could be intimidating bastards when they wanted to be. There'd be no way she could keep whatever plan she and her brother had devised a secret when they interrogated her.

All he had to do now was wait for Brick to call him back so they could discuss arrangements to get him home without leaving a digital trace, make sure they knew he wouldn't be alone, that Maisy would be coming with him, and then wait for the right time to make his escape.

Whatever the reason he'd been brought here and lied to, Stone was done playing their game. By the time the sun rose, he'd be on his way home. To his *true* home. To the men and women who'd never lie to him.

CHAPTER TWELVE

"Where'd you go today?" Jason yelled in Maisy's face.

She flinched and tried to step away from him, but he grabbed her arm and hauled her closer.

"Did you hear me? Where'd you go?"

"J-Just for a picnic. Paige packed us a lunch," she stammered.

"Liar! You're lying! You went to the bank, didn't you?" Jason asked.

"What? No!"

Jason shoved her away hard, and Maisy went flying backward, hitting her hip on the edge of his desk before falling to the floor. She landed on her left arm, and it hurt. A lot. But she didn't like being on the floor when her brother was standing over her. She was way too vulnerable down there in range of his feet. He'd kicked her before. And it hadn't felt good.

She was scared out of her mind. Of her brother, yes... but something had happened to Jack today. One second he was there with her, and the next she felt as if he was a million miles away. She had no doubt his head hurt, she could tell by the stiff way he was holding himself and from his furrowed brow, but there was more to it than a simple headache.

He was distancing himself from her for some reason. She'd racked her brain to try to figure out why. Had she said something to piss him off? Done something? She didn't think so, but he was definitely acting different.

Of course, the most obvious reason he hadn't touched her even once after they'd started home was because he'd remembered something. But surely he would've said something, right?

Maisy wasn't sure. She didn't know how amnesia worked. She hated her brother a little more right then, for not bringing a doctor in to see Jack. What if he was permanently disabled by whatever had been done to him by the kidnapper Jason had hired?

"You were gone way too long for a fucking picnic!" Jason snarled as he stalked toward her.

Maisy crab-walked backward away from him, but she wasn't fast enough. Her brother reached out and grabbed her by the hair, hauling her upward as Maisy desperately tried to take the pressure off her head.

"Tell me where you went. What you did. Now!" Jason ordered.

"I swear, we didn't do anything! Jack wanted some different scenery, so we went to the park and hung out. Then we ate the lunch Paige packed for us and came home. Please, Jason, let go, you're hurting me!"

Her brother eyed her with a cold expression. Maisy shivered just seeing it.

"Beg."

"What?" Maisy asked, trying to pull herself out of his grip, with no luck.

"Beg me to let you go."

"Please, Jason."

When she didn't say anything else, he yanked on her hair. "More."

If she could've gone to the police right that second, Maisy would have. *This* was the man who'd killed his wife because she'd outlived her usefulness. *This* was the monster who'd likely killed their parents because of greed. She hated him. Completely and utterly.

"Please let go of me. I swear we didn't do anything other than have a picnic today. I wouldn't betray you that way. I'm begging you, Jason, let me go. Please, please please..." It was humiliating to lower herself this way, but she would if it meant getting away from her brother.

For the first time, it hit home what Jack had given her by not making her plead for anything. She'd brushed it off as being a quirk of his, but she was more sure than ever that at some point in his life, he'd had to beg for something, and he understood how demeaning it was. How hopeless it made you feel. Because at that moment, she felt lower than a bug. Jason was toying with her, and it felt awful.

He smirked, then shoved her away from him so hard, she stumbled and fell to the floor yet again. As she rolled, her face hit the leg of the chair opposite the desk. Pain bloomed in her cheek, but she didn't hesitate to jump to her feet.

"Don't fuck this up," Jason warned. "We have less than three months until we can get that money. All you have to do is keep your legs spread, keep his dick happy, and we're home free." He narrowed his eyes. "I know you're in love with him, it's obvious...and *pathetic*. But don't go thinking the two of you can live happily ever after. It's not gonna happen. We can't risk him remembering. All that matters is that the marriage certificate was filed and the countdown to getting what we deserve has started. Understand?"

"Yes."

"I mean it. He might be infatuated with you now, but that's because he's getting pussy on a regular basis. There's no way he'd ever fall for you if he didn't already think you two were married. You're too ugly and stupid to catch any *real* man. That's why I had to go out and find one for you. This was for your own good, Maise. Just be thankful that instead of bringing home a dildo, I bought you a real live dick."

He laughed then, an evil sound that made Maisy's toes curl. Any affection she'd once felt for her brother was long gone.

"Now, to make sure you don't fuck things up, I've talked to your doctor and he prescribed something new for you." Jason walked to his desk and picked up a pill bottle she hadn't seen before. "And because I don't think you're taking your medicine every morning like you're supposed to, I'm clearly going to have to take over *that* responsibility for you too. Here." He shook out a pill and held it out to her.

Maisy stared at it with trepidation. She had no idea what it was and no desire to take it. But she knew better than to protest. To defy him. She held out her hand, but Jason shook his head. "I don't think so, sis."

He moved so fast, she couldn't evade him. He grabbed

the hair at the back of her head and tilted her back so far, she was thrown off balance. Then Jason shoved the pill in her mouth and put his hand over her lips and nose, cutting off her air.

"Swallow it," he ordered.

Maisy's eyes widened as she stared at her brother. She tried to pry his hand off her face, but he was far stronger. She wanted to pretend to take the pill. Keep it hidden in her mouth until she could spit it out. But she hadn't counted on Jason depriving her of oxygen, something he'd never done before.

She didn't mean to swallow the damn thing, but in her desperation for air, as she thrashed and struggled, the pill accidentally slid down her throat.

"It's gone?" Jason asked.

Maisy tried to nod but couldn't move her head.

Her brother removed his hand and Maisy took a huge gulp of air. Then Jason held her mouth open as he inspected her as if she was a kid...or a dog. Finally, he ran a hand gently over her hair and murmured, "Good girl," as if she really was an animal. "See? As long as you do what I want, nothing bad will happen. Now, why don't you go and lie down? That pill is gonna kick in fast, and trust me, you aren't going to want to be walking around when it does." He chuckled, but there was nothing funny in the sound.

"What was it?" Maisy asked.

"Nothing you need to worry about. You've taken it before...just valium. But your previous dose wasn't enough, so I tripled it."

Maisy stared at her brother in shock. "Tripled? The regular dose made me feel out of it as it was!" she said.

Jason merely shrugged. "Well, now you'll *really* not worry about anything. That's my job. You've always had too much anxiety. Like I said, this is for your own good, Maise. All you need to think about is keeping your husband happy. And the best way to do that is to keep your legs open. If he's getting pussy, he won't think too much about anything else. Just a few more weeks, sis. Then this'll be over and done."

Maisy didn't ask what over and done meant...she knew.

She didn't want to think about what a triple dose of valium was going to do to her either. She'd be completely out of it, like she'd been for way too many years of her life.

"Go upstairs," Jason ordered in a low, mean tone. "The last thing I want is you passing out on me down here where I'd have to see your ugly face."

Maisy turned toward the door, her mind spinning. She needed to add this to her diary. Had to let the police know that her brother was drugging her once more. But Jack said he wanted some time alone. She couldn't go upstairs... but if she didn't, she was afraid of what her brother would do.

With no choice, and feeling bitterness well up inside her at how little control she had in her life, Maisy headed up the stairs. The difference was, this time, she was aware of her brother's manipulation. In the past, she'd thought he was actually trying to help her. She was grateful he was there. Now? She wanted to be anywhere but here. But Jason wasn't going to let her and Jack leave. He'd probably start drugging Jack too, which was unacceptable. Maybe she could pick a fight with Jack, make him hate her so much, he'd leave.

Her heart seemed to shrink at that thought, but having him away from Jason was preferable to him being dead, which was his fate if he stayed here. She had about fifteen minutes before the drug really began to kick in, based on experience with her normal dosage, and Maisy knew she'd have to do something drastic before that happened. Once she began to experience the floating feeling that valium always gave her, she'd lose the determination that currently swam through her veins.

Not thinking about anything other than convincing Jack to get the hell out of this house of horrors, Maisy opened the door to their room.

Standing at the window, Jack turned to face her, and suddenly her determination took a nose dive. She spun to face the door. He looked so...*angry*! And Maisy had never seen him like that before.

"What are you doing up here? I told you I wanted to be alone," Jack said.

Maisy couldn't stop the wince. She'd come to see Jack as her safe place. When things with her brother got too intense, she'd been able to count on her husband to soothe her. Having him speak to her just as harshly as Jason was a blow. She closed her eyes as she continued to face the door for a long moment, trying to gather her courage to incite his anger. To stoke it. To get him so pissed and frustrated with her that he left.

She turned away from the door to face him, opened her mouth to say something completely ridiculous and outrageous—but where he looked angry before, the absolute fury on his face *now* stopped her in her tracks.

"What the *fuck*?" he bit out as he stomped toward her.

Maisy cringed and stared at him as he approached. When his hand came up, she couldn't help it, she flinched and cowered slightly. Which seemed to make him even angrier. Well, her goal had been to make him so mad he left; at least she'd managed the first part. She just didn't know how she'd done it. Was he that angry at her very existence? It wouldn't surprise her; she seemed to inspire that in people.

Shit...she was already feeling the effects of the pill her brother had literally forced down her throat. Her thoughts were disjointed, and she found she couldn't pull up the determination she'd felt even moments ago when she walked toward her room.

"What happened to your face? And...are those fucking finger marks on your arm?" Jack growled. He didn't touch her, his hand was hovering over her face as if he was afraid to hurt her.

Smiling, Maisy took hold of his hand and placed his palm on her cheek. She tilted her head into him and closed her eyes.

"Maisy?"

"Hmmm?" she asked, lost in the feel of his palm against her overheated cheek. It felt so good. His hands were soft, but they also had calluses, which felt amazing when he ran them over her body. He was everything she'd ever wanted in a man, and he was hers.

"What's wrong? You're acting weird."

Was she? Maisy opened her eyes and stared up at Jack. His brown eyes were so beautiful. Reminded her of milk chocolate. Was there any in the house? She was hungry. Then she remembered that she was trying to make her husband mad, but couldn't really think of why.

Then it hit her. Jason was going to kill him. She had no doubt.

"You should leave," she blurted.

"What?"

"Leave. You need to go. But don't tell anyone. Just go, Jack. You have to go."

He studied her, and to her relief, didn't move his hand from her face.

"Why? Why should I leave?"

"Because. It's bad here. Bad things happen."

"Like what?"

But Maisy shook her head. "Can't say. You'll hate me. And I love you too much to purposely make you hate me. But I'm gonna fix it. Need to write in my diary."

"Maisy, did you take something?" Jack asked softly.

She liked this gentle Jack much better than the angry one.

"I'm trying to be gentle," Jack told her. "Now, tell me what you took."

Crap, she'd said that thing about gentle Jack out loud?

"Maisy, concentrate. Tell me what you took."

"Didn't wanna, but I couldn't breathe and had to swallow. He said it was valium. But triple dose. Didn't know they made those. Guess he can get his evil minions to make whatever he wants." She had no idea what she was saying anymore, and visions of yellow creatures like from that cartoon movie danced in her head.

"Fuck."

"Yeah. He said I was s'posed to do that too but...I'm tired. And dizzy. Can I rest for a minute before we have sex? Or maybe you can just do it while I'm sleeping? But then you gotta go." Maisy blinked, and it seemed to take way too much energy to open her eyes again. "Get away from here, Jack. I wish I could say where you came from, so you could go there. But I don't know. I'm sorry. I'm so sorry."

She seemed to wilt then, but she somehow didn't fall to the floor. She was floating. No, Jack was carrying her. She turned her head and buried it into the skin of his neck. "Smell so good," she told him, trusting him not to drop her.

She felt something soft under her and smiled. She recognized her mattress. "I love my bed," she said dreamily.

"Did Jason do this?" he asked, running his fingers up her arm.

Since he'd asked so nicely, Maisy nodded.

"And this?" Jason asked, and she felt his fingers on her cheek once more.

"Sorta," she said with a shrug. "I fell when he shoved me."

"And he made you take the valium?"

Maisy heard the skepticism in his voice, and it hurt. More than the bruises on her body. "You ever thought you were gonna die?" She didn't wait for his response before she went on. "His hand over my nose and mouth...cut off my air. I couldn't breathe. It was scary. He's gonna kill me, you know. Not today, because time's not up. But in a couple months, we're as good as dead. Should've just let him do it. Then you would've left. Been safe. And he wouldn't get it. Charity would get it all. Should've died a loooong time ago...then you wouldn't be here."

"Shhhh, *Stellina*, you're safe now."

She loved when he called her his little star. "Not safe,"

she disagreed, then she closed her eyes and couldn't find the strength to open them again. Maybe she'd take a nap, then she'd get up and do whatever it was she was supposed to do. At the moment, she didn't care about anything other than sleeping.

CHAPTER THIRTEEN

Stone stared down at Maisy with a frown. He'd been so pissed at her when she'd entered the room, but now he couldn't stop worrying. Her breaths were shallow and slow, and he couldn't stop staring at her chest, making sure it kept moving up and down as she slept. No, she wasn't sleeping, she was passed the fuck out.

He'd needed space from her after his memory had returned, but in taking that space, he'd left her alone with her brother. And she'd returned to him abused and drugged. It wasn't acceptable.

Stone's feelings about the woman on the bed were confusing. He hated her for participating in this crazy deception, but the love he had for her was still there. Simmering under the surface.

His phone vibrated, startling Stone so badly he jerked toward the door. Shaking his head, he answered, putting it on speaker. It wasn't as if he needed to hide the call or what was said from Maisy. Not when she was dead to the world.

Even thinking the word *dead* made him feel panicky inside.

"Stone."

"Fuck, it's good to hear your voice!"

Stone grinned. "Likewise, Owl. Are you and Lara really all right?"

"We're good. It's *you* we were worried about. Did you really have amnesia?"

"You really think I'd let you guys worry for this long if I didn't?" Stone asked a little harsher than he'd intended.

"No, of course not. I'm just so damn relieved that you're okay."

"What's the plan?"

"Stone, Brick here. I talked to the others and they agree that with all the questions about what the hell is actually going on, it's best if your exit strategy is covert. Ry's been working since the second she heard where you are and got the number of the phone you're using, and she seems to think the assholes who kidnapped you have no idea who you actually are."

"How does she know that?" Stone asked in confusion.

"How does she know *anything* she knows?" Pipe asked.

Stone grinned. "Hey, how's Cora?"

"She's good. We're thinking about fostering a seven-year-old boy."

"Can we please stick to the topic at hand?" Brick asked, but Stone could hear the pride and happiness for their friend in his tone.

"Great news, Pipe. You're going to be an amazing role model and father."

"If we get approved," Pipe said dryly. "People tend to

take one look at my tattoos and think twice. Not to mention my funny accent."

"Whatever," Stone said. "If Ry is as good as you guys say she is, she can just go in and approve the application, move it through."

"Hey, that's a great idea," Pipe said.

"No, it's not. Can we not encourage her to break the law any more than she's already doing in order to get Stone home?" Brick grumbled.

Stone heard chuckles, and realized all his friends were probably on the other end of the line. "Tonka? Spike? Is Tiny there too?" he asked.

"We're here," Tonka said.

"But Tiny's at his cabin hovering over Ry, as if he has any clue as to what she's doing on that computer of hers," Spike said with a laugh.

"Henley and Reese are good? Pregnancies going okay? Shit, I feel as if I've been gone for years instead of weeks," Stone said with a frown.

"We're all good. Just anxious to see you. Now, back to what we were talking about. Ry hacked into Jason Feldman's email and phone, and it looks like he's asked a couple of his friends to find intel on you, and no one's been able to deliver—which must make them the dumbest assholes on the planet, considering there's plenty of info about you online if they know where to look.

"It also seems that one of his more questionable acquaintances hired a friend of a friend to drive you to the house. The guy stole your wallet and is now in the wind. No one can find him. And the guy he hired to do all this doesn't even know the real name of the guy *he* asked to take care of your kidnapping.

"And another friend, some Don asshole—who isn't someone you want around anyone you actually give a shit about—sounds like a sick son-of-a-bitch. But regardless, they're all a bunch of amateurs...Ry's words, not mine. Although I happen to agree."

"Why me?" Stone asked the question that had been bothering him the most.

"If it's any consolation, I don't think it mattered who they kidnapped. It could've just as easily been me. But the motive is as old as time. Money," Owl said. "Ry's still working on figuring out all the details, but she's convinced it's tied into the marriage certificate that was submitted with your name on it."

The renewal of vows that was actually a marriage ceremony. But learning the motivation behind his kidnapping brought up even more questions. For instance...what would they have done if he hadn't lost his memory?

"Right, anyway, Ry contacted someone she knows from the dark web and he's going to meet you at oh-five-hundred at the airport with new identification. She's booked you on a six a.m. flight out of Seattle. And when she says no one will be able to trace you or the false name she's created, I believe her."

Stone's gaze went back to the woman on the bed. Maisy was completely vulnerable at that moment. He could literally do anything he wanted with her, and she'd have no idea.

The mark on her face seemed to mock him. She'd hurt him. Had lied to him and used him for *money*. And yet, it was more than obvious she was terrified of her brother. It was more obvious than ever that Stone couldn't leave her behind. She'd been alone with her brother for what, an hour? And she'd returned to his side covered in bruises and drugged out of her skull.

And Stone couldn't get her words out of his head when she'd asked if he'd ever thought he was going to die. Because he *had.* Memories of being a POW were burned into his brain. He assumed it was the reason why he'd had temporary amnesia. It was his brain's way of trying to protect him from reliving the horrible memories of being kidnapped the first time.

Other things Maisy said in her drugged state echoed in his mind.

It's bad here. Bad things happen.

I love you too much to purposely make you hate me. But I'm gonna fix it.

I guess he can get his evil minions to make whatever he wants.

Get away from here, Jack. I wish I could say where you came from, so you could go there. But I don't know. I'm sorry. I'm so sorry.

He's gonna kill me.

"I need two tickets and two IDs," Stone blurted.

"What? Why?" Brick asked.

"I'm not leaving Maisy here."

Utter silence greeted him for a moment. Then Owl said, "She was in on it, Stone. She knew you weren't her husband, and yet from what you've said, she went along with it."

"I know, but she didn't want to," Stone said, realizing he believed what he was saying one hundred percent. "She was the worst liar, but I was so confused and in shock from not remembering anything about who I was, other than my first name, that I ignored the signs. He abuses her, Owl. She's lying here on the bed in front of me, completely out of it from the triple dose of valium he literally forced down her throat, with bruises on her arm and face. And I've seen others. If I leave her here, he's going to kill her. Besides...there's a possibility she's carrying my baby."

He heard Brick mumble something about everyone being fucking pregnant, but then Owl spoke again. "Do you trust her?"

"No," Stone said without hesitation. "But all signs are pointing to the fact that she's my legal wife."

"She is," Spike said. "Ry found your marriage license. It was submitted all legal like and everything."

"Except it's not his name," Tonka argued. "So technically it's *not* legal."

"She's my wife," Stone insisted, not sure why he wasn't jumping on the idea that because his last name was wrong, he wasn't married. He'd made a commitment. Even if he was conflicted in his feelings about Maisy, he'd made a vow to protect her. And he wouldn't go back on that now. Not when he knew without having to think twice about it that if he left her here, she was as good as dead.

"Right, I've texted Ry and told her to add a passenger. It'll make you more recognizable if anyone starts looking for you, but I think if you wear hats or something, it'll help."

Stone nodded, frowning as he wondered what such a high dose of valium might to do a fetus. Reaching out without thought, he put his hand atop Maisy's belly.

"All right, you going to be able to get to the airport?" Brick asked.

"Yeah."

"Okay. Ry said to ditch your phone somewhere before

you get there. And I'm guessing that goes for Maisy's phone too."

"She has pictures on there that she's not going to want to lose," Stone said. Again, he was confused about his protective feelings for the woman who'd deceived him. But he recalled the look on her face when she'd showed him pictures of her parents. There had been such sorrow and love there, he couldn't bear for her to lose them, as it was obvious how much she still missed her mom and dad.

"I'll talk to Ry. I'm sure it won't be a problem for her to download them before you turn the phone off. Just shoot me her number after we hang up," Brick said.

"I appreciate this," Stone told his friend.

"Whatever," Brick said. "We're just thrilled that you're all right. And this is what friends do. A SEAL doesn't leave a SEAL behind," he said.

Stone chuckled. He'd heard that saying many times from the SEALs he'd transported in his chopper while he was in the military. "Yeah, but I'm not a SEAL," he said.

"True, SEALs smell better than you Night Stalkers."

The banter felt good. Normal. Suddenly Stone couldn't wait to be home. Back in his cabin in the mountains of New Mexico.

"You sure about bringing her with you?" Tonka asked in the slight lull.

"No. But I can't leave her," Stone answered honestly.

"Not sure where we'll put her, but we'll figure it out," Brick mused.

"She'll stay with me. I need to keep an eye on her. I don't trust her on her own," Stone told his friends.

"Sounds familiar," Pipe muttered.

"What do you mean?" Stone asked.

"That's what Tiny said about Ry," Owl told him. "Is it gonna be a problem to lay low until you need to leave?"

Turning his attention back on the situation at hand, Stone said, "No. Maisy's out. I mean, *completely* out. I'm hoping I can rouse her enough to get her out of the house under her own power later. And I can claim my head's bothering me and skip dinner. Besides, if I see Jason, I'm not sure what I'd do to him."

"Right. She needs to be conscious to get on a plane, Stone," Spike warned.

"I know." And he did. Her condition worried him, but he was more pissed that she'd been drugged against her will. He couldn't forget her description of how her brother had smothered her in order to get her to swallow the pill.

"All right. We'll let you go," Brick said. "I'll send you details about your contact and where to find him at the airport. Don't forget to ditch the phones, and we'll see you soon. Stone?"

"Yeah?"

"Glad you're all right. Things weren't the same here without you. Later."

"Later." Stone clicked off the phone, but didn't stand up from where he was sitting next to Maisy on the bed.

He reached out without thought and brushed her hair back. She sighed and turned toward him. Her hand reached out blindly, and when she touched his knee, she curled her fingers around it almost desperately.

"Maisy?" he whispered.

She didn't respond.

"Shit," Stone swore as he sighed. He'd been all fired up earlier. Ready to tear into Maisy, force her to go with him, to get her to The Refuge so she could be interrogated. And now all he wanted to do was hold her tight and protect her from anyone and everyone who might even look sideways at her. It was confusing as hell.

Looking at his watch, Stone saw he had hours to go before he needed to even think about leaving. He lay down next to Maisy and somehow wasn't surprised when she immediately curled into him. Her face was buried in his chest and her hands clutched the front of his shirt with a death grip.

"It's okay, Maisy. You're safe."

"Not safe," she mumbled.

"You are when you're with me," he said, running a hand over the back of her head.

"But you aren't safe with me," she said so sadly, Stone moved back to see if she was awake and lucid. But she wasn't. Her eyes were still shut and she was lax in his arms.

On the one hand, he liked that she wasn't hiding anything from him, and everything made much more sense now that he knew more about why he was taken. But he couldn't reconcile the woman he'd come to know with someone who apparently was greedy enough to go along with a plan to kidnap a man and force him to marry her for money.

But as soon as he had the thought, it occurred to Stone that it was possible she hadn't had a choice. Had Jason planned everything without her knowledge? Maybe...but then again, she'd gone along with it. Had stood in front of him and vowed to love and cherish him as if they really were madly in love. And she'd had plenty of opportunities to tell him the truth.

Nothing made sense, but Stone wouldn't get any more answers to his questions tonight. Maybe not even tomorrow. But eventually he and Maisy were going to sit down and she'd tell him everything. She owed him that much.

* * *

"You need to get up, Maisy."

Sighing, Maisy shook her head and tried to block out Jack's order.

"Please, *Stellina*. I need you to concentrate. We need to go."

She couldn't resist him when he used that pet name. She loved it. Almost as much as she loved him. No, that was a lie, she couldn't love anything more than she loved Jack. She rolled over and forced her eyes open.

The room was dark, but with the light coming from the bathroom, she could see her husband sitting next to her with a worried look on his face.

"There you are. I need you to get up. Can you do that?"

Maisy nodded, then clumsily she sat up and tried to shift her legs off the side of the bed. She felt uncoordinated and the room seemed to spin around her.

"That's it. Let me help you. Lean on me. Good girl."

His praise felt good, but then she frowned. She didn't deserve praise. She was a horrible person, but didn't remember what she'd done to feel that way.

"I'm going to help you to the bathroom, you need to pee before we leave, but first, drink this."

Blinking, Maisy saw Jack holding a large bottle of water to her lips.

"It's warm, but it'll have to do."

For a split second, she panicked. She didn't want to be forced to drink the water. She felt as if she was drowning when Jason did that...but then the man next to her came into focus. It wasn't her brother, it was Jack. Her husband. And he wouldn't hurt her. Not like she'd hurt him.

That thought made her frown, but she reached for the bottle of water anyway.

Jack held it steady for her as she drank but didn't tip it up, forcing her to take more than she was comfortable with. The second the water hit her tongue, she realized how dry her mouth felt and how thirsty she was. She gulped the water down as fast as she could.

When Jack gently took it away, she whimpered.

"I know you're thirsty, and water's good to flush your system out, but I don't want you getting sick. You can have some more in a bit. Come on, let's get you to the bathroom."

She should've been embarrassed that he had to help her undo her jeans and get her underwear down, but this was her husband. He knew every inch of her body intimately.

Maisy's eyes widened slightly when she heard Jack swear quietly, his gaze narrowed on her hip. She looked down as his fingers gently brushed over a large bruise, and she frowned, but she couldn't recall how she'd hurt herself.

With a tight jaw, Jack helped her sit on the toilet. She refused to let him wipe her, but had to hold onto him again when she stood so she didn't fall on her face.

Once her pants were fastened, Jack turned her toward him and held her close as he stared at her with a serious expression. "We're leaving, Maisy. Now."

She felt as if she was floating, watching them from above. "Okay."

"I need you to understand what I'm saying. We're

going to the airport and we're leaving Seattle, and not coming back anytime soon."

She nodded and said again, "Okay." Then thought about what he'd said for another moment. "Good. You need to leave. Did you find your people?" Maisy wasn't sure what she meant, but she knew it was important.

"Yeah, I did."

"I'm glad. I bet they were worried. It probably feels good to be worried about. Be free, Jack. Don't come back. Ever. You aren't safe here. Martha wasn't either, and now she's in the yard. I don't know for sure, but that's what I think. She wasn't safe, and I didn't know until it was too late. But *you* know, and you can leave."

"You're coming too," Jack said.

It took a second for that to sink in. Maisy shook her head. "I can't. I have to sign the papers. If I'm not here, he'll be mad."

"Then he'll have to be mad, because I'm not leaving without you."

Maisy's eyes widened. "You have to! You have to go!" she said, pushing against his chest urgently.

"Not without you. You could be carrying my baby. I'm not leaving you here."

Her hand went to her belly, and she sagged in his arms. "A baby," she breathed.

"Yeah, so you're coming with me."

"Okay."

"Okay?" Jack asked.

Maisy nodded. "He'll hurt the baby. Less money for him. Wish I could get rid of it."

"Get rid of our child?" Jack asked.

She didn't like the hurt tone of his voice. She shook her

head so hard she got dizzy. "No! I'd *never* hurt my child. *Ever!* The money. I wish it wasn't there. Mom and Dad would still be here, and Martha, and you would've never come but that's okay. Everyone else would be alive."

"It's okay, Maisy. You're all right. I just need you to come with me now. You're still pretty out of it from the valium, but I need you to be as lucid as possible so you can get on the plane."

"We're going on a plane?" Maisy asked.

"Yeah, is that a problem?"

"I've never flown before. Wanted to, but Jason said it wasn't a good idea. That I was too sick."

"You weren't sick," Jack said in a tone Maisy couldn't understand.

But she nodded anyway. "I was sad," she said with a deep-seated knowledge.

"Yeah."

"I'm not anymore," she told him honestly. "I have you, and I love you."

"Right. We need to go if we're going to make our flight."

"Can I have the window seat?" she asked as Jack steered her out of the bathroom.

"Yes."

"Goodie!"

The floaty feeling remained as Jack helped her down the stairs. It was a good thing he was there because it was dark and she probably would've fallen on her face if she'd been alone. But she had Jack, she wasn't alone. Her husband would take care of her.

He quietly led them outside instead of to the garage, and Maisy was confused. But then Jack told her that they were taking a taxi so they didn't have to disturb anyone in the house, which made sense.

Time had no meaning as they entered the airport. Maisy didn't even question why they didn't have any suitcases, she was too tired, and excited to actually get on the plane. Jack met a friend in the airport, which was confusing because she didn't remember him having any friends here, but she dismissed it when he checked them in using the computer thing and they waited in line for security.

Once through, Jack seemed much more relaxed, and she leaned against him as they sat and waited for their flight to board. She missed the announcement that they could board, but she let Jack help her down the hallway to the plane. He pointed at one of the first rows of chairs for her to sit and Maisy looked up at him.

"First class?" she whispered once they were seated.

He grinned at her, and Maisy felt as if she could lose herself in that smile.

"Apparently."

"Cool."

"Good morning, Mr. and Mrs. Henderson, can I get you something to drink before we take off?"

Maisy frowned, not sure who the woman was talking to, but she decided she must have heard her wrong because Jack told her they'd both take some water.

"You can have mine," he said after she'd eagerly drained her plastic cup.

"Are you sure?" she asked.

"Very."

Her husband's intense gaze hadn't left her, and if she'd been able to think clearly, Maisy might've wondered what he was thinking about so hard, but because she still felt removed from reality, she simply drank his water down too. Suddenly, her eyes felt too heavy to keep open.

"Sleep."

She reached over the console between them and grabbed his arm. "You won't leave me?"

"No."

"Promise?"

"You think I'd get up and leave you like this on your own, on a plane?" he asked with a frown.

Maisy shrugged. "If I was you, I would. I'm bad."

"Close your eyes, *Stellina*. It's going to be okay."

She did as he asked, and soon felt her worries slipping away. But before she let the floaty feeling take over, she whispered, "Love you."

Maisy didn't even notice that he didn't return the words, because she was once more lost in the safety of the clouds in her head.

CHAPTER FOURTEEN

Stone closed his eyes as he hugged Owl. Hard. He was glad to be home. Well, almost home. Owl and Brick had come to Santa Fe to pick up him and Maisy, and he hadn't realized how stressed he'd been until that moment.

Having good friends to watch his back felt incredible. He was pretty sure he'd gotten out of Seattle undetected, but knowing he had backup now was a huge load off his shoulders.

Maisy had been pretty out of it throughout the trip, but she currently looked more aware than she had since she'd walked into their room back at the house in Seattle the afternoon before.

"Is she okay? She doesn't look okay," Owl asked when he stepped back.

Brick was currently off to the side making small talk with Maisy, so she was out of earshot.

"Actually, she's doing a lot better now than earlier."

"This is better?" Owl asked skeptically.

"He forced her to take a triple dose of valium. Yeah, this is better."

"Does she understand what's happening?"

"I don't know," Stone said honestly.

"Does she at least know your memory returned?"

"No. At least I don't think so. I didn't have a chance to confront her. To tell her I knew everything. I was going to, but then she had that encounter with her brother and the drugs took effect before I could talk to her."

"Well, shit. This is going to be interesting," Owl mused.

"You ready to get going?" Brick asked as he walked up to the two men.

Stone looked at Maisy. She looked lost and confused, but her gaze was locked on him. As if he was her safety net in a world that had suddenly turned upside down.

"Jack?" she asked softly.

Stone wanted to keep his distance. Couldn't forget her role in everything that had happened. But with her looking so unsure and worried, he couldn't stop himself from reaching for her. He pulled her to his side and let her snuggle in close. "It's okay, Maisy. We're okay."

She nodded and let him take some of her weight.

"Come on, let's get home."

Home. Man, that sounded good.

They walked toward Brick's Jeep and Stone got Maisy settled in the backseat then climbed in after her. She fell asleep almost as soon as they pulled out of the parking lot. Stone spoke quietly with Brick and Owl about the last few weeks as they drove toward Los Alamos and The Refuge. Less than an hour later, Brick pulled up next to the main lodge and Stone couldn't help but smile at seeing the group waiting for him outside.

He roused Maisy and got her out of the Jeep, but lost track of her almost immediately when he was surrounded by his friends. Stone hugged Lara hard, pulling back to look into her eyes, wanting to make sure she was all right.

She smiled up at him. "I'm good, promise."

"Heard you flew the shit out of that chopper," Stone told her.

She blushed. "It wasn't pretty."

Stone was so damn thankful that things had turned out the way they had. "You're here, so I'd say it was fucking beautiful." Then he hugged her again and whispered into her ear, "Thank you for saving my best friend."

Her eyes were filled with tears when she finally let go of him. Then Stone made the rounds, hugging all the women and giving man-hugs to his friends. Even Robert, The Refuge's cook, was with the group, promising to make Stone's favorite pork chops the next night to welcome him home.

Satisfaction coursed through Stone. When he'd first agreed to invest in The Refuge, he wasn't sure if he would stay long-term. Now he couldn't imagine himself anywhere else.

A niggling voice in the back of his mind told him that he'd been ready and willing to make a life in Washington with Maisy, and that he would've been perfectly happy doing so, but Stone ignored it.

Thinking about Maisy made him wonder where she was. He felt guilty that he'd completely forgotten about her for a moment.

Turning in a circle, he searched for her, momentarily panicking when he didn't spot her immediately.

"Ryleigh's got her over there," Tiny said, pointing to a bench on the lodge's porch.

Turning, Stone saw Maisy slumped on the bench with Ryan—no, her name was apparently Ryleigh, or Ry, as most people called her. Maisy's eyes were cast downward and she looked uncomfortable and out of place. Stone was moving before he'd given it much thought.

He walked over to where Maisy was sitting and knelt in front of her, putting his hands on her knees. Stone nodded to Ry, then turned his attention to Maisy. "You feel all right?" he asked.

She nodded but didn't look up. Stone frowned. He looked at Ry again. "Thanks for sitting with her. I've got her from here."

Ry stared at him with a look he'd never seen before. The housekeeper had generally kept to herself around the place. She'd been polite and friendly, but now that Stone thought about it, she hadn't really opened up to anyone. She'd stayed on the peripheral. But now she met his gaze with a look so intense, Stone was surprised he didn't burst into flames right there on the spot. It was a little irritating. He hadn't done anything wrong. Maisy was the one who hadn't told him what her brother had planned. But he couldn't help but like how protective Ry was over Maisy. He felt the same protectiveness toward her...even after everything that had happened.

"Be good to her," Ry told him with a bite to her voice.

It instantly made Stone feel defensive. "I'm thinking you know nothing about what's between us," he retorted.

But instead of making Ry back off, her back straightened at his tone and she narrowed her eyes at him. "You haven't been here, so I suppose I should cut you some slack. But here's the deal...I'm the one who found Jasna, who tracked Reese's tile so you could fly in like a hero and snatch her before she was taken across the border. I'm also the one who's been working nonstop to find your ass and make sure you came home.

"Since you called Brick less than a day ago, I've read every text message you sent, every email, and seen every picture on your phone. That guy from the ranch you interviewed with wants to hire you, by the way, and has sent an email offering you the job, so I'm guessing you need to let him know you won't be working there after all. But more importantly—I've done the same with Maisy's phone."

She took a deep breath before continuing. "I have all her pictures, all her emails, and she even made some recordings that I can only assume were done in secret because of what was said. I know your wife probably better than *you* do in some cases, and I'm telling you that you need to go easy on her."

Stone's eyes narrowed. "What recordings?"

"Between her and her brother, who's a real dick if you ask me."

"He is," Stone agreed. "I don't suppose you took a break from hacking into my life long enough to look into Jason and figure out why the fuck he picked *me* to kidnap and lied his ass off to my face?"

"I'm working on that," Ry said. "All I'm saying is," she said in a less-biting tone than before, "your wife is both stronger than you could ever imagine, and far more vulnerable than you realize."

"That makes no sense," Stone said, wanting to be done with this conversation.

Ry shrugged. Then she took a deep breath and looked away briefly, toward their group of friends. "I'm sorry. I'm being a bitch. You haven't done anything wrong, and I'm taking my frustrations out on you. You have every right to be angry. About what happened to you, and with Maisy."

Stone was surprised at her abrupt change of demeanor. "Thank you."

Ry nodded at him.

"Excuse me?"

Both Stone and Ry turned to Maisy at the quiet interjection.

"You have my phone?" she asked Ry.

"No, I'm sorry." The other woman's tone was soothing, calm, friendly.

"I had to ditch them before we got to the airport," Stone told her.

"But I was able to recover all your pictures," Ry quickly added.

"Oh...good."

"You were a cute kid," Ry told her. "That one picture of you between your parents in front of that boat is adorable."

Maisy smiled and had a faraway look in her eyes. "Yeah, we went whale watching. Jason didn't want to go and stayed with a friend. But we had the best time."

Ry patted her hand. "I have some stuff I need to do, but if you need anything, you find me and I'll get it for you. I'm in cabin number ten, it's the one with the green door, west of the one you'll be in. Okay?"

"Okay," Maisy said absently.

Ry looked at Stone once more, and the soft look on her face was replaced by a stern one. "Easy," she said, before squeezing Maisy's shoulder and standing. She didn't get ten feet off the porch before Stone saw Tiny breaking off from the group still standing outside the lodge chatting and head after her.

"You got your memory back."

Stone turned to look back at Maisy. She was still sitting on the bench, was still clutching her hands in her lap, but she was looking right at him. He shifted until he was sitting in the seat next to Maisy that Ry had just vacated, and nodded. "Yeah."

Maisy looked around for a moment before saying, "This place fits you."

"It does," Stone agreed. All of a sudden, he wasn't sure what to say to the woman next to him. He'd spent the last few weeks by her side and they never had a problem finding something to talk about. But now she felt like a stranger, and it sucked.

"I'm sorry I—"

"No," Stone interrupted. "Not now."

Maisy frowned.

"We'll have our talk, but not when you're still a little out of it from that valium. I want you clearheaded and with no excuses for not telling me every damn thing I need to know."

Maisy pressed her lips together, but she nodded. "Why'd you bring me with you if your memory has returned?" she asked after a moment.

"How else was I going to get answers if I didn't?" Stone said. If he hadn't been looking into her eyes at that very moment, he would've missed the flash of hurt that leaked out before she was able to control her emotions. Their relationship was a sham. Fake. Why would she be upset that he had no other reason to want her here?

"Right," she said with a nod.

Stone felt like an asshole, which made no sense. He hadn't said anything that wasn't true, but if he was honest with himself, that wasn't the only reason he hadn't been able to leave her behind. He could've reminded her about the possible pregnancy. Also...she was under his skin, but he'd *never* admit that. And no matter what she'd done, he couldn't leave her to suffer her brother's wrath. Especially not after seeing the bruises on her skin and knowing he'd drugged his own sister, apparently without a second thought.

"It's been a long day and it's only a little after lunch. I'll get you settled and come back up to the lodge and grab us something to eat. I'm sure there's nothing edible in my cabin."

Maisy stared off into the distance and said, "He's not going to be happy about this."

Stone knew who she was referring to. "I don't give a fuck."

She turned at that and met his gaze. "He's going to come after me."

"He'll have to find you first," Stone told her. "And I've been told on good authority that'll be easier said than done."

"You don't understand," Maisy said with a frown.

"You're right. I don't. But for now, you need to sleep, let the rest of that drug work its way out of your system. Tomorrow, we'll talk. I'll tell you what I know, and you can tell me why the fuck your brother had me kidnapped, and why you went along with his lies." His words came out sharper than he'd intended.

Maisy simply sighed and nodded.

"You'll tell my friends and me everything?" he asked, not yet willing to believe getting answers from her would be easy.

"Yes. But he won't stop. He needs me."

"Then we'll have to *make* him stop," Stone said simply. But he had a feeling it wasn't simple at all. "Come on. After lunch, I could use a nap too. I was up most of last night."

"Doing what?" Maisy asked as Stone helped her stand.

"Making sure you were breathing," he said bluntly.

Maisy tripped over her feet and would've fallen to the ground if Stone hadn't been there to keep her upright.

"Easy," he said, wrapping an arm around her waist as he walked her away from the lodge toward his cabin. "Alaska said she and the others are going to get you some clothes and toiletries. You can wear something of mine until they get back from town."

"I don't want to be a bother," Maisy told him.

"You won't. This is what they do."

They continued walking and, after a moment, Maisy said softly, "I knew you had friends like this. People who were worried. Who would care that you disappeared."

Stone gritted his teeth. "And yet you still lied to me," he couldn't help but point out.

Maisy didn't respond, but it was just as well. Stone was still a little too raw about being betrayed by her to be forgiving right then. It felt as if he was being torn in half. Part of him was thrilled beyond belief to have Maisy here with him, at his real home. The other part was pissed as hell and didn't even want to see her face.

But she was his responsibility. Just as he hadn't been able to leave her in Washington to face the repercussions of him vanishing into thin air, he couldn't manage to give over responsibility for her to one of his friends. For better or worse, she was his. Fake or not, they had a marriage certificate filed in some computer database in Seattle that said so.

When he got to his cabin, Stone saw that someone had already unlocked it for him, which he appreciated since he had no idea where his keys had gone. Brick had told him on the way home from the airport that Ry was working to get his identification cards replaced, and he'd have new credit and bank cards in a few days. She'd deactivated his old ones the second they learned he was missing. He made a mental note to thank her for that.

He also had the thought that it was actually pretty handy to have a computer genius working at The Refuge.

He opened the door to his cabin and with his hand on the small of Maisy's back, guided her inside. She stopped just through the door and took in his space.

The main room was open-concept, with the kitchen on one side, a sectional taking up most of the living room, and a dining table breaking up the two spaces. He had a gray rug on the living room floor, a fireplace opposite the sofa, and a huge bookcase on another wall. But the best part, in his opinion, were the floor-to-ceiling windows that faced the forest. They made it feel as if the cabin was completely open on one side. Like he was camping in the trees.

"It's..."

Stone held his breath as he waited for her thoughts.

"...perfect," she said reverently.

"Yeah," he agreed. "Come on. I'll show you where you'll be sleeping."

He led her through the room toward a hallway. He had an office of sorts, with a love seat that opened up into a bed.

"I'll get some sheets and stuff for you. Wait here." When he returned a minute later, Maisy was standing exactly where he'd left her. She didn't move as he made up the bed, simply stepped out of his way so he could complete the task. He left once more to grab a shirt and a pair of gym shorts for her, and once again, when he returned, she was still standing where she'd been a moment before.

"Here," he said, holding out the clothes. "They'll be big, but more comfortable to sleep in."

She looked down at the clothes in her hands and nodded.

Stone didn't like the distant look in her eyes. Even though she was right in front of him, she might as well have been a million miles away. "I'll get you some water. Drink it. It'll help flush your system. There's a bathroom in the hallway if you need it. You can shower when you get up."

"Okay," she said softly.

Stone wanted nothing more than to take her hand and bring her down the hall to his room, to his bed. But everything was different now. He didn't even know this woman. And now that his memories had returned, the reasons why he shouldn't take her to his bed were even more dire.

His nightmares. How violent he became.

But again, that voice in his head reminded him that he'd slept with Maisy for weeks and not once had he ever hurt her. In fact, he'd slept better than he had in years, since he and Owl had been rescued from that hellhole overseas.

Mentally sighing, Stone backed out of the room. He didn't know what else to say. So instead of saying something he might regret, he simply closed the door and left Maisy alone.

An hour later, Stone couldn't stand it any longer. He had to check on her. He hadn't heard anything from the guest room/office since he'd shut the door earlier.

He knocked softly but didn't get a response. Worried that something might be wrong, that she could've stopped breathing because of a delayed reaction to the drugs, Stone didn't hesitate to crack open the door.

The curtains in the window were open, and there was plenty of afternoon light coming in to illuminate the room. Maisy was on her side at the very edge of the mattress, curled into a tight ball. She hadn't gotten under the sheet or blanket, and she was clutching his clothes to her chest, her nose buried in the material. She looked small and vulnerable.

Stone had actually taken two steps into the room toward her before his brain caught up with his heart. He froze, filled with indecision. He wanted to go to her, take her into his arms and tell her that everything would be fine. But he also wanted to rail at her, shake her and force her to confess everything. Explain why she'd betrayed him so badly. Ask if all her pretty words about love and taking care of him were nothing but lies.

He did neither of those things. He simply backed up

until he was once more in the doorway. Then he shut the door quietly and went back to the sofa. He sat and stared into space. He was exhausted and his head still throbbed. But there was no chance of him being able to sleep. Hopefully tonight when it got dark, he'd be able to catch a few hours of rest. For now, all he could do was sit and run the last few weeks over and over in his head. Trying to understand the motives of the woman he'd married.

Tomorrow. Tomorrow, he'd get answers. He'd decide what to do after he heard what Maisy had to say. Until then...all he could do was obsess over every little thing she'd said and done since he'd first met her.

CHAPTER FIFTEEN

Maisy felt like she was going to throw up. She was sitting at a table in a conference room at the main lodge of the retreat Jack apparently co-owned. All his friends were there, staring at her expectantly. They wanted information and were waiting for her to give it to them.

She'd slept through the afternoon and night. When she'd woken up this morning to the smell of bacon, her first thought had been pleasure. Paige didn't make bacon or sausages very often because Jason felt they were too fattening.

But when she opened her eyes and found herself in a room she didn't recognize, Maisy remembered. She wasn't in Seattle anymore. Paige wasn't here. And Jack's memory had come back.

She knew the moment it happened. When they'd been in the park and that helicopter had flown over.

Now he hated her, and she had no one to blame but herself.

Traveling to New Mexico was a blur. She didn't

remember much of what happened after her brother had forced her to swallow the valium. She had vague memories of the flight they'd taken, but that was it. She'd met a lot of people the day before, and surprisingly, most had been nice to her. If she'd been in their shoes, she wasn't sure she would've offered as much grace as the men and women of The Refuge had shown her.

Things had been awkward between her and Jack since she woke. She'd showered, they'd eaten, Alaska had come by with some clothes, and as soon as she'd changed, Jack informed her that they'd be going up to the lodge to talk with his friends.

And now here she was.

She still felt a little off...but the fog that had consumed her because of the valium had cleared. When he'd asked if she was okay this morning, the temptation to tell Jack that she still wasn't feeling like herself had been strong, but it was time she owned up to her part in what had been done to him. The sooner she told these men what she knew, the sooner she could leave.

Because she had no doubt whatsoever that her brother would come for her. He'd hire whoever it took to find her because without Maisy, he wouldn't be able to access her trust. And he wouldn't have any compunction about hurting anyone who stood between him and what he wanted—her money.

She had to leave. As soon as possible. Where, she had no idea, but she'd figure it out. Maybe she'd ask Ry if she could help her change her name and start over somewhere. The other woman had been extremely kind to her the day before, and Maisy vaguely remembered her saying that she was a computer genius and had been able to save all her pictures from her phone, which was probably buried in a landfill somewhere right about now.

"Why did your brother kidnap Stone?" Brick asked.

Maisy mentally shored her shoulders and took a deep breath. The men had been more than patient, making sure she was feeling all right, offering something to drink and asking if she was comfortable. But they had a right to know why their friend had been taken. And Jack needed to know too.

"To answer that, I need to go back in time..." Maisy started.

"My parents were rich. They'd invested well and Dad had a good job in Silicon Valley. They moved to Seattle when I was little, bought a big house where my dad worked remotely. Hired a few people to help around the place, and were very generous with their money in the community. Jason is seven years older than me and he seemed happy, even though he had to leave all his friends behind when we moved.

"When I was around fourteen, Jason started to change. He was about to graduate from college and Mom and Dad were on his case about doing something with his life, but he was content to stay on his friends' couches and stuff. Things seemed tense between him and our parents, but honestly, I was too into my own stuff to pay attention. Typical teen. I wasn't part of the popular crowd or anything, but I had a few good friends I loved to hang out with.

"When I was fifteen, I was at a sleepover at a friend's house when my parents were killed. Jason came to my friend's and got me and brought me home. He told me that Mom and Dad had been out to dinner and when they went back to their car, someone shot them and stole their vehicle. Dad died instantly, but Mom lived long enough to crawl over to his side and was found with her hand on his head. The police think she was trying to stop the bleeding."

Maisy ignored the sympathetic noises coming from the men. They wouldn't last, and she didn't want to feel their concern and then have to give it up once they heard the entire story.

"The cops didn't find their killer or killers. There was no physical evidence at the scene, no bullet casings, no blood other than from my parents, no fingerprints on either of them. There wasn't even any surveillance video because the restaurant's cameras were broken or something. So no one ever answered for their deaths.

"I didn't take it well. I was hysterical at the thought of never seeing them again. Jason moved back into the house and became my legal guardian. He took care of me, making sure I saw doctors for my depression and anxiety. I couldn't go to school...couldn't make myself care about *anything*. I dropped out, but Jason helped me study for the GED test. I passed, barely, but I wasn't interested in going to college anyway.

"The first twelve years after my parents' deaths are a fuzzy blur because I was taking so many meds. They made it impossible to care about what was going on around me. I didn't have to worry about anything because Jason was there. My parents had life insurance policies, and Jason got his money right away. I assumed he used my portion to pay for my expenses...drugs, medicals bills, that sort of stuff. But honestly, I was too drugged to ask.

"When I was around twenty-two, Jason met a girl. Her

name was Martha. I liked her. She was shy and sweet. She helped me get a little stronger, and I was able to stop taking some of the daily meds I'd been on for so long. She and Jason got married down at the courthouse, and she didn't seem to have a lot of friends, so she and I hung out a lot. But around four months after she and Jason got married...she disappeared."

"Disappeared how?" Pipe asked.

"One day she was there, and the next she was gone. All her things were gone too. Her purse, a suitcase of clothes, the jewelry Jason had given her. The police investigated, but with all their other cases, and with no evidence of foul play, eventually I think they simply wrote her off as an adult deciding to leave her husband. She had no family to encourage the police to keep looking into things."

"Your *brother* didn't do that?" Brick asked.

"At the time, I thought he was too upset and humiliated that she'd left him. He'd hinted at the possibility of her cheating with someone else, and I thought he wasn't willing to stoop to begging for her to come back."

"And now?"

Maisy turned toward Owl. Jack was sitting next to him...on the other side of the table from her. When she'd sat down, and saw Jack pull up the chair next to his friend, as far away from her as he could get, it hurt. A lot. But she wasn't surprised. She'd known this day would come from the first lie that passed her lips.

"As I said in the beginning, my parents had a lot of money. It was split between the two of us upon their deaths. But my parents were...quirky. They believed in soul mates, and they wanted their kids to experience the kind of true love that they had. So in order to try to help us find it, the money they left us had strings attached." She didn't wait for someone to ask what those strings were before continuing.

"In order to access the money in our trusts, we had to be married for at least three months. Only then would we be able to have it released. There's a monthly stipend that we got, whether we were married or not, but the bulk of the money was only accessible after we were married."

"Ah..." Tiny said with a knowing look in his eye.

Maisy felt her cheeks heat. She knew what these men were thinking. That she was a money-grubbing bitch who'd come up with a plan to access her fortune.

They were so far off it wasn't even funny. But why would they believe her? All evidence was pointing toward the fact that she was exactly what they probably thought.

"So your brother got married and after gaining access to his money...his wife disappeared?" Jack asked.

Maisy nodded.

"Convenient," Tonka mused.

"Not for Martha," Maisy couldn't help but say. Then she sighed. "He killed her." The three words felt heavy in the room, but the weight that had settled on her shoulders from the moment she'd realized what her brother had probably done, suddenly lifted. She wasn't sure anyone would believe her, but at least she was sharing her suspicions at last.

"I don't know how the murder actually took place, but one day, very shortly after she went missing, Jason hired someone to put in that basketball court in our backyard. It was weird, my brother isn't exactly the athletic type. But a company came, dug a big hole, then it rained for days and days, as it does in Washington. They came back about a week later and filled it in and put the concrete pad over it, but I think Jason put Martha's body in that hole."

"Why?" Spike asked. "It seems risky to put a body in a hole someone else is going to fill in."

"I know. I never said it was a smart plan. But I woke up one night after a nightmare and went downstairs to the kitchen. He was coming in from the back covered in mud. He yelled at me and told me to get back upstairs. I think he was preparing to move her body to that hole. And her stuff too. Martha wasn't a big woman, only a little over five feet. I think he put her in there, maybe even digging a little deeper so the contractors wouldn't notice, covered her up with some of the dirt the excavators had removed to create the hole, and then when the contractors came back, they helped him by filling in the hole with concrete and putting that stupid basketball court over it. I think he went out like three times after that to shoot hoops, and that was it."

"But you have no proof," Jack said.

Maisy forced herself to meet his eyes and shrugged. She had something that *might* be proof, but wasn't sure it was enough.

The room was silent, and it felt as if she and Jack were the only ones in the world. She wanted him to believe her. To trust that she wasn't simply lying to cover her own ass. When he averted his gaze, her heart dropped.

"So your brother allegedly killed his wife after he got her money. Where does Stone come in?" Owl asked.

"Right," Maisy said, forcing herself to continue. This was the hard part. "So he was happy for a while. Jason had lots of money and he didn't have to work for it. But just like he made his way through the life insurance payouts, eventually he spent all the money he got from his trust."

"How much?" Brick interrupted.

"Four million."

Brick whistled low. "That's a lot of money."

"Yeah. And he didn't like that he couldn't spend willy-nilly anymore. He had my monthly stipend, but it wasn't enough."

"Wait—*your* monthly stipend?" Jack asked.

Maisy nodded. "Since I was a minor when our parents died, he arranged for it to be deposited into his account, which was legal at the time because he was my guardian. And when I turned eighteen, I was in no shape mentally to manage it myself. So it continued to go into his account. By the time I started to get better, not taking as many of the drugs and had the presence of mind to ask, years had passed, and he told me he'd been using the money to make sure I had everything I needed. Food, a roof over our heads, medicine, paying Paige's salary...things like that. He insisted I still wasn't ready to take care of that stuff on my own."

"So all these years, he's been stealing your money too," Tiny said.

Maisy looked down at the table and shrugged. "It wasn't as if I needed it. But after Martha disappeared, and he spent all his money...he stopped administering all of my drugs. Started encouraging me to find a boyfriend." She sighed. "I guess he needed me clearheaded if he wanted to marry me off.

"I wasn't interested in any of that. I'd barely left our house in years, I knew *nothing* about dating. But he signed me up for some dating sites anyway, arranged for me to meet some guys. He had the men come to the house, and it was *beyond* awkward. I didn't like any of them, they only seemed interested in sex, not a relationship. Jason didn't care, he kept pushing me to stop being such a prude. But I didn't want any of those men."

"So he went out and found you a husband," Brick concluded.

Maisy couldn't read the expression on his face, and she refused to look at Jack. "Yeah," she said quietly. "I don't know how he did it. I mean, he has some really horrible friends, but I never thought he, or they, would do what they did."

"Friends like Don Coffey?" Tiny asked.

"Yes."

"Who?" Owl asked.

"Don Coffey. Ryleigh found texts and emails between him and Maisy's brother. He wasn't the guy he worked with to kidnap Stone. But they did other shit together. Sick stuff, like drugging women in bars and taking them to motels, leaving them there to wake up alone with no memory of the night before."

"Assholes," Spike muttered.

Maisy couldn't agree more. She hadn't known her brother and Don were doing stuff like that. It made her sick and even more ashamed of herself for not going to the police sooner. For letting her brother manipulate her so thoroughly.

"Why didn't this Don guy marry her?" Spike asked. "If Jason wanted to get his hands on her money, why not just have one of his friends do it?"

"Because then someone else would know," Maisy said. "I thought about that too. Don's horrible. He was always saying crude things to me, touching me when Jason wasn't around. But if my brother had to pay Don to marry me, he'd have to tell him why, and then probably have to share some of my inheritance with him as well. And Jason's greedy. He wouldn't want to have to pay any more than necessary."

"So, he arranged to have someone kidnapped. To what? Force him to marry you? That shit doesn't happen today. Maybe back in the old days with shotgun weddings, but today? No way," Owl said with a shake of his head.

"What was he going to do if I didn't have amnesia?" Jack asked.

Maisy forced herself to look at him. He was the wronged party here, not her. *He* was the one who'd been kidnapped and lied to. She'd had plenty of time to separate herself from her brother, and she hadn't. "Shotgun weddings might not be a thing today, but he wouldn't have hesitated to hold a gun to your head, or mine, to make you go through with it."

Her words were calm, but Maisy's heart was beating a mile a minute, and she felt a little light-headed. But she forced herself to continue.

"All he needed was your signature on that marriage certificate. Once he had that, he would've locked you in the safe room in our basement for three months, until I signed the papers to accept my inheritance, and then he would've killed you."

The room went electric.

"Are you fucking kidding me?"

"Holy shit."

"No fucking way!"

"Jesus."

Maisy couldn't blame the men for reacting the way they were.

"What about you?" Jack barked.

Maisy couldn't stop herself from flinching. "What *about* me?" she asked.

"What would've happened to you after the three months were up?"

"He would've killed me too. Can't risk me telling someone what he'd done."

"Did he really think he'd get away with more people in his life just disappearing?" Brick asked.

"I don't think he really thought about it much," Maisy said honestly. "As long as he had access to the money, he didn't seem to care about the details."

"But that didn't happen," Owl said. "Stone woke up and didn't remember who he was. When was the decision made to make him think you were already married?"

Jack had obviously already told his friends the parts of the story he knew.

"Jason came up with it on the fly. As soon as Jack woke, the moment Jason figured out he didn't know who he was, he said something about being his brother-in-law and things spiraled from there."

"And why did you go along with it?" Brick asked in a hard tone, leaning forward.

Maisy knew that question was coming, but she was no closer to knowing how to answer it than she was before.

"You see that bruise on her face?" Jack replied for her.

Maisy's gaze swung back to him.

When everyone nodded, Jack went on. "She's got more on her arms, and a huge one on her hip. She's had others. All over her body. She always told me she was clumsy, but I never saw her so much as stumble when we were together."

Maisy's face flamed with embarrassment, but she didn't interrupt.

"When I first woke up, I heard Jason being nasty to her. I didn't understand what I was listening to, and I figured maybe I'd misheard things because my head hurt so badly. But I'm guessing if the man was willing to put a gun to his sister's head in order to force me to marry her, he wasn't above threatening her to get her to do what he wanted...namely, stay quiet and go along with the story about us being married. Let me guess, it was his idea to tell me I was a bounty hunter?"

Maisy nodded, more relieved than she could say that he'd figured things out on his own. "He said it was a solitary profession and would explain why you had no friends."

"And living in Spokane, the fire at my apartment complex?"

Once again, Maisy nodded.

"The renewal of vows ceremony was actually genius. I didn't suspect a thing."

She had no idea what to say. No, that wasn't true. "I'm sorry," she whispered.

"Are you?" Jack asked.

Maisy bit her lip. She was sorry for deceiving him. That he'd gotten caught up in her brother's greed. But was she sorry about the last few weeks? About being his wife? About everything that came with the title?

No. She wasn't sorry about that in the least. Even with dread hanging over her, she'd been happier than she'd been since her parents had died. Jack made her feel as if she was worthy. Like it wasn't an obligation to take care of her, but a privilege. She wasn't in the way, she wasn't a pain in his ass. She was his wife, someone he cared about and wanted to protect because she was important, not because he was beholden.

But she didn't think saying all that would be in her best interest at the moment. So she simply said, "Yes."

Jack didn't look happy, but he also didn't look as if he wanted to spring across the table and strangle her either. She was counting that as a win.

"So, now what?" Pipe asked. "You're back. Asshole kidnapper doesn't know where you are. But you're presumably legally married, so that means the clock for Maisy getting her money is still ticking."

"They really *aren't* married," Owl said. "The name on the license isn't his. Jack Smith doesn't exist. And we all know Ry could make that marriage license disappear in a heartbeat."

Maisy's heart skipped a beat. She hadn't liked deceiving Jack, but she was surprised at the pang of sorrow she felt at the thought of not actually being married to him.

"That's not going to solve any of the issues here," Jack snapped. "You think Jason is going to give up on getting his hands on Maisy's money?"

"You could get divorced, that should stop the clock," Brick volunteered.

"But then what? We send Maisy home so he can kidnap someone else and do the same thing?" Jack asked as he shook his head. "No, not an option."

Maisy's heart swelled. He might hate her and what she'd done, but at least he wasn't willing to make her go back to her brother. Or put anyone else in danger of being kidnapped to satisfy her brother's greed.

"What happens when three months is up, Maisy?" Pipe asked.

She turned to look at the tattooed man. "What do you mean?"

"How do you get your money? Is it automatic?"

"Oh, um, no. There are papers and stuff that need to be signed. I need to appear before the guy at the bank, and the lawyer who's in charge of the trust, to get the money released."

"What was your brother going to do after you signed?" Jack asked.

"As I said before. He told me he'd kill you, because he couldn't risk your memory coming back." She looked away. "And he mentioned something about me having an 'overdose' because of my grief. After that, I assumed he'd live happily ever after with his millions, plus the proceeds from our life insurance policies."

"Wait—what life insurance policies?" Brick asked.

Maisy sighed. "The one he made me sign for Jack, and the one he apparently took out on me at some point."

"Holy fuck, I do *not* like this guy," Owl growled.

"I need to talk to Ryleigh," Tiny said.

"I thought you didn't trust her," Brick said.

"I don't. But there's no doubt the woman knows her way around a computer. Maisy, I'm assuming the money from your trust is supposed to go into your brother's account?"

"Probably."

"Right...so, what if it didn't? What if it went into an account set up in your name?"

"But wouldn't that lead Jason right to me?" Maisy shook her head, already panicking. "No! I don't want him anywhere near here."

"Ryleigh's sneaky enough to set something up that no one would ever be able to trace back to you or The Refuge. She could also probably get those life insurance policies canceled. And get the marriage annulled after the three months is up as well."

"She can do that?" Maisy asked with a raised brow.

"She can do anything with that computer. Which is why I don't trust her. I'm thinking we need to get her input on this."

"I agree," Brick said. Everyone else nodded as well.

Everyone but Jack.

"Stone? What are you thinking?" Owl asked.

"I'm thinking it's all well and good to get Ry to work her magic from a keyboard, but that doesn't prevent Maisy from needing to show herself in person to get access to her money. And I don't want her anywhere within a hundred miles of that asshole brother of hers. There's no telling what he'll do when he realizes how royally he's been fucked. He'll be desperate to get his hands on that money."

He was right. Jason would be beyond furious if his plans went down the drain. He was truly unstable, Maisy understood that now, and she didn't know what he'd do if he saw her again.

But if she wanted to start over, she needed that money. Oh, not all of it. She never wanted to put herself into the position of being taken advantage of again, and millions of dollars in her bank account could do just that. Besides, she'd never needed millions to this point in her life, and she didn't need them now. She just needed enough to take care of herself. Maybe she'd see if Ry could help her give most of it away.

She'd keep enough to buy a small home and live comfortably, find a job somewhere, and try to forget the man who'd been tricked into marrying her...and who she'd love for the rest of her life.

But she wouldn't be able to do any of that if she didn't do the right thing. Do what she should've done long before now.

"I need to talk to the police. Tell them what I told you," she blurted.

"We can arrange for you to do that here," Brick told her.

Maisy shook her head. "No. I mean, that would be okay, but there's an officer in Seattle...I think he's always been suspicious of Jason. He checked in on me a few times after Martha died but could never talk to me alone."

"We can get the detectives here to talk to him," Brick reassured her.

But Maisy knew she'd eventually need to go back to Seattle. She needed to face her brother. Let him know that she was done being manipulated by him. But it wasn't just that. "I have evidence," she admitted in a whisper.

She immediately had the attention of everyone in the room.

"What evidence?" Jack barked.

Maisy swallowed hard. "I wrote it all down, just in case something happened to me. Put it in a diary and told Paige where I hid it, and told her to get it to the police."

Jack's shoulders relaxed a fraction. "Okay, but nothing

did happen to you, so you can tell the detectives everything that you wrote down."

"I also took pictures," she said in a tone much calmer than she felt.

"What? When? Of *what*?" Jack asked.

"That night when he came in covered in mud. I was suspicious about what he was doing. So when I went back upstairs, I snuck into the hall bathroom, which overlooks the backyard. I had an old-fashioned camera. You know, the kind with actual film? Jason went back into the yard, and I took pictures of him doing something in that hole. I don't know if they'll be any good, it might've been too dark, but that roll of film might prove there's something there, under the court. If the cops dig up that stupid basketball court, they'll find Martha. I just know it."

"Holy shit," Owl breathed.

"Where's the film?" Spike asked.

"In the hole in my floor, with the diary. And that's not all."

"What else?" Jack asked.

"I have Martha's wallet. I found it on the floor in Jason's backseat. He was taking me to a doctor's appointment, and he always made me sit in the back when we went because I threw up once and it made him gag. The wallet was on the floor and I picked it up. I didn't understand why it was there, why it would be in Jason's car if she supposedly left town with her purse and a suitcase full of her stuff."

The men all exchanged glances, and Maisy wished she knew what they were thinking.

"We could get this Paige woman to grab that stuff, as Maisy asked her to," Pipe suggested.

"If Jason catches her, she'd be as good as dead," Jack said.

Maisy winced. She hadn't meant to put her friend in danger when she'd told her about the hiding place, but now she realized it probably wasn't the smartest thing she'd ever done. There was a chance Paige had already retrieved the diary, as she'd asked. But an even bigger chance that Jason had lied to the staff about where she and Jack had gone, to hide the fact they'd fled the house.

"Right, so we'll tell the detective where the items are hidden and *he* can go and get them," Jack said.

"Not without a search warrant," Spike said with a shake of his head.

"But after Maisy tells them what she knows, and what she saw in her yard, they should have probable cause," Jack insisted.

"Hearsay," Tiny said.

"Fuck." Jack ran a hand through his hair.

"I can go. I *want* to go," Maisy blurted. "I never intended to put anyone else in danger. Especially not Paige. And...I need to face Jason. Let him see that he hasn't beaten me. That he didn't win."

"She wouldn't be alone," Brick suggested. "We'd go with her."

"No," Jack said.

"Go to the house, get the evidence, and go the cops."

"I said, *no*."

"Yes," Maisy said, straightening in her seat.

Jack glared daggers at her from across the table.

She didn't look away from him as she spoke. "I fucked up. This is *my* mistake. *My* fault. I should've gone to the police back when Martha disappeared. But I didn't. I was a coward. And when Jason dragged you into the house and informed me that he'd gotten me a husband, I should've stood up for us both. But instead, I went along with his stupid plan because I was afraid. I knew it was wrong, and yet I did what I've always done—let my brother dictate my every action.

"I don't give a shit about the money. I wish it wasn't there, because then none of this would've happened. My parents might be alive, Martha would *definitely* be alive, and you wouldn't be married to a woman you never would've chosen in a million years. I need to do this, Jack."

"This isn't your fault," he said after a moment.

He was wrong. This was *all* her fault. "It's not yours either," she told him. "You didn't ask to be kidnapped, to be so traumatized that your brain shut down in order to cope. I didn't ask to lose years of my life lost in a fog of anxiety and antidepression drugs. You once said you'd never make me beg for anything...but I will. I need to do this. To move on. To have closure."

Jack's jaw ticked as he stared at her. Then he growled, "*Fine*. But I have conditions. If you're pregnant, you aren't getting anywhere near your brother. I won't endanger my son or daughter."

Maisy heard a few murmurings from the men around them, but she kept eye contact with Jack. It sucked that he felt as if he could endanger *her*, but not his baby. But she understood it. She did. "Deal. If I'm pregnant, I'll wait until after the baby is born before going to Seattle."

Jack sighed, then nodded. "And you won't go alone."

Maisy nearly sagged in her chair in relief. She didn't *want* to face Jason alone. There was no telling what he'd do if she showed up on her own. She'd probably end up in a hole in the backyard like Martha or drugged to the gills, at the very least. She was still feeling the effects of the valium he'd forced her to take. She nodded at Jack.

"And you won't ever lie to me again. I want to know everything. Where you are, where you're going, who you're emailing, who you're calling—*everything*, Maisy. No more secrets."

She had no problem with that. It wasn't as if she had any friends to email or call anyway. "Okay."

"I mean it. I won't abide any more lies."

"I said okay," Maisy told him a little testily. "When will we leave?"

"When will you know if you're pregnant?" he returned.

She frowned. "I don't know."

"You can make an appointment with Henley's doctor in town," Tonka said.

"I think Cora might have some of those tests you pee on," Pipe added.

"We'll do both."

"It might be too early for either. It depends," Brick suggested.

"How the hell do you know that?" Tiny asked.

Brick grinned. "I just do."

"Anything you want to tell us?" Spike asked his friend.

"Nope. And even if I did, Alaska would kick my ass if she wasn't the one to share any good news we might have."

"You had your period just over a week ago, right?" Jack asked Maisy.

She blushed furiously. Jack was purposely making their business public, and while she didn't like it, she knew she deserved it. And *he* knew darn well when she had her period.

He'd seemed upset that he hadn't already knocked her up, and when she protested his advances, saying she wasn't sure she wanted to have sex while she was bleeding, he'd managed to override all her concerns. He'd protected the bed with towels, made love to her in the shower, and made sure she was cleaned up and good to go before they fell asleep.

But they'd made love plenty of times since then. And while the timing might not be ideal, she wasn't so naïve to think she couldn't get pregnant right after her period was over.

She nodded at Jack in acknowledgement.

"So we have a few weeks before we'll know," he said in a flat tone.

Maisy swallowed hard. Did she want Jack's baby? Yes... and no. Yes, because she loved him so damn much it almost hurt. And no, because it would make moving on with her life so much less complicated.

"That's probably better anyway. Give the asshole time to stew, and Ryleigh time to do what she needs to do on her end," Tiny said. "Not to mention, it doesn't make sense to go up there twice. You have to go up to see the banker once the three months is up, so we might as well wait and kill two birds with one stone."

"In the meantime, we'll have you see a doctor here regardless, just in case the drugs your brother made you take all those years have done any lasting damage, and you can get your feet under you again," Jack said.

Maisy took heart that he was using the "we" pronoun and not saying "you." She wouldn't blame Jack for washing his hands of her, but realizing that he wasn't made the ball of anxiety in her gut recede a smidge.

"You want to see the progress on the hangar?" Owl asked Jack with a smile.

"Hell yeah! I didn't even ask, what's up with the chopper?"

"We're getting her. She's currently grounded in Washington until all the investigations into Grant are done, but after that, she's ours."

"Awesome," Jack said.

"Yeah, so...you want to walk out there with me?"

"Yes. I'll get Maisy settled in the cabin and meet you back here."

Everyone stood, the meeting obviously done. Maisy felt awkward. Jack was right, it would be a few weeks before she'd know if she was pregnant. What was she supposed to do until then?

Jack didn't give her any time to think about it. He gestured for her to walk in front of him and they left the conference room. Alaska waved at her from the reception desk, but it was obvious Jack was anxious to meet up with Owl. So Maisy gave her a small smile and kept walking.

Before she was ready, Jack was opening the door to his cabin. He stepped inside with her but hovered by the door. "I'll be back later," he told her.

Maisy nodded.

Then he turned and walked back through the door, shutting it firmly behind him.

Maisy was alone—and she wanted to cry. She hadn't expected Jack to take her in his arms and tell her he forgave her and still loved her. But she'd expected...*something*. Maybe more talking once they were alone. She didn't think he'd dismiss her entirely.

She walked over to the couch and sat, staring through

the wall of windows. She wasn't sure she could survive the next month in this cabin if this was how Jack was going to treat her.

Then she shook her head. No, she could. This was her penance. She'd been weak, had deceived the best man she'd ever known. She'd take whatever punishment he wanted to dole out. And whatever happened between them when everything was said and done, she'd accept it with as much grace as she could.

Jack wasn't hers. As much as she wanted to keep him forever, he'd entered her life under false pretenses. It didn't matter if she loved him with every fiber of her being. To him, she would always be the sister of the man who'd kidnapped him. The woman who'd lied to him.

She kicked off her shoes, then brought her knees up. She put her feet on the edge of the couch cushion and clasped her arms around her legs. She rested her chin on her knees and sighed. She wondered what Jason was doing right that moment. Was he pissed? Was he worried at all?

Shaking her head, Maisy knew he wasn't. He was worried that he wouldn't be able to get her money in a few weeks, but that was about it. Her brother cared about himself and *only* about himself. And soon he'd get what was coming to him. Karma would find him. Maisy had to believe that, otherwise she probably wouldn't be able to find the strength to confront him, to turn him in. To admit to her part in everything he'd done.

She was guilty by association. She hadn't spoken up when she'd had the chance. Instead, she'd hidden evidence first because she didn't want to believe the brother she knew and loved could be a killer...then because she was convinced he was capable of killing *her*.

But any love she'd had for him was gone. Jack had all her love now, and she'd do whatever it took to keep him safe. Even if that was from herself.

* * *

"Find her," Jason snarled at Don.

"What about him?"

"I don't give a shit about him!"

"So when I find them, I can kill him?" Don asked with an evil grin.

"Did you not hear me? He's *nothing*. I have what I need from him—his signature on a marriage certificate. But I need my sister. Alive. She has to present herself at the bank after three months to get that money transferred."

"And I'll get twenty K, right?" Don asked.

"Yes," Jason said between clenched teeth.

"I'll find them. They couldn't have gone far. I've already checked with a guy I know who works at the airport. He's fucking one of the chicks who works at the front counter. She looked them up, and they didn't get on a plane, so they have to be around here somewhere."

"And if we can't find them soon, my sister needs that money to survive. She'll be back after the three-month mark. She'll go to the bank like the greedy bitch she is," Jason fumed. He *hated* Maisy. She'd been a pain in his ass for years. He'd resented having to look after her, every fucking penny he'd had to waste on keeping her alive. If she wasn't around, all of his parents' money would have been *his*.

"Any chance I can have a go at her before you get rid of her?" Don asked.

"You want to fuck her, go for it. But she's no longer the tight bitch she used to be. Her husband has stretched that pussy for sure."

"Don't care. She's looked down on me for as long as I've known her. It'll be a pleasure to put her in her place."

"Then fine, but if you do, you'll have to get rid of her," Jason said.

"Not a problem."

"Good."

"What are you going to do in the meantime?" Don asked.

Jason scowled. "Whatever the hell I want. I've already fired all the hired help. I was only keeping them around for appearance's sake and to babysit my sister."

"Well, shit. I liked the biscuits that cook bitch made."

"Whatever," Jason said, rolling his eyes. Anger rose within him once more. When he woke up and realized that both Maisy and her fucking husband were gone, he'd been shocked to the core. Then he'd panicked. He didn't give a shit about whoever the fuck Jack really was, but he needed Maisy. At least for another month or so.

For the first time since the kidnapping, he wished he'd asked more questions about the man he'd paid to be kidnapped. He hadn't specified anyone in particular, just said he needed someone he could force to marry his sister. The man his buddy's friend hired was a ghost. Jason had no way of contacting him, and the guy probably wouldn't respond even if he *did* have his number. As soon as he was paid, the man was as good as gone.

As a result, Jason had no idea who Jack was. Not his last name or where he came from. Hell, he had no idea if he had friends in high places who could help him disappear with Maisy as if into thin air—like they seemed to have done.

But it didn't matter. Eventually the bitch would come back. She had to if she wanted to get access to her inheritance. And whenever she returned, Jason would be ready.

He hadn't done what he'd done all these years, only to fail now. No, he had her inheritance, plus the life insurance policies to cash in on. Once he did that, he'd be set. He could sell this fucking house for another couple million and move to Mexico. It was cheap as fuck down there and he could live like a king, getting all the pussy he wanted.

He was too close to his goal to let his sister screw it all up now.

He turned his back on Don and stared out at the backyard. The basketball hoop was looking pathetic and in need of repair. He needed to take care of that before he put the house on the market. Thinking about what lay buried under the concrete made him smile. He was smarter than everyone. The police officers were idiots, he'd outsmarted them all. No one had any suspicions about him, and soon he'd be a millionaire once more and could start his life over, without the ball and chain of his sister around his ankle.

The only wild card was Jack. But ultimately, he didn't matter. Jason would get rid of him as easily as he did his sister. He should've done what he'd planned in the first place and locked him in the safe room in the basement. It was too late now, but Jack would get what was coming to him.

The door to the office closed, and Jason heard Don walking down the hall toward the front door. His old friend would probably need to be taken care of as well. He could join Martha in the backyard. Or maybe he'd call that tip line and give him up to the cops, after the idiot offed his sister. Kill two birds with one stone. Don would be locked up, and he wouldn't have to pay him a dime.

Smiling, Jason decided he liked that plan. He didn't care that the body count was rising exponentially. All that mattered was money in his pocket. He'd do whatever it took to get it. *Had* done what it took. He only needed a few more weeks, and if he didn't find Maisy before the three-month anniversary of her wedding, she'd come to *him*.

He knew his sister, knew how she thought. She'd be back, if only to claim her money.

And when she did...she was as good as dead.

CHAPTER SIXTEEN

Maisy sat in Brick and Alaska's cabin and had to pinch herself. The women who lived at The Refuge had been so...*nice*. She hadn't expected it, especially after they'd learned all about her part in Jack's kidnapping. Or at least the fact that she hadn't immediately told him the truth and had gone through with the sham of a wedding.

Alaska had invited her to come over tonight for an impromptu baby party. That's what she called it, and apparently it was an excuse for everyone to get together and talk about "girl stuff."

It had been a week since Maisy had arrived, and she wasn't sure she was going to last until the three-month point in her marriage.

Jack hadn't been mean to her, hadn't treated her like a prisoner or a pariah, but he wasn't the man she'd come to know and love. Not that she blamed him, she wasn't sure she'd be able to be all that civil if she'd been treated like he'd been.

But she hated sleeping in the guest room. Hadn't actually been sleeping very well at all, and she didn't think Jack was either. She sometimes heard him calling out during the night during one of his nightmares. She wanted to go to him, soothe him like she used to, but since that wasn't an option, all she could do was lie on the pull-out couch and listen to him suffer.

He was overly polite when he *did* speak to her, which cut her to the bone. It was as if they were strangers, which hurt more than anything else that had happened in recent months. He might find it easy to turn off the memories of their time together, but she couldn't. She loved him still. And it sucked to realize that he didn't care about her the same way in return, no matter what he'd said before regaining his memory.

When Alaska invited her to come over and hang out with her and the other women, Maisy jumped at the chance. She shouldn't. Shouldn't try to make friends with these women because as soon as the three months were up, she'd be leaving. But if she had to sit in the cabin for one more night with Jack acting like she was a stranger, a house guest he barely tolerated, she was going to go crazy.

The cabin was crowded, but no one seemed to care. Alaska was currently in the kitchen pouring drinks for those who weren't pregnant. Jess, one of the housekeepers, was shuttling snacks and drinks back and forth from the kitchen to the living room, and everyone else was sitting around laughing and talking.

Maisy was sitting on the floor, leaning back against the couch next to Ry. Cora and Lara were on a love seat. Henley, Reese, and Luna—who was the daughter of the main chef at The Refuge—were all on the couch behind her and Ry. The mood was relaxed and happy, and Maisy realized that she'd never experienced anything like this. At least not since she'd attended some sleepovers when she was in high school.

"What has Stone told you about all of us and the crap we went through?" Henley asked Maisy.

She shook her head. "Nothing."

"What do you mean, nothing?" Reese asked.

"Just that. Nothing," Maisy said slowly.

"What do you talk about at night?" Cora asked.

"Um...nothing."

"Right, they probably have better things to do," Jess said with a grin. But no one else looked as if her comment was amusing...proving they all knew things weren't going well between her and Jack.

"No, it's not like that with us," Maisy told Jess, trying to sound casual and not let the devastation that surged through her show. Looking around at the women, she felt a sudden need to confess all her sins. She had no idea what they thought of her—although she didn't think they hated her; if they did, she wouldn't be here right now. But she wanted them to know she was sorry. Sorry about her role in what happened to Jack. Sorry about going along with her brother's scheme, not that she had much choice, but still. Sorry about all of it.

"Jack's the most amazing man I've ever met. He's everything I ever wanted in a partner. The few weeks we were together were...the best." Her voice lowered at the last two words. They seemed so inadequate for how Jack made her feel. "But I knew as soon as he got his memory back, that brief time would be over. And it was. My brother, he's...evil. I don't know why. We had the same upbringing. But he's decided that money is the most important thing in the world to him. I don't know for sure, but I think he killed my parents. And I *know* he killed Martha, his wife. All for money. And then he decided he wanted my inheritance too."

Maisy was rambling, but she couldn't stop. She was also talking fast, but she didn't want to be interrupted for fear she wouldn't be able to get out everything she wanted to say. "Since I had to be married in order to get my money, he kidnapped Jack and was going to hold a gun to his head, or mine, probably both, and force him to sign the marriage certificate. Then I guess he planned to keep him locked in our basement for the required three months until I could claim my inheritance, then kill him. And me. I didn't want to do it. Marry Jack against his will, that is, but I didn't have a choice.

"No, that's not true. I *did*. I could've said no. Could've told my brother to go to hell, but I didn't, too afraid of the consequences. So it's my fault as much as it's my brother's that Jack's married to me. And now he hates me for it."

She was out of breath by the time she was done, and Maisy had a momentary pang of guilt that she'd brought the mood of the room down so much. But she felt so much better now that she'd gotten all that out.

"It's not your fault," Henley told her.

"I went along with my brother's claim that we were already married. Lied to Jack, perpetuated the story. And Jason *wasn't* holding a gun to my head. I was alone with Jack all the time. I could've told him. Told him to get the hell away from there. But I didn't," Maisy said sadly.

"What would your brother have done to you if you didn't go along with his story?" Reese asked.

Maisy shrugged. "Kidnapped some other unsuspecting guy? Locked me in my room. Hit me."

"Exactly!" Reese exclaimed so fiercely it made Maisy jerk in surprise. "Sorry, didn't mean to scare you, but seriously, you had no choice. If you didn't do what your brother wanted you to do, it wouldn't have gone well for you. You're just as much a victim as Stone was."

Maisy appreciated Reese trying to cut her some slack, but she wasn't at a point where she could forgive herself.

"And Stone doesn't hate you," Alaska said as she came out of the kitchen and joined everyone. She sat on Maisy's other side and put a hand on her knee. "He doesn't," she insisted when Maisy gave her an incredulous look.

"He barely speaks to me. Most of the time it's like I'm not even there. He's overly polite when he does, and he goes out of his way not to touch me or even get too close to me at all. I understand, of course I do, I'd hate me too if I'd been through what he has, but...it hurts." Maisy took a deep breath and looked around the room. Most of the women here, other than Ryleigh and Luna, were married. Had men who would scorch the earth to make sure they were safe. Probably told them every night how loved they were.

"We were together almost twenty-four hours a day for weeks. And I...I made the mistake of getting too close. Of believing that we really *were* a couple. He rarely went two minutes without touching me. Sitting so close that our thighs were pressed together. Always keeping a hand on my leg, or brushing his fingers along my cheek. And at night..." Maisy's voice cracked as she looked down at her lap. "He'd hold me so tight, I used him as a pillow. And now if he so much as accidentally brushes his fingers against mine, he acts as if he's touched a live wire. It was all a lie. But it didn't *feel* like a lie," Maisy said so softly, she wasn't sure anyone could hear her.

"It wasn't a lie," Lara said firmly. "For either of you. He watches you. When you aren't paying attention, he can't keep his eyes off you. He's constantly assessing, making sure you're all right."

But Maisy shook her head miserably.

"The other day, when you were at the barn with Tonka, he burst into the lodge wanting to know where you were, telling Brick and Spike that he couldn't find you. He sounded frantic," Henley said.

"My dad told me that he specifically requested he make a green bean casserole, because it was one of your favorite things the cook at your house in Seattle used to make," Luna added.

"And he's been almost as bad as Tiny, hovering over me while I work, insisting I be extra careful and not let your brother know anything about where you are so he can't get his hands on you," Ry told Maisy.

Their words felt good. Really good. But Maisy couldn't take them to heart. If she let any speck of encouragement seep into her soul, it would hurt that much more when Jack washed his hands of her. He was simply waiting for the three-month anniversary of their wedding to pass so she could access her money. Once that happened, he could be done and not feel any guilt about signing annulment papers and kicking her ass to the curb.

"Don't give up," Alaska said urgently, tightening her fingers around Maisy's leg for a moment. "More than anyone, I know how it feels to love someone and not have them return those feelings. But here I am...with the man I've loved my whole life."

Maisy turned to her. "I don't believe that Brick hasn't always loved you. You're everything to him, it's obvious."

"I am *now*, yes," Alaska said. "But it wasn't always that way. You really don't know our stories?"

Maisy shook her head.

"Well, sit back, sister. Do we have some tales to tell."

The next hour was eye-opening for Maisy. She had no idea these women had been through such awful situations. They seemed so...normal. Happy. She was even more in awe of them after hearing about what they'd gone through. Felt even more out of her league.

"See? Things can work out. You just have to have faith," Alaska told her when everyone had finished sharing.

But Maisy could only huff out a disbelieving breath. "Not one of your situations involved you lying to your men. Deceiving them. Participating in a freaking *kidnapping* scheme," she protested.

"Listen to me, Maisy. Seriously," Lara said, leaning forward and pinning Maisy in place with her intense gaze. "Owl and Stone have been through hell together. I got curious one night and looked up one of the videos online that their captors posted, when they were POWs, and I made it through about ten seconds before I had to shut it off. What happened to them was *horrible*. And it made them question everything about their lives and what they believed in. Despite that, I've never met two men more suited to being in relationships. They both have a huge well of love inside them. They want to take care of the world. But more than that, they're loyal to those they love. Protective of them. I thought Owl was going to lose his mind when we couldn't find Stone and didn't know what he was going through.

"From what I've seen, Stone looks at you the way Owl looks at *me*. As if he can't believe I'm in his life. That I'm with *him*." She looked at the others and grinned. "I mean, I'm totally aware that he'd like to keep me safe and protected in his cabin twenty-four hours a day, just to make sure no harm comes to me. And now that I'm pregnant? That need is even stronger. But he doesn't because of course he knows I'd hate that. So he suffers through his insecurities and fears that something could happen to me or our child anytime I step outside our front door, and he lets me go about my normal day. But that doesn't mean he isn't there watching. Waiting for me to need something. When I do, he's there. No questions asked. And it makes him feel good. Fulfills a deep need within him."

"She's right," Henley said softly. "You'd make a great psychologist," she told Lara with a smile.

The other woman simply rolled her eyes. "No, I just know my man. Anyway, I do have a point here. As I said, Stone watches you like Owl watches me. He might be acting like he doesn't care, but I think it's a self-defense mechanism. His world has been rocked, hard. And I'm not saying that to hurt you, it's simply a fact. He was so freaked out that his brain shut down and wouldn't let him remember his past as a protective measure. But now that his memory's returned, he's trying to figure out how to mesh together his love for you, with what your brother and, I'm sorry to say, what *you* did to him. Like Alaska said, do *not* give up. The feelings Stone had for you aren't gone. They're still there. They're just jumbled up with all the other feelings he's trying to reconcile. But if the shit hits the fan, he'd give his life for you regardless. I have no doubt about that."

Maisy wanted to believe her. She longed to see something in Jack's eyes other than wariness. But she had no idea what to do to make up for what happened. If she even could. She wasn't sure life could turn out as good for her as it had for everyone sitting around her, but she wanted it to. God, how she wanted that.

"Right, so on that note...can we talk about babies now?" Luna asked. "I can't freaking wait for you guys to start popping those kids out!"

Everyone laughed, including Maisy. It was a relief to break the tension in the room.

"I don't know about anyone else, but I'm more than ready to push this kid out," Henley said as she rubbed her belly.

"How far along are you?" Maisy asked.

"About seven months. Reese is a month behind me, Lara just found out she's pregnant not too long ago."

"I'm so freaking excited!" Alaska exclaimed.

"I have news," Cora said a little shyly. "Our application to foster was accepted."

Everyone whooped and cheered at that.

"When are you getting your first kid? Do you know how old? A boy or girl?" Jess asked, not giving Cora a chance to answer between questions.

"I don't know. We actually requested older kids. Not babies. There are so many children who need safe homes. And we don't care if it's a boy or girl."

"Didn't you say you guys decided to put in your application because of a specific kid?" Ry asked.

"Yeah. There was a seven-year-old boy who Pipe heard

about, but his grandparents decided to take him in and raise him." Cora shrugged. "I'm sure there will be others. The agency could literally call at any time now that we're approved."

"I think that's so great," Lara said, hugging her friend. "I'm so excited for you guys."

"And Jasna is going to be thrilled. She likes babies, but I think she'd be happier with someone she could play with and show the ropes around here," Henley said.

As the women talked about pregnancy cravings, what to do if the upcoming babies have colic, and other kid-related topics, Ry leaned forward and whispered into Maisy's ear, "Can we talk?"

Looking at the other woman, and not knowing what she could possibly want to talk to her about, Maisy shrugged and nodded.

Ry immediately stood and grabbed Maisy's hand, pulling her to her feet as well. "Maisy and I are gonna go chat about something other than babies," she informed her friends.

"You're gonna miss some serious awesomeness about how our cooters are gonna stretch to the size of bowling balls if you go!" Henley teased.

"Oh Lord, is it too late to change my mind about having a kid?" Lara asked.

Everyone laughed as Ry kept hold of Maisy's hand and pulled her into the kitchen. The cabin wasn't huge, and it was open concept like Jack's, but it didn't seem as if anyone was paying any attention to her and Ry in the corner of the kitchen.

Ry dropped Maisy's hand and leaned a hip against the counter. "I've been doing some digging."

That's all she said.

Maisy frowned in confusion. "Okay?"

"You know what I can do, right?"

"Uh...yeah. The guys said something about how you're good with computers?"

Ry didn't crack a smile. She raised a brow. "I'm not good with computers," she said. "I'm freaking *good* with computers. There's no one better than me. *No one*. I can hack into the FBI and CIA databases, get Russian nuclear weapons codes, find out exactly what the Chinese leaders are planning from day to day and wipe clean any and all research on those damn spy balloons they have, and any progress North Korea has on illegal biological warfare. Hacking into a company's database and canceling life insurance policies, or changing where money is being transferred from a trust fund...those are pieces of cake for me. Do you understand?"

Maisy stared at the woman in front of her. She knew Ryleigh was talented when it came to working on the computer based solely on what the guys had all said. But she had no idea *how* talented. "I think so," she said after a moment.

"Good. I just wanted to make sure you weren't going to freak out when you logged into your bank account and saw your balance."

"What did you do?" Maisy whispered.

"Nothing anyone didn't deserve. First, I changed the monthly deposit routing details from your brother's account to yours—the new account I made for you in town—so you're now getting the monthly stipend you should've been getting for years. Tiny also told me about the life insurance policies Jason took out on you and

Stone. That shit's been canceled, so you don't have to worry about those. I also changed ownership of the house from your brother—which wasn't supposed to happen in the first place; the house was left to both of you. The asshole somehow got that changed so it was only in *his* name—to you. Just for fun, I also put it on the market. Jason's gonna be surprised the first time someone shows up to see it."

Maisy gaped at her in disbelief.

"What? I'm sorry, did you want to live there after we evict your brother?"

"No! I mean, I loved that house once, but now it holds too many bad memories. I don't ever want to live there again."

"Good. So you'll get the proceeds when it sells then, which will make up for the stipend he's been stealing all these years. Not sure how long that will take, as I'm sure Jason will refuse to leave, but the offers will come to me, and I'll share them with you so you can decide what to accept. I listed it at a *very* competitive price, so I'm thinking you should get several good offers."

"Holy crap," Maisy said, completely in awe of Ry.

"The only thing I *can't* do is get around the requirement that you come in to sign for your inheritance in person. I'm sorry. So you'll still have to go back up to Seattle to take care of that. But I heard from Tiny that you already knew that."

Maisy nodded. "I want to go."

Ry stared at her for a moment. Then said, "You want to show your brother that he didn't win."

"Yeah."

"Good for you. Stone needs someone with a backbone.

I haven't been here as long as some of the others, but I like him. He's intense, but in a good way, if that makes sense."

It did. Maisy nodded.

"I wasn't thrilled when I heard he was missing. Felt guilty that I wasn't able to get to Lara, Owl, and Stone before he was taken. And it sucked that I didn't pull the right thread necessary in order to find him. Your brother's an asshole, but he's not completely stupid. Actually, I take that back—he's an idiot. He had no idea who Stone was, who he'd kidnapped. I bet if he knew he was a former special forces pilot and had badass friends who would stop at nothing to find him, he would've picked another man. But then, you wouldn't have fallen in love with just any man, so even though Jason's a moron, I'm glad he picked Stone."

Maisy's brain spun with Ry's words. She couldn't keep up. But luckily the other woman didn't seem to expect a response. She kept talking. "I was fully prepared to not like you, Maisy. My fingers were itching to cause as much mayhem as possible in your life, but then I realized you had all sorts of mayhem going on already. Your brother had isolated you, drugged you, threatened and hurt you. All for money. And I saw the way Stone looked at you too. Then he made me promise that nothing I did electronically would come back to you in any way. He obviously loves you."

Maisy's head was shaking even before Ry finished speaking.

"He does. And I agree with everything Lara said in there. If you don't fight for that man, you're not the woman I *think* you are. It won't be easy, but nothing worth having is, right?"

"I don't know what to do. He won't talk to me. Won't touch me. Won't even *look* at me."

"Seduce him," Ry said without hesitation.

Maisy almost choked. "What?"

"Take off all your clothes and climb into bed with him. He won't be able to resist you."

"Or he could shove me away from him and make me die of embarrassment," Maisy said incredulously.

"Not gonna happen. Trust me."

Maisy wanted to. She really did. But she couldn't bear it if Jack rejected her when she was at her most vulnerable.

"Tell me the truth...do you think you're pregnant?"

Maisy sighed. "No."

"If you *get* pregnant, that man isn't going to let you out of his sight," Ry mused.

"I don't want to trap him. The last thing I want is to worry about whether or not he's with me for the sake of his child or because he loves me."

"Yeah, that's a problem," Ry said with a sigh. "I still say amazing sex will make him stop ignoring you."

Maisy wanted that. Badly. She lived on the memories of the way they'd made love, before the shit hit the fan. And having Jack's baby would be a dream come true. He'd be the best father any child could ever hope to have.

"Right," Ry said, studying Maisy's face closely, with a small smirk on her own. "So while you're waiting to confront your asshole of a brother, you still have time to convince Stone that he can't live without you."

"How, though?"

"I don't know. But you're smart, you'll figure it out," Ry

said easily, leaning back against the counter as if she didn't have a care in the world.

"I'm *not* smart," Maisy protested. "I dropped out of school, barely passed my GED. Jack was only the second guy I'd ever been with. I have no idea how to convince him that I really do love him and hate my brother for what he did."

"Wait, what?"

"What, *what*?" Maisy asked, confused herself.

"What do you mean, you barely passed your GED?"

"Just that. Jason told me that I scored so low, I was one point from failing."

"And you believed him?" Ry asked, her expression showing exactly how ridiculous she thought that was.

"Um...yes?" Maisy said.

"Look, while I was digging into info about your twat-waffle of a brother, I looked into you too. You scored a seven eighty-five."

"Yeah, which is sixty-five percent," Maisy said with a shrug.

"What? No, it's not! Good Lord. Look, we know Jason isn't exactly an upstanding guy, but if he told you the max score for the GED was twelve hundred, he was lying. Hell, that's not a score for *anything*. The SAT is sixteen hundred for a perfect score, and it's thirty-six for the ACT.

"The GED test is split up into four subjects. Barely passing is one hundred and forty-five on each section. Getting between one sixty-five and one seventy-four on a section? That generally means you're college-ready. Above that means you're eligible to get college credit. Maisy, you scored a one hundred and ninety in math—which was your *lowest* score, by the way—two hundred on reasoning through language arts, one hundred and ninety-seven in social studies, and one hundred and ninety-eight in science. Girl, you're practically a genius!"

Maisy stared at Ry in confusion. "I didn't almost fail?"

Ry laughed. "No, Maisy. You got a perfect score in one section and almost perfect on two others. You certainly didn't *almost* fail."

"Oh my God," Maisy whispered. "I always wondered how I could do so poorly. I used to get straight A's in school. But I'd already started taking so many meds that I guess...I guess I just thought maybe the drugs were the cause. Regardless, I took Jason's word for it, like everything else."

"Your brother knew how smart you were. He also knew you were *definitely* smart enough to eventually figure out he was a low-life scum. So I'm guessing he kept you drugged for years so he could spend money that was meant for you."

He had. Maisy already hated Jason, but now she hated him even more. All her life, she'd thought she was worthless. Stupid. And her own flesh and blood had perpetuated that belief. And for what? Money. "I hate him," she said between clenched teeth.

"Me too," Ry said almost breezily. "But I'm taking care of him. Did you know that your inheritance has grown over the years?"

Maisy raised a brow and gave her a look.

"Right, sorry. Of course you don't. It's no longer four million dollars. It's almost ten."

"*What?* Seriously?"

"Yup. You're quite the millionaire."

But Maisy shook her head. "I don't want it."

"What? The money?"

"Yes. I don't want it. Money has caused me nothing but heartache. It turned my brother into a monster, made him kill my parents, murder an innocent and nice woman, and kidnap Jack."

"I thought I liked you before, but now I think I love you," Ry said with no trace of amusement or humor. "Money is definitely the root of all evil. And I don't blame you for not wanting it. But you'll need something to live on when your brother is no longer a threat."

"I'll figure something out."

Ry studied her for a long moment. "How about you keep some, like a million, and give the rest away?"

"A million's too much," Maisy said.

But Ry laughed. "No, it's not. You have no idea how fast that money'll go, especially if you have a baby. But luckily you have a friend who knows the best stocks and bonds to invest in."

Maisy narrowed her eyes at her new *friend*.

Ry chuckled. "Right. We'll get into my abilities as an investment broker at a different time. So, if you don't want the money, what do you want to do with it?"

"Donate it."

"Good choice. And I just so happen to be an expert on legit charities, as well. Where do you want it to go?"

"I don't know. I like animals."

"I can recommend several very worthy rescue groups that really need the money," Ry said.

"And kids. Oh, and veteran groups. Can we give some to The Refuge?"

"Yes. Although it's a little tricky, because Brick and the rest of the guys are pretty sensitive to receiving charity.

But I've been funneling money here already. Do you know they have a donate button on their website? I've set up an automatic donation to be sent in through their site every four days." She smiled. "And they have no idea. It's awesome. That hangar they're building for the helicopter? It's being built solely with donations."

"Which came from you?" Maisy guessed.

"Yup. I mean, there are other donations too that I didn't initiate, but it feels damn good to get these guys what they need to make this place even more awesome than it already is. They do truly great work here."

"Where are you getting the money from?" Maisy asked.

And just like that, the happy, satisfied look on Ry's face slipped away. "It doesn't matter. Okay, so animals, kids, veterans...what else?"

Maisy wanted to ask more questions, but it was obvious Ry wouldn't answer them. "Um...there was a woman who worked in the house. Her name is Paige. I heard that Jason fired her, along with the others who worked for us. Which isn't right. She'd been working for us for decades, and I'm sure he was underpaying her."

"You're right, he was. I'll make sure she and the others who worked for you guys are compensated properly. Anything else?"

Maisy made a few more suggestions, but honestly, she had no idea how to even go about giving away nine million dollars.

"I'll start with your suggestions and we'll go from there, how about that?" Ry asked gently.

Maisy swallowed hard, suddenly overcome with emotion. She'd arrived here in New Mexico a week ago expecting to be shunned, to be ostracized. Instead, she was brought into the fold by these women as if she'd always been there. And Ry...Maisy couldn't come up with the words to thank her.

"It'll be okay," Ry said gently.

Taking a deep breath, Maisy nodded. "Yeah. It will be. Because I'm going to turn him in."

"Your brother?"

She nodded. "I can't prove he killed my parents. But I'll do what I can to prove he killed his wife. I have a few blurry pictures I took in the dark, I have Martha's wallet—which is relevant, because Jason told the police she took it with her when she left—some recordings of my brother being awful to me, and a diary where I wrote down every single thing I could think of that can hopefully be investigated."

Ry stared at her for a long moment before saying, "I have emails. And texts. I downloaded them from his phone. It'll help with Martha, but maybe not your parents. That was too long ago. I'll print them out and you can take them with you when you meet with the police in Washington."

"You do? You *will*?"

"Absolutely. Anything that will help take him down and keep you safe, I'll do."

"Why?"

"Because he shouldn't get away with what he's done. Because he's a greedy asshole. And because I like you, Maisy. We're a lot alike. More than you know. You had to do things you didn't want to do because you had no choice. You had to stay silent for your own safety. I get it. I *so* get it. You deserve a second chance, and I want to help you make that happen."

"You do too." Where the words came from, Maisy wasn't sure, but she had a feeling this woman deserved that second chance as well.

Ry smiled sadly. "I'm not so sure about that. My sins are way bigger than yours. I wasn't forced into lying. I made the former housekeeper here at The Refuge leave through deception so I could get the job. And I'm not sure anyone can forgive me for having information about the women when they were in trouble, and not sharing."

"From what I just heard, you *did* share," Maisy protested.

Ry shrugged. "Too little, too late. I'm sure that's what the men think. Besides, I know stuff about The Refuge. Things they don't want anyone knowing, and I won't tell them how I found out. Although it should be obvious. Nothing electronic can hide from me. Tiny definitely doesn't trust me."

Maisy bit her lip, but since they were laying all their cards on the table, she decided to ask what was on her mind. "Why are you still here? I mean, I doubt you actually need the housekeeper job."

"I don't. And I stayed because I wanted to find Stone," Ry said.

"Well, he's here. And fine."

"You want me to leave?" Ry asked with a tilt of her head.

"No! Not at all. But with all the talk about Jack and how he looks at me, I can't help but notice how Tiny barely lets you out of his sight."

"Right, because he's afraid I'm going to bankrupt this place or something," Ry said with a roll of her eyes.

"I don't think so."

"No," Ry said with a shake of her head.

"No, what?"

"Don't go thinking there can be anything between Tiny and me. I'm still here at the moment because I'm working to fuck over that brother of yours. Sorry, but if you have even the smallest shred of love left for him, you need to get over it. He's a monster."

"I know he is. But, Ry—"

"Please don't," the other woman whispered in a tortured tone.

Maisy wanted to push. Wanted to do more for Ry, but it was obvious there was a lot going on with her she didn't know about, and it wasn't as if she knew Tiny all that well either. She just didn't like to see her new friend so... resigned. To what? Maisy didn't know, but she didn't like it.

"All right. I don't know what I could ever do to repay you for your help, but if you need anything, I'm here for you, Ry."

"Thanks. You don't know how much that means to me."

"I do, actually."

"Don't let Stone go," Ry whispered. "He loves you. I know he does. It'll take him some time to get over what happened, but he will. Do what I told you. Seduce him. I've never seen two people more meant to be together than you and Stone."

Maisy wasn't so sure about that. She hadn't downplayed how awkward and bad things were between her and Jack. But she didn't want to think about that anymore. "Do you know why everyone calls him Stone? I can't do it. In my head, he's always been Jack, but I'm curious."

"When he was training to be a pilot, they had to do this drown-proofing thing. It sounds horrible, and the videos are even worse. They put them in a simulated helicopter and turn it upside down in the water. They have to stay put for thirty seconds before attempting to get out. And once they do, they turn on these jets that blow bubbles up from the bottom of the pool, I guess they're for divers who are learning, so they don't hit the water too hard. Anyway, they turn them on and there's immediately no visibility and the water is all churned up. It looks scary as hell. Stone isn't the best swimmer, and every time he got out of the fake helicopter, he sank straight to the bottom of the pool."

"Sank like a stone," Maisy said with a small smile.

"Yup."

"How'd he pass then? I mean, he had to get past that in order to become a Night Stalker, right?" Maisy had heard all about how amazing Jack and Owl were. How very few people were able to become legendary Night Stalker pilots in the Army. Hearing that wasn't surprising, she already knew how amazing Jack was, but she was impressed nonetheless.

"He was allowed to retake the test at the end of the class. He spent every spare second he had at the pool, trying to learn how to swim. He got to a point where he didn't immediately sink when he was in the water, but he still wasn't a strong swimmer. He was able to get to the surface during his re-test, and while he got the lowest possible score he could get, he passed. The nickname stuck after that."

"How in the world do you *know* that?" Maisy asked.

Ry simply lifted a brow.

"Right, sorry. I forgot. Super computer hacker," Maisy said with a small chuckle.

"And he hasn't always worn glasses either."

Maisy was confused. What did his nickname have to do with his glasses?

Ry didn't make her wait long to figure out her line of thinking. "Helicopter pilots have to have perfect vision. They can't be flying around in the desert and get a speck of sand in their eye and fuck with contacts or something. And if their glasses fog up in the middle of an op, that wouldn't be good either."

"Right," Maisy agreed.

"He didn't need them until a few years ago. He resisted it as long as he could—because he's a guy—then finally went in to see an eye doctor. The prescription isn't all that strong, but he still wasn't thrilled that he needed them."

"I like them. He's kind of like a sexy librarian, but a guy. Wait, that sounded sexist. Of course men can be librarians."

"Yup. Tonka's former partner who lives out in Virginia is a librarian."

"Really?"

"Uh-huh."

"Cool. Anyway, maybe I should say he's like one of those older professors I'm always reading about in romance books," Maisy said. Then blushed. She hadn't meant to admit to reading that kind of thing.

"Ooooh, I love those," Ry agreed, making Maisy feel better about her choice of reading material. Which was stupid. Why did it matter what she enjoyed reading? And romances were awesome. They always ended happily and made her feel really good inside, convinced that things could work out for people. Gave her hope for herself.

Then Ry shocked the crap out of Maisy by reaching out and pulling her close. She hugged her tight, and it felt so good to be touched once more. Maisy hadn't realized how touch-deprived she was until Jack came along. And now that he was going out of his way to avoid making even the smallest bit of physical contact with her, this hug meant even more.

"Do what one of those heroines in a romance would do. Go into his room in the middle of the night, naked, then jump him before his brain has time to catch up." The words were whispered in Maisy's ear, and then Ry pulled back, smiled, opened the fridge and grabbed another pitcher of whatever sweet concoction Alaska had mixed, before heading back into the other room where all the girls were still chatting away about nothing in particular.

As Maisy watched the women in the other room talking, she realized that she actually felt pretty good at the moment. She'd been in a funk for days, and knowing Ry had her back was nice. And not only her. All the women had been more than kind.

She suddenly understood why Jack was so loyal. If she had friends like this, she'd do whatever it took to make sure everything was right in their lives. She had no idea what the future held, but Maisy would make sure nothing she said or did negatively impacted The Refuge or anyone who lived and worked there. The world needed more people like them.

Honestly, confronting her brother scared the crap out of her, but before she could move on, she needed to do it. Wanted him to know that he hadn't beaten her. That no matter how badly he'd treated her, she would rise above it. If she had to stoop to his level to make him understand how serious she was, so be it. She wasn't going to fall for his tricks and manipulation ever again. Hopefully he'd end up in prison for what he'd done, but if not, she didn't want him trying to get back at her for the rest of her life.

Maisy wanted to be free. Wanted Jack to be free. Because one thing she knew about her brother was that he held a nasty grudge. And if there was even a one percent chance he could get to Jack and hurt him, he would. Which wasn't acceptable. Maisy needed to right the wrong that had been done to Jack, and maybe wipe her slate clean in the process.

Jason would be pissed, would probably try to hurt her. But she didn't think he'd kill her. Because if she died, her money would go to charity, not to him. She'd say what she needed to say, then get the hell away from him.

She didn't think *Jack* would want to confront her brother. Nor did she think Jack would allow her out of his sight for long, knowing what Jason was capable of. So she'd have to take whatever time he was willing to give her. Even if it was only one minute, that would be enough.

Feeling a little better about the upcoming trip back up to Washington, Maisy rejoined the rest of the women. She let Ry refill her cup and enjoyed the feeling of being part of a close-knit group for the first time in her life.

CHAPTER SEVENTEEN

Something had to give. Stone wasn't sure he could continue on like this for much longer. With every day that passed, it was more and more difficult to keep his distance from Maisy. The more he tried to keep away from her, the more he wanted to *be* with her. Especially when she was trying so hard to fit in. To help out around The Refuge.

He found her in the barn with Tonka and Jasna one day, shoveling shit out of the stalls. Another day she was in the kitchen with Robert and Luna, laughing as she made a huge bowl of salad. And yet another day, she was hiking with some of the guests and Brick, making small talk and keeping them happy as they walked.

But things between the two of them weren't good. Stone just wasn't sure what to say to her anytime they were in a room together.

Ry had cornered him just a few days ago and shoved a thick sheaf of papers at him and told him to get his head out of his ass. That if he thought Maisy wasn't as much a prisoner in that house as he was, he was an idiot.

By the time he'd finished reading through the emails and texts from Jason to his so-called friends, he was ready to fly back up to Washington that second and take the man out.

The correspondence went back several years. He regularly made fun of Maisy, telling his buddies that she was pathetic and a "tight prude." He despaired of ever finding anyone to marry her because she was so fat, stupid, and ugly. He thought he was so smart, using antianxiety drugs to keep her compliant. Other emails complained about how bad his wife was in bed, and he didn't show one ounce of concern when she "disappeared."

But it was a recent conversation between Jason and his friend Don that had Stone rethinking the thoughts about Maisy. It was a couple of weeks after they'd been married. Don had asked if Maisy was causing any trouble with the new brother-in-law living under the same roof. His response was burned into Stone's head.

no. my sistr is so in love wth him she does whatevr I tell her to

Maisy had told him that she loved him more times than Stone could count. And yet after his memory returned, he'd doubted everything she'd ever said. Now that he'd had more time to think, to come to terms with what had happened, he had a feeling she hadn't been lying about loving him.

He'd never been with a woman who was so in tune with him. Anytime his head hurt, she knew, and she'd lie down on their bed with him. They didn't talk, but feeling her against him somehow made him feel better.

And they didn't have sex...they made love. He seriously doubted any woman could be as good an actress as Maisy seemed to be when they were alone. He'd had a one-night stand or two, and they'd seriously lacked the connection he and Maisy had between the sheets. She eagerly did anything he asked of her, even when she was obviously nervous. There wasn't a chance in hell that she'd slept with him because she'd been ordered to do so by her brother.

In fact, she'd gone out of her way to avoid being alone with Jason, something Stone had fully approved of and encouraged. The few times she'd been unable to avoid him, she'd returned to Stone with bruises.

The signs had always been there, but because of his hurt and betrayal, Stone had refused to acknowledge them. But after reading the communications between Jason and his dumbass buddies, the full scope of the hell Maisy had endured for years hit him hard. Yes, he'd been a victim of the man's evil plan, but Stone had been treated reasonably well because Jason didn't want to risk him getting suspicious. Obviously he didn't have the same concern when it came to his sister.

Maisy had been completely reliant on her brother. She'd been a minor when her parents had died, when her world had been shaken from its foundation. And the person she thought was fully on her side was actually the enemy in disguise. He'd drugged her for years, stolen from her, then came up with the kidnapping scheme and threatened to kill not only Maisy, but whoever he brought in to marry her as well.

And then Stone took her away from everything she'd ever known, forced her to live with him, told her that he would be annulling their sham of a marriage as soon as possible, and treated her as if she had a communicable disease.

The problem was, he didn't know how to fix it. His

feelings for Maisy were confusing as hell. He didn't want to be near her, but he couldn't imagine not having her with him in the living room each night. He wanted to know all about what she was doing each day to stay busy, but every time he heard her voice, he got mad about her deception all over again.

The nights were the worst. He wasn't sleeping well. At all. His bed seemed too big, too empty, without her in it. And, *God*, he missed the feeling of being inside her. Of seeing her above him, smiling down at him, as she rode his dick. Of how she always seemed so damn surprised when she orgasmed. It was cute. And such a massive turn-on.

She made him feel as if he could do anything. Like he could be her protector, her rock, the man she turned to when she was upset.

All that had been ripped away with the return of his memories...but again, now that some time had passed, Stone couldn't help but wonder if not *all* of what happened had been a lie.

Tonight had been the worst yet. He'd made them a simple taco dinner, and they'd eaten in complete silence. Then he'd turned the TV to a baseball game. They'd sat on opposite ends of his couch without saying a word. He could smell her unique apple scent—she'd obviously ordered her favorite shampoo and had it delivered—and every time she shifted, Stone had to force himself not to turn to her and ask if anything was wrong.

Eventually she'd sighed, told him quietly that she was going to go to bed and read, and left the room. The second she was gone, the room seemed empty in a way he'd never felt before. Stone wanted so badly to talk to her. To tell her that he forgave her. To ask if their marriage had been real in her eyes or simply a way to keep her brother from hurting her.

By the time he'd shut off the television in disgust and gone to bed, Stone was heartsick. He still wanted Maisy. Wanted to be her husband. Wanted to hear her talk excitedly about her evening with the girls the other night. Instead, he'd overheard her telling Carly all about it the previous afternoon, while she'd been helping her clean one of the guest cabins.

Stone was missing out on everything Maisy was doing, everything she was thinking, anything she might be planning for her future...and he *hated* it.

He lay in bed for a long while, his ears straining for any sound coming from the room next to his. He wished things were different. That he had the guts to pull Maisy onto his lap and make her talk to him. No, that wasn't fair. *He* was the one who wasn't talking. Who was going out of his way to make her feel unwelcome. This was all on him. Not Maisy.

Eventually he fell asleep, but his brain wouldn't settle. He kept thinking about every minute he'd spent in that house with Maisy in Washington. How...happy he'd been, despite everything. And it was because of her. She made all the difference.

* * *

Maisy wasn't sleeping. She hadn't had a full night's sleep since...well, since she'd last fallen asleep in Jack's arms. She was safe with him. Her brother hadn't come into her room once after he'd arrived. He was like a wall between her and Jason, keeping him from saying mean things, pinching her, pushing her to the ground. And without him at her side, every noise felt as if it could be Jason returning to take revenge on her for leaving. For ruining his plans.

By now, he'd have realized he wasn't getting her monthly stipend. He might have even gotten notice of the canceled life insurance policies. Possibly even realized somehow the house got put on the market and it wasn't in his name anymore. He must be freaking out. Trying desperately to figure out a way to get control back. Control of her, of her money, of the situation.

Because she was awake, she heard the soft knock on the front door. She was confused for a moment, then leaped to her feet. It was eleven-thirty, way too late for someone to come for a social visit. Something had to be wrong.

Maisy rushed out of her room and automatically looked at Jack's door as she exited. It was shut tight. He did that every night, closed his door, making it clear she wasn't welcome in the private sanctuary that was his bedroom.

Not thinking about anything other than finding who could be knocking so late, if someone was hurt—or worse, if Jason had figured out where she and Jack had gone, and was now on his way—she rushed to the front entry. Without looking through the peephole, she unlocked and opened the door.

Owl was standing there.

"What's wrong?" Maisy blurted almost desperately.

"Nothing. I mean, I hope not. I was just...Stone seemed off today, and I wanted to check on him."

"Oh, good! I mean—no, not good that something

might be wrong with Jack, but that it's not anything more serious. Come in." She stood back and held the door open.

"I know it's late," Owl said, not moving. "Lara told me I was being ridiculous, but I just couldn't shake the feeling that I needed to come over. Make sure he was all right."

"It's fine. It's not that late," Maisy said in a soothing tone. Owl looked stressed, and once again she was fiercely glad Jack had a friend like him. They'd been through some intense experiences together, and his disappearance had to be even worse for Owl than the others.

Reaching out, she took his hand and pulled him inside the cabin, then she shut the door quietly behind him. "We called it an early night, so we've both been in bed a while. He's probably asleep, but I'm sure he wouldn't mind if you went and woke him up."

"Oh no," Owl said quickly. "I'd never do that."

"Why not?"

"He doesn't do well being woken up when he's asleep. You know about his nightmares, right?" Owl asked.

Maisy nodded. "Yeah, he got them every now and then when we were in Seattle."

"Did he hurt you?"

"Jack? No! Why would you even ask that?" Maisy asked.

"Because when he has a nightmare, he loses a part of himself. He's not in his right mind. And if he's touched, he gets violent."

"No, he doesn't," Maisy said, confused.

"Yes, he *does*," Owl countered. "He's punched me more than once when I've tried to wake him up. I've learned to keep my distance and do what I can to snap him out of it." Then Owl seemed to realize what Maisy had said. "Wait, he doesn't get violent when you try to wake him up during a nightmare?"

She shook her head.

"Wow. Okay, that's...that's awesome."

Maisy was still confused, more questions on the tip of her tongue, but a sound down the hall made both her and Owl turn and look in that direction.

"Fuck," he swore. "Sounds as if my intuition was right on tonight. Stay here."

But Maisy couldn't. She recognized the agonized sounds coming from Jack's room. She heard them every other night. He was having yet another nightmare, and every whimper and pleading word for faceless men to stop hurting him tore at her insides.

She pushed past Owl and practically ran down the short hallway.

"Maisy, wait!"

She ignored him and opened Jack's door. As she'd expected, he was thrashing on the bed, the covers tangled around him as he fought an imaginary foe. Not imaginary, that wasn't the right word. As he fought the memory of those who'd tortured him years ago.

When he briefly settled on his side, facing away from them, Maisy didn't hesitate. She climbed onto the bed beside the man she loved. No matter what had gone on between them, she still loved Jack. With all her heart. She'd go to the grave loving him.

"Maisy—"

As far as she was concerned, it was only her and Jack in the room. "It's okay, Jack, you're okay. You're safe here at The Refuge. Those men can't hurt you anymore."

He rolled suddenly, making Owl gasp, and pulled Maisy

against him so roughly, she grunted with the impact. But he didn't hurt her, simply buried his nose in her hair and held her to his chest almost desperately.

"I've got you, you're good. Owl's here," Maisy murmured.

"Owl! Get out! Run!"

Shoot, maybe mentioning Owl's name hadn't been the right thing to do. Maisy did her best to wiggle an arm free, and once she succeeded, she wrapped her hand around Jack's nape. "He's safe. He and Lara are good. She's pregnant. You're going to be an uncle."

Her words had Jack going still.

"And Henley and Reese are too. You're going to be an uncle three times over. Well, four if you include Jasna in there. Oh, and Cora and Pipe are on the short list for a foster kid. Things are good around here, Jack. Promise. You're home safe, those men can't touch you anymore."

"*Stellina*," Jack whispered. He hadn't opened his eyes yet.

"That's right. It's me. I'm here."

"I'm going to go," Owl whispered.

Maisy nodded in acknowledgement but didn't take her attention away from the man in her arms. Her only goal was to settle him down. To soothe him. She distantly heard the bedroom door click closed but immediately dismissed it.

"I'm sorry," Jack said quietly.

Maisy blinked in surprise. She had no idea what he was apologizing for. "It's okay," she told him.

Then his eyes opened, and she was startled to see them so clear. So focused.

"Jack?" she questioned, stiffening. It was one thing to

climb into his bed when he was having a nightmare and had no idea what was happening; it was another when he was lucid. Especially considering how things had been between them.

"I'm sorry," he repeated.

"Um...okay?" It came out more as a question than a statement.

"I've been a dick. You didn't deserve that."

Maisy was afraid to get her hopes up. He was usually kind of out of it after a nightmare. It was likely he wouldn't remember this conversation in the morning.

"Actually, I deserve anything you want to dish out," she said a little sadly.

Jack's arms tightened around her. "Can we talk about it?"

Maisy knew exactly what "it" was. And no, she definitely didn't want to talk about it. "Now?"

"I'm awake, you're awake, and the last thing I want to do is think about what I was just dreaming about...so yeah, now."

Sighing, Maisy closed her eyes. She didn't want to talk about how horrible she'd been. How she'd lied to him time and time again. She was right where she'd wanted to be for the last week or so. She'd craved this, him. And now that she was in his arms, in his bed, she didn't want to do or say anything that might rip that away from her again.

"Please?"

That did it. The last thing she wanted was to make this man beg her for anything. Especially with his abhorrence for the act. "What do you want to know?" she asked.

"Anything you'll tell me. Obviously, I know that your brother had me kidnapped so I could marry you and start the clock ticking on your inheritance. Was everything you told me about our relationship his idea?"

Maisy nodded against him. She'd opened her eyes and was staring at his chest. "I went to Jason and told him it wasn't going to work. That you'd have questions about why you had no belongings at the house, what you did for a living, things like that. He told me what to say. And when I still expressed doubts about his plan...well, he made it clear I didn't have a choice."

Jack's arms tightened around her for a moment before he relaxed again. "I couldn't understand why the hell I'd up and leave and go to Spokane. It made no sense to me. Even if we weren't getting along, that didn't feel like something I'd do."

She couldn't help it, she snorted against him. "Kind of like now. You hate me, and yet you won't let me stay anywhere else."

Jack rolled then, forcing Maisy onto her back. She stared up at him with wary eyes.

"I don't hate you."

"Yeah, right," she said, the sarcasm easy to hear in her tone. "I lied to you over and over, pretended to be your wife, tricked you into marrying me, all because I was scared of what my brother would say or do if I defied him. I should've told you the truth. Gone to the police. *Something.*"

"You did lie, but it was for a good reason. You knew that if you said no to your brother, bad things would happen. And if you told me that we weren't married, that I'd been kidnapped and had amnesia...I'm not sure I would've believed you. It would've sounded extremely outlandish."

Maisy stared up at Jack. He'd taken his glasses off to sleep and his brown eyes seemed even more intense without them. His hair and beard had been trimmed at some point since they'd arrived in New Mexico, and she longed to feel his cheeks and lips against her own.

Ry's suggestion about seducing her husband flashed through her mind, but she wouldn't do that to Jack. He'd been forced into doing way too many things against his will already. The last thing she wanted to do was add one more thing to that list. If there was a chance for them, she wanted it to be his choice.

"I forgive you, Maisy."

She jerked. Afraid she hadn't heard what she hoped she had, Maisy asked, "What?"

"I forgive you. I had a long talk with Henley today, and she made me think about stuff I hadn't considered before. Mostly about how scared you had to have been. Your brother brought an unconscious man into your room and informed you that he was going to be your husband. With every day that passed since our wedding, a huge clock's been ticking. You, more than anyone, know exactly what your brother's capable of, and not only were you trying to deal with him, but you had to continue to lie to me, worry about what would happen if I regained my memories, and how your brother would react. You had a lot on your plate, and I haven't stopped to consider everything from your perspective."

Maisy's heart was thumping hard in her chest. She would grab onto the olive branch Jack was extending with both hands. She had no right to ever hope that things might go back to the way they'd been, but not being hated by Jack...it would be enough.

"The thing is, I can't forget how things were between us," Jack went on. "It had been a long time since you'd been with anyone before our wedding night...hadn't it?"

Maisy briefly closed her eyes. She knew she was blushing; she could feel the heat in her cheeks. She was so embarrassed. "Since I was fifteen," she whispered, her eyes fluttering open.

She'd clearly shocked him, based on his expression. "I can't stop thinking about that night. How brave you were. I thought we'd made love hundreds of times. That you'd seen every inch of my body before then. I was so excited to get a second chance to make love to my wife for the first time that I rushed you. I should've been more gentle. Should've gone slower."

"It was perfect," Maisy whispered, hating that he thought for even two seconds that she hadn't loved everything they did. "I have a lot of regrets about what happened. About the lies I told you, about not being strong enough to stand up to Jason. But I have *zero* regrets about our physical relationship." She couldn't believe she was admitting that out loud, but she needed Jack to understand. "My brother might have whored me out, but when it was just you and me...I felt special. As if it really was my wedding night. You really were my husband."

"It *was* our wedding night," Jack said in a tone she couldn't interpret. "And I *am* your husband."

"It was all a lie," Maisy said uneasily.

"Was it?" Jack countered.

She wouldn't lie to him again. Never again. "Not to me."

"Not to me either. The thing is, I knew something was wrong. I heard the way Jason spoke to you. I didn't like it, not at all. I couldn't understand why I couldn't access my own bank account, couldn't picture myself as a bounty hunter. It wasn't clicking, and now, obviously, I know why. But with you, Maisy...right from the beginning, I felt as if I was right where I belonged. It's why I didn't question what was happening. I was enjoying my wife too much."

Maisy couldn't believe what she was hearing. Maybe she was dreaming. The words coming out of Jack's mouth were a miracle.

He was still lying over her, keeping her trapped beneath him. She had on the T-shirt he'd given her that first night in his cabin and a pair of underwear. That was it. He was wearing a pair of boxers. And now that she was thinking about it, she could feel his erection against her belly.

Need rose hard and fast within her. Maisy might have gone years without being sexually active, but Jack had flicked a switch inside of her. She wanted him with an urgency she'd never felt before. Her nipples hardened under her shirt and she felt wetness between her legs.

"Do you forgive me for being an ass?" he asked.

"Of course."

He smiled. "There's no 'of course' about it. I wouldn't blame you if refused to have anything to do with me."

"Kind of hard to have nothing to do with your husband," she told him. "Especially when he refuses to let you stay anywhere but in his cabin."

"Hated every second of you being in the room next door. I wanted you here. With me. In my bed."

He was killing her.

"I don't care about anything that happened before now," Jack said, sincerity oozing from his words. "About being kidnapped, about your brother being a dick, about any lies you had to tell me in order to keep yourself safe. Wait, no, that's not true, I *do* care about one thing...I made a vow, Maisy. To have and to hold, for better or worse, for richer or poorer, through sickness and health, I pledged myself to you. And I take my promises seriously."

What was he saying? Maisy could barely breathe.

"I don't want the annulment," he said, blowing her mind. "I want you. I want children. I want to start over. With no lies between us. Do you think you could ever forgive me enough for that to happen?"

Maisy couldn't believe what he was saying. She let out a small noise in the back of her throat and wiggled until she could get her arms out from under him, throwing them around his back. She lurched upward until her nose was buried in the space between his shoulder and neck and wrapped her legs around his waist. She held onto him as tightly as she could and burst into tears.

She couldn't speak, could barely wrap her mind around what he was saying. He wanted her? For real?

Thankfully, Jack didn't seem alarmed by her reaction. He eased upward so he was sitting on his ass and she was in his lap, still clinging to him. One hand went behind her head to hold her against him and the other went around her lower back, pressing her closer.

When Maisy had a little more control over herself, she lifted her head so she could look into his eyes. His hand stayed at the back of her head, holding her protectively.

"Forgive you? You did nothing wrong. *Nothing*," she said heatedly. "I have no idea why you want anything to do with me. My brother is most likely a murderer, definitely a kidnapper and an asshole. You were forced to marry me under false pretenses, and if my brother ever finds out where we are, he'll likely do whatever he can to make our lives hell."

"None of that has anything to do with you. Us," Jack said simply.

Tears filled Maisy's eyes again. "Yes, Jack. I want all of that. I love you. I think I loved you that first night when you were so gentle with me. So worried that you were hurting me. I knew then that you were a good man down to your soul, and you just proved it again."

"I take you, Maisy, to be my lawfully wedded wife, to have and to hold, for better or worse, for richer or poorer, through sickness and health, till death do us part."

Shit, she couldn't stop crying. "I take you, Jack, to be my lawfully wedded husband, to have and to hold, for better or worse, for richer or poorer, through sickness and health, till death do us part."

Then Jack's head lowered, and he kissed her with the most loving and gentle meeting of lips she'd ever felt in her life. He lifted his head and his hands came to her face, wiping the tears from her cheeks.

"We're gonna make this work," he vowed.

"Your friends are gonna wonder what the hell is wrong with you," Maisy warned.

He chuckled. "No, they aren't. I've already been getting side-eye from all of them. They don't like how I've been treating you. They're on *your* side, Maisy. Even with everything your brother did, they understand that you're the best thing that's ever happened to me. Yeah, getting kidnapped sucked, for both of us, but in the end I came out a winner. And just think about how us being together for real will piss off your brother."

Maisy couldn't help but laugh at that. Yeah, her being happy would chap Jason's ass for sure.

"You good?" he asked.

"Yeah. You?"

"I'm perfect."

"Owl told me that you hit him once when he tried to wake you up while you were having a nightmare." Maisy wasn't sure where this was coming from, but she wanted to make sure he was really okay, and this whole conversation wasn't somehow because he was sleepwalking or something.

"Yup. More than once. No one could ever get near me when I was dreaming. It didn't turn out well for them."

"You didn't hurt *me*," Maisy said.

"No, I didn't. And I won't. Ever. You're the only one who can reach me when I'm lost in my nightmares, and I wouldn't want it any other way." Then he moved, putting Maisy on her back once again. He hovered over her, and this time one of his hands fingered the hem of her shirt at her hip.

And just like that, arousal swam in Maisy's veins. "Yes, Jack. I need you."

"Are you sure?"

In response, feeling braver than she'd ever felt, Maisy wiggled and shifted until she got her shirt off. Then she lay under him in nothing but her underwear.

The lust and pleasure in his eyes made her feel like the sexiest woman in the world. He didn't speak, simply lowered his head and took a nipple into his mouth.

Maisy groaned. Jack's hands and mouth on her felt *right*. She felt as if she'd finally come home.

This time, there were no secrets. He knew who she

was, and who she wasn't, and he wanted her anyway. It felt like a miracle. Somehow this felt as if it was their true wedding night. They'd re-pledged themselves to each other with no lies between them.

But unlike their first time, there was nothing slow and easy about their coming together. Jack ripped his boxers off and Maisy slid her underwear down her legs and kicked them away. Jack's hand went between her legs and drove her right to the brink with hardly any effort. She was soaking wet. Needy. Desperate.

"I'm ready. Now, Jack. Now!"

He didn't ask if she was sure again. Didn't hesitate. Pushing her legs apart with his knees, he pressed inside her in one long, hard stroke.

They both moaned.

"Can't go slow," he warned.

"Don't want you to," she panted.

He took her then. With no mercy. And Maisy loved every second of it. Jack kept his gaze locked onto hers, and it felt as if he was finally seeing all of her.

Her orgasm took her by surprise. One second she was admiring the color of Jack's eyes and how they seemed to change right in front of her, and the next, she was flying over the edge.

"That's it, *Stellina*. Come on my cock. Squeeze me hard. Fuck, you feel so good."

His words prolonged her pleasure. She felt as if she was flying. When he grunted and slammed into her as hard as he could and stayed planted there, she knew he was coming too.

They were both sweaty and panting by the time he

lifted his head. He stayed lodged deep inside her body, something Maisy never thought she'd ever feel again.

"I'm not giving you up," he told her as casually as if he was asking what time it was.

"Good, because I don't want you to," she returned.

"I'm not an easy man to live with."

Maisy couldn't help it, she laughed.

"What? What's so funny about that?"

"Jack, I know that. When you take off your socks, you leave them in the middle of the room. You hog the covers, but since I'm usually plastered against your side, I'm okay with that. You're kind of a picky eater—and you get grumpy when you haven't eaten—and you aren't exactly a morning person. You're protective, and kind, and loyal to a fault. You have more integrity in your little finger than anyone I've ever met. I love you. All of you. And you saying you're not easy to live with is ridiculous considering I've lived with a man who loved to torment me, belittle me, and physically hurt me when he could get away with it. With you, I feel as if I can finally be the person I was always meant to be."

"You can. And I'll never hurt you, Maisy. I give you my word."

She wanted to hear him say that he loved her once more, but she was more than content with him not glaring at her or trying to keep his distance.

"Stay here," he ordered, then gently eased out of her body.

Maisy couldn't hold back the small wince. Even though it had only been a week since they'd last made love, Jack wasn't a small man, and as promised, he hadn't been gentle.

He was gone less than a minute and returned with a

warm washcloth. He cleaned her up, making Maisy squirm in the process, then climbed back under the covers after a quick trip back to the bathroom. He pulled her close, and Maisy settled against him as she'd done so many other nights.

"Good?" he asked.

"Good," she confirmed.

A moment later, he said, "Missed this. You, clinging to me like a baby monkey."

She might've been insulted if he didn't sound so darn content. "Me too," she admitted. "You're always so warm."

"And you're always freezing. Your feet are blocks of ice, woman."

Maisy giggled. She felt him kiss the top of her head before relaxing fully.

He fell asleep in what seemed like seconds, and Maisy lay against him reveling in being able to hold him once more. She never thought this would happen again. Not only had it happened, but it seemed as if she and Jack were...remarried?

That made no sense, and no one would understand if she tried to explain it. But they'd literally exchanged vows earlier. This time they meant so much more because she wasn't living a lie. Jack didn't have amnesia. And his forgiveness meant everything to Maisy.

But deep down inside, she wasn't content to let things stay as they were. Jason was still out there. Like a black cloud hovering over her and Jack. He wouldn't stop trying to get her money. She knew that as well as she knew he'd murdered their parents.

And if she wanted her happily ever after, she'd have to fight for it. She was scared out of her mind to confront

Jason, but she needed to. Needed to show him she wasn't the same little sister he'd bullied for half her life. Oh, she wouldn't do anything stupid, but she wanted him to feel some of the fear he'd instilled in her for years.

She thought she'd have to confront Jason alone, even if Jack and his teammates were willing to escort her to Seattle to settle her financial affairs. But now that Jack had forgiven her, and seemed to want a real relationship, she wanted him there to see her stand on her own two feet. She didn't want to be the pathetic, spineless woman he'd first met, but she also didn't want to be TSTL. Too stupid to live. She'd learned that phrase online, in a review for a book. The heroine had a stalker and yet she'd insisted on being independent and going off on her own to do something. Shop, maybe. And the reviewer was right. The heroine had been too stupid to live.

So maybe instead of trying to confront Jason on her own, she'd ask Jack to be there. And maybe Brick and Tiny as well, who'd already volunteered to go with them to Seattle. Having two former Navy SEALs and Jack at her back would give her courage, and dissuade Jason from doing something stupid...like punch her, or drag her down to the bank by her hair and force her to sign over her inheritance.

She just needed a few minutes. Long enough to finally tell him that everything he'd done had made *him* the pathetic one, not her, as he'd so often called her.

Maisy felt good about her plan. She wasn't sure how to make it happen if Jason was no longer living at the house, and she had a feeling it wouldn't be easy to talk Jack into letting her confront her brother, but in order to move on with her life, she had to do it.

Sighing, Maisy eased a leg up and over Jack's thigh and smiled when his arm tightened around her.

"You okay?" he murmured, sounding mostly asleep.

"More than okay," she told him.

She fell asleep with his scent in her nose and his warmth seeping into her bones. She had no idea what the future held, but for once in her life, she was actually looking forward to whatever came next.

CHAPTER EIGHTEEN

Stone's three-month wedding anniversary had come and gone. Things with him and Maisy were better than ever. He hadn't realized how tense he'd been until Maisy was back sleeping in his arms and they'd worked things out between them.

Maisy wasn't her brother. *She* hadn't kidnapped him. She was as much a victim in what happened as he'd been. It had taken that talk with Henley to truly and honestly see that. Once he stopped to think about what her life had been like, it wasn't a hard decision to forgive her.

Being back at The Refuge was therapeutic for Stone. He loved the corner of the world he and his friends had carved out and couldn't imagine living anywhere else. Thankfully, Maisy was fitting in perfectly. She helped out where she could, and everyone had embraced her wholeheartedly.

But neither of them could forget that her brother was still out there. Likely fuming over losing Maisy's monthly stipend and not being able to find her to force her to change what Ry had done electronically.

The time was approaching when they needed to head back to Washington so Maisy could meet with the lawyer and sign the papers that would give her full and legal access to her inheritance. Stone didn't like it, but in order to cut ties with Jason once and for all, it had to be done.

Maisy had talked to Stone about her plans for the money. She didn't want it, felt as if it was somehow tainted, which he didn't agree with, but he'd never tell Maisy what to do with her own money. She and Ry were working out plans on what charities to donate the bulk of it to, and he'd never been as proud of anyone as he was of his wife.

Wife. Stone hadn't planned on getting married, hadn't really thought much about it all. But now that he was, he couldn't imagine not coming home to his cabin every night and having Maisy there. Couldn't even *think* about sleeping without her in his arms. The sex was amazing, but it went deeper than that. The connection they had, the emotional bond, was more intense than he ever could've imagined.

When it became obvious to his friends that he'd forgiven Maisy and they were now more than simply roommates, he was on the receiving end of a barrage of teasing. But he didn't care. They could rib him all they wanted, he'd never been happier.

Though he'd be more relaxed once their trip to Seattle was over and done with. He wasn't thrilled that Maisy wanted to go back to her house and get her diary, the pictures she'd taken years ago, and the other evidence, but ultimately, if they wanted Jason to go down for his crimes, they needed that stuff. The case against her brother was mostly circumstantial as it was, the police would need the other evidence to get a search warrant so they could dig up the basketball court in the backyard and hopefully find poor Martha's body.

Brick had suggested to Maisy that he and Tiny go to the house to get everything, but she'd refused. It had taken a bit of talking to find out why she was so determined to get the evidence they needed to take to the police herself, but eventually she'd given in and told them that she needed to see her brother one more time. To say all the things she hadn't felt safe saying before. And with him, Brick, and Tiny at her back, she was confident no harm would come to her.

Stone wanted to protest, tell her it was asinine to get anywhere near her brother, but he also understood her need for closure. And the fact that she was smart enough to not do it on her own, to literally want some muscle behind her, ultimately made Stone give in.

Not to mention, he had some things to say to Jason as well.

So they'd be leaving in two days. They'd called the lawyer in charge of the trust and he'd agreed to meet them at the bank manager's office first thing in the morning the day after they arrived. Then they'd go to the house and get the evidence Maisy had left behind, along with anything else she might want, since Stone had gotten them out of the house without even a suitcase. He'd let her say what she needed to say to her brother—if he was even at the house—then they'd spend another night at the hotel before heading out the following morning.

All in all, the trip would be as short as possible. Even thinking about going back to Washington made the hair on the back of Stone's neck stand up. He felt antsy, hyped, just as he used to feel before a dangerous flight when he'd been in the Army.

This morning, Brick was having their weekly check-in meeting. Everyone would talk about what they were doing on The Refuge, discuss things they wanted to change or implement, and generally keep everyone's finger on the pulse of their business. Stone honestly enjoyed these meetings. Liked hearing his friends' ideas for the place. It felt as if so much had happened in the weeks he'd been gone.

Tonka started, giving an update on the animals he looked after, then Brick gave a rundown of their financials and donations, which were up five hundred percent over a few years ago. Owl discussed the progress on the building of the hangar for the helicopter, and Brick added that hopefully in another month or so, the investigation into Carter Grant and what had happened out on his island would be wrapped up and they could arrange to have the chopper delivered to The Refuge.

Stone was more excited than he could express about having a helicopter on the property. He hadn't realized how much he'd missed flying until he and Owl had flown down to the Mexican border to save Reese. And even though it was now evident that Grant had used the helicopter as bait to get his hands on Lara, Stone couldn't deny that he'd loved the Bell when he and Owl had test-flown it.

"What are Ry's plans?" Pipe asked Tiny.

"Why?" he asked sharply, eyes narrowed.

"Easy, man, I'm just wondering," Pipe told his friend.

"Sorry," Tiny apologized. "I don't know. She's been working with Maisy to fuck over her brother. After that's done...I'm guessing she'll be leaving."

"Where will she go?" Spike asked.

"Don't know."

"Do you care?" Brick asked.

The room was silent, with everyone's attention on Tiny.

"Why should I?"

"Because you like her," Tonka said baldly.

"No, I don't," Tiny disagreed.

"Riiiight. That's why you won't let her out of your sight," Owl said with a sarcastic snort.

"She lied to us. Deceived us. She could literally steal us blind and we'd have no idea until it was done. She's possibly the most dangerous person I've ever met in my life, simply because every time she touches a computer, she could do immeasurable amounts of damage. To The Refuge, us personally, the US. Did you know she used to hack into the president's email for fun?"

Brick leaned forward and stared at Tiny with an intense glare. "She wouldn't hurt us."

"You don't know that."

"I do, but the fact that *you* refuse to see it means you're not willing to open your eyes and see what the hell's right in front of your face."

"And what's that, Brick?" Tiny growled.

"That Ry's scared shitless," Brick told him.

Tiny laughed. But it wasn't a humorous sound. "Right."

"She is," Brick insisted.

"The only thing she's scared of is not being able to play with people's lives if she gets thrown in jail."

Stone had no idea if Tiny was trying to convince himself or them that he believed what he was saying. He didn't know Ry all that well, she didn't let anyone at The

Refuge get too close, but what he *did* know, he liked. Ry was kind, always willing to help out, and she didn't like to gossip. And the fact that she apparently had the ability to get her hands on enormous amounts of money, but was still working as a housekeeper at The Refuge, said a lot about her.

"You're being an ass," Spike said, sounding uncharacteristically harsh. "She didn't *have* to figure out how to track Reese. And if she hadn't, I'm not sure I would've gotten her back."

"And the fact that she rescued Jasna, and didn't ask for or want any thanks, tells me all I needed to know about her," Tonka added.

"She found out about our bunkers!" Tiny argued. "We all agreed that we'd never tell anyone about them. And yet, she not only knew about them, but rubbed it in our faces by putting Jasna in one. Why didn't she simply bring her back here? Why the subterfuge?"

"I'm guessing she found out about them the same way she knows everything," Pipe said reasonably. "Because she somehow discovered the plans online somewhere. Or maybe saw a stray email back when we were having them built. I don't know. But you know what? I don't care that she knows. I'm glad she used her knowledge to keep Jasna safe."

"Me too," Tonka said, which wasn't a surprise, given Jasna was his stepdaughter.

"What I want to know is, *why*," Brick added after a moment.

"Why what?" Tiny asked.

"Why she worked here for months without letting on what she can do. The woman's a freaking genius. Tex has admitted that she's better than *him* at computer shit, and we all know that's a huge deal. She could've been sipping margaritas on a beach somewhere, living off ill-gotten millions. And yet she chose to be *here*, in the middle-of-nowhere New Mexico, cleaning toilets and washing towels and sheets. There's a story there...and I want to know what it is."

Stone agreed wholeheartedly.

"Well, I don't," Tiny grumbled.

"If she left today, you wouldn't care?" Brick challenged. "You wouldn't think twice about her? Wouldn't wonder what she was running from? And don't roll your damn eyes at me, we all know she's running from something. Hiding. And if we don't do anything, she'll be gone. Vulnerable to whoever or whatever she's obviously afraid of. And if that happens, we'll never find her. She'll take a new name and be lost to us forever." He shook his head. "Maybe you hate her, Tiny, but I don't. I actually like her. So does Alaska. I don't want her to leave without at least trying to find out what's wrong, to see if we can help her."

"Me too," Tonka said.

"Same," Owl agreed.

"She saved my Reese, that's enough for me to do what I can to help her."

Stone was on the same page as his friends. Ry was doing a hell of a lot for Maisy, without asking anything in return.

"I don't hate her," Tiny said after a moment.

"Could'a fooled us," Brick said.

Tiny ran a hand through his hair in agitation. "She... confuses me. I don't understand her motivation for anything she's done."

"Maybe she does things because she's a good person," Stone volunteered.

Tiny sighed. "Sometimes when she doesn't know I'm watching her, I catch her with her guard down. She looks... haunted. Whatever she's hiding from, it's not good. And call me selfish, but I don't want whatever it is to come back on *us*. I have a feeling whatever it is could destroy The Refuge."

"All the more reason to find out what it is and convince her to let us help her," Brick insisted.

"You need to back off, Tiny," Tonka said sternly. "She saved Jas. You don't have to help, but I'll throw down for Ry, no matter what her name is."

"Same," Spike agreed.

"She's been a miracle for most of us," Owl added.

"Fine. I hear you. I'll back off. But don't blame me if we wake up one day and all our bank accounts have been drained and she's taken off," Tiny said, tossing his hands in the air.

Tonka scooted his chair back so fast, it fell to the floor behind him. "You're an asshole," he said in an even, controlled tone. "I was like you for a long damn time, man. Refusing to see what was right in front of my face until it was too late. Ry's not going to stick around here if she doesn't feel welcome. If she thinks you believe the worst in her. She's already got one foot out the door. The only reason she hasn't left already is because Maisy needs her. The second that's done, she's gone. And that would suck, because she saved my daughter's life without asking for a damn thing. She was willing to confront a serial killer in the making to bring Jas home.

"Ry's not going to steal our money. She could've done

that the first week she was here and we wouldn't have had any idea it was her. Get your head out of your ass, Tiny, before it's too late. Now...I'm gonna go check on Melba. One of her hooves has been bothering her."

With that, Tonka marched to the door and left without looking back.

Silence filled the room until Brick broke it. "I'll go get Savannah and tell her we're ready for her report."

Stone frowned. Tonka had been much more talkative since he and Henley had gotten together, but he wasn't the kind of man who went out of his way to foist his opinion on others. The fact that he'd taken Tiny down a peg was a huge deal. But he couldn't help but feel sorry for his friend. He was obviously struggling with his feelings about Ry.

"You gonna be okay going up to Seattle?" Stone asked Tiny quietly once everyone was talking amongst themselves.

"Yeah, why wouldn't I?"

Stone shrugged. "Wasn't sure you'd be comfortable leaving Ry in your place without you being there."

Tiny sighed. "Brick's right. Tonka too. I've been an asshole. I just...I have a very bad feeling about Ry. Not about her personally, but about what she's hiding from. What she can do is so far out of my league, but I know whatever's wrong...it could ruin all of us."

Stone nodded. "We'll only be gone a couple of days. When we get back, we can all sit down with her and reassure her that we don't want her to go, that we want to help."

"Yeah," Tiny said.

"Whatever it is, we'll figure it out," Stone said firmly.

"I hope so. Because if we don't, I have a feeling *we'll* be the ones paying the price."

Stone opened his mouth to say more, but Savannah entered the room with Brick on her heels. Now wasn't the best time to discuss Ry's situation, but they definitely needed to have another serious chat with the computer genius. Soon.

CHAPTER NINETEEN

"Do you have enough snacks?" Luna asked.

Maisy chuckled. "Yes, we're good. Half my carry-on is full of food."

"Make sure you do whatever they tell you," Alaska warned. "Drake knows his stuff. And since Tiny was a Navy SEAL too, so does he."

"We aren't going to war," Maisy said wryly.

"I'm thinking you shouldn't underestimate that asshole brother of yours," Lara said.

She wasn't wrong. Maisy nodded.

"Enough. You guys are freaking her out," Jack said, wrapping an arm around Maisy's waist. She looked up at him and saw a muscle in his jaw was ticking. He was doing his best to seem nonchalant about this trip, but it was obvious, at least to her, that he was anything but.

If there was any way to get her inheritance without this trip to Seattle, Maisy had no doubt Jack would've insisted on it. They'd tried to arrange for her to see someone here in New Mexico, but the lawyer in charge of the trust was the only one who could release the money, and he wasn't willing to travel to New Mexico because of family commitments.

Maisy understood. He couldn't be expected to fly all over the country on his clients' whims. And she actually appreciated that he stuck to the letter of the law. If he didn't, it was likely her brother would've already found a way to get his hands on her money.

Besides, there were some things she wanted from the house...the evidence against Jason at the top of the list, of course. But also keepsakes, clothes, her dad's handkerchiefs he always carried that she kept in her dresser, her mom's wedding ring. They were just things, but they were some of the only items she had from her parents.

Brick, Tiny, and Jack were all tense, as if they really *were* getting ready for a mission. Maisy wanted to reassure them that with any show of force, her brother would cave. Bullies always did. Around anyone weaker than them, they talked a good game, but the second someone pushed back, they gave in. Her brother was no different. Of course, this knowledge was too little, too late for her, but she was secretly looking forward to Jason coming face-to-face with the guys. He'd crap his pants for sure.

Best of all, he wouldn't be able to hurt her. Not with Brick, Tiny, and Jack there to protect her. She could say what she needed to say without fear of retribution. She was actually looking forward to seeing her brother.

They finally finished saying their goodbyes and headed toward the airport in Santa Fe. They only had carry-on suitcases, so check-in was a breeze. She sat between Jack and Brick on the plane, with Tiny in the row behind them.

Before she knew it, they'd landed in Seattle and Tiny was driving them toward their hotel.

Their appointment at the bank wasn't until the morning, and before they'd arrived, the timing of everything seemed fine, but now Maisy wished they could go to the bank right this second. She stayed tense as Tiny drove, afraid somehow her brother would've found out she was here and would do something to prevent her from getting to the bank to sign the papers.

"Relax, you're good," Jack said, as if he could read her mind.

He couldn't hear what she was thinking, but he probably *could* read her body language. Feel the stress in the way she clung to his hand almost desperately.

"Even though it's not legal, Ryleigh's idea to use those fake IDs you and Stone used to leave Washington the first time was smart," Tiny said as he drove. "If your brother *does* have a way to monitor who's flying in and out of Seattle, he won't know you've returned until it's too late for him to do anything about it."

Tiny was right, she knew he was, but it didn't stop her from fearfully glancing at everyone in the vehicles around them.

"We'll check in, then order room service. We'll find something to watch that'll take your mind off everything," Jack said.

Maisy appreciated him doing what he could to help her calm down, but the last thing she wanted was to sit in the room and think about all the ways Jason could mess things up. "What if we went down to the restaurant in the lobby?" she asked. She wasn't stupid enough to suggest they go out sightseeing or anything, but maybe he'd agree to them eating downstairs.

"I don't know," Jack mused.

Brick interjected from the front seat. "I think that'll be fine. We can request a booth in the back of the restaurant, away from the windows."

"You sure?" Jack asked Maisy.

She nodded enthusiastically.

"All right. Should we meet downstairs in about an hour and a half after check-in?"

Everyone agreed, and Maisy tried to force her muscles to relax. This was okay. Everything was okay.

And it was. They checked in without any issues; Brick and Tiny were sharing a room down the hall from her and Jack. They met in the lobby for dinner, and Maisy found herself laughing and forgetting about what they were going to do the next day...at least for a little while.

Then Jack brought her back upstairs, put on a movie that neither of them really had any interest in watching, and pulled her into his arms.

This was what she needed. Maisy always felt safe with Jack around. Tomorrow was going to be fine. They'd do what they came to do, then go back home and move on with their lives.

"Tomorrow's gonna be fine," Jack said softly.

Maisy chuckled.

"What's funny?" he asked.

"I was literally just thinking those same words."

"Great minds think alike."

Maisy smiled at that. "Jack?"

"Yeah, *Stellina*?"

"Thank you."

"For what?"

"For being here. For not freaking out when I said I needed to confront Jason. For making me feel safe. For forgiving me."

"You don't have to thank me for any of that, Maisy. We might not have started our marriage in a conventional way, but I take my vows seriously. If you want something, I'll bend over backward to get it for you."

"I don't need anything but you," she said.

"You've got me."

And that was a miracle. Jason had done this man so wrong. Had kidnapped him and forced him to marry his sister. And yet, he was the best man Maisy had ever met. Not only was he good-looking—which was the least of her desires when it came to a partner—he was smart, forgiving, understanding, empathetic, and kind. She literally couldn't have done better if she'd picked her own husband. Which kind of galled her, because she didn't want to give Jason even one little iota of credit for how happy she was right now.

"I love you," Maisy whispered as she snuggled into Jack's side.

He squeezed her affectionately in return. He hadn't said he loved her since he'd regained his memory, but Maisy could be patient. It was crazy that she was so in love with him after such a short amount of time, but she didn't care. She needed him to know how she felt, even if he didn't feel the same in return. She hoped he would someday. Hoped he'd be able to love her as much as she loved him. He'd said the words before, when he didn't know who he was, and she had faith he'd say them again.

* * *

Neither she nor Jack slept all that great, but at least neither had a nightmare. They'd gotten up, prepared for a long day, then met Brick and Tiny downstairs before heading over to the bank to be there right when it opened.

Everyone was tense, and Maisy regretted eating as much for breakfast as she had. She prayed she wouldn't throw it all up from nerves. Brick and Tiny were on high alert, and for the first time, Maisy got a glimpse of the Navy SEALs inside the men. Their heads were on a swivel and they kept themselves between her and anyone who might approach them at all times.

Jack's hand was locked around hers, even refusing to let go when they'd arrived at the bank, insisting she scoot across the seat and get out on his side of the vehicle. Truthfully, while their actions were freaking her out, Maisy was relieved they were so vigilant.

And thinking about how this would've gone down if Jason had gotten his way, with him dragging her down here, probably holding her arm tight enough to leave bruises, threatening her the entire way...yeah. She was happy to have the three overly protective men at her side instead.

To her surprise, signing the paperwork was actually anticlimactic. After all these years, after all the stress and pain, they met the gentleman in charge of her trust and were led into the bank manager's office, where signing the papers to gain access to ten million dollars took less than thirty seconds.

After it was done, she was reassured the papers would be filed immediately and the money would be transferred to her new account—the one Ry had opened for her in a bank in Los Alamos—within a week. He apologized that it would take so long but because of the amount, certain protocols had to be followed.

Then they were back in the car and the atmosphere felt twenty times lighter.

"That was...different than I expected," Maisy said when Tiny started the engine.

"What did you expect?" Brick asked from the front seat.

"I'm not sure. More security, more...something."

Jack smiled. "It's done. Your brother no longer has any control over what you do, where you live, or how your money is spent."

It hit her then. "It's over."

"Yes, his reign of terror is over," Jack agreed.

Then Maisy burst into tears. They were a mixture of relief, sadness for her parents, and happiness that her brother could no longer hurt her.

"Shit! She okay? Should I pull over?" Tiny asked a little desperately.

Brick grinned. "You have a lot to learn about women. She's good. Just a little stress relief, right, Stone?"

Maisy felt Stone nod as she did her best to get control over her emotions. The easy part was done, but she still needed to face Jason, find the evidence, and pack. Later tonight, she could have another breakdown, but now she needed to get her shit together.

Taking a deep breath, Maisy sat up.

"All good?" Jack asked.

Maisy shook her head but said, "Yes."

Jack chuckled. "You're good," he said firmly. Then he

wrapped his hand around her nape and pulled her toward him, kissing her forehead. "Proud of you," he whispered.

His words made Maisy tingle from head to toe. She hadn't done anything but walk into a bank and sign a piece of paper, but knowing Jack was proud of her meant the world.

"So, the plan's still the same?" Tiny asked after a moment.

They'd talked about how to proceed at the house last night at dinner, but Maisy understood Tiny was just reaffirming what they'd already decided.

"We'll drive around the block, get the lay of the land. Then we'll park a few houses down, Maisy will use her key to get in. No knocking. If her brother had the locks changed, we'll go around to the kitchen door, break one of the windows and go in that way," Brick said.

"You still want to do this? We could still go to the police first and have them get a search warrant to get the pictures and your diary," Jack said.

"I thought there was a chance it wouldn't be approved if we did it that way?" Maisy asked. "Something about it being my word against his and not enough proof."

Jack didn't reply, simply held eye contact, and she knew she was right.

If possible, Maisy fell more in love with him right then and there. It was obvious he didn't want to go back to her house. Didn't want *her* there either. Definitely didn't want Jason anywhere near her. But he was willing to go with her because it was something she needed to do.

"I need to make sure he's punished for what he did to Martha. And if he did have anything to do with Mom and

Dad's murder, for that too. And I need those pictures and Martha's wallet to back up what I tell the detectives."

"We could go in and get them for you," Brick offered.

Maisy appreciated all of them so much. But this was something she needed to do. She should've done it way before now. Hated herself for letting so much time go by and letting her brother get away with his crimes. "We'll be quick," she told the guys in the car.

"Damn straight we will," Tiny said.

"In, upstairs, get the stuff, and out," Brick agreed.

Maisy wanted to remind them that she wanted to confront Jason, but the closer they got to the house, the more her stomach rolled and the worse that idea seemed. The last thing she wanted was to hear her brother's hateful words. And she had no doubt that he'd lash out the only way he could—verbally and emotionally. He knew her better than anyone, and thus he knew exactly how to hurt her the most.

For the first time, she crossed her fingers that Jason wouldn't be home when they got there. But her hopes were dashed when they drove by the house and she saw his car in the driveway. For some reason, he never parked in the garage, liked to pull up right outside the front door and enter that way. As if he had servants who would move the car for him...which he didn't.

Tiny pulled over a few houses down and turned off the engine.

"Let's do this," he said firmly.

Some of his confidence seeped into Maisy. She wasn't doing anything wrong. This was her house too. She could go in if she wanted to. Taking a deep breath, she tightened her fingers around Jack's as she climbed out of the backseat.

They walked toward the house as if they had every right to be there—because they did. They didn't slink around, didn't cross through yards like burglars. Maisy held the key to the house tightly in her hand and tried to slow her heartbeat as they neared the front door. Holding her breath, she pushed the key into the lock and breathed a sigh of relief when it turned.

They stepped into the house, and Brick shut the door behind them. The house was eerily quiet. It was still early, at least for Jason, and because he'd gotten rid of Paige and the other women who worked in the house, no one was around. There was no smell of breakfast coming from the kitchen, and even in the few weeks she'd been gone, the lack of a housecleaner was obvious. There was dust and trash everywhere. Takeout bags lay discarded on the floor, as if whoever had dropped them assumed someone else would pick them up. The house smelled a little funky too, as if Jason had thrown a party, alcohol had been spilled, and no one had cleaned it up.

"Come on, Maisy, let's find this evidence," Tiny said in a barely there whisper.

Nodding, Maisy pointed toward the stairs. As they climbed, she glanced over at Jack. The muscle in his jaw was ticking again, and she knew this house held some not-so-great memories for him too. True, he didn't know he'd been kidnapped for most of the time he was here, but that wouldn't matter.

They walked silently past Jason's room toward hers. When the door swung open, Maisy couldn't stop the gasp that left her mouth at seeing the destruction in front of her.

Not one item in the large room had been left untouched.

Drawers were opened and their contents strewn all over the floor. The bedding and the mattress itself had been shredded, stuffing spilling out and joining the other stuff on the floor. The carpet was stained with what Maisy assumed was red paint, but the effect was creepy because it looked like blood. The clothes that had been in the closet were torn down and tossed everywhere.

Stepping into the room, Maisy walked in a daze toward the bathroom. Her toiletries had been emptied all over the counter and floor. Toothpaste, shampoo, even the small bottle of perfume her mom had given her when she'd turned thirteen had been emptied.

She knew without a doubt Jason had done this. In a fit of rage, he'd come in here and destroyed everything.

Instead of getting upset, Maisy was furious. He'd had a temper tantrum like a toddler because he hadn't gotten what he wanted—money that wasn't his to begin with. He'd kidnapped Jack, lied to him, treated her like shit, and *he* was mad!

For the first time, Maisy realized what a lucky escape she'd had. If he hadn't kidnapped Jack, if he hadn't been such a greedy asshole, she probably would've joined Martha under that slab sooner rather than later.

"Where'd you hide the stuff, Maisy?" Brick asked gently.

Pressing her lips together, Maisy turned away from the mess in the bathroom and headed for the window. Once upon a time, she'd loved to sit on the small window seat her dad had made for her so she could read books comfortably while looking outside. The books that had sat lovingly for years on the small shelf under the seat were all destroyed now. Their pages ripped out, covers bent and stomped on. Paint poured over everything.

Maisy knelt on the floor and pushed some of the mess aside. She held her breath as she reached for the loose board. There was just enough room at one edge to get her fingernail under. She pulled it up—and heard Tiny swear when he saw nothing in the hole under the floor.

She simply grinned to herself and reached down. The hole was long, and she'd stuffed the evidence all the way back, out of sight, just in case someone *did* find her hidey-hole.

She didn't realize how tense she'd been until her fingers brushed against the small bag she'd hidden back there. Sitting up, she pulled it out and held it up to the others.

"That it?" Brick asked.

She nodded.

"You sure?"

She nodded again.

"I'll hold onto it for you," Jack said, reaching for the small blue bag.

Without hesitation, Maisy let him take it from her. He stuffed it into a pocket on the vest he was wearing. She'd wondered why he'd packed it, because it didn't seem like something he'd usually wear. Then she'd realized how handy it was when she saw the multiple pockets held things like knives, zip-ties, and other objects that could come in handy for a badass like her husband.

Bag secure, he held his hand down to help her up off the floor.

"The next step was to pack your things, but..." Brick's voice faded as they all looked around the room.

Maisy was sad for a moment when she saw her favorite sweatpants covered in paint on the floor. The picture of cows she'd always loved, broken in half and also paint-splattered. All her belongings, destroyed.

But she took a deep breath. As she'd thought earlier, it was just stuff. Alaska and the other women had gone out of their way to make her feel comfortable and bought her so many cool clothing items. Jasna had drawn her a picture of Melba the cow to make her smile, and it was tacked to the wall back in Jack's cabin.

Thankful that she'd put her mom's ring, one of her dad's handkerchiefs, and a picture of her parents in her hiding place months ago, for safekeeping, Maisy turned to Jack. "I don't want anything from here. I have everything I need back at home."

Home. People threw that word around without thought. She'd always done the same. But the thing was, a home wasn't four walls and a roof. It was anyplace—or any *person*—that made you feel safe. And this house hadn't been safe for years. Ever since her parents were killed. She hadn't felt safe first because the person or people who'd shot her mom and dad were still on the loose. Then because of Jason. He'd made her life a living hell, and she'd been happy to lose herself in the fog of drugs to escape it.

Her home was wherever Jack was. It didn't matter if it was in Washington, New Mexico, or the other side of the moon. As long as Jack was by her side, she was home.

"Right, then let's get the hell out of here," Brick said brusquely.

Jack once more took Maisy's hand in his and they

followed Brick, with Tiny bringing up the rear as they headed out of her room and down the hall. They made it downstairs, but that's when their luck ran out.

Jason was standing in the living room, and he looked up in surprise as Maisy and the others appeared.

"Well, well, well," he drawled. "If it isn't my baby sister and her husband, returning home."

Maisy gaped. Jason looked *awful*. His hair hadn't been combed, brown tufts were sticking up all over his head. He hadn't shaved in what had to be a few days, and she could smell his body odor from where she was standing across the room. He obviously hadn't showered in quite a while, and his clothes hung off his gaunt-looking frame.

She was shocked by his appearance. Her brother had always prided himself on his looks. Now, he simply looked like a bum.

"Jason," she said, not sure what else to say.

"I'm guessing since you're here, that means you've completely fucked me over," Jason said.

Maisy frowned. "What?"

"You did it, didn't you? Signed the papers."

Understanding dawned. "Yes."

"You stole this house, and the money from my account too," Jason accused.

"It wasn't your money," Jack said, speaking up for the first time. "It was Maisy's."

"It was mine!" Jason shouted, making Maisy jump.

Jack steadied her, and she felt Tiny come up closer behind them.

"*My* money! Who took care of you when Mom and Dad died? Me! Instead of taking the job I was offered, I came home to babysit my little sister. You were a fucking mess! Couldn't function without me. You would've killed yourself if I hadn't gotten you to a doctor. You were out of it for years. *Years*, Maise! And this house isn't cheap! There was the mortgage, the housekeepers, the cook, the electricity. I took care of it all while you wallowed like a pathetic worm!"

Maisy clenched her teeth. She hated when Jason reminded her of that time. It was true, she hadn't coped well with the death of their parents, but he hadn't done much to help, simply encouraged her to take the drugs to make her forget everything.

"And what thanks do I get? Letters in the mail informing me that you've canceled policies, stolen my money, taken my name off the accounts—you're a fucking *bitch*!"

"I canceled the life insurance policies you took out on me and Jack without our permission," Maisy said evenly. "And you were stealing my monthly stipend because you'd spent your inheritance *and* all the life insurance you got from Mom and Dad."

She felt calm. Her heart was beating fast and she was a little shaky, but it felt good to be able to stand up to Jason for once.

He took a step toward her, but Brick was there, stepping between him and Maisy.

Jason scowled. "Who's this? You fucking him too? You liked taking your husband's cock well enough, we all heard you moaning and gagging for it. You're a fucking *whore*. Sleeping with a man you only knew a few days. If I'd known how much you loved cock, I would've sold your body for some extra cash long ago. Made a little money off all my friends. And make no mistake, I *bought* your husband. No one else would have you because you're fucking pathetic and hideous!"

Maisy blanched. She wasn't ashamed of what she and Jack had done. Their lovemaking was beautiful, and Jason's crude comments couldn't change that. But she didn't like him talking about Jack that way.

"You kidnapped him," Maisy said between clenched teeth.

"Because you weren't gonna find a man on your own!" Jason yelled. "I did it for *you*! You're so naïve. Did you really think you could just continue living here, no job, no way of making money, for the rest of your life? I did you a favor. Besides, it looks like you don't have any complaints now."

"You're done," Jack said, pushing Maisy behind him.

"Fuck you!" Jason said with a sneer. "You think I give a shit what you think? You're even more pathetic than my sister. A real man would've fought. Wouldn't have lost his mind—literally—after being stuck in a trunk for what, twenty minutes? You bought my story hook, line, and sinker. Without even blinking. You were just happy to stick your dick in my sister's holes. If you weren't so weak, so laughable, you would've known you hadn't met my sister until the moment you woke up."

Maisy could feel Jack vibrating in front of her. She felt sick at hearing Jason's words. Couldn't imagine what Jack was feeling.

"The only reason you took her with you when you left was because you realized you could get your hands on her money. She's loaded. Fucking rich as hell. And if you think you'll get that money because you're her husband, you're wrong!" Jason laughed then, a high-pitched, hysterical laugh that made the hair on Maisy's arms stand up.

"Your marriage wasn't legal. How could you be stupid enough to think it was? Your real name isn't on the stupid certificate. It was good enough to fool the government and that asshole at the bank, but it wasn't real. Everything was forged. Even the guy who married you didn't have the credentials. So if you think you'll get one damn cent, you're stupider than I thought you were."

"We're done here," Brick said in a low, furious tone.

Maisy wanted to roll her eyes. She'd always known her marriage to Jack wasn't legal. But Jason was right—it *had* been good enough to fool the bank. And once that money hit her account, she could give it to anyone she wanted... married or not. Now that she was out from under her brother's thumb, she certainly wouldn't be giving *him* any of it.

"Go ahead and leave, sister dear. But this isn't over. You owe me!"

"Owe you?" Maisy said incredulously. "I don't owe you a damn thing. You've stolen my money for years. You hurt me, Jason. Over and over. You're an abusive bully, and I'm done taking your shit. And this *is* over. I'm going to do what I should've done the day Martha disappeared."

Jason's eyes narrowed. "And what's that?"

"You *know* what. I know, Jase. I know what you did. To Martha and probably to our parents."

"You don't know shit," Jason said, not correcting her on his nickname for the first time Maisy could ever remember.

"I know you kidnapped an innocent man. And I know you won't come after me, because you'll be too busy trying to come up with more lies to cover the ones you've already told. Do you remember all the details about what you told the cops all those years ago when Martha disappeared, seemingly out of thin air? I've heard it's really hard to remember lies and tell them the same way every time. Karma, Jason. It's coming for you."

Maisy felt proud of herself. She'd finally stood up to her brother and it felt really good.

But then he moved, coming at her so fast, Maisy stumbled backward over her feet.

She ran into Tiny, who immediately steadied her, then swung her around so she was behind all three men, who'd formed a kind of wall between her and her obviously unhinged brother.

Brick pushed Jason back so hard, he fell on his ass. He leaped back to his feet, and the hate in his eyes made Maisy flinch.

"Get her out of here," Jack ordered Tiny.

"We should all go," Maisy said desperately.

"I'm thinking your brother and I need to have words," Jack said.

"No, Jack. Let's just go. He doesn't matter."

But it was as if Jack didn't hear her. His back was ramrod straight and when she touched him, she could feel every muscle in his back tense.

"Please, Jack," she said again. "I'm begging you, let's just go." He'd once told her that he'd never make her beg for anything. She was using his words against him. She knew it, and she didn't care. Anything to get them away from her brother's poisonous tongue.

"This isn't done!" Jason yelled as Brick and Jack began to back toward the front door.

Maisy didn't care what her brother said, it *was* done. Her brother would hopefully be going to prison for a very long time as a result of what he'd done to Jack, to Martha. Ry would send over the electronic evidence she'd discovered, and maybe if the police dug hard enough, they'd even be able to find who Jason solicited to kill their parents.

She felt sad and relieved all at the same time. She was finally free of her brother's control. She couldn't think about his final shouted threat. She was too focused on getting out of this house once and for all.

Maisy didn't breathe a sigh of relief until all four of them were out of the house and the door had slammed behind them. Jack took her arm and hustled her down the sidewalk toward their car. No one said a word as they climbed in and Tiny drove off.

But Maisy was internally freaking out. Not because of what Jason had said. Not because she now had to go to the police station and convince a detective that her brother was a murderer.

No, it was because Jack was sitting next to her, looking out the window...not touching her.

In the last twenty-four hours, he'd touched her every second possible, like he had before his memories returned. He'd held her hand on the plane, in the car, had his hand on her thigh as they ate, held her all night...and now he was inches away, but it might as well have been miles.

His jaw was tight, head turned away, his eyes focused on the landscape as they passed. Maisy had no idea what he was thinking. Which of her brother's insults he'd taken to heart. But it was obvious something Jason said was affecting him now, making him distance himself from her.

She wanted to beg him to talk to her, but with Brick

and Tiny in earshot, this wasn't the place. All she could do was bide her time. Pray that he'd realize Jason was desperate, full of shit, and would say anything to get a rise out of either of them.

* * *

Stone sat in a chair in the police station staring straight ahead. He'd rebuffed both Tiny and Brick's attempts to talk. He couldn't stop replaying the words Maisy's brother had spewed. He'd already been furious over the shit he'd said to his sister, and for some reason hadn't been ready for the venom to be turned his way.

He should've been. He'd heard worse when he was a POW. But the things Jason had said to him had hit their mark with deadly accuracy.

A real man would've fought.

It was true, Stone hadn't fought at all. He'd been caught unaware and had been knocked unconscious before he even knew he was in danger.

Wouldn't have lost his mind—literally—after being stuck in a trunk for what, twenty minutes?

Instead of figuring out how to get out of that trunk, disabling the brake lights, using the emergency release handle that all cars had now, Stone had freaked out. His mind had shut down, unable to deal with the stress of the situation. What kind of man did that make him?

A pathetic one, just like Jason had accused.

You bought my story hook, line, and sinker. Without even blinking.

That was true too. Many of the details Maisy had given him about his past hadn't rung true. But Stone hadn't truly second-guessed the idea that he was married. Hadn't offered much in the way of hesitation because of how "right" things felt between them. And all his training, all the things he'd seen and done, all he'd been through at the hands of international terrorists, hadn't been enough for him to do something about the clear threat he'd sensed from her brother from the moment he'd awakened.

If you weren't so weak, so laughable, you would've known you hadn't met my sister until the moment you woke up.

He *should've* known. His instincts should've kicked in. Instead, he'd been happy enough to lose himself in Maisy, to ignore all the warning signs that were screaming at him that something wasn't right. Not only that, but he'd let Jason continually abuse Maisy, telling himself not to cause even more trouble between a brother and sister who already had a tumultuous relationship.

He'd screwed up so badly. He *was* pathetic. Brick, or Pipe, or Owl...*none* of his friends would've fallen for the story he'd been fed. They wouldn't have been weak enough to let their brains shut down to begin with. Henley had explained to him that he'd experienced trauma-induced amnesia, which was sudden and rare, though a bit more common among combat vets and abuse victims...but that didn't make him feel better in the least.

He was lost in a fog of self-loathing, and not even the sight of a pale and trembling Maisy coming toward him after being in an interrogation room for two hours could shake him out of it. In fact, seeing her made him feel more ashamed. He'd done *nothing* to help this woman. Because of him, she'd been put through even *more* hell. All her things were destroyed. Every last possession she owned.

Stone stood, but he couldn't make his legs work.

Couldn't make himself walk toward her. Brick did what he should've, going to Maisy and wrapping a protective arm around her shoulders.

"What's wrong with you?" Tiny hissed. "Get your head out of your ass, man."

Stone nodded...but still didn't move.

Tiny grabbed his shoulder and turned toward the door, practically shoving him toward it.

The ride back to the hotel from the police station was a blur. Stone heard Brick and Tiny questioning Maisy about her visit with the detectives. Asking if she thought they believed her. A part of him was relieved when she said they were going to look into it immediately and get a search warrant as soon as possible, but as much as he wanted to participate in the conversation, he couldn't.

Pathetic.

Weak.

Stupid.

The words echoed in his head. He tried to block them out, but it was impossible.

When they got back to the hotel, Tiny asked, "You want to eat at the restaurant for lunch? Or maybe for dinner again tonight?"

"Um...I don't think so. I just want to go to the room and crash," Maisy said. "I'm not hungry."

"All right. If you change your mind, let Stone know. He can order takeout," Brick told her.

"I will."

"We'll meet you downstairs in the morning at six. We have an early flight. We'll be back home before you know it."

"Good. I'm looking forward to getting out of here. I

know I'll probably have to come back for the trial, if there ever is one, but for now, I can't imagine stepping foot back here anytime soon."

Brick and Tiny both hugged Maisy before they all got into the elevator to take them to their floor.

Brick held Stone back as Tiny walked Maisy down the hall to their room.

"What's up with you?" he asked.

"Nothing."

"Bullshit. Maisy's been through hell, you need to snap out of whatever funk you're in and help her deal."

"I will," Stone said, knowing full well he was lying. Maisy deserved better than him. She should have someone who could stand up for her when the shit hit the fan. And he obviously wasn't that man. Who knew when he'd have another panic attack and freak out? Their marriage wasn't legal, the best thing to do would be to let her go. Free her to live her life. She had the money now to go anywhere, be anything she wanted to be. He had no doubt Ry would figure out a way for her to keep the inheritance even if it came out that her marriage wasn't legal.

Brick eyed him, then shook his head. "Don't fuck this up, Stone. I mean it. She's the best thing that's ever happened to you."

Stone knew his friend was right. Knew it down to his bones. But he wasn't the best thing for Maisy. Not even close.

He nodded, then turned and walked down the hall.

The door closed behind him, then it was just him and Maisy in the room. She stared at him for a long moment before sighing and turning toward the bathroom. "Just being around Jason made me feel gross. I'm going to take another shower."

"Okay," Stone said, still feeling disconnected to her and everything that had happened at that house.

He paced the room for a few minutes after he heard the water in the bathroom turn on.

He couldn't stay here. The room was too small. The walls were closing in on him.

He quickly changed into a pair of shorts and a T-shirt, then knocked on the bathroom door.

"Yeah?" Maisy called out.

Stone cracked the door open an inch. "I'm going downstairs to work out. Don't leave the room for any reason. Okay?" He wasn't so lost in his head that he'd ever forget to warn her to stay safe.

"I won't. Jack?"

"Yeah?"

"Are you okay?"

He should be asking *her* that. Another failure on his part. "Yeah, I'm good. I just need to let off some steam. I'll be back."

"All right."

Closing the bathroom door, Stone took a deep breath and left the room.

* * *

Maisy let the tears fall from her eyes unchecked. The water from the shower immediately washed them away. She wasn't sure why she was crying. Everything had gone pretty well. She'd gotten her inheritance, picked up the evidence against Jason, confronted him, and even convinced the detectives that they probably had a pretty solid case against her brother.

But somewhere between the confrontation and the police station, she'd lost Jack.

She didn't know how or why, but he'd definitely checked out. He was there, but wasn't.

Her brother's rants were horrible, but nothing she hadn't heard before. He loved to tell her how pathetic she was. The words barely registered anymore. Besides, he was a freaking murderer, how could she take anything he said to heart?

But maybe Jack had? Or maybe after seeing Jason again, being in that house, he'd changed his mind about forgiving her?

She had no idea, and it sucked. All she knew was that Jack didn't seem to want anything to do with her now. Hell, even at a hotel, he'd gotten as far away from her as he could.

Taking a deep breath, Maisy wiped her eyes. She'd brought this on herself. How could she think for a second that things with her and Jack could work out, given how they'd started? Her brother was right, she'd fallen for a complete stranger. Had gone to bed with him without a second thought.

But she loved him. Even after only knowing him a short time, she well and truly loved Jack.

Sighing, she got out of the shower and dried off. Going into the hotel room, she put her clothes back on, knowing she wouldn't be able to sleep like she'd planned, and sat on the bed. It would be a long day and an awkward night, what with Jack avoiding her and only one bed in the room. But it was big, they should be able to share without touching.

The thought depressed her. One of her favorite things in the world was snuggling up to Jack while they slept.

Maisy had no idea how long she'd been propped up against the headboard, arms around her legs as she stared out the window into the cloudy afternoon sky, when she heard a knock on the door. Thinking Jack had probably forgotten his key in his haste to get away from her, or maybe it got demagnetized or something, she got out of bed. Without looking through the peephole, she unlocked the bolt and opened the door.

The second her brain registered who was standing there, Maisy knew she'd made a huge mistake.

She tried to slam the door but was punched in the face before she could even get it shut halfway. She collapsed to the floor in a heap. Then she was hauled upright by a brutal hand on her upper arm.

She whimpered as Don Coffey began to drag her down the hall. "Don't make a sound. Or I'll kill that asshole working out downstairs. Understand?"

Maisy nodded immediately. She had no doubt that Don would do exactly what he threatened. He obviously wasn't the kind of man who thought twice about hitting a woman in the face or shooting a complete stranger.

He bypassed the elevators and dragged her into the stairwell. They went down, Maisy stumbling over most of the steps because of his fast pace, and exited out a side door into the parking lot. Before she knew what was happening, Don shoved her into his car and was driving away.

Away from Jack.

Away from safety.

Probably taking her to Jason.

She was as good as dead. She just prayed Jack would realize she hadn't left of her own accord. That he'd know she didn't want to leave him, she'd just made a mistake. That she'd had no choice.

Terror threatened to overwhelm her, but she took a deep breath. She had to stay strong. Jack, Brick, and Tiny would find her. Would realize what happened and who took her. She just had to hang on until then.

Surreptitiously glancing around her, she tried to come up with a plan to get away from Don. She inched her hand toward the door handle, but he simply chuckled.

"Go ahead and try it," he told her.

So she did. Nothing happened. The door definitely didn't open.

"Child locks. They come in handy for times like this."

Maisy did *not* like this man. I mean, who thought like that? There was no telling how many other women he'd prevented from escaping with child locks.

But she wasn't giving up. No way. Not when she was on the cusp of being free once and for all. Free to do what she wanted. To live the rest of her life with Jack...at least, she hoped that was the plan. After today, she wasn't so sure. It figured that her brother would manage to mess up the best thing that had ever happened to her.

She tried to remain calm and not freak out as Don drove the familiar roads back to her childhood home. He pulled around the back of the house, turned off the engine, climbed out, then reached back in and grabbed Maisy's arm once more.

She winced in pain as she did her best to move quickly, trying to avoid having her arm pulled out of its socket when Don yanked her from the car. She stumbled as he marched her to the kitchen door and pushed her through. She wasn't in the least surprised when he walked her toward her brother's office.

He opened the door and shoved her in, hard. Maisy went down on her hands and knees, quickly scrambling to her feet as she pushed her hair out of her face.

"Thank you. Now get out," Jason said coldly.

Confused, Maisy looked toward the door.

"Not you, bitch," Jason said with a huff. "You." He pointed at Don.

"I'm gone...as soon as I get paid."

"Right. Go ahead and take the TV from the other room."

Don snorted. "Is that supposed to be a joke? I want the money you promised me."

"I don't have it. Not yet."

"What the fuck?" Don asked, sounding extremely pissed off.

Maisy did her best to appear invisible. The last thing she wanted was to get in the middle of the fight that was clearly brewing between her brother and his friend. She couldn't help but think about Lara's story. How the serial killer who'd kidnapped her and Owl, and the guy he'd hired to do the actual kidnapping, had gotten so pissed at each other, the two men ended up killing each other in a shootout. Maybe she'd be lucky enough to have that happen here too.

Jason stood up from the desk so fast, his chair screeched on the hardwood before teetering and falling backward, clanging to the floor.

"You'll get your money as soon as I get *my* money!" he yelled.

"This is bullshit!" Don told him. "You said twenty K. Follow your sister and her asshole fake husband and snatch her when I had the chance. Well, I got the chance. The guy went down to the gym. I went up and knocked on the door. She opened right up, even though she obviously couldn't check the damn security hole. I should know—I had my finger over the lens."

"How'd you know what room I was in?" Maisy asked, not able to keep quiet.

"I seduced the maid," Don said with a sneer. "And by *seduced*, I mean I threatened her after I took what I wanted from her."

Maisy pressed her lips together. She *really* didn't like this man.

Don turned back to Jason. "I want the twenty thousand you promised me."

"And you'll get it. My sister's got millions now."

"Fine. I want *fifty* K then," Don told Jason.

Her brother narrowed his eyes at his so-called friend. She held her breath and prayed they'd both pull guns out from their waistbands and start shooting each other.

"This is why I didn't ask you to marry her," Jason said in a somewhat calm tone.

Maisy's dreams of a huge shootout died. She recognized that tone. He was planning something. Was going to double-cross Don. She had no doubt. He used that tone with her right before he informed her of something she wouldn't like.

"I need time to...talk...to my dear sister. I'll have your money tomorrow."

Don's eyes narrowed. "You better."

"I will," Jason reassured him. "We've known each other a long time. You know a lot about me. You know I'm not going to screw you over."

Maisy wanted to snort-laugh. Her brother would screw over anyone and everyone if it meant he got what he wanted. He'd killed his own *parents* for money. Besides, it wasn't as if Don was going to whine to the police that Jason didn't give him the money he promised for kidnapping his sister.

"Fine. I'll be back tomorrow. Noon. You better have my dough."

"I'll have it. I'm sure my sis will be cooperative. And if she's not...well, it's not as if she needs any of the fingers on her left hand to add me to her account, since she's right-handed."

Both men laughed, and Maisy felt as if she was going to throw up.

"You need help getting her to the basement?" Don asked after a moment.

"The day I need help getting this bitch to do what I want is the day you might as well lock me up and throw away the fucking key."

"Just checking," Don said, then he stared at her with a look that made her feel dirty just for being on the receiving end. "Maybe tomorrow you'll let me have that time with her you promised, before you do whatever it is you're ultimately going to do with her."

Jason shrugged. "Not sure why you'd want her. She's hideous."

"Don't have to look at her face to do what I'm gonna do," Don said with a grin.

Once again, Maisy felt bile rise up in her throat.

"Fine. Works for me."

"Good. Tomorrow. Have my money, Jason, or I'm not going to be happy."

"I'll have it," Jason said confidently.

Don nodded, then turned and walked out of the office.

"Jason—" Maisy started, but her brother came at her so quickly, the words died in her throat as she stumbled backward. But there was nowhere to go. Jason grabbed her arm in the same place Don had, making her wince, and headed for the door.

She tried to pry his hand off her arm, with no luck. Next, she tried pulling her arm out of his grasp, but he only tightened his fingers around her harder. Then she panicked, and began fighting him in earnest. It was almost ridiculous how easily he subdued her. No matter what she did, how she tried to kick or bite, he managed to keep her firmly in his grip.

"Enough!" he barked, shaking her so hard it made her head wobble on her neck.

"Please, Jason, we can talk about this," Maisy pleaded. She wasn't going to sign anything. She'd rather die than have him take one more dime from her. But it wasn't about the money, not really. It was about standing up for herself for the first time in her life. For not caving to her brother. Did she want to die? No. Not when she had so much to live for. But if it was a choice between giving her brother what he wanted and dying, she'd choose the latter.

"Time for talking's done, sis," he said. "You made your choice. That asshole over me. A guy you just met. His dick must have magical qualities or something if you would choose him over your brother, your own flesh and blood, the guy who took you in when no one else would, when you would've ended up in a foster home. Who made sure you got the meds you needed so you didn't end up in a nuthouse. Fine. Good. Whatever. Now, I want what's *mine*."

Maisy wanted to scream at him. Tell him that he'd *had* his inheritance. That it wasn't her fault he'd spent it all. Wasn't fair that he wanted to steal *her* money too, that he'd already stolen enough over the years. But she was concentrating too much on staying on her feet as Jason quickly dragged her toward the door to the basement.

"I'm thinking a little time in the safe room will change your attitude. I still have some things to do this afternoon. But come tonight, we'll be having a chat. And by chat, I mean you signing papers that will add me to your bank account, that will grant me sole decision-making in how that money is spent. In the morning, I'll head over there, tell those assholes that you're bedridden and can't come in —something about your period, men hate talking about that shit. Then I'll get Don's money, come back here, let him have some quality one-on-one time with you...then, Maise...I'm sorry, but you have to go."

Her blood ran cold. "Jason, if I disappear, people will notice. I have friends...a husband."

"Oh, I'm counting on it," he said with a laugh as he flicked on the light at the top of the stairs that led to the basement. "I'll call and make a missing persons report. Tell them all about your recent mental breakdown, how you married a guy after only knowing him for five days, how he was able to get control of your fortune, and now you're gone. Eventually, they'll find your body in a field somewhere...and when they do a rape test, they'll find my dear friend's DNA inside you. Don'll be blamed. Bim, bam, boom. Done. He'll go to prison, and I'll be home free. The grieving brother."

Maisy gaped at her brother in confusion. What was he even talking about? Don? He'd tell the cops that she'd married *Don*? How could he be so stupid? He had a marriage certificate with "Jack Smith" named as the groom. And his so-called "friend" would tell the cops everything about her inheritance—and everything Jason had done to get it.

And then there was Jack and his friends. They'd probably go to the police the second they found her missing. There could only be one person to blame, and Jack, Tiny, and Brick knew exactly who that person was.

Not to mention, hiding her at their house was ridiculous! It would be the first place everyone would look for her.

Her brother had lost it. There were enough holes in his story to drive a semi-truck through. He was clearly unhinged.

"I'd forgotten about Don wanting to have a go at you, but that'll work out better than I even planned. I'll have to see if I can't snag his phone while he's busy with you...take it with me when I dump your body. So when the cops check his digital trail, they'll see him in the area your body was found—and my phone will be here at the house, giving me an alibi."

God, there was virtually no way his plan could work. But that didn't mean she wasn't in danger.

She missed the last step and went to her knees, but Jason didn't slow down. It took her a moment to get to her feet again, and by the time she did, her brother was in front of the safe room. Her parents had it built because they worried about someone targeting them for their money. Ironic, considering their own son was now going to use it to torture and eventually kill his sister for the money they'd left her.

He opened the door and walked Maisy over to the other side of the room, where he'd attached chains to the wall. He'd obviously planned this, or more likely, he'd planned to keep Jack here after he'd forced him to marry her. Maisy fought once more, but she was no match for Jason. He snapped the manacles on her wrists and stepped back.

The chains fastened to the cuffs were affixed to the wall at about hip level, and were roughly three feet long. Long enough for her to stand up and move around a little, strong enough that she wouldn't be able to rip them out of the wall or anything else heroines in movies typically did to save themselves.

"Don't piss or shit on the floor. If you do, I'm not cleaning it up. Go in there," Jason said, pointing to a bucket against the wall within her reach. "I'll be back later. Be good." Then he laughed before turning his back on her.

"Jase, please! You don't have to do this," Maisy told him desperately.

Her brother turned. "How many fucking times do I have to tell you *not* to call me that?"

Then he left without another word, shutting the door behind him. Thankfully, it locked from the inside, not the outside. He couldn't actually lock her in, but the chains attached to the wall kept her from getting to the door to lock him out. Besides, it wouldn't do her any good. If she locked herself in the room, she was still screwed. Yes, Don and Jason couldn't get to her, but she'd eventually die of thirst. Once upon a time her parents had stored months' worth of provisions in this room, but those were long gone.

Putting her back against the wall, Maisy slid down until her butt touched the floor, then she wrapped her arms around her knees and cried. Cried for the brother she used to know. Cried because she was scared. Because she knew when Jack got back to their room, he'd freak out when he found her gone.

But then she took a deep breath. She had no idea what had spooked Jack earlier. Why he was so out of sorts. But she had complete faith in him. As soon as he realized she wasn't down the hall visiting with his friends, or anywhere else in the hotel, the first place he'd think to look was here. He'd come for her. Even if he'd decided he didn't want to be married to her, that she was too much trouble or he just couldn't forgive her after all, he wouldn't leave her in the hands of her brother. She had no doubt about that.

She had to hang on until he and Brick and Tiny came for her. She just hoped whatever it was Jason was doing took long enough for the cavalry to come to her rescue. Before her brother could return to torture her.

The craziest thing of all was, once upon a time, if Jason was the brother she remembered, if he'd just *asked* her, she probably would've gladly shared her inheritance.

Swallowing hard and wiping her cheeks on her arm, Maisy lifted her head. She couldn't waste any more time sitting here like a freaking damsel in distress. She needed to figure out a way to escape. When Jason returned, she'd do whatever she could to get away. If she could manage it, she'd tell the cops everything, then hopefully go home to The Refuge with Jack. They could work on whatever it was that was bothering him.

She wasn't ready to give up. She loved Jack with all her heart. Would fight for the right to stay by his side.

CHAPTER TWENTY

"What the hell are you doing?" Brick growled.

Stone ignored him as he clicked on the link Ry had just sent. It hadn't taken him long to realize he was being an idiot. He'd let Maisy's asshole brother's words get to him, just like the man wanted.

He'd been running on the treadmill in the small workout room at the hotel and literally came to an abrupt halt, barely preventing himself from being thrown against the wall behind him by the fast-moving tread. He wanted to kick his own ass.

Somehow, Jason had known exactly how to make Stone doubt not only himself, but Maisy as well. He wasn't weak. Shit, he'd survived something most men wouldn't have been able to last five minutes through. He'd been tortured by fucking *terrorists*, and yet, here he was.

He and Owl had been through hell, and they'd somehow managed to find women who didn't pity them, didn't think they were lesser men because of what they'd gone through. They loved them exactly as they were. And their experiences made them the men they were today.

He'd been such an ass. Maisy had needed him to be supportive and encouraging, and he'd fucked that up completely. He hadn't been there for her when she'd talked to the detectives, and that had to have been extremely hard for her. He hadn't insisted he stay by her side while she told her story. Hadn't done a damn thing.

Taking the stairs two at a time, he'd rushed back up to their room to apologize. To grovel. To tell Maisy what a dick he'd been—but she hadn't been there. Stone hadn't panicked, not at first. Had simply gone down the hall to Brick and Tiny's room, having no doubt that's where Maisy would be found.

But she wasn't there either. He was confused for half a second—then terror set in.

Jason had gotten to her.

Sure, maybe she went down to get ice, or to the lobby for a snack, but deep down, he knew she wouldn't do either of those things. Not by herself.

There was only one person in the world who had a reason to hurt Maisy. Her own damn brother. And Stone had left her alone and vulnerable. Another mark against him. Another thing he'd have to make up for.

Brick had rushed off to search the common areas of the hotel. And while Tiny had tried to reassure him, offering reasons why Maisy could be gone and where else she might be—eating by herself down in the restaurant, swimming in the pool—Stone had been busy texting Ry.

Unbeknownst to his friends or Maisy, he'd had a long talk with the woman before they'd left for this trip. He was intrigued by her abilities. And since he'd been uneasy about bringing Maisy back to Seattle, he'd wanted to see if she had any suggestions for keeping her safe.

Ry did.

"Seriously, Stone, what the fuck are you doing? We need to go look for Maisy." Also from Brick, who'd returned a few minutes ago, his search unsuccessful.

"I know where she is," Stone said as he stared at the map in front of him.

"What? How?"

"Where?"

He wasn't surprised at his friends' questions. "Ry gave me trackers," he told them. "I've got one, and I gave one to Maisy. Well, I didn't *give* it to her. I slipped it into her pocket this morning. It looks like a quarter, but it's not."

"No shit?" Brick asked.

"No shit. I talked to Ry, who apparently consulted with Tex. He suggested the tracker."

"Well, that's not a surprise. The man does love his freaking tracking devices," Tiny said.

"Exactly."

"How'd you know you'd need it?" Brick asked.

"I didn't. I mean, I hoped I wouldn't, but if her brother was willing to go to the extreme of kidnapping a complete stranger and incarcerating him for three months, then probably killing him, just to get his hands on Maisy's money...I wasn't taking any chances."

"So he took her?" Tiny asked.

"I don't know. But I'm guessing probably not. He wouldn't want to chance having his face on camera anywhere, so he could claim he didn't know what was happening. Ry's working on hacking into the surveillance cameras here at the hotel, so we'll know for sure. But ultimately it doesn't matter. He's got her. She's at the house."

"What are we waiting for? Let's go get her! We can definitely take that asshole!" Tiny exclaimed, heading for the door.

"You guys aren't going anywhere," Stone informed them.

"What?" Brick and Tiny asked in unison.

"I need you to rally the troops. Maisy laid the foundation today when she told her story to the detectives. I need you guys to contact one of them, tell him that Jason's got Maisy and is holding her under duress to try to get her money, then come to the house."

"And what are you going to do?" Brick asked.

Stone narrowed his eyes. "I'm gonna go get my wife back."

"That's not a good idea," Brick warned.

"The hell it's not. Look, she's gone because I was a dumb fuck. I let that asshole get to me."

Brick glared at Stone. "If you're referring to his fucking speech about being weak, he was talking out his ass."

"Yeah, I realize that now, but I took his words to heart at the time. Look, I'm not like you and the others. Neither is Owl. We're damn good behind the controls of a chopper, wouldn't hesitate to fly into a sandstorm or a fucking hurricane, but boots on the ground isn't our thing...obviously. I fought when our chopper went down overseas, both Owl and I did, but it didn't matter, we were still captured and tortured. When Jason's goon did his thing, I didn't have a chance to fight back because I was hit from behind. And he was right, when I was in that trunk, I panicked. I didn't even try to escape. I'll have to live with that, but in the end...I got the best thing that has ever happened to me out of the ordeal."

"Maisy," Tiny filled in unnecessarily.

"Exactly. What happened, happened. Jason played dirty, and it's time I beat him at his own game."

"What's your plan?"

"While you and Tiny are convincing the cops to get a search warrant—which shouldn't be hard once we get the footage from the hotel cameras from Ry, and they see the map with the tracking info, combined with the shit Maisy told them today—I'm gonna walk right up to the front door and demand to see my wife."

"What? That's insane!" Tiny exclaimed.

"Actually, it's perfect," Brick said with a nod. "You said you don't have boots-on-the-ground skills."

"Jason could shoot him," Tiny warned.

"He could. But I don't think he will. He wants to see his sister suffer as much as possible. If we time things right, Jason will be too wrapped up with Stone's arrival to even think about it being a trap or wonder where *we* are. By the time he does, it'll be too late and he'll be done for."

"And if he hurts him? Or Maisy? Can you live with that?" Tiny asked Brick.

Brick met Stone's gaze head on. "I trust Stone. He can handle shit at the house until we get there."

His words meant the world to Stone. Brick was right. Jason could shoot him in the head the second he saw him. That would definitely hurt his sister in a way nothing else could. But even though he was taking a risk...he agreed with Brick. Jason was crazy. And with Stone at his mercy, he wouldn't be able to stop himself from gloating to his sister about how he had all the control. It would be his downfall. Stone would bet his life on it.

Was betting his life on it.

"And I'd say that even if it was Alaska in that basement, and Jason was that asshole trafficker who wanted to get his hands on her."

And *that* was why Brick was one of his best friends. The loyalty. The trust. The absolute certainty, even though he wasn't a Navy SEAL or a Delta Force Operative, that Stone could handle the situation at the house until help arrived.

Just then, a text notification sounded from Stone's phone. Looking down, he saw it was from Ry. Another link. Clicking on it, Stone watched as a man he definitely recognized knocked on his hotel door. The time stamp was from an hour ago.

As soon as Maisy opened the door, Don punched her, then reached down and grabbed her, hauling her out of the room with a grip that looked painful, forcing her down the hall. Stone's teeth clenched.

"What've you got?" Tiny asked.

Instead of answering, he sent the link to both his friends. "You can show that to the cops."

He waited while Brick and Tiny watched the short video clip, their bodies going tense when they witnessed what Maisy had endured.

"She probably thought it was me. I know she was worried about where my head was at. I left so fast after we got back to the room, she probably assumed I forgot my key. I'm gonna fix this. Once and for all. Her brother won't be an issue after tonight."

"No, he fucking will not. Go," Brick said. "Take the car.

We'll get a taxi to the police station and meet you at the house."

After getting the keys from Tiny, Stone headed for the door. He was still wearing shorts and a T-shirt, his standard workout gear, but the only thing on his mind was getting to Maisy. She had to be terrified. Wondering if he'd come for her.

He'd made a vow, one he had no plans to break. Once this was behind them, he'd make sure his wife never had a reason to doubt him again. He'd done nothing but break her trust, and if she took him back, he'd make sure it never happened again.

Maisy was the most amazing woman he'd ever met. Life kept kicking her in the face, and yet she could still see the good in people. Open herself up to others. She embraced a group of strangers at The Refuge and made them fall in love with her after a few short weeks.

Just as he had.

He loved Maisy. He hadn't said the words out loud since he'd regained his memory, and Stone regretted that deeply. She'd told him time and time again, probably hoping she'd hear the words returned. One more way he'd been an ass. But no longer.

She was his. Legal marriage license or not, she was *his*. Just as he was hers.

Time to prove it to Maisy.

CHAPTER TWENTY-ONE

Maisy had no idea what time it was. No idea how long she'd been in the safe room. All she knew was that her ass was numb from sitting on the concrete floor. And she was cold. And hungry. But those things were the least of her worries. She'd be hurting a lot more once Jason returned.

It was still hard for her to believe her own brother planned to cut her fingers off if she didn't sign the papers he put in front of her. But then again, he'd killed Martha, probably killed her parents, and had plans to frame his friend for *her* murder. What was a few fingers in the scope of things?

A sound from outside the room had Maisy jerking where she sat, the chains attaching her to the wall clanking. Her heart was pounding and every muscle was tense. She wouldn't make it easy for Jason to touch her. He'd have to sit on her to get to her hand. She'd use her fingernails to claw him so his DNA would be found on her body as well. Mark him as much as possible so maybe the cops would be suspicious.

Using a knife on her would also cause her to lose a lot of blood. If she could somehow get him to cut himself at the same time, and his blood mingled with hers, the people at the labs would be able to figure out that he'd had something to do with hurting her, as well as Don.

Her mind was going a mile a minute. All the murder shows she'd watched flashed through her brain as she tried to figure out a way to make Jason pay for his crimes, even after she was dead and gone.

The very last thing she expected to see when the door opened was Jack.

For a moment, her spirits soared—then her heart fell into her stomach when she saw Jason behind him, pointing a gun at his head. Her heart shattered into a million pieces. All it would take was Jason threatening Jack and she'd do whatever he asked. He could cut off every finger and every toe and she wouldn't make a peep of protest. Not if it meant keeping Jack safe.

"Hey, sis! Look who decided to join the party!" Jason said jovially as he entered the room. "Over there," he told Jack in a much harder tone.

Without complaint and as if he was joining them for an afternoon spot of tea, Jack went over to the wall on the other side of the room from her and sat where Jason had pointed.

"Put them on," Jason ordered, gesturing to the handcuffs with the gun in his hand.

Again, without a word, Jack did as he was told, clicking the handcuffs around his wrists.

Maisy tried to catch his eye. Tried to tell him without words to stop. To fight. *Something*. But Jack didn't look at her until he was as trapped as she was.

"Jack," she moaned in despair.

"It's okay," he told her.

"Yeah, sis, it's okay!" Jason crowed.

He tucked the gun into his waistband, and Maisy prayed it would misfire and shoot his dick off. Would serve him right. She should've been shocked at the bloodthirsty thought, and ten minutes ago, she might've been. But now that Jack was here? And at her brother's mercy? She didn't feel bad in the least.

"Let him go," she begged her brother.

"No." The word was flat and unequivocal.

"Please, Jason! You want me to sign everything over to you? Fine. I'll do it. Give me the papers. Just don't hurt him. He has nothing to do with any of this. Has *never* had anything to do with it."

"Don't, Maisy," Jack said.

She ignored him. "I'm serious! Let him go! I'll sign whatever you want."

"Oh, you'll give me my money," Jason told her. "But it's too late to let him go. You should know that by now."

"It's not," Maisy protested.

"This is all your fault!" Jason suddenly screamed, making Maisy snap her mouth closed and lean back against the wall. "If you weren't so stupid, so needy, so fucking hard to kill, this wouldn't be happening!"

Maisy stared at him with huge eyes. "What? What are you talking about?"

"Jason, what's your plan here, man?" Jack asked.

But her brother also ignored him. "Jesus, I drugged you for *years*, and instead of making you suicidal like the warnings said, the shit just made you more goddamn compliant.

Then I drugged you up to your fucking eyeballs! And instead of making your heart stop, it just put you to sleep—and you woke up *every goddamn time*! So I tried to create a nonprofit, so you could sign some papers to give your inheritance to my charity when you died, but it was too much frickin' work. I had to provide all this proof and shit to show the charity was legit. So that plan was out. I couldn't kill you without you being married, because all the money would go to *other* charities. Fucking Mom and Dad! Bloody do-gooders! Why couldn't they've had a normal will like everyone else?"

"You killed them," Maisy said in a low, even voice. Almost unemotional. She'd suspected it, had even told the police earlier that she was certain her brother had hired whoever had shot their parents, but she'd still held out a tiny shred of hope that she was wrong. That her brother wasn't *that* much of a monster. But that hope was now dead.

"Of course I did," Jason growled. "They were stingy as fuck. Did you know they refused to pay for my last two years of college? They had millions of dollars and wouldn't shell out a couple thousand for my tuition. They made me get a job! Fuck, no wonder my grades sucked. It was *their* fault, not mine!"

"What did you do?" Maisy asked.

"What I had to. I didn't want that stupid job they were so excited about. They ruined my life! And yet here *you* were, the favorite. Their angel. Good grades, doing all the extracurricular shit they wanted *me* to do that I hated. You could do no wrong. Anything you wanted, you got. It wasn't fair!"

"You killed them because you were *jealous?*"

"No. I killed them because I wanted their money. Money I *deserved.* Money I shouldn't have had to beg for every month!"

Maisy had no words for what she was hearing. But she figured while she had him talking... "And Martha?"

Jason snorted. "You *know* why that bitch died. She served her purpose."

"You aren't my brother. You're a monster," she hissed.

But Jason simply laughed. "Whatever. I don't care what you think. And it doesn't matter anyway, because soon I won't have to worry about you fucking things up for me anymore."

"You really think you'll get away with any of this?"

"I already have," Jason said smugly. "I wasn't even a suspect in Mom and Dad's carjacking. I was the poor grieving husband when Martha disappeared, and I've already told you who's going to get blamed for your rape and death."

"What about Jack? What's your excuse going to be for him?" Maisy asked, honestly curious as to what her brother was thinking.

"*Him?*" He snorted. "Some loser? Who cares. No one will trace him back to me."

Maisy couldn't help it. She laughed. And once she started, she couldn't stop. Which pissed Jason off.

"Maisy," Jack warned, but she kept her gaze locked on her brother as she laughed harder. This was between the two of them, and she was done tiptoeing around the asshole.

"Stop it. Shut up!" Jason ordered.

But Maisy couldn't stop. Her brother was so conceited.

So *stupid*. He'd always called her dumb, but thinking he could get away with killing Jack was just too much.

It wasn't until he stalked toward her, and Jack again said her name in warning, that Maisy managed to control herself. Just in time too, because Jason was obviously ready to kick her. Looking up at him, she said, "You have no idea who you kidnapped, do you?"

Jason curled his lip. "It doesn't matter."

It mattered. *Jack* mattered.

"His name is Jack Wickett. He was a Night Stalker in the US Army. That's one of their hotshot helicopter pilots, if you didn't know. He was a POW and his face was plastered all over the internet by his captors. When he was rescued, the country literally rejoiced. There were parades, commendations." She was laying it on a bit thick, but she didn't care.

"When he got out of the military, he joined some of his buddies, former Navy SEALs, Delta Force, other special forces guys, and they started a retreat in New Mexico. It's won awards, the pictures of the owners again all over the internet. You kidnapped one of the most recognizable faces in the country, brother dear. I'm not surprised none of your dumbass friends didn't recognize him. But now? If he disappears again? I promise you, his friends will plaster his face all over social media—with all the details about his kidnapping and our fake marriage. The entire *world* will know who he is...and what you've done."

Maisy was a little concerned he might ask why his friends didn't do a media blitz the first time, but given Jason's angry scowl, and the way his face was getting redder and redder, she figured he was too furious with her to think about anything else right now. And that's what she wanted.

"You might get away with killing Mom and Dad, Martha, and even me. But there's no way, *no way*, you'll be able to hide the fact that my husband was *the* Jack Wickett. And that he mysteriously disappeared at the same time as I did. The cops are gonna be all over you. All over this place—especially after what I told them this morning. You'll be at the top of their suspect list for sure."

"*What*? What did you tell them?" Jason asked, his anger increasing, if that was even possible.

"Everything, Jason. I told them *everything*," Maisy said, looking straight into his eyes as she did.

"*Fuck*... Fuck, fuck, fuck, *fuck*!" Jason exclaimed, as he paced back and forth.

Then he pulled the gun out of his waistband and pointed it straight at her forehead.

Maisy stopped breathing. For all her bluster, she didn't want to die. Not now. Not after finding Jack.

"Shooting her isn't going to fix this," Jack said firmly from the other side of the room. Maisy saw from the corner of her eye that he was standing now, but she didn't dare look at him.

Because her brother didn't lower the weapon.

"No. But it'll make me feel better," he said, his voice eerily calm.

"Put down the gun! Now!"

The new voice from the doorway made Maisy jerk, but she didn't take her gaze from the barrel of the gun pointed at her head.

Jason didn't move. But Jack did.

Her brother went down hard, his forehead hitting the

concrete floor as he landed. Maisy let out a squeak of surprise and fright, but before she could do much of anything, two men wearing all black, including bulletproof vests with a number of pockets that rivaled Jack's vest from earlier, joined him in restraining her brother.

The gun Jason had been pointing at her was kicked away and his hands were cuffed behind him before Maisy could blink. Then Jack was there. Kneeling in front of her, blocking her view of what was happening with her brother.

"You idiot," Jack murmured lovingly as another one of the men in the very crowded safe room used a key to remove the handcuffs around her wrists. Jack picked her up as if she weighed nothing at all and carried her out of the suddenly claustrophobic room, through the basement, and up the stairs. He didn't stop in the living room but walked her through the house—which was also full of uniformed officers—out the door and straight to an ambulance.

"How did you get out of the cuffs?" she asked.

"I had a key in my hand. Your dumbass brother didn't even check. I was waiting for a chance to subdue him, and you provided that. Although I'm not thrilled you riled him up so much that he pointed that weapon at you. I swear I just lost ten years off my life."

"Jack, I'm okay," she said after swallowing several times to find her voice.

"Humor me. That didn't quite go as I'd planned," he muttered as he gently lowered her to a gurney.

Maisy didn't get a chance to ask him what the plan was before the paramedics were buzzing around her, taking her vitals and asking her questions about how she felt.

After about ten minutes of them fussing over her, they

finally decided she wasn't in dire need of a ride to the hospital.

"Can you give us a minute?" Jack asked.

Without hesitation, the paramedics stepped out of the back of the ambulance, giving them some privacy.

"We're gonna have to talk to the cops again, but before they descend, I wanted to tell you how amazing you are. I was prepared to do whatever it took to buy some time for Brick, Tiny, and half of the Seattle police force to get to us, but I didn't have to do a damn thing. You did it for me."

"What were you even doing here? Did Don get you too?" Maisy asked.

Jack shook his head. He was kneeling by the gurney, one hand on her arm, his thumb stroking her skin, and Maisy wasn't sure if she was dreaming or not. She'd left a man behind in the hotel who seemed ready to break off everything between them, and now he was looking at her the way he had before he'd regained his memory. With love.

She had to be shellshocked or something.

"No, I walked up to the door and knocked."

Maisy's mouth fell open. "What? Why would you *do* that?"

"Because I knew you were somewhere in that house."

So many questions rattled around in Maisy's head. "How?" she asked after a moment.

"I slipped a tracker into your pocket this morning."

"What?" Maisy asked, truly shocked.

"Long story short, I talked to Ry, and we both agreed that just in case, it wouldn't be a bad idea for someone to be able to know where we were at all times while we were here. After what happened to Lara and Owl...hell, most of the women at The Refuge...she didn't hesitate to get me two trackers. It was all she could get her hands on at the time, otherwise Brick and Tiny would've gotten trackers too. When I pulled my head out of my ass and came back up to the room, you were gone. It was a simple matter of getting in touch with Ry and asking her to track you. I saw you were here, sent Brick and Tiny to the police, and I came straight to the house. I figured I could distract your brother long enough for the good guys to arrive. But again, you didn't need me."

Maisy shook her head. "I'll always need you."

Heat flared in his eyes and she prayed that was a good sign. His hand tightened on her forearm. "Also, you did what I didn't think was possible."

"What's that?"

"You got your brother to confess. To everything. He's going away for good, Maisy. He's not going to ever be a problem for you again."

"It'll be my word against his."

"Nope. Those trackers Ry gave me? They're also small microphones. She activated them as soon as she heard you were gone."

"But it was in my pocket. There's no way she could've heard what Jason said," Maisy protested, even as her hopes rose that maybe by some miracle, a recording of what Jason said would be audible enough to be used against him.

"Yours was—but mine wasn't," Jack said with a small smile. "I had it in my hand and planned to plant it in the basement. If anything had happened to us, eventually someone would've found it and figured out what it was. Even if they didn't, Ry would've certainly sent the audio files to the authorities."

The ramifications of what Jack was telling her began to sank in. "It's over?"

"It's over," Jack confirmed.

Maisy closed her eyes and sighed in relief.

"With his own words used against him, plus the pictures you gave the detective, Martha's wallet, and I'm guessing Don's testimony—especially after he hears how Jason was going to frame him for your murder, and for leniency in his role in your kidnapping today and all the shit he's done for Jason in the past—he's done for."

She felt his hand on her cheek and opened her eyes to stare into Jack's beautiful brown gaze.

"I'm sorry. He's your brother. I know this is hard."

Maisy scowled. "He's *not* my brother. Not anymore. I refuse to think about him in that way for one more second. He's a monster. A serial killer. I hate him. But, Jack...are *you* okay?"

"Me? Why?"

"I said some things...I didn't mean to say anything that might bring back bad memories for you."

But Jack shook his head. "You were magnificent. I'm not thrilled with the way you baited him. That had been *my* plan, to get him to turn his attention to me so he'd leave you alone, but nothing you said makes me love you any less."

Maisy blinked. Afraid to believe he'd said what she *thought* he'd said.

He stood up from his crouch and sat on the edge of the gurney. He took her face in his hands and leaned in. "I love you, *Stellina*. I'd walk through the fires of Hell to have the right to be your husband. I've done a shit job of being yours so far, but I promise I'll be better...if you give me the chance."

Maisy didn't hesitate, she threw her arms around him and held on as tightly as she could. She felt Jack chuckle against her.

"I take it that's a yes?" he asked against her neck.

"I love you too," Maisy said in reply.

"I'm gonna do better," he told her after pulling back so he could meet her gaze.

"Impossible. You're already the best man I've ever met. And I love you so much."

"How about we head outside, make sure Brick and Tiny are good, go to the police station to talk some more with the detective, get some sleep, then go the hell home?"

All of that sounded good to Maisy, except maybe for the talking to the cops part, but it had to be done. She knew that. "Yes. But can we maybe get a change of clothes first? Get into something clean that isn't tainted by my brother and his basement?"

"I'll send Tiny back to the hotel to grab our bags and have him meet us at the station."

Emotion swamped Maisy. Probably delayed reaction from everything that happened, but she didn't think anyone would think less of her for it. She rested her head on Jack's chest and did her best not to break into a million pieces.

"It's okay, *Stellina*. I've got you. I'll always have you."

They didn't move for a minute or two, then Maisy sat up. "I'm good now."

"So damn strong. Love you."

She'd never get tired of hearing those two words. "I

love you too. Now, let's do this. The sooner we can get home, the better."

"Amen," Jack said. Then he stood, helping her off the gurney, holding her until she was steady on her feet, and led her out of the ambulance.

EPILOGUE

A month had passed since Maisy's brother had tried to kill her, and Stone's nightmares had morphed from dreaming about being a POW to watching Jason shoot Maisy in the head while he did nothing but stand there and watch.

Maisy had her own nightmares, but they'd been there for each other, holding each other in the middle of the night, reassuring each other they were all right. That Jason couldn't hurt either of them ever again.

Her brother was in prison up in Washington and the last time they'd talked to the DA, he'd said he was confident they could get a conviction on all three counts of premeditated murder, plus two counts of kidnapping, and a host of other charges. At a minimum, he'd be facing life in prison, at best it would be without a chance of parole.

His friend Don was also going to see prison time, and they'd learned just the day before that detectives had been able to track down one of the men Jason hired to kill her parents. It had been a tough day for Maisy, but Stone was in awe of the way she was able to bounce back, to see the positive in the latest development. At very long last, her parents were seeing some justice.

This morning, Maisy had woken up with the sun, as usual, had met Tonka and Jasna at the barn to help with chores, then headed over to the lodge to assist Luna and Robert in setting up the breakfast buffet for guests. Stone was as proud of her as he could be, and he wanted nothing more than to shelter her from all the shit life liked to sometimes throw at people. She'd had her share, and if he could help it, she'd experience only goodness from here on out.

Ry had asked to speak to him three days ago, giving him one of the most thoughtful gifts he'd ever received. He wasn't sure what Maisy would think, but he hoped she'd be as pleased as he was.

Stone had wanted to ask Ry if she was staying, but she seemed a lot more...fragile lately, and he didn't want to do or say anything that might push her to make any rash decisions about her future. Personally, Stone wouldn't mind if Ry stayed forever. He liked her, yes, but more than that, having someone as talented as she was when it came to electronics and information would be a very good thing for The Refuge, as far as he was concerned.

Yes, he was a little worried about her penchant for breaking the law while she gathered information, but she'd promised him and the rest of the guys that she wouldn't ever do anything that would bring attention to The Refuge. As a man who'd benefited from her abilities, legal or not, Stone was willing to trust her word.

He had no idea what was going on between her and Tiny. Most of the time his friend seemed irritated with his new roommate, but when anyone suggested any other living arrangement—like converting one of the conference rooms in the lodge into a temporary living space for her, or having her move into the family and friends cabin they'd built—Tiny immediately vetoed the idea.

So, Ry was still living in Tiny's cabin, even though the two of them were like oil and water. Half the time they didn't even seem to like each other, and yet...she was still here.

Alaska had texted him and given him a heads-up that Maisy was on the way back to his cabin, so Stone was ready and waiting for her when she walked in.

"Hey!" she said happily.

In the month since they'd returned from Washington, nightmares aside, Maisy had blossomed. She'd lost the haunted look she sometimes got in her eyes, and she seemed to walk taller. She was becoming more and more outgoing. Stone loved the changes, loved that she was gaining confidence in who she was. Her brother had told her often enough that she was stupid and weak, when in reality she was anything but.

Stone had heard about her scores on the GED and was encouraging her to look into taking classes at The University of New Mexico at Los Alamos. She was considering it, but she didn't know what she wanted to major in. There was a lot of time for her to figure out the rest of her life, and honestly, Stone was just thrilled to have her there with him, and for them both to finally be able to live a normal, if hectic life.

She'd taken to living at The Refuge as if she'd been here forever. She loved hiking with the guests, helping Lara and Cora plan activities for the children of guests the next time they opened The Refuge up to families, and every time he turned around, Maisy was helping someone else with their job.

They'd finally hired a new housekeeper, since Ry's... skills...were better served elsewhere. It was Maisy who'd showed the guy, Joshua, around The Refuge and introduced him to everyone. Jess and Carly liked the young man, and he seemed to be fitting in really well.

Stone had finally had a chance to call his parents and bring them up to speed with everything that had happened in his life. About losing his memory, although he'd downplayed the part where he'd been kidnapped... again. They'd been through enough when he was a POW, and he simply wanted to protect them. He did tell them all about Maisy though. About being married. They, of course, were thrilled, and while they couldn't come out to New Mexico to see them just yet—they had a three-month cruise that was leaving in a week or so—they'd insisted on FaceTiming with him and Maisy so they could meet her. The call went on for two hours and by the time it was over, Maisy had won them over completely simply by being herself.

The helicopter The Refuge had bought was finally scheduled to be delivered next week, and both Stone and Owl were beyond excited. Brick had hired a team of pilots to fly it down this time, after everything that had happened. Owl, Stone, and Brick would meet the men at the airport in Los Alamos, go over the paperwork, do an inspection of the bird, then Owl and Stone would do one more test-flight to make sure all was well. Then they'd fly her to the lodge. The landing pad and hangar had been completed the week before, and everyone was excited to start a new chapter at The Refuge.

But Stone had something very important he needed to talk about with Maisy. And he was extremely nervous.

"Are you okay?" Maisy asked with a small frown as she walked toward him.

Stone nodded. "Yeah. You have a good morning?"

Maisy beamed. "Yes! Tonka's talking about getting a couple more goats, and maybe selling their milk to a woman in town. She makes the most divine goat cheese and yogurt. And...goats!"

Stone loved seeing her so excited, so exuberant.

"Luna's been talking to me about her classes, and...I think I do want to at least dip my toe in next semester with her. I mean, I haven't been in school in forever, and I'm not sure I'll remember how to study, but I want to try."

"You'll do awesome," Stone told her.

"Anyway, I also chatted with one of the guests. I don't know how Henley does what she does. I get so sad and upset for people when I hear what they've gone through. And before you say anything, no I didn't ask her to tell me anything about her PTSD, she volunteered the info."

"I didn't think you had, *Stellina*," Stone told her. The last thing his wife would do was pry into anyone's demons.

"Anyway, I guess after the story about what happened to us made the rounds on social media, she saw it and wanted to tell me she was sorry. She empathized with me because she also had a bad experience with family. I guess she had a sister who was their parents' favorite. Like, *really* their favorite. They treated her like a princess, and locked our guest in a closet, barely fed her, made her sit in her own waste, and she wasn't allowed outside or to go to school or anything!"

Maisy was getting worked up, but Stone couldn't blame her. He'd read the info sheet on the guest she was talking about, and her story was horrific. Over the years, he'd heard stories about this kind of thing happening, but hadn't allowed himself to think too hard about the details. And for good reason. After reading the details on this poor woman, it reminded him of how horrible humans could be.

But then there were people like his Maisy. People who bent over backward to do the right thing, to be kind, to help where they could.

"Anyway, it sucks. But the good news? She's doing wonderful," Maisy said with a smile. "She had an incredible foster family who adopted her when she was *seventeen*. I even got to meet her fiancée. She's amazing and they're so cute together!"

Stone grinned. He'd met the couple when they'd checked in earlier that week.

"That's good," he told Maisy.

His wife wrinkled her nose. "Sorry, I'm going on and on and haven't even asked about your day."

Now he chuckled. "Maisy, it's nine thirty-one. I haven't had much of a chance to even *have* a day yet."

She giggled. "Okay, good point, but it's been what, three hours since we got up? What have you been doing while I was gone?" She leaned into him, staring at him with so much love, it was all Stone could do not to toss her over his shoulder and throw her back down on their bed. He'd woken up in the middle of the night with a sudden urge to make love to his wife. He hadn't had a nightmare, hadn't really dreamed much of anything, but the need to make sure Maisy knew how much he loved her had prompted him to slide a hand up her side and then between her legs.

She hadn't complained about him waking her up, and they'd made long, slow, sweet love to each other. Every time he was with her, Stone was more certain she was his perfect match.

"Jack?"

And that was another thing. He loved how she called him Jack. Everyone else, and he meant *everyone*, called him Stone. But not his Maisy. She insisted on using the name she'd first known him by. She was her Jack, and he freaking loved that.

"Sorry, was thinking about last night," Stone told her.

Her cheeks flushed as she gave him a shy smile. "Yeah?" she asked.

"Yeah. And while I'd love nothing more than to drag you back to bed, there's something I want to talk to you about. Something important."

"Jason?" she asked, her brow furrowing.

"No!" Stone practically shouted. He took a breath and forced himself to relax. He hated even hearing her asshole brother's name. He'd made her life hell, and he wanted nothing but good for her from here on out. "No," he said a little more calmly. "But if I do hear anything else, I'll be sure to tell you right away. It's something else."

Now that he was doing this, Stone suddenly felt unsure.

"Okay. Whatever it is, it'll be fine. We'll figure it out together."

This woman. He loved her so damn much. It was obvious he was nervous and she was doing what she could to soothe him. He took her hand and pulled her over to the table that separated the living room from the kitchen. He picked up a piece of paper and held it out to her.

"I got this from Ry. She took it upon herself to fix things."

Maisy looked confused—and Stone couldn't blame her. He wasn't explaining this well at all. She took the paper he was holding out to her and lowered her head to read it.

Stone saw the second the words sank in. Her head flew up and her eyes met his. "This is our wedding certificate," she whispered.

"Yeah. Since my real name wasn't on our marriage license that means the money from your inheritance was obtained illegally, which could come back to haunt you. And it means technically we were never married. But...as I said, Ry fixed it."

Maisy looked back down at the piece of paper in her hand and ran a finger over his signature. Instead of saying Jack Smith, as he'd signed it on that day months ago, it now said Jack Wickett. And hers said Maisy Feldman, instead of Smith, as she'd signed her own.

"What? How?" she asked incredulously.

"Ry's got skills," was all he said. Now wasn't the time to go into details about how she'd hacked into the Washington state database and changed the original document that had been scanned in. How she'd taken his signature from one of the many forms he'd signed here at The Refuge and replaced the one he'd used to sign his marriage license.

"I know we've talked about getting married here in New Mexico, just to make sure our bases are covered...but we don't have to now. Unless you still want to. I mean, if you want a party with our friends, I'm sure everyone would be thrilled. And you deserve the wedding of your dreams. The white dress, the aisle, the whole shindig. I just wanted to make sure you were all right with this. With us being married already. For real."

He was babbling, but Stone couldn't read what Maisy was thinking, and it was killing him.

In response, Maisy put the altered marriage license on the table...then turned and walked away from him.

Stone could only stare at her in dismay. His heart was in his throat, and he thought he was going to barf. This was more painful than anything he'd ever experienced. Including his time as a POW. If his Maisy rejected him now, he wasn't sure he'd ever recover.

She entered their bedroom, but a moment later she was walking back. Her face was inscrutable. Stopping in front of him, she held something out in her hand.

Looking down, Stone's heart skipped a beat. He immediately knew what he was looking at. His gaze flew back up to hers. And this time, she was smiling. Huge. The happiness and satisfaction in her expression was blinding.

"Once upon a time, you said I couldn't leave because I might be pregnant. Well...it looks like you're going to be stuck with me. Us."

"You're...we're...a *baby*?" Stone choked out as he clenched the positive pregnancy test in his hand.

Maisy giggled. "Yeah. You can't be that surprised, considering neither of us has been using any kind of protection. And since your favorite thing in the world seems to be coming deep inside me..." Her voice trailed off.

Stone dropped to his knees and wrapped his arms around her, burying his face in her belly. He felt her hands in his hair as his eyes filled with tears. He hadn't cried in years. Even when he was being tortured, he hadn't cried. But thinking about this woman having his baby made him lose it completely.

Looking up, he said, "Please don't ever leave me. I couldn't handle it. I love you so much, *Stellina*. How we met was fucked up, but you're literally the best thing to ever happen to me. I'm begging you, don't ever leave me. If I piss you off, tell me what I did so I can make sure it doesn't happen again. Anything you want, I'll bend over backward to give to you. Please, Maisy, please."

She shook her head as her own eyes filled with tears and she tried to pull him to his feet. But Stone didn't budge. He couldn't. There was no way his knees would be able to hold him up.

"Don't," she said. "Don't beg. It isn't you. Besides, it's not necessary. I don't want to go anywhere. The day I met you was the beginning of my new life, and I'll fight like hell to keep it. And I don't need another wedding. Maybe in twenty years, we can do the renewal of vows thing for real, but for now, I just want to enjoy being Mrs. Jack Wickett and starting a family with you."

The hell with his plans. They'd talked about going for a hike out to Table Rock and he was going to get down on one knee and give her back the rings he'd bought for her in Seattle. But the thought of going anywhere other than to their bed was abhorrent. He needed to show his wife how much he loved her. How excited he was for their baby. She was right, he did love coming inside her. But since she didn't seem to mind in the least, he didn't either.

Finding the strength, Stone stood. Then he wrapped an arm around her waist and led her back down the hall the way she'd just come. He went to the little table next to their bed and pulled open the drawer. He pulled out the rings they'd worn before his memory returned and reverently took her hand in his. He slid the rings down her ring finger and as soon as they were seated, it felt as if everything in Stone's life settled into place as well. He put his own ring on, then leaned down and kissed Maisy, long, slow, and deep.

Without a word, he stripped his wife in record time and joined her on the bed after taking his own clothes off. Instead of pulling her against him, Jack pressed her onto her back and crawled between her legs. He rested his forehead against her stomach, much as he'd done in the other room.

"Hi, baby," he whispered as he stroked the soft skin of Maisy's belly. "I'm your daddy. And I'm gonna be the best daddy in the world. We'll go hiking, and fishing, and I'll teach you to fly. You'll not go one day without hearing the words 'I love you.' We'll travel, laugh, and probably fight. But no matter what, you're already loved."

Hearing a sniff, Stone looked up and saw Maisy bawling her eyes out. But he wasn't worried; he knew she was crying because she was happy. He inched his way up her body until they were touching from their toes to their chests. Reaching down, he settled his rock-hard cock between her legs, then slowly eased his way inside.

Maisy smiled up at him, even as she widened her legs, making room for him. She was tight, and definitely not wet enough to take him hard and fast, but Stone didn't mind, and she didn't either. He simply needed to be connected to her at that moment. He felt her core gradually soften around him.

"I love you," he told her as he gazed down into her beautiful brown eyes.

"I love you too."

"I'm gonna be the best husband and father. I give you my word."

"You already are," she whispered.

They made love with all the devotion in their souls, then they fucked hard and fast. By the time they orgasmed, both were drenched in sweat and breathing hard.

"Well, now that we've gotten our workout for the day... I'm thinking a nap is in order," Maisy said with a small smile as she cuddled against him in the tangled covers.

"I agree," Stone told her, ignoring the fact that he'd told Owl he'd meet with him later, and that Maisy was supposed to meet with Cora to help her get their cabin ready for their foster child, who would be joining them in a few days.

As Maisy began to fall asleep in his arms, Stone pushed her onto her back, then rested his palm over her belly as he gazed at his beautiful wife.

"Are you going to do that for the next eight or so months?" Maisy mumbled sleepily.

"Do what?"

"Stare at me."

"Oh, that. Yup," Stone said easily.

"Whatever."

She fell asleep with a smile on her face and her hand over his on her belly.

Stone closed his eyes and reflected on his life. How he'd ended up here, he had no idea. He was a lucky son-of-a-bitch, and he knew it. If he'd known when he was a POW that this was where he'd end up, he wouldn't have believed it. But everything he'd experienced in his life, the highs and the lows, were worth it to be where he was today. The fact of the matter was, he deserved this. Maisy. And she deserved him right back. They'd lived through hell and this was their reward.

He needed to call his parents. Let the others know that he and Maisy wouldn't need a marriage ceremony after all...and of course, inform everyone that there would be another baby on The Refuge soon.

He chuckled softly. Four new babies, plus Cora and Pipe's new foster child. Lord, their plan to have an adult-only resort had been thrown out the window in short order.

Lowering his head onto the pillow next to Maisy's, Stone fell into a light doze. There would be challenges in their future, he was sure of that, but with Maisy by his side, they could weather anything.

* * *

It was time for her to leave. Ryleigh knew that, but she was having a hard time actually doing it. She'd stayed too long already. Everyone was safe, there were no new crisis happening. She'd done everything she could for the men and women at The Refuge, and now she needed to go.

But every time she made plans to sneak out in the middle of the night and disappear into thin air, something stopped her. Jasna asking for help with her homework. Maisy asking how she was doing—and honestly seeming interested in her answer. Stone asking her to fix his marriage certificate. Jess and Carly asking her to come chat while they folded towels...

Ryleigh had never been treated as...nicely, as she had here at The Refuge.

And in return, she'd deceived them. Was *still* lying. They didn't know all the things she'd done. Didn't understand that simply being around her could get them into serious trouble. She was poison, her father had told her that time and time again, and no matter how much she tried to deny it, to block his voice in her head, she couldn't.

Her father had taught her everything he knew, which meant she was as much a criminal as he was. It didn't matter that she'd tried to atone. That she'd fled from her good ol' dad, that she'd used everything he'd taught her *against* him. The cops, the Feds, no one would believe she hadn't had a choice. She'd be locked away just as her dad would be...if she was caught.

And the longer she stayed in one place, the more comfortable she got here, the better the chance she'd be tracked down. She wasn't scared of the police...she'd take the punishment they doled out because she deserved it. It was her father who terrified her.

He wouldn't be content to make her feel like the worst daughter in the world. No, he would destroy her. And not only her, but everything she held dear. And for the first time in her life, she had something she valued. The Refuge, and everyone who lived and worked here.

Her father wouldn't hesitate to destroy it, little by little.

So she had to go. Before it was too late.

But she had a feeling it was *already* too late.

And it was all her fault.

She'd known better than to use Brick's computer when he'd scooted it angrily across the table at her, when Lara and Owl had been kidnapped and Stone had disappeared. She knew it would leave a crack that her father could exploit.

And it had.

It was starting.

Her father's revenge.

He'd waited years for the opportunity to find his daughter and make her pay for double-crossing him, for using the skills he'd taught her against him.

The first clue was the ten-cent deduction from The Refuge's bank account. It was only ten cents, but it might as well have been a million. Her father was playing with her. Letting her know he'd found her. That he was out there. Watching. Biding his time.

He'd destroy The Refuge without a single qualm about the lives he would ruin in the process. Even if he didn't know how much the people here meant to her...he'd ruin them anyway. Simply because she'd been living among them. And the only person who could stop him was *her*. Leaving now wouldn't help. Wouldn't make him stop.

Her phone vibrated with a text, and Ryleigh picked it up.

Henley: Did you hear the news? Maisy's preggo! We're all meeting at the lodge in fifteen minutes!

. . .

Ryleigh should've been happy. And she was. Maisy and Stone were adorable together. But it also meant one more person she needed to protect. The pressure she felt was immense. She wasn't sure she could handle it.

But then again, she had no choice.

Looking out the window, she saw Tiny in the distance. He was with one of the couples staying at The Refuge that week, gesturing at the ground, probably showing them tracks from a rabbit or deer.

Her heart beat unsteadily, and Ryleigh frowned. The man hated her, and she couldn't blame him. She'd lied. Deceived not only him, but everyone here. And she refused to answer most of the questions he fired at her when they were alone. She didn't want to lie to him, so instead she kept her mouth shut.

He would never forgive her, which sucked. Because she actually liked the former SEAL. He was loyal and giving, and a little rough around the edges, which turned her on. She'd grown up surrounded by nerds. Men and boys who stared at computers all day. She longed to have a manly man. Someone who could wield a power tool, who wasn't afraid to get his hands dirty, and who preferred to spend his time outside, getting sweaty and doing physical labor.

And she'd had more than one fantasy of Tiny shoving her up against the wall and taking her hard and fast. Not letting her say no—not that she would—and giving her more pleasure than she could stand.

But Tiny could barely look at her. Forget about ever wanting anything more intimate.

Sighing, Ryleigh picked up her phone and typed out a quick response to Henley, letting her know that she'd meet her and the others up at the lodge as soon as she could.

Then she turned her attention back to her computer. She had to find a way to seal off The Refuge electronically. Not leave even one small hole where her father could get in. She'd already locked down the bank account as best she could, but with the number of vendors The Refuge paid electronically, there were plenty of threads her dad could follow.

Pressing her lips together, Ryleigh inhaled deeply. Once she was sure The Refuge was locked down, she'd leave. By then, her secrets would probably all be exposed. No one would be sad to see her go...except for herself.

Hopefully Tiny can get over his grumpiness in order to accept Ryleigh and find out what exactly she's running from. Read the conclusion to The Refuge series in *Deserving Ryleigh*.

Scan the QR code below for signed books, swag, T-shirts and more!

Also by Susan Stoker

The Refuge Series

Deserving Alaska
Deserving Henley
Deserving Reese
Deserving Cora
Deserving Lara
Deserving Maisy
Deserving Ryleigh (Jan 2025)

SEAL of Protection: Alliance Series

Protecting Remi
Protecting Wren (Nov 5)
Protecting Josie (Mar 4, 2025)
Protecting Maggie (Apr 1, 2025)
Protecting Addison (May 6, 2025)
Protecting Kelli (TBA)
Protecting Bree (TBA)

SEAL Team Hawaii Series

Finding Elodie
Finding Lexie
Finding Kenna
Finding Monica
Finding Carly
Finding Ashlyn
Finding Jodelle

Eagle Point Search & Rescue

Searching for Lilly

Searching for Elsie
Searching for Bristol
Searching for Caryn
Searching for Finley
Searching for Heather
Searching for Khloe

Game of Chance Series
The Protector
The Royal
The Hero
The Lumberjack

SEAL of Protection: Legacy Series
Securing Caite
Securing Brenae (novella)
Securing Sidney
Securing Piper
Securing Zoey
Securing Avery
Securing Kalee
Securing Jane

Delta Force Heroes Series
Rescuing Rayne
Rescuing Aimee (novella)
Rescuing Emily
Rescuing Harley
Marrying Emily (novella)
Rescuing Kassie
Rescuing Bryn
Rescuing Casey

Rescuing Sadie (novella)
Rescuing Wendy
Rescuing Mary
Rescuing Macie (novella)
Rescuing Annie

SEAL of Protection Series

Protecting Caroline
Protecting Alabama
Protecting Fiona
Marrying Caroline (novella)
Protecting Summer
Protecting Cheyenne
Protecting Jessyka
Protecting Julie (novella)
Protecting Melody
Protecting the Future
Protecting Kiera (novella)
Protecting Alabama's Kids (novella)
Protecting Dakota

Delta Team Two Series

Shielding Gillian
Shielding Kinley
Shielding Aspen
Shielding Jayme (novella)
Shielding Riley
Shielding Devyn
Shielding Ember
Shielding Sierra

Badge of Honor: Texas Heroes Series

Justice for Mackenzie
Justice for Mickie
Justice for Corrie
Justice for Laine (novella)
Shelter for Elizabeth
Justice for Boone
Shelter for Adeline
Shelter for Sophie
Justice for Erin
Justice for Milena
Shelter for Blythe
Justice for Hope
Shelter for Quinn
Shelter for Koren
Shelter for Penelope

Ace Security Series

Claiming Grace
Claiming Alexis
Claiming Bailey
Claiming Felicity
Claiming Sarah

Mountain Mercenaries Series

Defending Allye
Defending Chloe
Defending Morgan
Defending Harlow
Defending Everly
Defending Zara
Defending Raven

Silverstone Series

Trusting Skylar

Trusting Taylor

Trusting Molly

Trusting Cassidy

Stand Alone

Falling for the Delta

The Guardian Mist

Nature's Rift

A Princess for Cale

A Moment in Time- A Collection of Short Stories

Another Moment in Time- A Collection of Short Stories

A Third Moment in Time- A Collection of Short Stories

Lambert's Lady

Special Operations Fan Fiction

http://www.AcesPress.com

Beyond Reality Series

Outback Hearts

Flaming Hearts

Frozen Hearts

Writing as Annie George:

Stepbrother Virgin (erotic novella)

ABOUT THE AUTHOR

New York Times, USA Today, #1 Amazon Bestseller, and #1 *Wall Street Journal* Bestselling Author, Susan Stoker has spent the last twenty-three years living in Missouri, California, Colorado, Indiana, Texas, and Tennessee and is currently living in the wilds of Maine. She's married to a retired Army man (and current firefighter/EMT) who now gets to follow *her* around the country.

She debuted her first series in 2014 and quickly followed that up with the SEAL of Protection Series, which solidified her love of writing and creating stories readers can get lost in.

If you enjoyed this book, or any book, please consider leaving a review. It's appreciated by authors more than you'll know.

www.stokeraces.com
www.AcesPress.com
susan@stokeraces.com

facebook.com/authorsusanstoker
x.com/Susan_Stoker
instagram.com/authorsusanstoker
goodreads.com/SusanStoker
bookbub.com/authors/susan-stoker
amazon.com/author/susanstoker

Made in United States
Orlando, FL
25 September 2024